PRAISE FO[...]

The
Reunion

"Like every iconic Hollywood love story, *The Reunion* sparkles incisive industry detail over the moving and deeply sweet romance of its stars, who learn with each other how to reboot their lives unscripted. Olson's debut romance is one to obsess over like a new show and cherish like a favorite film."

—Emily Wibberley & Austin Siegemund-Broka,
authors of *The Roughest Draft*

"A heartfelt, poignant look at the ups and downs of life in the spotlight. Ransom and Liv's chemistry leaps off the page, and their journey is sweet, emotional, and thoroughly satisfying."

—Ava Wilder, author of *How to Fake It in Hollywood*

"*The Reunion* swept me off my feet. As vivid as it is sweet, I was totally immersed in this behind-the-scenes look at two actors getting their oh-so-satisfying second chance at love. I completely adored it."

—Bridget Morrissey, author of *A Thousand Miles*

"With an original twist on a friends-to-lovers romance, *The Reunion* is a page-turning peek at the life—and love—of a Hollywood starlet and her co-star: the boy of her teenage dreams who might just be the man of her grown-up heart. This fun romance, set in the world of Hollywood glamour and celebrity gossip, is not to be missed."

—Meredith Schorr, author of *As Seen on TV*

"*The Reunion* was utterly charming, the perfect mix of behind-the-scenes Hollywood and heartstring-tugging romance."

–Kate Spencer, author of *In a New York Minute*

ALSO BY KAYLA OLSON

The Sandcastle Empire
This Splintered Silence

The Reunion

A NOVEL

KAYLA OLSON

ATRIA PAPERBACK
NEW YORK LONDON TORONTO SYDNEY NEW DELHI

ATRIA
PAPERBACK

An Imprint of Simon & Schuster, Inc.
1230 Avenue of the Americas
New York, NY 10020

Copyright © 2023 by Kayla Olson

First Atria Paperback edition January 2023

For information about special discounts for bulk purchases, please contact Simon & Schuster Special Sales at 1-866-506-1949 or business@simonandschuster.com.

The Simon & Schuster Speakers Bureau can bring authors to your live event. For more information or to book an event, contact the Simon & Schuster Speakers Bureau at 1-866-248-3049 or visit our website at www.simonspeakers.com.

Interior design by Lexy East

Manufactured in the United States of America

1   3   5   7   9   10   8   6   4   2

Library of Congress Cataloging-in-Publication Data

Names: Olson, Kayla, author.
Title: The reunion : a novel / Kayla Olson.
Description: First Atria Paperback edition. | New York : Atria Paperback, 2023.
Identifiers: LCCN 2022018514 (print) | LCCN 2022018515 (ebook) | ISBN 9781668001943 (paperback) | ISBN 9781668001950 (ebook)
Subjects: LCGFT: Romance fiction. | Novels.
Classification: LCC PS3615.L75252 R48 2023 (print) | LCC PS3615.L75252 (ebook) | DDC 813/.6—dc23
LC record available at https://lccn.loc.gov/2022018514
LC ebook record available at https://lccn.loc.gov/2022018515

ISBN 978-1-6680-0194-3
ISBN 978-1-6680-0195-0 (ebook)

For all the Emilys who inspired and encouraged me
while writing this book—

✧ Emily Bain Murphy, my friend through
every mountain and valley;
✧ Emily McClendon, who sharpens me on
and off the tennis court;
✧ Emily Wibberley, whose books made me
fall in love with rom-coms;
and
✧ Emily Henry, whose rom-coms made me
finally decide to write one of my own

And for everyone who always

✧ wished for Topanga's hair;
✧ cheered/cried when Ross and Rachel finally
had their first kiss;
and
✧ had Big Opinions on whether Joey should
choose Dawson or Pacey in the end.

This one's for you.

Girl on the Verge Lands Twentieth-Anniversary Reunion Special at Fanline

By Elijah Jones // Senior Editor, Arts & Entertainment, *Sunset Central*

Beloved teen drama *Girl on the Verge*—hailed by critics as "iconic" and "trailblazing"—has officially been picked up by streaming giant Fanline for a long-rumored twentieth-anniversary reunion special.

Shattering record after record over the course of its six seasons, the breakout hit launched its young actors to superstardom, most notably Liv Latimer and Ransom Joel, whose fictional counterparts were on-screen sweethearts. The success of the pop culture juggernaut remains unmatched by any teen drama.

While undeniably a hit, *Girl on the Verge* was not immune to criticism: with great devotion came great expectation, and the fandom proved tricky to please when the show took its final bow. With its infamously abrupt cut-to-black ending—in the middle of Liv Latimer's final line, no less—many fans have vocalized their desire for closure (numerous think pieces defended the choice, however, praising it as "brave" and "borderline revolutionary").

Fans and critics alike have to wonder: Will the world finally get the answers they've begged for in this reunion special?

Whatever the case, it will be good to see the original cast together again. In the (nearly) fourteen years since the polarizing series finale, its stars have gone on to varying degrees of success in Hollywood but never on the same silver screen. Ransom Joel has headlined many a box-office smash since his days on *Girl*, most recently as Hunter Drew, the titular character in a trio of espionage thrillers. Liv Latimer took a decidedly quieter route, pivoting to the world of low-budget indie films, turning out magnificent performances in each. Sasha-Kate Kilpatrick and Ford Brooks, who rounded out *Girl*'s original core cast, have both appeared in a number of projects but have yet to break out in a significant way beyond the show that made them household names.

Sources close to the project report that scheduling conflicts nearly prevented the entire original cast from returning for the reunion, but at long last, the fully scripted, hour-long episode is a go. Shooting is scheduled for this summer, with plans to air in the fall.

Subscribe to *SUNSET CENTRAL* breaking news alerts for the latest on all your favorite shows, stars, and more!

I'd forgotten just how hot it feels under a spotlight.

"All right, Liv, we're going live in five . . . four . . . three . . ."

A production assistant motions for quiet, and the chorus of chatter fades in the *Java with Jade* studio. For a split second, it's just me and Jade Johnson and the hum of the electricity powering her sunny morning-show set. I shift in my seat, a plush armchair upholstered in brightest white. It's comfortable, even if I'm not entirely so.

My relationship with the press: it's complicated.

I pick a focal point, anything that will ground me here in this singular moment—the coffee, dark in its bone china cup—and just like that, I'm prime-time TV starlet Liv Latimer again, not just Liv who regularly tosses her hair up in a messy bun and wakes up with morning breath like the rest of the population.

"Liv!" Jade says, her voice a song even with just the one syllable. Her teeth are next-level perfection. "It is my *absolute pleasure* to have you here on the show—can I admit I'm just a little starstruck right now?"

She laughs, and I laugh, and it all goes down like honey. "Thanks, Jade. Can I admit the feeling's absolutely mutual?"

"It's not every day I get to sit down with someone who was such a fixture of my adolescence," she goes on. "And now I'm dating us both—it cannot possibly be two decades since *Girl on the Verge* premiered!"

"Unbelievable, right?" I match her energy, careful not to surpass it. "I think it feels like less time has passed because we were on the air for so long."

"Six seasons." Jade takes a sip from her coffee and sets the mug back down on the low table between us. "What was that like, growing up with the whole world watching?"

It's hardly the first time someone has asked—I've gotten every question under the sun. *People will take as much as you give them, Livvie*, my father used to say. *Be careful to keep some things for yourself.* I need something sharp and quotable, something relatable and true that doesn't actually require me to part with some private piece of myself I'll never get back.

"It was exactly how you'd expect," I say, like even this doesn't feel like giving too much away. You'd think I'd be used to it at this point, scraping slices of my soul into sound bites, but it has never gotten easier. "It was a lot of pressure but also a lot of fun."

"Let's talk about the pressure. Your character on the show—Honor St. Croix—was Miss Americana to the extreme, and honestly, it never looked like a stretch. Honor never crumbled under the pressure she felt, and from what I can tell, neither did you. How did you handle it all?"

Jade wasn't there for my rather jagged twenties, or any of the behind-the-scenes days that led up to them. There's a difference between crumbling and cracking. Honor and I *absolutely* did both.

"It all comes back to being grateful," I say. It's a line I've practiced many times over in my head, and one I *think* is true? "Being grateful, even for the hard things, and starting fresh each new day no matter how tough the day before felt."

"But they did feel tough," Jade says. A fact: not a question.

I look her straight in the eye. "People go through harder things every day," I say, choosing my words carefully. *I've* gone through harder. "But yes, the expectations on me back then were unreal."

The schedule, the interviews, the tours. There was pressure everywhere, so many eyes on me, always.

I loved the acting itself, though—unsurprising, given that it's practically a family legacy on the Latimer side. The chance to escape into someone else's skin, to be someone as perfect as Honor St. Croix while my own personal universe was falling apart? Even at a young age, it was never lost on me what a privilege that was. It worked out well that I was *good* at it. Good enough that no one ever had to know exactly how hard things were on me when my father—three-time Oscar-winning Hollywood heartthrob Patrick Latimer—was killed in a car crash up in the canyons during our second season.

"It certainly seemed like an intense experience for all of you when the show took off overnight. At least you clearly had chemistry with your castmates," Jade says, eyes glittering under the lights. I know where *this* is going. "You and Ransom Joel seemed especially close."

And there it is: I've been down this road a thousand times—in interviews, in daydreams, in sleepless nights where I tried to piece together where everything went wrong between us. We were best friends, closer than anyone else on set. The closest.

Slipping into Honor's life was exactly the escape I needed when my father died. And when the cameras stopped rolling, it was Ransom— and *only* Ransom—who got the real me.

"You and Ransom were inseparable in those years, and more than a few people speculated you were secretly dating." She leans in conspiratorially, as if it's just us having a chat over coffee without millions of viewers hanging on our every word. "I know you both adamantly denied it, but I have to know—was there ever any truth to those rumors?"

It takes every ounce of professional poise to not break character: Liv Latimer, perfectly unruffled talk show guest. Behind my ultra-calm facade, I'm wondering how this question possibly slipped past my publicist.

"They were rumors," I say evenly, putting on a smile that's anything but easy. "Never anything more."

I don't tell her how we were so close it *felt* like dating sometimes, how there were days when he mattered more to me than the show itself. I especially don't tell her about the painful drama between us at the end of our final season, the purposeful step back from our friendship— Ransom's idea, not mine. How it felt like a breakup.

It's always been easier to deny the rumors than to admit I once wished they were true.

"Have you and Ransom seen each other since the show ended?" Jade's question is so casual, so blissfully unaware of all that went down between us.

"I've certainly seen him on social media!" I reply, deflection-with-a-smile at its best.

"Oh, haven't we all!" Jade says, pivoting with me without missing a beat. "I admire how he uses his platform to put good out into the world. Is he really that good of a guy behind the scenes?"

That good and more, I think. So good it hurts.

"He once took in a stray kitten and kept it in his dressing room—it was an entire week before the studio found out and made him take it home!" The memory of him smuggling a bag of kitten food under his hoodie in the middle of a heat wave makes me smile for real, no acting required.

Jade's eyes light up. "I can only imagine how many pets have been adopted thanks to his activism—did you know he even did a calendar to raise funds for the ASPCA one time? My niece gave me one for my birthday a few years ago!"

Ransom, when the clips from this interview inevitably go viral, will not love this turn of conversation. His photos have taken on a markedly dark filter as of late, veering decidedly away from teen heartthrob into *GQ* cover–worthy territory.

Not that I've been keeping up with his daily posts.

Or the six to ten stories he posts on the regular throughout each day.

Or his Snapaday Lives, which my personal-assistant-slash-best-friend Bre peeks at for me on her account every so often, just so he won't know exactly how often I tune in to see what he's up to.

Jade leans in, as if she's about to tell me something extremely confidential.

"Let's circle back to the reunion special. For those who haven't heard, it's an all-new hour-long episode that's rumored to pick up where the series finale left off. Fans everywhere are dying to know—without giving away any spoilers here—will we finally get closure on that one big thing the show left hanging in the balance?"

I let out a long exhale, relieved to be back in preapproved-question territory. "I've read the script, Jade, and I think it's safe to say it will have been worth the wait."

"Were you surprised by anything in the script?" she asks. "Or have you always known what would've happened next? I've got to admit, I screamed when the series finale cut to black in the middle of your last line!"

"Honestly, I didn't know for sure."

People have never believed my answer to this question, but it's the truth. If I had known how many times people would ask—*Did Honor stay with Duke in California or take her dream job in New York?*—I would have begged the writers to give a more conclusive ending.

"I obviously had my own theories after playing Honor for so many years," I go on. "I felt such a strong connection with her and had this gut feeling about the choice she would've made. I'm happy to report that my gut feeling was spot-on."

"I love that," Jade says, looking absolutely sincere. "Is what I'm hearing true—that we might get even more than just one new episode? Is *Girl* getting a reboot?"

Calm, Liv, calm, I coach myself. This is extremely confidential news, and it's not a sure thing yet. If the numbers from streaming and the reunion special are high enough, we'll almost certainly get the green light, but it would be completely irresponsible—not to mention a breach of my contract—to tell her so.

I'm also still not entirely sure I *want* to go back to such a sprawling set full-time; it's not a coincidence I've taken only a handful of roles since we wrapped fourteen years ago, all of them on small, intimate indie films. It's definitely not for lack of opportunities.

"As of this morning, all six seasons are streaming on Fanline for everyone to enjoy," I say, turning my charm factor up to distract from my nonanswer. "If you love them, let the producers know you want more by spreading the word on social media!"

Jade runs with my lead and closes out the interview by telling them where to find me in various corners of the internet—because a few million followers are only a fraction of what I *could* have, according to my publicist. I should share more of myself, be more relatable instead of a *beautiful, mysterious recluse*, as she once referred to me.

To some extent, she's right. That's why I hired Attica in the first place, to help me find balance—left to myself, I'd be off the grid entirely (maybe not the electric one, but most certainly the Snapaday one).

"Well, get ready, Liv!" Jade says, eyes bright. "I think it's safe to say you're going to have an entirely new generation of fans."

The very thought of being in the spotlight again fills me with butterflies . . . and also a few reluctant moths that aren't sure they're ready to fly out of the shadows. I want it, and I don't. I want it more than I don't, though, so I'm doing the brave thing: putting myself back out there a little at a time—but only what I want to give.

✧

Back in my dressing room, I take a moment just for me—it might be the last of its kind, at least for the next few weeks.

Girl on the Verge was the most-watched teen series for six years straight, beloved by critics and fans and even a few university professors who've devoted entire courses to dissecting the things our writers did right. Even though we've been off the air for a while, the general consensus is that *Girl on the Verge* remains a timeless hit and will hold up—which means I should probably prepare myself for a decent amount of attention in the days to come. Months or years if the reboot happens.

I slip my phone out of my handbag. Missed messages fill the screen: there are nearly half a dozen short texts from my mother (who's still fiercely supportive of me even though she's traded Hollywood for the Outer Banks of North Carolina), three notifications from Bre, at least ten one-off texts from various people from the fringes of my life, and one from . . . Ransom? His name on my screen is such a surprise I nearly choke on my coffee.

It's been a while.

I swipe it open on instinct.

do you have any idea how many kittens are in my mentions this morning? i'm drowning over here!

According to the time stamps on our text history, it's been over a year since I last heard from him—a brief congrats for the award nominations, then dead silence after I sent an ecstatic GIF back in reply. Before that, we texted sporadically here and there, mostly on birthdays and whenever one of us had a premiere making waves.

It's hard to believe we were once inseparable, even harder to believe he was my safe place and I was his. Before the end of our last season, anyway, when everything came crashing down.

Despite it all, I feel an undeniable thrill at the sight of his name at the top of my screen; his words are rock candy at the bottom of my stomach, jagged but sparkling, a sweet aftertaste that leaves me feeling a little fizzy inside.

My body is a traitor.

There are worse ways to drown! I write back. *You're welcome.*

I tap out of the window and into my thread with Bre. *CALL ME ASAP*, her most recent message says, on the heels of two others sent just before and just after my interview—*You'll be amazing!* one says, and the other simply says, *Killed it, Liv!*

Once I'm all tucked in to the back seat of the shiny black Mercedes I arrived in, sunglasses firmly in place, I call her back.

"Liv?" Bre's voice is loud in my ear. "My inbox is blowing up with requests passed along from Mars and Attica—there's a magazine in Spain that wants you to shoot a cover for them, I think that's one of the best ones, but point is, I'm going to send you a list in twenty minutes, and I need you to approve at least eight of the opportunities and no more than twelve. That's a request from Attica."

Attica, my twenty-six-year-old publicist, has the energy of a rabbit and the instincts of a tiger shark. Bless her. She's a relatively new addition to my team—I hired her a few years back to help with press when the first indie film I did started to take off. Marsden, on the other hand, has been my agent since the beginning, a tour de force of patience and wisdom and razor-sharp intuition.

"Mars will work with legal to handle the contracts," Bre goes on, "and I'll make sure all the scheduling works out. Oh, and Liv, your social is absolutely *exploding*—between your interview with Jade and the GIFs the new fans are starting to circulate and the kittenpalooza over on Ransom's account, you're trending everywhere. If you could work in a post or two before noon and a story or two by three p.m.— where you're talking to the viewer and where we can clearly see your face, but definitely with a tone that says *I'm oh so natural and relatable, everyone!*—that would be great. That's another request from Attica, by the way. Oh, and—"

"Bre?" I cut in. Her energy is *necessary*, but on a normal day, it's never as frenetic as this. "I'll look out for your email, thanks, and I'll do my best with the social media. Pass my thanks to Mars and Attica, too, okay? Now take a breath. Are you breathing?"

"I am. Yes. Yes, thank you—today's a bit more hectic than usual and—"

"Bre. You're amazing. I couldn't live without you, and I'm beyond grateful," I say. "But I think you should take an hour and go get some gelato. Tell me you're going to get some gelato, okay?"

A beat of silence passes. "Okay. Okay, yes, you're right. Thank you." The way her energy starts to settle is palpable, even over the phone. "I'll go right after I send the list your way. We're still on for quarter to six tonight?"

"Unless you have more interesting plans that come up between now and then," I deadpan. As we are both very much single these days, Bre has agreed to be my plus-one for the fancy dinner Fanline's throwing for the cast and crew tonight to kick off the show's anniversary festivities. She—Bre Livingston, who makes new friends in the snacks aisle at Trader Joe's—went full-on speechless when I invited her. I'm not sure I've ever seen another person so excited.

"I *was* thinking about finally getting started on knitting an ugly Christmas sweater for Sergeant Moonbeam . . ."

"Oh, yes, I can see how knitting your cat a Christmas sweater *in June* might take priority," I say, smirking into the lid of my flat white.

"When you put it that way, I guess I could put it off for another day or so."

"Such sacrifices! I know you're not looking forward to this *at all*."

"Only for you, Liv. Only for you."

"You're the best," I say. "See you tonight."

This barrage of requests pouring in all at once? It's not normal for either of us. When *Girl* was still on the air, no one ever asked for my input—I've since learned that having a say in things is a blessing and a curse. So is being back in the public spotlight more significantly than I have been in quite some time.

Speaking of, did she say I'm *trending*? I open my Flitterbird profile and . . . oh. Four million followers and growing, more than double the number I had when I last checked a couple of days ago. I don't dare look at my mentions. Before I can stow my phone away in my handbag, though, it vibrates with another new text.

Ransom—again.

Not for the first time this week, my mind trips over the fact that he'll be at the dinner tonight in the flesh, sharing the same air as me. We haven't been in the same physical space in fourteen years—it feels like fire to think about, something warm and familiar and captivating that could burn if I let down my guard and get too close.

GQ wants to do my shoot this afternoon with a literal pile of kittens surrounding me, WHAT HAVE YOU GOTTEN ME INTO, LIVVIE

I can't help myself, I smile.

And then I remember how close we were, and then how close we weren't, and it fades.

You know you love it, I write back. He's never been one to say no to attention, has never felt the crushing weight of the spotlight like I have—only its warmth.

I tuck my phone away, look out the window instead to watch the world pass by. I've been in a thousand cars just like this one, done a thousand interviews—but today feels different. New. Like a beginning, like the start of something big.

Like a landslide.

Get ready, Liv.

Handsome Ransom Sends "Kittenpalooza" into Tailspin

By Zenia DiLitto // Editor in Chief, Pop Culture, DizzyZine.com

HELLO, Spinners—have I got a treat for YOU! I don't know about you, but my bedroom walls were absolutely covered in Ransom Joel posters back in the day. (I'm not ashamed. My money's on the fact that yours were, too.) You're probably also one of his 4.3 million Snapaday followers—find him at @ransom_notes if you haven't already to see a glow-up like none other! His transformation since his days playing Duke Beaufort on *Girl on the Verge* is a wonder to behold—and that's saying something, because the boy was already *quite* the stunner!

ANYWAY. THE KITTENS.

Let's start at the beginning.

Earlier this morning, Ransom's former costar Liv Latimer (talk about another glow-up, amirite? And it's not like she wasn't already gorgeous—time has been KIND to this cast, y'all!) gave her first interview in ages to none other than America's #1 talk show host, Jade Johnson. Liv was so kind as to remind the world of the adorable animal activism phase Ransom went through after *GotV* wrapped/before he went full-on sexy twentysomething. I think I still have that ASPCA calendar somewhere, not to mention I definitely still have the pair of cats I adopted after seeing a few of his cat-of-the-week posts. (Cantaloupe and Clementine send their regards.) Show of hands, who else saved some cats thanks to Ransom's activism? Good for all of you!

If you've been anywhere online today, you've probably been equal parts mystified and entranced by the number of kitten GIFs/photos/videos being flung Ransom-ward . . . so now you know where it all started. Ransom hasn't directly responded to any of the thousands of messages that have piled up, but he did post a simple directive that prompted even more of a tailspin (pun intended): "Adopt, don't shop," he wrote in his latest tweet, which is now pinned to the top of his feed, along with a simple yellow cat emoji. Rumor has it that adoptions have spiked all over the country today, so let me repeat: Good for all of you!

Now, if we can just get a fresh post of sexy thirtysomething Ransom snuggling a kitten or two, that would be greeeeeeeeaaaaat. Hear that, Ransom? The internet has spoken!

In the meantime, fire up your Fanline accounts and start bingeing *Girl on the Verge*—their twentieth-anniversary reunion show is coming up soon, and I, for one, will be dropping everything to watch.

2

My home is an oasis, afternoon light streaming through the wall of windows that overlooks the ocean. The salt air and the sea calm me on even my hardest days, while the pristine, unbroken sand is reassurance that this little slice of shore delivers the privacy I've craved for as long as I can remember.

I fill a tumbler with iced water and head out to the patio. Once upon a time, it wasn't just me here—I had a boyfriend, Noah, who might have become a fiancé had he not suddenly shown his true colors the moment I picked my career back up. I'd just taken a role in an indie film after a several-years-long hiatus, and at first it was *You'll be gone for how long?*, which turned into *I'm not comfortable with you kissing him, even if it is part of the job*, which blew up into a myriad of shrapnel from the single grenade of *Honestly, I just prefer Quiet Liv to Famous Liv*. He'd met me at low tide, when I'd pulled as far away from Hollywood and everyone in it as I possibly could. When I realized I wasn't creatively fulfilled—I missed the art of it all, the challenge, the chance to slip in and inhabit someone else's skin for just a little while—things that were in my blood every bit as much as my aversion to the press—a riptide swept through, and it destroyed us.

I haven't been serious with anyone since. Noah was the first person I truly opened up to after Ransom, and yet—at the end of the day—when it was over, our breakup felt inevitable.

It's possible I haven't given anyone the chance to get that close again.

From what I can tell, Ransom took the exact opposite approach in the decade that followed our years on the show: a string of spy thrillers and huge, flashy blockbuster hits that have made him typecast for his chiseled, incredibly handsome face. (And, for the record, his body. He has *definitely* put in some work.) Girl after girl after girl, nothing too serious until last year, when he started dating Gemma Gardner, his literal girl next door from childhood who moved out to Glendale to open an adorable independent bookstore called the Garden. She's petite and demure, and they've looked effortlessly happy together in every photo I've seen.

At least there's that: They're happy. *He's* happy.

I've never admitted this to a single soul, but for a long time I secretly wished he wanted that happiness with me. He never thought of me like that, though, like a girlfriend—we were Liv and Ransom, inseparable best friends.

Until suddenly we weren't.

I've done my best not to go down Ransom rabbit holes in the years since the show, especially in the recent months since our reunion special got the green light—a knot forms when I start to think too much about slipping into our former roles after all this time and all that happened between us.

About kissing him again on camera.

About everything else.

My phone vibrates on the glass patio table beside me: a text from Bre asking my preferences for the dinner tonight. It's an easy choice—oysters and chardonnay, crème brûlée for dessert.

Tonight's dinner will kick off the celebration of the show's twentieth anniversary. Even though the reunion special itself will only be an hour-long scripted episode, Fanline is making an entire two-week ordeal out of the whole thing. Some people are traveling in from far corners of the world to make it happen—like Annagrey Siebert, who played my mother and eventually retired off the coast of Greece, or Pierre Alameda, who played my tennis coach (and, unlike me, was chosen for the part because he was a tennis professional in real life—he now coaches full-time at a tennis academy in Spain).

Others, like Sasha-Kate Kilpatrick, still live right here in Los Angeles and make the city feel too small; we've run into each other a dozen times since wrapping the show, and it's been awkward every time. She and I originally auditioned for the same role on the show, so I've known her since the very beginning, even longer than Ransom.

We were never close. She was cold to me right from the start, cast as one of my character's sisters instead of in the starring role, and it only got icier from there. I've long suspected Sasha-Kate's influence lit the fire that led to all the drama in our final season; I'm not exactly looking forward to sharing a set with her again.

It will be a few days before we start filming, though. This first week will be full of media hits—interviews, photo shoots—and costume fittings, along with tonight's dinner and another more casual get-together this weekend at the home of our writing team, Dan and Xan Jennings. Next week will be all about the show itself, starting with a table read on Monday, our first since the series finale. When we sat around the table that last time, scripts in hand, we never imagined we'd get the chance to do it again. For better or worse, I'm glad it's happening: the fandom has been begging for closure for as long as we've been off the air.

If I'm honest, I've needed a bit of it myself.

✧

I'm in my closet, freshly showered and about to change into the perfect dress for tonight—solid black silk, high neckline, plunging V in the back, so glossy and posh it's like I've been dipped in lacquer—when my phone buzzes.

tell me again how there are worse ways to drown, Ransom's text says, punctuated with a side-eye emoji. A second later, an image comes through: a screenshot of a Snapaday post, someone's very bare—and extremely tattooed—back filling the entire frame. I can't help it, I burst out laughing.

Is that supposed to be your face? I mean, clearly, that's a cat tattoo on the left, but the other tattoo beside it . . . uhhhh . . .

The artist (and I use that term loosely) has taken quite the abstract approach to the size and placement of Ransom's various facial features, and it doesn't exactly look purposeful.

His reply is immediate.

yes. yes it is.

And now I'm crying, both *at* the unfortunate tattoo and *for* the person who now has it permanently affixed to her skin.

The resemblance is uncanny, I text back. All these years of silence and, somehow, out of nowhere, it's like we never left off. *I think my favorite part is how the artist has attempted to make it look like Tattoo Ransom is gazing fondly at Tattoo Cat.*

He sends back a skull emoji, followed quickly by *can you imagine asking someone to put this on your skin permanently? or . . . at all?*

I've never seen anything so perfectly hideous, I write. *The more I look at it, the more I kind of want one.*

nothing says liv latimer like a botched tattoo of my face gazing long-ingly at someone else's cat, he replies.

He still knows exactly what will make me laugh, and for one sus-pended moment, it feels like nothing's changed.

We're not the same people we were all those years ago, I remind myself.

And yet.

Another message bubble appears before I can write back.

on a serious note, i'm looking forward to seeing you tonight, livvie. it's been too long.

My laughter catches in my throat, and now I'm blinking back tears for a different reason altogether. I don't know how to respond. It's not that I'm *not* looking forward to seeing him—I am, I think, despite all our complicated history. It's more that I feel myself start to unravel a bit when I try to imagine *how* it will be to see him. How I'll feel, being so close again after all the distance that's been between us. If it will be awkward—if it will hurt.

These texts help, at least.

On a serious note, I eventually write back, *I'm looking forward to unveiling the freshly botched tattoo I plan to get on the way to dinner! I'll be the talk of the red carpet for sure.*

Almost as soon as I hit send, a dot bubble pops up but disappears just as quickly.

I really should finish getting ready.

I can't bring myself to set the phone down.

A moment later, another dot bubble pops up. Instead of disappearing this time, though, it's replaced by a new message. Three little words, no punctuation, and the effect is like a dizzying shot of pure oxygen straight to my brain:

you always are

#5Facts: Sasha-Kate Kilpatrick— Look at Her Now!

By Octavia Benetton // Staff Writer, *Love & Lightning Rounds*

What's up, Lightning Bugs—welcome to a shiny new round of #5Facts! Seems like everyone and their llamas are losing their minds over the upcoming reunion of the *Girl on the Verge* cast . . . yours truly included! If you've been around here for any amount of time, you know this site stans the *other* It Girl from back in the day: Sasha-Kate Kilpatrick, fictional sibling—and longtime real-life rival—of beloved pop culture icon Liv Latimer. Liv has soaked up enough of the spotlight over the years, yes? Let's give Sasha-Kate the moment in the sun she deserves! Here are five things you might not know about Sasha-Kate:

1. Sasha-Kate may have played Liv's younger sister on TV, but she's actually two months older than Liv!

2. Rumor has it that her feud with Liv began when Sasha-Kate auditioned for the part of Honor St. Croix but was passed over for it due to her height. She's a full four inches shorter than Liv!

3. Sasha-Kate is the only cast member who sat out on the Australian leg of their world tour. Her brother played on the professional junior tennis circuit for a few years, and she cut out of the tour early to go watch him play in the semifinals at Wimbledon! Psssst: tennis runs in their family, and it's another reason Sasha-Kate resented Liv's casting as Honor!

Liv had never picked up a racquet prior to her role on the show, sources confirm, while Sasha-Kate was practically born with one in her hand (her mother played competitively for Romania before a wrist injury cut her career short).

4. Ransom Joel isn't the cast's only animal activist. Sasha-Kate poured a huge portion of her earnings from the show into the Save the Whales movement, and has cochaired a number of fundraising events to promote general awareness for the protection and preservation of our oceans.

5. And finally, looooook at baby Sasha-Kate from S1:E1 of the show. Remember how they always had her hair in double Dutch braids for those first two seasons? I had almost forgotten, especially since her hair became EVERYTHING in later seasons (surely you remember the Bianca, since every girl on the beach that one summer had those billowy sand-blond ombré waves that looked like the *actual* beach at low tide?? Or is that just me?).

Group watch party starts tonight at six, PST—live chat under hashtag #LBWatchParty! Post a photo of your Sasha-Kate-inspired Dutch braids if you wear them!

3

I'm putting on a careful coat of mascara, turning Ransom's last text over in my head, when my phone buzzes again: it's Attica, my publicist.

Any chance you're suddenly interested in adopting a kitten? Or maybe Bre and I could find a fundraiser for you to chair, like maybe for snow leopards?

A kitten? I send back. *SNOW LEOPARDS? (??)*

Almost immediately, she sends a link over. Something about Sasha-Kate in the headline, from a site I've never heard of. I skim the post, grateful Attica's not here in person to see how dramatically I've just rolled my eyes.

We've reached the point where texting is inefficient. She picks up on the first ring. "So what if Sasha-Kate wants to save the whales?" I say in lieu of an actual greeting. I glance out the window—Jimmy, my driver, is set to pick me up in ten minutes. "It's not a competition."

"You say that now," Attica says. "But it does matter, Liv. I know that's just a random blog post, but it's not the only one that's popped up lately—you want a reboot green-lit after the reunion special, and not just some mediocre spin-off where you get cut out of it. You need to make sure the audience is firmly Team Liv."

"I was never under the impression they *weren't*." I'm not even sure I *want* a reboot green-lit—not that Attica can be blamed for assuming so, since I'm still working through my feelings and haven't told her otherwise—but it would be beyond insulting to be cut out of it. *Girl on the Verge* without its original girl? Surely they wouldn't.

"Oh, they love you, Liv, always have! But we're talking kittens and whales here—if any of those Sasha-Kate fan sites wanted to make you look cold in comparison, they could."

I bristle at her words but resist the urge to defend myself.

"How about this," she goes on. "Think of something that feels right for *you*. Once you land on your thing, let me know and I'll work my magic. Forget about the snow leopards?"

"Already forgotten."

"Okay—rest up, think about it, get back to me when you can. How are you feeling about tonight? The carpet, the press?"

"Eh," I say. "I'll survive it."

"You've got this." She's made of confidence, and I want so badly to believe her. "Just do your whole mysterious enigma vibe if there's anything you don't want to answer, okay?"

"So that would be preferable to, say, biting their heads off in very public fashion?"

"Only slightly. But yes."

When we end the call, it's like the air has physically stilled in the room. Attica's energy is palpable even over the phone, just like Bre's. If not for Mars—calm, cool, and collected to the extreme, a mostly ideal personality mix for an agent—my team would skew too heavily toward the frenetic. I'm somewhere in the middle: my whole life, people have attached words like *magnetic* and *charismatic* to my name, even though I've got a relatively calm way of moving through the world. Some of that poise came naturally, and some came through practice; my first publicist back in the day coached me by saying, over and over again, words that could have come straight from my father's mouth: *Starlight is full of energy, but it stays fixed in the night sky. You're a star, Liv—act like one.*

The girl staring back at me in the mirror took that advice to heart a long time ago, for better and for worse. Sparkling eyes, cherry lips, smoky shadow beneath perfectly arched brows: a familiar face to go with a household name, even if she's fiercely devoted to keeping parts of her life locked away, just for herself. Luminous but distant.

I peek out from my bathroom window and see Jimmy's Mercedes idling in my circle drive, only a little bit early. I touch up my lipstick one final time and head downstairs.

✧

Bre's outside and ready when we pull up. Her green dress perfectly complements her red hair and fair complexion; her heels could kill. She slides into the open seat behind Jimmy.

The ride gets off to an uncharacteristically quiet start. Bre fidgets, riffling through her slim handbag for who knows what.

"You good?" I ask, and she meets my gaze with dreamy eyes.

I've seen *that* look before—and never in a million years expected it from Bre. Not once have I ever seen her nervous or intimidated in the presence of another person.

"I'm *so excited*, Liv," she breathes. "I thought I'd be chill, but—ahhhh—I'm so mortified right now that I'm like this. Sorry, I'll try to pull myself together."

I laugh. "Breathe. In and out. You'll be fine, just be your normal lovely self."

I never considered that an event like this would faze her even slightly. I forget the people who'll be in the room tonight are iconic household names from her childhood—all of us together with the litany of producers, directors, and writers could be more intimidating than I realized. To me, they've always just been the people I grew up with.

They weren't part of Bre's world until our paths crossed a few years ago, when I'd freshly settled back in LA after my years off the grid. A stranger at the time, Bre came to my rescue when a starstruck group of tourists spotted me jogging on the Strand—I'd craved the view of the Pacific while in Montana and had almost gotten away with being on a public beach when the tourists started flocking to me. Bre was on a run, too, and expertly extracted me from the situation like we'd been best friends for ages. All these years later, we actually are as close as we pretended to be.

We pull up to the venue just as the sunset fills the sky with the most extraordinary explosion of colors, pinks and oranges and purples and rays of gold. The timing couldn't be better—it will make the most gorgeous, dramatic backdrop for all the photos that are about to be snapped as soon as we step out of the car.

"Ready for this?" I say, turning to Bre. She looks better than before, but I know her well enough to know her calm facade is taking a *lot* of work.

She gives a subtle nod. "Let's do it."

I climb out first. The shock of flashes almost takes my breath away—so many, all at once. Bre follows, and together, we make our way toward the venue's entrance. Spotlights that match the sunset illuminate the expansive exterior granite wall, with the *Girl on the Verge* and Fanline logos projected in gigantic bright white letters.

The questions blend together: *Liv! Can you tell us any details about the reunion special? Liv! Is it true—are we getting a reboot? Liv! There are rumors circulating that Ransom bought a ring for Gemma Gardner—any comment? Liv! Can you confirm that Sasha-Kate is in negotiations to take a more prominent role in the reboot, if there is one? Liv! Liv! Liv!*

They fly like arrows, the questions, burrowing straight into my thick, scarred heart—especially the one about Ransom, and to a lesser extent, Sasha-Kate. These questions don't mean any of it is *true*. Reporters like to get a rise out of us, spinning up eye-catching headlines that will pull traffic to their sites.

I give a demure smile, even though I'm a mess on the inside. "You'll just have to watch and see!" I say over and over again, swallowing all that I *could* say but very much shouldn't.

All at once, there's a commotion at the end of the carpet as everyone turns, collectively, looking at something behind me. I turn to see what's caught their attention, and—

"*Oh* my gosh, Liv!" Bre's hand squeezes mine so tightly I'm surprised my bones don't crack. "Ransom's here, and he looks *good.*"

My heart stutters. Bre's right—he *does* look good. Very, very good. His tux is midnight black, tailored in a way that's both elevated fashion yet still perfectly, casually Ransom; black oxfords gleam at his feet. His hairstyle is extremely *GQ*—thanks to his shoot with them earlier today, no doubt—and he's got just the right amount of stubble darkening his jaw.

In all the hours I spent turning this moment over in my head—what it would be like to see him again, in the flesh, after all this time—I never imagined it feeling like *this*. I expected nerves, or regret, or the lingering sting of bitterness. Not once did it cross my mind that it might feel like returning to a favorite place, like going home—if said home had undergone some substantial upgrades, anyway. Gone is the Ransom I knew in our teenage years, with his boyish charm and adorable boy-next-door vibe. In his place is a full-fledged *man*, one who radiates confidence and looks like he knows his way around bourbon and bedsheets and yachts off the coast of various glittering European vistas.

He's also, notably, alone.

At the exact second I register this observation, he looks up through the sea of flashbulbs. His eyes lock with mine immediately, and they light up.

I light up—I can't help it. It's been so many years, and old instincts die hard.

"Ransom, where's Gemma tonight?" a reporter asks, his voice cutting through all the others.

Before he gives an answer, though, the sound of my own name pulls me out of my head. "Ms. Latimer!" someone is saying, just off the carpet in front of me. "May I inquire as to whether you're considering any more roles in independent features?" It's an impeccably dressed reporter, extremely polished and polite in her British accent and tailored black dress. "You were stunning in *Love // Indigo*."

This catches my attention, and not in a bad way. Hardly anyone mentions *Love // Indigo*—it was the second independent film I did, a low-budget romance with more silence than actual lines. The cinematography was beautiful, with a distinct melancholy tone to it, all set largely on the shore of Bay Head Beach in the dead of winter. I took the role because it had fantastic range to it, and a small, intimate set. I knew it would be a quiet release—and quiet turned out to be an understatement—but it's possibly the role I'm most proud of.

"Thank you," I say, meeting her eye. "I loved that film, loved Vienna's vision for it. I'd love to work with her again in the future."

Her entire face lights up. "I hope you do," she says sincerely. "Her writing is so underrated. If you ever do team up again, here's my card. I'd love to do a piece on it."

She effortlessly produces a card from her handbag and slips it to Bre. Wow, she's good—I never give a commitment on the carpet, but I will absolutely take this woman up on it if anything happens down the line.

"I'll keep it in mind, thanks." I flash my best smile before Bre and I move on.

The rest of the carpet is a sea of insipid questions, one of them actually quite hostile—*Liv! Don't you think you should just sit the reboot out and let Sasha-Kate finally have her time to shine?* I mean, what am I supposed to say to that? Nothing they want to hear, that's for sure.

Just when I think Bre and I will make it all the way through without someone going too far, it happens: "Liv!" a reporter calls out, a thin man in a trim navy suit. "What do you think your father would say if he could see you now?"

My poker face slips ever so slightly, and suddenly it feels like I'm fourteen all over again on that blisteringly hot September afternoon. A rash of heat climbs my throat—

A hand closes gently around my arm, just above the elbow, steadying me.

It takes a moment to register the scent—it's subtle but sensual, cedar and citrus and spice—most definitely masculine. Unfamiliar but not unwelcome.

"Liv's done some amazing work in the years since the show, yeah?" Ransom says with an easy smile, not so subtly redirecting the conversation. Chastened, the reporter gives a curt nod, tucking his voice recorder back inside his jacket pocket as if he never said anything at all.

Heat radiates from the places where Ransom's fingers rest on my arm, searing my skin even though his touch is featherlight. And he seriously smells so *good*, distractingly so. A heartbeat later, he presses in ever so slightly, a silent reminder that my Louboutins are not, in fact, one with the carpet.

Wow, Bre mouths, just to me, as the three of us move on without another word.

I'm tangled inside, gossamer spiderwebs linking old wounds to the pleasant reality of what just happened. What's happen*ing*. Being this close to Ransom is everything I never wanted to lose—and I still have no explanation as to why he's here alone, why Gemma Gardner isn't by his side with the rumored engagement ring sparkling under all these lights.

As if Ransom can still read my mind, his fingertips fall away from my skin as suddenly as they settled there. Only the ghost of feeling lingers, a chill in the absence of his warm touch.

"Well, *that* was an experience," Bre says under her breath once we're finally through the gauntlet. "It looks so much more enjoyable in pictures."

"It'll be smooth from here," I say, to myself as much as to Bre, nodding to the pair of security guards who stand still amid the bustle. "No press past those guys."

Fanline went all out with the decor, and we haven't even made it inside yet—there's a posh-looking cocktail area off to our left, including a strategically lit photo op wall made of live succulents; our bright pink *GotV* logo is emblazoned on it in curving, curling neon lights.

From just off the carpet, one last reporter calls Ransom's name.

"Excuse me for just a minute," Ransom says with another light touch, his fingers grazing the bare skin of my lower back. He leans in close, like there's a secret he can't wait to share. "I can't help but notice," he says, breath hot in my ear, "the distinct lack of botched tattoo on your back."

I can't help it, I laugh—and he flashes me his moneymaker smile before breaking away to go answer the reporter's question. That smile is megawatt bright, the kind that would stop traffic (possibly even of the space travel variety). Despite all our complicated history, I've missed it.

"Okay," Bre whispers, once he's out of earshot, eyebrows so high I worry they'll leap right off her face. "What was *that*?"

"It's nothing."

The alternative is that it is *something*, which is impossible, because Ransom has Gemma and I have a scarred heart.

"It didn't look like nothing."

I glance his way, watch the reporter's eyes fill with stars as Ransom answers her question. He's always been good at making a person feel like they're the only one in the room; his natural charm is magnetic, and it's intense. It's impossible not to feel safe with him.

"Well, if it isn't Livvie Latimer—girl of my dreams!"

My head whips up at that distinctive drawl. There's only one person who's ever called me *girl of my dreams*.

"Ford Brooks!" I greet him. "It's been a million years. What have you been up to over there in London?" He's got a smile that rivals Ransom's, though it's lopsided and usually goes hand in hand with whatever joke is on the tip of his tongue.

Ford politely thanks the reporter he'd been talking with and heads our way. When he pulls me into a hug, I look over his shoulder to see Bre mouthing, wide-eyed, *Girl of my dreams??*

One week in our third season, Ford and I were shooting some tennis scenes, and he started having the most bizarre dreams. One night I was riding a triceratops onto the court, another night we were both mermaids playing tennis with our fins. This went on for a solid week, then stopped as suddenly as it started—ever since, he's called me *girl of my dreams*.

"No Juliette tonight?" I ask, when we're face-to-face again. According to many a tabloid cover, he and actress Juliette Wells are one of London's hottest couples—he met her shortly after moving there from the States.

"She's shooting in Iceland right now," he replies, beaming with pride. "Another Jonathan Cast project."

Bre gasps beside me, and I don't blame her—it's a really big deal.

"Wow, congrats to her!" I say. "I look forward to seeing it."

"Another year or two, hopefully," Ford says. Jonathan Cast is notorious for blowing budgets by shooting three times longer than he needs, then being ruthless and meticulous in the editing room until every single second is perfection. He gets away with it because the final results are brilliant, always.

Ford turns his attention on Bre and smiles. "I don't believe we've had the pleasure . . . ?"

"Ford, this is Bre Livingston, who's technically my assistant but is also a close friend—Bre, meet Ford."

A hint of pink flushes in her cheeks. For a split second, I worry she'll go speechless, but she recovers smoothly. "So tell me all about London—are the double-decker buses as fun as they seem?"

They chat for a bit as we make our way inside, past the security guards who let us through without a hassle. I glance back over my shoulder to see if we should wait for Ransom, but he's chatting with another reporter now; while I tend to hold everything back with the press, he's overly generous. He relishes it, I think, though he would say I'm wrong about that.

If I thought Fanline had gone all out with the exterior decor, the inside is every bit as amazing. The lofty ceiling is starlit, dotted with countless twinkle lights that make it look like the night sky. Foliage covers the walls—it feels like we've been transported straight into the most beautiful modern garden, and the room is intimate despite its expansive height. Fifteen circular tables are draped in pristine white linens, set with delicate bone china and an array of glasses waiting to be filled. A stage spans the length of the far wall, on which there is also a huge screen; like everything else, it boasts our logo along with Fanline's.

For a moment, it's like the world stands still: I'm hit, suddenly, by just how rare this all is. That I was *part* of it—part of something iconic—that the show has been trending daily, now that it's streaming and a new generation has started bingeing our old episodes. Maybe I'm just nostalgic after seeing Ransom and Ford, but it's not lost on me how incredible this is.

"Oh, look, Liv!" Bre calls from where she and Ford ended up while walking and talking. "Here's my table!"

I can hear the relief in her voice. She'll be sitting at the plus-ones table—she's been legit terrified she'd end up starstruck to the point of speechlessness if she somehow landed a seat with me and the rest of our core cast. I go to join them and see her name scrawled on a white card in fun bright pink hand-lettered cursive; the card itself is nestled neatly atop the thick, fleshy leaves of a miniature potted succulent.

"Let's see who you're with," Ford says, circling the table. "I don't know any of these—oh, wait, here's Havilah Loren!" He picks up the tiny pot with Havilah's name on it and smoothly switches it with one marked *Caroline Crenshaw*, originally seated next to Bre.

"Havilah Loren," I say, trying to place why it sounds so familiar, and then it hits me. "Isn't that Hālo's given name?"

All the color drains from Bre's face. "Hālo, as in *super mega chart-topping pop star* Hālo?"

"That'd be the one," Ford says, grinning. "She's friends with Sasha-Kate."

So much for Bre not being starstruck, I think, stifling a laugh. It's cute that either of us ever thought she could contain her chill.

"Who's friends with Sasha-Kate?" a deep voice says, one I'd recognize in my sleep. Ransom appears beside me, pulls me in close for a side hug. It's smooth, especially considering this is new territory, only a ghost of how it once was between us.

"Time's been good to you, Liv," he says, his voice muffled in my hair, turning all of me to honey.

"And me?" Ford says, pulling us apart and giving Ransom a gigantic hug of his own.

Ransom laughs. "Time's been good to you, too. Where's Juliette? She shooting with Cast already?"

"She was disappointed to miss out on this, yeah," Ford says. "And Gemma? Those rumors true, man?"

I, too, would like to know if those rumors are true.

Ransom grimaces. "Had to get my watch battery replaced a few weeks ago, and the jewelry shop was right around the corner from one of my shoots. Half hour later, the world thinks we're getting engaged." He glances over his shoulder, as if he's afraid the wrong person might hear. "Things had actually been shaky with Gemma for a while," he goes on. "The engagement rumors broke us up for good."

My heart skips.

They're not engaged—they're not even *together*.

"I'm sorry, *what*?" Ford says, emphatic enough to distract from how completely and utterly frozen this revelation has left me. "How did you manage to keep that out of the press?"

Ransom's gaze flickers over to mine. "Tried my best to make sure our private life stayed private. For her sake." The briefest shadow clouds his face, but then he's bright and beaming. "But, ahhh, hey—on the bright side, the internet took a nice break from analyzing my romantic life for most of today."

"You forgive me for the kittens, then?" I tease, and his dimples deepen.

"I should buy you *dinner* for the kittens," he quips back. "Adoptions have shot through the roof—"

"And so has your social media following," Bre says, finally finding words again. That was the longest she's ever gone without speaking for as long as I've known her.

Ransom laughs. "You, I like."

"Bre, Ransom—Ransom, Bre," I say. "My wonderful assistant—"

"Slash best friend," she finishes for me.

"Pleasure's all mine," Ransom says, flashing his best grin, the one that's likely responsible for kicking off his entire career. "What about you, Liv? No date tonight?"

"Did you just give her the *twinkle*?" Ford exclaims, and here we go—it's like we're all sixteen again. Ford and Ransom together were always a charismatic mess, feeding off each other's energy. "I detected a distinct sparkle in your eye, Rance."

"I saw it, too!" I add, because Ransom has always adamantly denied the existence of the twinkle, and I can't help myself. And then reality sets in, and I'm hit with the full weight of the question I've just been asked: Ransom Joel is curious about my dating life.

I'm not ready to think about what that means.

"No—no date." I consider adding more—that it's been years since I've even been on a *first* date, let alone been one half of a steady relationship—but the silence blooms between us, taking up all the space where my words should go.

"So, Bre," Ford says pointedly, "want to check out the drinks with me?"

Bre's not oblivious. Ford hooks his arm into hers, and together, they head off in the general direction of away from us.

"It's good to see you, Liv," Ransom says, once it's just us, eyes locked on mine. "I wanted to ask—wanted to make sure—"

His voice drops off, and he runs a hand through his hair. "The way we left things, back when the show ended . . . I just wanted to say I'm sorry. I've had a lot of time to think over the years, and in hindsight, I don't think I handled what happened as well as I could have." He's quiet for a beat, and I know the same dark memories must be playing across both our minds. "I'm sure you've moved on from it, but I just wanted to tell you, because we've got some, um, scenes to do next week. And I want to make sure you know I never meant to hurt you before we get that close again. In the scenes."

Right. In the scenes.

It's never been the scenes I've worried about. I can be someone else completely when the cameras are on, pretend he's someone else, too.

"Thanks for what you did back there," I say, dodging the subject, taking in all the depths of his eyes, light green with subtle flecks of gold. "How you handled that reporter when he asked about my dad. It meant a lot."

A flush of pink spreads on his cheeks, a rare shy moment.

"They should know better by now," he says quietly, studying me. I used to be able to read his thoughts, but right now, I can't begin to guess what he's thinking.

"This is surreal, isn't it?" he finally says.

I breathe in the moment, survey the room. So many familiar faces weathered by time and age.

"*Surreal*'s the word," I say. "Did you ever think it would all turn into *this*?"

The first time I ever stepped foot on *Girl*'s set, it was the strangest feeling in the world to have cameras pointed at me and not my father. He'd rehearsed with me the night before, made sure I'd nailed my lines. After my first day of shooting, we went for milkshakes, extra cherries on top.

I really do wish he could see me now and all the show became.

Ransom's quiet beside me. He's always been the sentimental one of the group; whereas his soft side used to read as adorable boy next door, those tendencies now manifest much moodier, more mature. It suits him more than I'm ready to admit.

"We're the lucky ones, Liv." His gaze flickers to the starlit ceiling, then back to me. It's so intense, so classic Ransom, my stomach does a flip. I'm not immune to how devastatingly attractive he is. I'm not immune to the twinkle, either, not even a little bit.

A beat passes, and I'm still feeling around for the right words—but then a dress as bright as our logo catches my eye, layers upon layers of flashy pink chiffon that somehow manage to be over-the-top and elegant at the same time. Ransom turns, looking over his shoulder.

Say what you want about Sasha-Kate, but the girl knows how to make an entrance.

"Guess the party can start now," Ransom says with a wry grin.

Star-Studded Turnout
to Fanline Dinner as Entire Cast of
Girl on the Verge Descends Upon
West Hollywood

By Ithaca Alexander // Staff Writer, Arts & Entertainment, *Sunset Central*

The stars came out in full force under tonight's unbelievable sunset—all eyes were on the red carpet outside the John and Carol Harris Center for the Arts as, one by one, the big names rolled in.

Sweetheart writing duo Dan and Xan Jennings were among the first to arrive, looking chic as ever in Armani and Oscar de la Renta, respectively. Always nice to see a couple stay together in Hollywood, especially when they're responsible for one of the most iconic teen dramas of all time.

Showrunner-director Bryan Cortado, along with producing team Nathaniel Ezzo and Gabe Holcomb of Wild Mustang, arrived next, with a slew of Fanline execs close behind—of note, Fanline CEO Shine Jacobs stood out amid the veritable boys' club in vintage silver Chanel.

Ford Brooks was the first of the main cast to make an appearance, arriving in a loud emerald Gucci ensemble only he could pull off, and notably alone. Longtime girlfriend Juliette Wells—a British actress known most recently for snagging multiple award nominations last season—is rumored to be shooting a new Jonathan Cast picture up in Iceland.

Liv Latimer looked every inch the starlet she is in an ink-black Christian Siriano dress and Louboutins to match. Looks like a girls' night for Liv, whose assistant—Bre Livingston, sources confirm—joined in on the fun and looked stunning in vibrant green.

Ransom Joel took a solo trip down the red carpet, wearing all black Dolce & Gabbana and a five-o'clock shadow, looking undeniably classy and timeless. Another notable absence: amid engagement rumors, girlfriend Gemma Gardner was nowhere to be seen.

Finally, rounding out the cast's most prominent quartet, Sasha-Kate Kilpatrick stole everyone's hearts in bold pink Chanel, a frivolous dream of satin and chiffon daringly cut all the way down to her navel. Sasha-Kate never arrives without her #girlsquad these days, and tonight was no exception—resort heiress Garbiñe Itiriti, publicist Caroline Crenshaw, and singer-songwriter superstar Hālo were also in attendance, in addition to SK's beau-du-jour Nikola Milošević.

Annagrey Siebert, Laurence Williams, and Millie Matson—mom, dad, and adorable kid sister of the fictional St. Croix family—were also in attendance, along with Aurora Cove's hottest tennis coach, Pierre Alameda. (Two solid reasons to tune in to the reunion special when it airs, if you weren't already convinced: little Millie Matson is all grown up now and looking fantastic, and said tennis coach hasn't aged a day!)

What's going to happen in the reunion special? Post your best guesses below in the comments! We'll be live-tweeting the show when it airs, so spend these next weeks catching up on old episodes and be sure to follow @SunsetCentralBuzzzzz!

"Is it just me, or does Sasha-Kate have half of Hollywood with her?" Ransom murmurs.

I laugh. "How did she pull *that* off? The invite said plus *one*, not plus ten."

"Hundred bucks says that guy will be at our table," Ransom says, pointing at a lithe, long-haired man who somehow manages to make his tan, boxy, oversized suit look completely fashionable.

Our table turns out to be the liveliest one in the room, and the guy—Nikola—is, indeed, seated with us. I'm between Ransom and Ford, Sasha-Kate and Nikola are on Ford's other side, and to round out our table is Millie Matson, who was eleven years old last time I saw her. Now she's twenty-five, with glowing skin and makeup done to perfection. She's best known for the two pop albums she released over the past few years—particularly her most recent one, *Peaches*, which landed a top-twenty spot on the charts as soon as it was released.

"That's Hālo over there, isn't it?" Millie asks Sasha-Kate, trying (and failing) to look chill and not overeager. There's a reason Millie pivoted toward music instead of acting—when she was cast at age five, the acting didn't matter as much as her charisma.

"Why, you want an introduction, Millie?" Sasha-Kate says with a sly grin. She takes a sip of chardonnay, her lipstick immaculate.

If Millie is a rising pop star, Hālo has been borderline supernova for years now. Leave it to Sasha-Kate to demand a seat at our table for some guy she'll probably break up with by next week and relegate the rest of her star-studded entourage to a table on the other side of the room; Sasha-Kate isn't big on being outshined.

"I'm a big fan of her work," Millie says, a blush creeping into her cheeks. "Her album *Hallowed* was—it was just—I have sooooo many questions on the production side of things!"

Ford, meanwhile, has struck up a conversation with Nikola, who's backed his chair up so they can talk around Sasha-Kate. That just leaves Ransom and me.

Ransom plucks a roll from the basket and smears on a soft pat of butter. "Got all your lines memorized yet?" he asks, a nice, innocuous entry point for our new *let's try to maybe be friends again* situation. It's such basic small talk you'd think we'd never spent an hour in each other's company.

You'd never guess we've kissed on camera countless times.

You'd never guess we've seen each other cry. That we've *made* each other cry.

We've never had to start over before, though.

So. Small talk it is.

"Still working on them," I admit. "Things have been nonstop lately getting ready for the press blitz, and I've had to squeeze in some extra sessions with my trainer, and on top of all that I'm supposed to be making my way through a stack of novels Mars sent over from the agency. . . ."

"Wait, wait—you actually read the books they send?"

"You *don't*?"

"I mean, I read them if we move forward on the project but never when we're trying to settle on one— What? My team reads them and sends over the summaries—?"

"I just can't imagine committing to a project without reading the whole thing," I say, laughing. "Don't you feel like you're missing out on all the subtle things about the characters? How do you know which ones are right for you?" I sip my chardonnay, watch as he takes a bite out of his roll, leaving neat teeth marks behind.

Suddenly his teeth are all I can think about. And his full bottom lip, and how the last time I tasted it, it tasted like the mint ice cream we'd just eaten before filming our final scene together, and—

"Roles in my queue aren't necessarily known for their *subtleties*, if you know what I mean," he says, pulling me out of my head. I quickly avert my gaze before he notices how hard I'm staring at his lips. His eyes are bright, but past the surface, I see a flash of something else, something a bit . . . unsatisfied.

Having seen his last few feature films: he's not wrong. Knowing some part of him is unsatisfied? I never would have guessed.

"You, though—" he says, changing the subject before I can dig too deeply. "You've had some great roles, Liv, I mean it. You were absolutely killer in *Love // Indigo*."

My heart swells at the compliment, and not just because it was my favorite film I've worked on yet—Ransom saw me in it.

Ransom thought I was *killer*.

"You saw that one?" I take a quick sip of water to cool the heat rising in my face.

His eyes catch mine, and it's like he's looking straight into me— and I can't look away.

"I've seen all your films, Livvie. You've been fantastic in every one." His voice is as smooth as honey, and it stirs something in me. I need another sip of water, *fast*.

Before I can thank him, a swell of music fills the speakers as the lights dim overhead. A spotlight focuses on center stage, where Fanline CEO Shine Jacobs takes the podium.

"Good evening, everyone!" she says, her smile bright and beaming. She projects ease and power like she was born to lead—it's not at all hard to imagine why she was listed at the very top of a recent "World's 50 Most Influential Women of Color" feature in *Time*.

"It's my pleasure to welcome you to our kickoff dinner for the Fanline *Girl on the Verge* reunion special!" She pauses to make space for the applause that rises up in the room. "Like all of you, this show has a special place in my heart. I was an intern in a talent agency mail room when your pilot premiered, and I didn't know a soul out here in LA. One of the other interns knew someone on set over at *Girl*, so I ended up joining their weekly watch parties. By the time we'd all moved on to other industry jobs, your show was so popular, so respected, that one of my stodgiest old professors was teaching a writing course on it—he was that impressed with the work you were all doing. Side note for a moment, can we just take a second to honor Dan and Xan, the heart behind all of this and the reason we're here in this room today?"

The applause now rivals the first round of it, and one by one, everyone stands. At the next table over, Dan and Xan Jennings share a loving glance with each other. I've always found them so inspiring; they are the perfect example of partners who love and respect each other, both as a writing team and as husband and wife.

"Thank you, Dan and Xan, for all you've done," Shine continues, once we're all seated again, "not just for those of us here in this room but for everyone at home who felt better equipped to navigate their world after falling in love with your show. It was certainly invaluable to me on both a personal and professional level—I'm honored to be spearheading the reunion special, and to be face-to-face with all the people who brought the original series to life."

I don't know if it's the chardonnay, or the way Ransom's eyes light up when he glances my direction, or the fact that the CEO of Fanline is so personally invested in our success—probably all of it—but I'm buzzing with hope and anticipation. Signing on for the reunion special brought up so many complicated feelings for me, but right now, in this moment, I can't believe I ever considered saying no. The idea of a full-on reboot still feels complicated, but at least this is a good chance to test the waters of how it might be to do the show again. Tonight is a promising start.

Shine speaks for a little while longer, and then our showrunner takes the stage. Bryan is the closest thing to a cyborg you'll find in the director's guild: he's got a photographic memory and exceptional attention to detail, and is notorious for his no-nonsense attitude on set. He's got plenty of heart beneath his machinelike exterior, though, which makes his more intense moments feel worth it. He directed nearly every one of our episodes, and his specific gifting and personality type brought the show to life in ways he rarely gets credit for.

Bryan takes a few moments to echo Shine's praise for Dan and Xan, then introduces the short montage we'll be watching. The stage lights dim, and the boppy melody of our theme song streams out from the speakers. I haven't heard it in ages—it's not like *I* sit around watching old episodes—and the nostalgia of it all hits hard.

"Holy crap, Liv, we were *infants*!" Ransom whispers as our barely-even-teenaged faces grace the screen.

"Millie looks the same, though, wouldn't you say?" Ford stage-whispers, loud enough for the whole table to hear. Millie turns and gives him a smoky-eyed look—she's definitely not the five-year-old from our first season anymore.

"Your *hair*, Ford!" Sasha-Kate exclaims, and we all laugh. For the first three seasons, production insisted Ford's glorious shoulder-length mane be worn exclusively in a man bun—a trend that wasn't trendy until he made it so. It wasn't until he became an official romantic interest for my character, Honor, that they let him wear it down for the first time. Our ratings skyrocketed when that happened, and it became his official look for the rest of the series, far outlasting the brief romantic detour between our characters.

The scenes flash by, six years of our best moments—and a number of our best bloopers—condensed into a twenty-minute compilation. By the end of it, I have tears in my eyes. I'm not the only one.

Dan and Xan take the stage to close out the presentation.

"I'm supposed to give a speech here," Dan begins, "but as it turns out, I'm speechless." He surveys the crowd and lingers a little when he meets eyes with me; he gives me an almost imperceptible nod. "You have all left me speechless. What a legacy this show has left since its premiere! Twenty years—it seems like no time and forever all at once." A wave of applause fills the room. Dan takes a sip of the water he's brought onstage with him, and Xan puts her hand on his back. "Thank you all for being our dream cast—I'm not exaggerating when I say that Xan and I would never have done a moment of it differently."

Xan leans over to the mic. "This show was the ride of a lifetime for us," she adds. "And we're excited and grateful for the opportunity to experience the ride again—thank you to Shine and to Fanline and to everyone else who had a hand in making this reunion possible. Thank you to every one of you for signing on to return!" She looks at our table when she says this, at Ransom and at me, and then raises her glass. "To twenty years!"

We all raise our glasses, drink to the occasion. The rest of the night is a blur of faces and half-finished conversations, of chardonnay and music and laughter under the starlit ceiling.

Ransom and I are pulled in opposite directions almost immediately. He gets caught up with Annagrey and Laurence—who played my character's parents—and I find myself trapped in a particularly longwinded, one-sided conversation with Edna Arcadia, who's looking *good* for eighty-four; she played one of our teachers on the show. Ransom and I keep catching each other's eye, and it makes everything a little more bearable. He's a life preserver, keeping me afloat. Until one of the Fanline execs cuts in and steals him away, that is, and then I'm on my own.

When Bre eventually rescues me, I can finally breathe again.

"Okay, so Hālo's amazing—she told me to call her Lo, what her friends call her, and it took everything I had not to tell her about how my favorite Peloton instructor includes at least one song off *Hallowed* in every ride!"

I laugh. "I take it you're having a good time?"

"That's an understatement, Liv, it's been incredible. Hālo even offered to take me on a tour of her studio sometime."

"Think you can handle an entire studio tour without spilling your deepest, darkest secrets about your Peloton obsession?" I laugh.

"Absolutely not," she says. "But at least I didn't lead with that!" She takes a sip of rosé, which appears to have been freshly refilled. "And it seems like you're having a good time, too?" She glances at Ransom across the room, then gives me a look.

I feel a blush creeping into my cheeks. "Oh yeah," I say. "Edna Arcadia is a *scintillating* conversationalist."

Bre smirks. "That's not what I meant, and you know it."

"I have no idea what you're talking about."

"Sure," she says, barely containing her grin. "Guess I just imagined your blazing-hot costar whispering with you during that heartwarming montage."

"We were all whispering, the whole table, not just Ransom and me."

She arches a single eyebrow.

"Okay," I admit. "It's possible the majority of commentary came from the two of us."

She's won this one, and she knows it. "He's into you—I could see it from a mile away." *And you're into him*, she doesn't add, but it's written all over her face.

"We're just friends," I protest, but Bre knows better. "Or . . . we were."

I scan the room on instinct, see him up near the stage, looking devastatingly handsome as he chats with our producers and Shine.

I don't know what we are now, but I do know this: Ransom Joel being *into me* is the last thing I need.

Out of nowhere, Ford hooks a casual arm around my shoulders. "Want to go chat up some Fanline execs with me?" he says, a wild gleam in his eye.

I've never loved this part of the job—cozying up to the execs, passing it off as if I truly believe they're the most important people on the planet. "Not really," I say, "but it would probably be a good idea."

While most everyone else in attendance seems to be having a blast tonight, the Fanline execs—other than Shine Jacobs—have proven hard to read. There are four of them, interchangeable in their black suits and impassive expressions.

We make our way over, and Ford takes the lead. It's impossible not to crack a smile when Ford focuses his full attention on you, and it turns out this is a good move: the execs aren't exactly warm, but Ford is able to pull a hint of a smile out of three of them, and I count that a success. We keep it surface-level, keep it grateful, and then move on before it can turn flat.

By the end of the night, when things are winding down and the guests have emptied out by half, Ransom and I have chatted up almost everyone in the entire room but never quite managed to circle back around to each other. Bre and I are saying our goodbyes to Ford when

Ransom finally makes his way over to us, close enough I feel heat radiating from his body even though we're not technically touching. Somehow he smells even better than he did at the start of tonight; I silently scold myself for noticing.

I get the feeling he wants to say something, something for my ears only, but we never get a chance to break away from Bre and Ford on our way out.

"Tonight was great," Ransom says, holding the door open as Bre and I climb into Jimmy's car, leaving me to wonder what he would have said to only me, alone.

It's a quiet ride home—Bre and I used all our words on everyone else, apparently. She's got a contented smile on her face, eyes closed. I watch the streetlights pass, listen to the gentle hum of the highway. Tonight really was a good one.

We're almost back to her place when she says quietly, "I'm right, you know."

I look out the window to hide my smile, and to hide the way it falls.

"I'm gonna need the whole story if you continue to deny all the feelings," she adds when I say nothing. "Maybe you don't have them, but I'm telling you, he totally does."

Aside from my mother, Bre knows more about my personal life than anyone else, but even she doesn't know everything. For the first time in fourteen years, part of me *wants* to talk about Ransom—how close we were before we suddenly weren't—if only to have someone there to help me untangle the thorns from my scars, to help me figure out if something's still alive in there after all.

"Jimmy, just take us both back to my place, please," I say, and he nods at me in the rearview mirror.

Bre lets out a little squeal, revived from near sleep in the seat beside me. "I hope you have popcorn in that gigantic pantry of yours," she says. "I was so excited tonight I kind of forgot to eat."

Spotted: Ransom Joel Flying Solo at Fanline Party

By Zenia DiLitto // Editor in Chief, Pop Culture, DizzyZine.com

Hello, hello, my lovely Spinners—anyone care to play a little game of ~speculation~ with yours truly?

If you're like me (and if you're here, chances are you totally are), you've spent all night spiraling down a rabbit hole of hashtags devoted to the incredibly heart-eyes-worthy *Girl on the Verge* party thrown by streaming giant Fanline—and you also may have noticed this little nugget dropped over at *Sunset Central* about how Ransom Joel inexplicably arrived without longtime girlfriend Gemma Gardner on his arm.

I know, I KNOW—THE HOPE, right?? Nothing against Gemma, she's lovely, but the prospect that Ransom Joel might be single again after all this time is just . . . yeah, I'm gonna need a drink of water, stat. Especially on the heels of the engagement rumors that leaked a few weeks ago, this was an unexpected twist.

Well, sorry to burst our collective bubbles, friends—my guess is he won't stay single for long. Ransom was spotted leaving the party alone at the end of the night, but the luminous Liv Latimer, BFF Bre Livingston, and Ford Brooks were right on his heels.

So! I'm not saying there's reason to read into any of this, but I'm not *not* saying that, either. Between Ransom flying solo tonight and the way he was spotted getting rumor-worthy close to Liv on the red carpet earlier (h/t to Brandon Alexander, photo used with permission, original photo <u>here</u>), it's safe to assume everyone's favorite TV couple spent at least a bit of the evening reminiscing about old times. At any rate, it doesn't look particularly good for Gemma. Maybe there's trouble in paradise after all? A girl can only hope!

(Sorry, Gemma.)

Drop your most elaborate conspiracy theories in the comments below, aaaaand . . . go!

5

Bre plucks the giant bag of freshly popped popcorn from my microwave and dumps it all in a bowl. We've both ditched our dresses for oversized sweatshirts and Lululemons—fortunately, we wear the same size, and I have plenty of extras on hand.

"Seriously, you've *got* to learn to live a little." Bre's muffled voice comes from the pantry, where she rummages amid packages of rice cakes and nori and rolled oats. "Please tell me you have some M&M's somewhere in here?"

"There *might* be some tiny packages leftover from Halloween last year?"

"Like I said"—she laughs—"you've got to live a little. Either dump it all in some lucky kid's plastic pumpkin or eat it all yourself before *eight months* pass. Aha!" She reemerges, triumphantly holding an unopened bar of gourmet dark chocolate. "Not what I had in mind, but this'll be even better. You're not saving it for anything, I assume?"

"Forgot I even had it," I say, and she laughs.

We settle onto the chaises on my patio, the bowl of popcorn between us on the low glass table. Bre chopped the chocolate up and mixed it throughout, along with a dash of salt.

"This is amazing," I breathe, licking a bit of melted chocolate from my finger.

"You can thank me in *information*," she says with a pointed look.

I ignore said look, choosing to focus instead on how clear the sky is, and on how so many bright white moonbeams catch on the waves as they roll in to shore. I've sat out here, thinking, on so many nights just like this. Usually, I sit out here alone.

"Okay, so," I say, testing the feel of words on my tongue. "You obviously know Ransom and I were best friends for basically the show's entire run, and that we very much aren't anymore."

"As your current best friend, I'd just like to take a moment to point out how *extremely patient* I've been in never prying for details on exactly what happened there," Bre says, popping a piece of popcorn in her mouth. "Especially since you are clearly still interested in keeping up with him via my Snapaday account."

I laugh. "Noted. And thank you." We would have had this conversation ages ago, had I not changed the subject every single time it came close to coming up—I can tell she's wanted to ask. I look out at the sea, watch as the tide crashes on the shore.

"Start at the beginning," she says, with another bite of popcorn. "I want to hear everything."

"Our first day on set," I begin, "we were both so nervous and trying not to show it." That day will forever be seared in my memory. "It was his first big role—he'd never landed anything major like that before—and everything was so new to him. I'd been on some movie sets, at least, watching my father, so I was a little more comfortable. But it was the first time either of us had been in the spotlight ourselves."

My father had been so proud of me that first day, and his presence made me feel calmer. In later seasons, I missed him terribly. I still do.

"Ransom and I became fast friends," I go on. "He was always making me laugh—I went through some incredibly hard weeks, and he somehow always knew exactly the right thing to say or do to make me feel better. Especially after what happened with my father."

The accident happened on a blisteringly hot day, early in our second season: my father died in a car crash up in the canyons, trying to outrun a paparazzo who'd followed him there.

"I hadn't had five minutes to process the news before twenty microphones were shoved in my face," I say. "Ransom was the one who pushed them away."

I decided then and there to never give an interview about my father, never answer a single question or give even the barest hint of comment on the subject. In my mind, the press had taken everything from me, and I had nothing more to give.

But oh, did they ask. They asked and asked and asked, and when I refused to answer, they talked about *that*.

Ransom was my safe space.

"No wonder you were so close," Bre says, reading my mind.

"Oh, yeah. We were inseparable after that." I grin, thinking of how many dark days I might have had if not for the brightness he brought to my life. "We went everywhere together and could practically finish each other's sentences. I remember entire conversations on set where neither of us said a single word."

"But you never dated?"

Her tone reminds me of the very first time a reporter asked if we were dating—the question caught me so off guard it made me laugh. *Absolutely not*, I replied on instinct. *We're just friends*.

I'd never thought of him as anything other than my best friend until that moment—but then the next time we were together, I started noticing things. The distinct color of his eyes, so many shades of light green that always seemed to catch the light. The angles of his cheekbones. His lips, his smile. The way his face lit up every time he saw me. The way he gave me his full, intense attention; the secrets we shared only with each other, our highest hopes and deepest fears.

There was a time I thought he might feel the same way—I could have sworn he was about to kiss me one time, on a flight to Shanghai for our world tour—but I was wrong. Wrong about all of it.

Definitely just friends, he told a reporter while doing press in Shanghai that same afternoon, less than an hour after confiding in me that he had a crush on someone else. He was dating her by the end of the tour.

I kept my feelings to myself—better to keep my best friend than admit how I felt and risk losing him altogether—and we stayed close, somehow even closer than before. Over and over and over again, we got the same question that started it all: *Are you secretly dating?*

Over and over and over again, we replied, *We're just friends.*

"Not each other," I finally tell Bre. It sounds more bitter than I intended.

"*Ah*," she says, fishing around in the popcorn bowl for a piece of dark chocolate. "Clearly, it didn't work out with whoever he was dating."

"It did not," I say evenly, an understatement. "Some huge drama went down, and they broke up. Over me."

Bre's quiet, taking it all in. "And that's why you and Ransom aren't close anymore?"

The crisp crests of the ocean blur, deep black waves blending into foamy surf. "He said he thought it would be best for us to take a step back from our friendship—that no one would ever want to date either of us if they thought we were in love with each other."

Bre studies me for a long moment. "Were you?"

"Were we what?" I say, as if I don't know exactly what she's asking.

"In love with each other."

I take a long, deep inhale, relishing the salt coming off the sea. "I was so in love with him it hurt."

It's the first time I've ever confessed those feelings out loud, and the relief of it is a tidal wave, catching me off guard.

"What about him?" Bre asks, pulling me out of my head. "You're sure he never felt the same way?"

"I mean, if *you* were in love with your best friend, wouldn't you try to keep them around instead of basically suggesting a platonic breakup?" Of all that happened, this is what I come back to when I can't sleep at night. "Especially since the point of taking a step back was essentially so we could find blissful, romantic love *with other people* without them wondering if we were actually secretly in love with each other?"

Bre lets out a long exhale. "Good point. *But*."

"But what?"

"What if he just never *realized* he was in love with you?" Bre's on the edge of her seat now. "I saw the way he looked at you tonight, Liv.

He might not have realized how into you he was back then, but he is *definitely* into you now. He's missed you, I can tell."

I've missed him, too. Our step back was never supposed to become this much of a chasm, but I didn't know how to do casual with Ransom—and honestly, I didn't want to. Knowing he didn't want to be as close with me made it painful to try to be close at all. So we drifted, little by little, until weeks passed, and then months. Years.

Taking that step back—*because* I loved him and wanted him to be happy, even if it wasn't with me—was the hardest thing I've ever gone through aside from losing my father.

It's been hard to get close to anyone since. It's been hard to *want* to.

Moonlight winks off the waves; we watch in silence for so long Bre falls asleep, curled up on her chaise under the stars. I nudge her into semiconsciousness and she follows me inside.

✧

It's almost eleven when I wake up, sunlight bright and streaming through my bedroom window. Bre's still here, and she's definitely already up—I know because I can hear her doing some sort of workout on the other side of the wall.

I take my time making coffee downstairs, using the French press my mother sent for Christmas years ago. My head is in the clouds this morning, and I'm pretty sure it isn't only because of the late night. My timer goes off, but when I go to pour the coffee, I realize I forgot to actually *grind* the beans before pouring the boiling water into the press. The second attempt, my mind wanders back to the red carpet— Ransom's fingers at my lower back, his breath hot on my ear—and I realize far too late that I forgot to set the timer. The third attempt, finally, is a success.

I'm curled up on my couch, still in the chic floral pajama set I slept in last night, when Bre finally comes downstairs. Her hair is freshly towel-dried and smells like the jasmine shampoo I keep on hand for situations exactly like this; she's dressed in a fresh set of athleisure wear from the guest bedroom drawers.

"Hey," she says, flopping onto the opposite end of the couch and kicking her bare feet up onto my bohemian-style leather ottoman. "How are you this morn— Ohmy*gahhhhh*, that coffee smells incredible, is there any left?"

"It's probably lukewarm by now, but I can make more." I meant to put some into a travel mug for her to keep it hot, but again: head in the clouds.

She waves me off. "That's what the microwave is for."

"Blasphemy!" I call after her as she disappears into the kitchen.

A few minutes later, she returns, face practically buried in her mug. "So? Doing okay?"

"Better than expected," I admit, and it's true: it was an impeccable night of sleep, somehow, full of the best dreams that were entirely at odds with my worst memories. "Thanks for listening last night."

She smiles above the rim of her mug, takes a long sip of coffee. "That's what I'm here for." She gestures to the open book resting facedown beside me. "Is that one of the ones from Mars?" She picks it up, scans the description on the back cover.

Mars sent a stack over two weeks ago—apparently there's a book-to-film agent who's trying to set up a package deal with talent attached. *No pressure to read them*, Mars wrote on a slip of stationary I've been using as a bookmark. *But if you see yourself as the lead in any of these, let me know and I'll pass word over to Erica.*

"It is, yeah." This one caught my eye—a survival novel set on a futuristic, technologically advanced Antarctica. What I read of it had me on the edge of my seat when I started it, but today, I can't seem to read more than half a sentence at a time.

"Let me know if it's good," she says, setting it back down exactly as it was. "Ugh, I wish I could read all day. Or, you know, binge the next season of *Flower Wars*. Or anything but run the thousand errands on my to-do list. You're off today, right?"

"Technically, yes." I've got a rare day off, my last before the *GotV* press blitz goes full whirlwind tomorrow—it's unusual to have all of us in town at the same time, so the schedule is a bit intense. "Practically . . . not so much." I'm only about thirty pages into the book, and I need to go over my lines for the scenes I don't know by heart just yet.

"Well, if you need anything, let me know. I've got you." Bre might *say* she wishes for time off to binge shows on Fanline, but there's literally nothing she enjoys less than an unstructured day. She gets restless with too much free time, thrives on making things happen.

A few minutes later, her Lyft shows up just as my phone starts to buzz—Attica calling.

Bye! Bre mouths as she lets herself out, taking the ceramic mug of coffee with her before I can offer an actual travel mug in its place.

Hopefully it won't be a bumpy ride.

"Can I just reiterate how *gorgeous* you looked in that Siriano gown last night?" Attica says as soon as I pick up, an extremely Attica greeting if I've ever heard one. "Everyone's talking about it! You were stunning." There's a muffled voice in the background, and her muffled reply in return. "Sorry, Liv. Anyway—people are also loving your little Ransom moment! It was the *perfect* thing to distract from how that reporter totally crossed the line. They love you together on the show, so we could play that up if that's something you're into. Also, hi, by the way!"

There is nothing I am less into than the idea of turning my romantic life into a publicity stunt. Not that there's any romantic life with Ransom to speak of. My cheeks grow hot, and hotter still as the memory of his touch on my bare skin takes root.

"Liv? Are you there?"

"Hi, yes, sorry," I say. "I'm glad people seem happy about last night." If I ignore her suggestion, hopefully she'll take the hint and leave it alone.

"Yes! They love you." I hear her clicking away at her laptop. "You're all set for tomorrow—*Vanity Fair* in the morning, *EW* in the afternoon?"

"All good, as long as Bre's been in touch with Jimmy about when to pick me up."

"I'm sure she's on top of it, but I'll double-check. Anything you need from me, you know where to find me, okay?"

It takes the rest of the day to shake off the phone call, the feelings that sprung up at Attica's off-the-cuff suggestion. There's a difference between *publicity for the show*—like tomorrow's photo shoot for the special edition *EW* is doing to celebrate our milestone anniversary—and *publicity stunt*. I'm fully up for the former: it's part of the job, to promote the show, and Ransom and I are the heart of the show. It's what we signed on for. But encouraging speculation about us as real, actual people—not just people who pretend they're in love on a scripted television drama? That is another thing altogether.

I pick up the book I'm reading, try to distract myself. It actually works for a while—it's good, and the character development is spot-on—but my mind keeps drifting back to Ransom, especially when the main character finds herself alone and under pressure and craving the company of the guy she's into but currently separated from by half the continent of Antarctica.

Ten chapters later, late in the afternoon, my phone buzzes on the table beside me: it's Bre.

LIV, LIV, HOLY CRAP is all it says at first. Another bubble pops up immediately. *HĀLO INVITED ME OVER FOR A STUDIO TOUR (!!!!!!!!!!)—SHE ACTUALLY REMEMBERED AND I AM STUCK IN ALL CAPS LIIIIIIIVVVVVV*

I laugh. *AMAGING,* I write. *When do you get to go?*

I hit send, and my phone buzzes with another message almost as soon as I've set the phone down. I pick it up, expecting another all-caps reply—but it's Ransom this time.

it was good to see you last night, he's written, with an old-school non-emoji :) to punctuate it.

It sends a rush straight to my head, and it's at this precise moment I know: I'm royally delusional if I try to deny it, the *feeling*—a pure and sparkling fizz sparking through my veins.

Logic and reason and history are all still there, bubbling under the surface.

But right now? Despite said history, nothing can argue with this visceral thrill, that Ransom enjoyed seeing me last night—that he's thinking about me right now, just like I can't get every moment we spent together at the party out of my head.

This . . . could be a problem.

Ones to Watch: Liv Latimer in Talks to Take Leading Role in Debut Novel Adaptation!

By Gregor Ives // Senior Editor, Books & Film, *West Coast Daily*

In today's edition of Ones to Watch: sources confirm that Liv Latimer has been approached by an unnamed (major!) studio to star in the screen adaptation of *AURORA*, an upcoming novel by debut author Emily Quinn. The novel, a survival story set in a futuristic Antarctica, won't publish until mid-October, but sources say Liv has her hands on an advance copy for her consideration. Updates to follow. Liv Latimer is represented by Marsden Heath at UTA; Emily Quinn is represented by Holly Taylor at Blossom & Co. Literary.

6

"Can it not be reworded?" I ask Mars, as Jimmy shifts lanes on the way from *Vanity Fair* over to *Entertainment Weekly*. My interview ran long this morning, so now we're pressed for time. "It makes it sound like I'm already committed. I'm not even done reading it!"

On the other end of the call, Mars sighs. "It was a leak from one of the publicists working on the book," she says. "I had nothing to do with it. But honestly, Liv, it'll only make you more in demand with the others who've sent material your way. Everyone else knows the game because they play it, too."

"The author's using my name to promote her book," I say. "There's more in it for her, I'd think."

"The *publisher* is using your name to promote her book," Mars replies. "The author hasn't said a word about it on any of her social accounts, and you've had the book for weeks now—don't hold it against her."

I glance out the window, watch the world pass in a blur. "You really think it won't lock me out of other options down the line?"

"You really think I'd let them get away with it if I thought it would pose even the slightest threat to what's on the table for you?" she shoots back, quick as ever. I love Mars. She's got a tongue as sharp as her instincts.

"Good point," I say, as we pull up to *EW* with barely a minute to spare. "Gotta go, Mars. We're here."

Inside, the nostalgia hits hard: twenty years ago, *EW* was the very first to feature us on a cover. They went digital-only a while back, but decided to go all-out with a collector's edition to celebrate our milestone anniversary. I'm greeted by a girl in light-wash skinny jeans, a sky-blue button-down, and purple leather flats; she wears glasses with thick clear frames, and her dark hair is layered around her face in waves.

"Hi, Liv, I'm Varsha," she says, with the hint of a lilting Indian accent. "I'll be directing the shoot today. We'll get you to hair and makeup first, and from there we'll start with the family shoot, then the friend shoot, and we'll close out the day with just you and Ransom. Sound good?"

She speaks quickly, walking as she talks, scanning us both through security. I follow her around a corner and down a long hallway.

"We have a flat white waiting for you, feel free to drink it while you settle in. Snacks are in the hall. Anything else you need, please ask. Millie and Sasha-Kate are finishing up at hair and makeup right now, so you'll be up next when there's an open chair. Hair and makeup will touch you up before your shoot with Ransom at the end of the day—oh, and Shanti will be pulling you aside at some point to get a few quotes. Since you're on all three covers, we'll have to squeeze it in during a break at some point. Is that okay? Any questions?"

She's a whirlwind—a nice, professional, very put-together whirlwind. Yes, it's okay, I tell her. No, no questions.

As promised, there's a flat white waiting for me—bless Bre for always mentioning how much I love them when setting these things up. I sip it as I wait for my turn, pick out a package of peppered cashews from the snack table. Soon after, I'm whisked away to hair and makeup, an empty seat beside me; of everyone scheduled for the first cover shoot, I was the last to arrive.

My phone buzzes with a text. I glance at it discreetly so my stylists won't get a peek—it's Ransom.

how was vanity fair? bet you killed it

It's like a blast of sunshine, warm and familiar and energizing.

Oh, the usual, I write. *Equal parts fashion and soul-probing interrogation, with a partial view of the Pacific*

so you def killed it, then, he writes back immediately. And then: *for what it's worth, i would take soul-probing interrogation over the same five questions i get every time. if i have to answer one more about that tiny triangle tattoo, so help me. why did i post that thing on social media*

I snort, startling my makeup artist. *Guess we'll have to get matching cat tattoos if you ever want a different question*, I send back. *Botched ones, in case that wasn't clear*

Even as I type it, I'm pushing away the thought of his tiny triangle tattoo. It's just beneath his hip bone, small enough that my thumb can cover it entirely. The memory of seeing it for the first time, about a month after he turned eighteen—of feeling hard muscle beneath my fingertips, his skin searing hot against mine—is doing some rather interesting things to my body right now.

obviously, he writes. *you at ew yet?*

In the chair now. You?

just got to lunch, but headed your way soon

I'm still overthinking the word *your*—not headed *that* way, or headed *to EW*—when another text comes through: *can't wait to see you again. this'll be fun*

I close my eyes, let the makeup artist do her thing as Ransom's words grow roots, tender tendrils working their way under my skin.

What's wrong with me? It should not sound fun to be face-to-face with the guy who wanted space when all I wanted was to be closer. It should not thrill me to see his name on my screen, or to think about his triangle tattoo, and my skin should be too thick now for such simple words to find their way through.

And yet.

I'm looking forward to it, too, I finally write back.

A little while later, the five of us who make up the fictional St. Croix family are the picture of perfection. They've put me in an emerald-green silk dress that contrasts beautifully with the deep scarlet shade of lipstick my makeup artist selected. Sasha-Kate is in yellow—a marigold that pops with her sleek chestnut hair—and Millie is in sapphire blue. Annagrey and Laurence are both dressed in black; time has turned both of them silver where they were once brunettes. The lights are bright, illuminating a taupe velvet chaise set against a light gray backdrop.

Varsha arranges us in a series of poses. First it's Annagrey and Laurence on the chaise with the rest of us behind them; then it's the three of us St. Croix daughters on the chaise with parents in the back; then it's just me on the chaise with Sasha-Kate and Millie on the floor leaning up against it, Annagrey and Laurence still behind us. Then Varsha does away with the chaise entirely, and we take a series of shots where we're so close we really do look like one big happy family—well, happy in the shots where we're laughing, and serious in the ones where she directs us to smolder at the camera lens.

A movement catches my eye from the far corner of the room: Ransom. Ransom, looking fantastic in the suit they've got him in—he definitely needs to ask if he can keep that one. Its deep navy blue and crisp, tailored cut accentuate his broad shoulders and trim waist; his legs look like they go on for miles. When did he start filling out a suit so well? A petite woman with long dark hair swept up in a high ponytail approaches him, smartphone in hand. Shanti, I assume, pulling him aside for his quotes.

"Liv?" Varsha says, and it has the distinct sound of something she's had to say more than once. "You with us?"

What was I thinking? I never lose focus like this. "Sorry!" I say. "Just getting a little thirsty, that's all."

Varsha checks her watch, then scrolls through the thumbnails of the photos we've taken so far. "That'll work, fam—looking good so far! Why don't you take fifteen, and then I'll see Liv and Sasha-Kate back here for the next round."

We go our separate ways. Fifteen minutes pass in the blink of an eye—it's really only enough time to take care of the basics in the bathroom and at the water cooler. I quite literally run into Ford on my way back to set.

"Nice dress," he compliments.

"Nice hair," I reply. Gone is the man bun he was known for back in the day—now it's cut stylishly short, with a little more length on top where it swoops up in the front. They also opted to leave him unshaven, and it is definitely a look, one that will sell all the magazines.

"Enjoy it while it lasts, Livvie, because I have no idea how to replicate it."

I laugh. "Just watch, this is totally going to be your look for the reunion special!"

Ford and I make our way over to set, where Sasha-Kate is already waiting. "Looking sharp, SK!" Ford says, pulling her into a hug.

Ransom is still over in the corner talking with Shanti, looking very intense, and—dare I say, as objectively as possible—exceedingly handsome. Varsha motions for them to wrap it up, then takes a moment to tweak the lighting for our next shoot.

Ransom joins us a moment later, and we lock eyes on instinct. He grins, and that's it. I have to look away.

"Now, for this one," Varsha says, "we're going to start with a pinwheel-type pose with your heads at the center, an overhead shot with all of you looking up at the camera. Liv, you'll be here"—she motions for me to lie down on a plush white blanket—"and Sasha-Kate, you'll be her opposite. Ransom and Ford, you'll each take a side. Does that make sense?"

When we've positioned ourselves, it's like our faces are the center of the pinwheel, our bodies the paper curls extending out from its axle.

"Won't this mean my face is upside down on the cover?" Sasha-Kate says, in a tone that says, *It very much better not be.*

Varsha gives a noncommittal hum. "If this arrangement turns out to be the favorite, that'll be up to the art department. Now, let's get a few where your faces say, *I'm on top of the world, everyone knows it, and I deserve to be there.*"

The photographer is on a rig above us, his massive camera lens pointed straight down.

I take the direction as best I can, settling on fierce eyes and a playful smirk that's *almost* a smile but not quite. Varsha seems pleased, and we move quickly on to a few poses where we're not lying down, all of which Sasha-Kate seems much happier with. The final arrangement is my favorite, with me looking straight at the camera, flanked on each side by Ransom and Ford. My arm brushes against Ransom's as we settle in; it's the lightest touch, but more than enough to spark a current of heat just under my skin. Sasha-Kate has her arms around Ford and her head resting on his shoulder. It's by far the most natural shot yet, and Ford keeps making little comments under his breath that have us in stitches, the sort of dumb jokes that hinge on his perfect delivery. I have a feeling Sasha-Kate won't have to worry about being upside down on the cover—these last ones were our money shots for sure.

We break for thirty, and it's not a moment too soon. I'm not sure I could have handled another moment of being so close to Ransom, hyperaware of the narrow space between us. It was always second nature to slip into Honor-and-Duke mode on shoots like this—but it's been a while, and the chemistry that made it so easy back in the day has taken on a new dimension with age.

"Ms. Latimer?" I turn, and see Shanti behind me; her alto voice radiates confidence. "Ready for your interview? It won't take long—we appreciate your time."

I follow her to a comfortably appointed corner outfitted with a pair of buttery leather chairs, a low coffee table made from the cross section of a tree trunk, and a woven black-and-white rug. None of the questions require me to dig too deeply for answers—the main article will be a spotlight on the show itself, and they've done more lengthy interviews with Dan, Xan, and Bryan. The rest of us will be featured in sidebar sections throughout, all giving our own perspectives on a series of the same questions.

When we've finished, I get a brief touch-up, then head back to work. Ransom's already there, chatting with Varsha. I stop short when I see the set: in the time it took to do the interview and refresh my makeup, the crew has switched the backdrop to bright white, and there's now a bed covered in a plush white duvet. It's a little confusing because Ransom's still in his perfect suit and I'm still in my green dress—we look like we're about to go to a fancy dinner party, not climb under the sheets.

The idea of both thrills me more than I care to admit.

"Liv, hi!" Varsha says when I walk up. "I was just telling Ransom my vision for this one. Here's what I'm thinking: The last time everyone saw you on-screen together like this, your characters were both eighteen. I want to do a headline that says *ALL GROWN UP*"—she spreads her hands in the air, like she's revealing the words as she speaks—"but it has to be the perfect balance of your new maturity mixed with the relative innocence your viewers are used to in the original series."

She goes on to direct us into position, both of us side by side on top of the thick white duvet. It's a bit intimate, even in our formal clothes—I haven't shared a bed with anyone in quite some time.

"Okay, now, Liv—turn on your side to face Ransom, yes, like that, only bend your knees a little more!" I feel someone spreading the skirt of my dress out behind me so it looks like it just happened to fall that way naturally. "Ransom, can you take one of her hands in yours, then put your other hand under your head and cross your ankles like you're living your best life?"

Ransom takes my hand in his, his gaze flicking toward mine. The corner of his mouth quirks up. A shiver courses through me, very much without my permission, at odds with the warmth of his hand intertwined with mine.

"Yes, yes," Varsha says. "Perfect!"

We try a few more poses, shifting the details along the way. By the final shot, we're shoulder to shoulder, my bare skin pressed up against the fabric of his suit jacket.

"Last one, guys, and then we're done," Varsha says. "Liv, can you tilt your head a little—yes, like that, just rest it on his shoulder, perfect. Snap a few of those, Ryan."

We stay there, breathing in the silence. It's comfortable, more comfortable than it should be after so many years apart. I guess that's how it is with someone you've known practically forever, who once knew your every shade and shadow: no matter how many ups and downs and detours creep in along the way, in the end, it's not hard to slip back to a baseline level of ease.

I need to be careful not to slip too quickly—someone could get hurt.

"Okay, great work, everyone—that's it for today! Take your time in the dressing rooms, Ransom and Liv, it'll be a while before our team is out of here."

"I think I'm stuck," Ransom says, still beside me on the bed. "This thing is like a cloud."

"Same here," I laugh. "I think it's softer than my bed at home."

He grins. Our eyes meet, and for a split second I'm sixteen again, the girl who was only just starting to realize she was falling in love with the boy in front of her and not just acting out the part.

I shake the memory off before it takes hold. I'm not sixteen anymore, this is *not* my bed, and even if it were, I'm not ready to consider the implications of the very real thought that just crashed through my mind: *I kind of wish it were.*

"Better get back to my dressing room," I say, a little more abruptly than I mean to. "They really caked this foundation on!"

His eyes are on me as I leave, I can feel them, so I walk a little quicker than I normally would. Because the truth is, if I'm honest, I like his eyes on me—and I don't like that I like it. We're actors, we've built entire careers out of making people fall in love with us.

I need to leave *now*, before I slip so hard I forget what's actually real.

Behind-the-scenes sneak peek of #GotV
cast—look for our trio of special edition
covers soon!
— @EntertainmentWeekly on Snapaday
June 14, 1:13 p.m.

@ZeniaDiLitto
OHMYGAAAAAAAAHHHHH those last
photos, tho

@abbeyyyyy17
they all look SO GROWN UP, i cannot even
handle this

@IthacaAlexander
Love that color on Millie

@GOTV_fanboiiii
PLEASE TELL ME RANSOM AND LIV ARE A
THING IN REAL LIFE, THEY ARE SO PURE
AND MORE THAN WE DESERVE

@GOTV_fanboiiii
seriously tho buying all three covers asap

@ShantiSrinivasan
Can't wait for everyone to see the final
covers. Cast was every bit as lovely as you'd
expect! xo

@Dan_and_Xan_stans
FORD'S HAIR

@authoremilyquinn
Anyone know if @EntertainmentWeekly will
be having a watch party for the reunion?
#GotVReunionSpecial

@Fanline
😌 👀

7

"So the Snapaday Live is tomorrow, yeah?" Bre says, on the other side of our FaceTime call, still slightly breathless from the Peloton ride she just finished.

"And my wardrobe check, too." I rummage through my fridge, ultimately decide on an omelet loaded with spinach, mushrooms, and bell peppers for dinner.

"Attica just sent some questions over for the Snapaday thing," Bre says, her eyes darting to one of the many browser windows she keeps open on her screen. "I'll send them your way now."

I refresh my email.

"Got it," I say, taking a quick second to scan what Attica's written. *The theme of the chat is #GirlsTalkGirls—they'll be touching on how each of your characters has been modernized to fit the present day. Here are some sound bites for you . . . make them your own so they don't sound scripted! xo, A*

"Perfect. How are you feeling about tomorrow?"

I've already filled her in on today. The basics, anyway—not the parts where my traitorous brain relentlessly dug up every single thought I tried to bury. I think Bre knows, though. She saw the teaser photos *EW* leaked on their Snapaday feed, and it's not hard to tell I looked absolutely, undeniably into the fact that Ransom was *right there*.

It's also worth noting that Ransom, for his part, looked equally into it.

I turn my focus to the omelet, careful to not let it burn.

"Tomorrow?" I say, after too long a pause. "It'll be nice to do a group interview, for once, a little less pressure. On the flip side . . ."

"It's with Sasha-Kate?" Bre fills in, knowing me all too well.

I slide the omelet out of the pan, flipping it over on itself. Perfect. "At the very least, it won't be boring." It's not always pleasant with Sasha-Kate, but boring? Never.

"Yeah," Bre snorts. "She's never met a camera she doesn't like."

"Truer words were never spoken," I say.

For a lot of reasons, Sasha-Kate and I never understood each other well enough to be real friends; one of the biggest was our feelings toward the press. I've always craved privacy to the extreme, yet my fierce devotion to it—ironically—created a paparazzi frenzy. Sasha-Kate, on the other hand, soaks up the spotlight like a snake basking in the sun: no matter how much she gets, it's never quite enough.

When the paparazzi chased me into hiding on numerous occasions, I wanted nothing more than to crawl in a hole and stay there for weeks on end—the panic attacks I experienced were intense, images of my father's car crumpled up in the canyons flashing across my memory every single time. I resented the attention, but Sasha-Kate resented me for resenting it—and especially for how the attention chased me in the first place.

As soon as Bre and I end the call, my mind runs straight back to Ransom. I tap over to the *EW* teaser photos again: they're just behind-the-scenes glimpses from the shoot today, not the official cover shots, but they're still pretty stunning. I take a screenshot of the best one before I think better of it.

Looking at it, you'd never know we hadn't spoken in over a decade before this week.

Looking at it, we appear to be every bit as in love as our on-screen counterparts.

I should maybe stop looking at it.

Just as I'm about to shut things down, a notification dips down from the top of my screen.

today was fun :)

I was just looking at the pictures EW posted, I write back. Why are my hands shaking? It's only Ransom.

me too, he replies immediately. *might make this one my new lock screen*

A warm, happy feeling spreads through me as I enlarge the photo he's sent—a candid where we're facing each other, both of our eyes crinkling at the corners.

That's my favorite, too. Today really was fun ☺

you look gorgeous, livvie

I blink at the screen, fingers frozen—his message popped up at the exact instant I pressed send on mine. Eventually, I settle on a slightly forward but absolutely true *You still bring out the best in me*

My thumb accidentally hits send even though I meant to add more to that thought—but before I can add to it, he sends back a single word: *likewise :)*

Those eight letters burrow down into my heart, cutting clean through the scar tissue.

It takes longer than it should to turn off my phone.

Millie Matson Drops New Single Ahead of *Girl on the Verge* Reunion Special

By Anna Lindell // Associate Editor, Arts & Entertainment, *Sunset Central*

Up-and-coming pop sensation Millie Matson dropped a surprise new single last night at twelve on the dot; fittingly, the new track—titled "Midnight"—is a rich blend of inky vocals and starlit mystery. Matson hinted at the title in a recent Snapaday image, a close-up of her cheekbone adorned with a silver crescent moon and stars to match (makeup artist: <u>Bekah Bell</u>); the post spawned hundreds of fan theories as to what her next single might be.

With infectious lyrics like "Take me to the moonlight, take me to the stars / I just wanna be with you where-ev-ever you are / I want your history, your mystery, your darkness, and your light / Wish upon a star with me—at midnight" set against a sparse backdrop of synth tones that explode into an undeniably addictive beat, Matson's clearly establishing herself as one of the most influential names in pop. The track soared to the number one spot on the streaming charts early this morning, just edging out longtime favorite "Hallowed" by Hālo, and looks unlikely to budge any time soon.

We think it's fair to say Millie has come a long way since her *Bubblegum!* days. Here at *Sunset Central*, we're eager to see what she has in store for the "Midnight" video, so keep an eye on this space—we'll share our reactions as soon as it goes live. Until then, drop your thoughts on the new single in the comments below! We, for the record, are fans.

Sasha-Kate and Millie are already at Snapaday HQ when I arrive. Its pristine, polished office is made of only white walls and spotless glass, while somehow still managing to project creative energy at every turn.

At the heart of the complex, floor-to-ceiling windows surround an indoor courtyard filled with palm trees, ferns, and tropical flowers. Sasha-Kate and Millie are dressed in all white, looking breezy amid the bright colors. I'm in a white crochet-lace top paired with short navy-and-white baroque-patterned shorts that make my legs look like they go on for miles down to my strappy platform wedge sandals, one of my favorite outfits from home. Hailey, one of our hosts today, likes my look so much she tells me not to bother with the dress they chose for me.

Marissa, who'll be conducting the interview, gives me a once-over. "I love it. A few quick touch-ups and you'll be good to go." They agree my hair is already exactly what they had in mind, too—I'm wearing it down, blown out in billowy waves that complete today's casual-but-posh aesthetic.

After a fast five minutes with the makeup artist, I head over to the trio of director's chairs that have been set up just for us. Sasha-Kate and Millie are sipping on water with cucumber slices in it, as if this is some kind of spa day.

"All right, ladies," Marissa says. "Clearly, you're all familiar with the Snapaday platform itself, so if all of you are ready, let's get to it!" We laugh—the entire *planet* is familiar with the Snapaday platform. For these takeovers, they always post some prerecorded spots, then do a live Q&A segment to follow.

They position us in the director's chairs; I'm in the middle, with Millie to my right and Sasha-Kate on my left. Millie is practically glowing today, buzzing with barely contained energy—by contrast, Sasha-Kate seems a bit dour, like she wishes her cucumber water were coffee instead, or perhaps something stronger. To her credit, she does a good job of hiding it once the cameras are rolling.

"Hello and welcome, everyone, to this week's Snapaday takeover!" Hailey says. The cameraman focuses only on her for now, where she's standing off to the side in front of a particularly beautiful section of the courtyard. "Today we'll be chatting with the ladies of *Girl on the Verge*. You know the drill, so get your questions ready—we'll be going live at noon!"

Hailey's take is perfect on the first try, so the cameraman shifts over to where Sasha-Kate, Millie, and I are waiting and sets up far enough back to capture all of us in the frame.

"Good to go, Mike?" Marissa calls out.

The cameraman gives her a thumbs-up.

Marissa nods. "Everyone ready?"

We confirm that we are. On the camera, a little red light blinks on.

"*Girl on the Verge* was known for touching on a wide variety of topics," Marissa begins. "Friendship and love, talent and ambition, hope and disappointment. While the focus was mostly on Honor's academics, creative passions, and talent on the tennis court—and, yes, her love life—there were other episodes along the way that centered on each of the St. Croix sisters. The writers have received abundant praise for prioritizing women's stories. Could you each share your own perspective on why *Girl on the Verge* has been such a force of empowerment to women of all ages over the years? Liv, why don't you start."

Even though I have an answer for this already, I'm glad I read Attica's sound bites on the way over—her words in the back of my head help to refine my own answer into something smooth and polished.

"*Girl*, at its heart, has always been all about giving girls the courage to try—and fail—and work hard—at their dreams," I say. "It never sugarcoated things, but it was also never bleak or without hope. I loved playing Honor because she grew up on the show believing she could be anything she wanted. Things weren't always easy for her, but she was allowed to feel and grow and learn along the way. I think it's important for girls, especially *young* girls, to see someone dreaming big, and to see them push through when things get tough."

Marissa and Hailey nod along as I speak—I can tell this will hit exactly the way I want it to.

"For me," Millie says, her energy palpable, "it wasn't just my character who grew up on the show—it was my literal childhood. I started playing Natalie at age five, and I think the writers did a really good job of not making her this clichéd sort of kid character, you know? She wasn't on-screen just for a laugh or the cuteness factor—they gave her actual lines and big emotions, and I've always respected that."

What Millie neglects to mention is that it took dozens of takes for her to nail those lines and big emotions—the audition that landed her the part had, apparently, been rehearsed and perfected within an inch of its life. Still, the writers continued to give her lines as the series went on, a testament to how committed they were to making sure her character had substance.

"I think we can all agree," she goes on, "that it's important for girls to know they're worth more to a story than just being cute, right?"

"Hailey, jot that last line down, we'll use it as a pull quote," Marissa says. "This is perfect so far, ladies. Sasha-Kate?"

Beside me, Sasha-Kate shifts in her chair. Even in this casual pose—legs crossed, somewhat slouched and leaning on one elbow—she looks very much in charge of the moment.

"I always thought Dan and Xan did a really good job balancing the romantic aspects of the show," she says, putting on the slightly deeper voice she uses whenever she does interviews. "Even though we all know Honor's love life was a *huge* focal point"—Millie and I laugh, because it's that true—"it was always dealt with in a way that made it clear that finding true love wasn't her be-all, end-all *purpose* in life. And she made mistakes along the way, like all of us do, but never let them define her."

I've never really thought about it like that, but she's right. I wonder whether it's something she came up with herself or if it's a sound bite she memorized on the ride over—knowing Sasha-Kate, it could go either way.

Hailey scribbles madly on her notepad. Marissa asks us a series of lightning-round questions—favorite episodes, favorite memories on set, scenes we're most proud of—before moving on to the individually tailored questions. Sasha-Kate's first this time, but halfway through Marissa's question, my phone vibrates at my hip, distracting me.

"Of course I did," Sasha-Kate replies, to a question I didn't hear. "There was always this sort of duality there, where I had to separate who I was on the show with who I was as a person—but the truth is, there was a lot of overlap. I ended up loving the role of Bianca, but it was hard sometimes because she had so much potential and, you know, never quite got her moment like Honor did. I'm happy with the reunion script, though. I think the writers have put Bianca in a good place—there's great potential for growth there if, you know, we get to do more."

I freeze. Even though there are rumors everywhere about us potentially getting picked up for a reboot, everyone from Dan and Xan all the way up to Shine Jacobs has made it clear we are *not* to acknowledge them—it goes without saying that they really don't want us feeding the fire with a wink and a smile like Sasha-Kate's just done.

Marissa, of course, is all over it. "Does this mean what we hope it means?" she asks. "We'd love to see a reboot! There's so much potential there for a modern, more mature take on how Honor—and Bianca and Natalie, of course—how all the girls navigate the world we live in today."

Sasha-Kate gives a slow, secretive smile, one that tells me she knows exactly how close to the line she's come because she's gone there on purpose. "I guess we'll see what happens!"

I don't know what she's up to. She's too careful, too calculated, to let things slip. Personally, I'm more than content to avoid the topic—better not to get people's hopes up, because if things go sour I won't have to be tagged in endless *But Liv basically promised it was HAPPEN-*

ING tweets. The Fanline execs are intimidating enough as it is, and I don't want to look like I'm reckless with matters of discretion. And on top of all *that*, I'm still not sure how I feel about the idea of signing on.

Marissa turns her attention to me. "I want to linger a minute on something Sasha-Kate brought up, how it was sometimes hard to separate who she was on the show with who she was as a person. Liv, we watched a recent interview where you touched on all the pressures that came with being Honor St. Croix—is that why you took such an extended break from acting after wrapping the show?"

"Oh, absolutely," I say. "Who wouldn't feel quite a bit lacking when held up to the impossible standard of Honor St. Croix? All of us have experienced that over the years, people expecting us to be like our characters. I needed a break from the scrutiny."

I needed a break from everything.

"You've famously turned down a number of offers for big roles since your time on the show, choosing to focus on only a handful of quiet projects," Marissa goes on, checking her notes. "How does it feel to be front and center in the spotlight again after staying out of it for so long?"

"It's different this time around." Not as bad as I expected, truthfully. "There haven't been as many cameras or microphones in my face—but thanks to social media, there are more voices in the mix."

A *lot* more. Millions, and growing by the day. It's best if I don't know exactly how many, or exactly what they're saying—thankfully, Bre and Attica are on top of all that. Everyone has a camera, everyone has a keyboard. Everyone has an opinion about what I should or should not do with my life.

"The blessing and the curse of social media!" Marissa says with a wink, gesturing to the Snapaday logo behind us. "I can only imagine what it's like for you, Liv. For all of you! What would you say the best part of that sort of visibility is?"

"The best part?" I repeat. "For me, it's been the freedom to pursue the projects I love without having to worry if they'll find an audience."

"And the worst?" Marissa says, leaning in.

"The false sense of intimacy it creates," I say. "It can be easy to think you know someone based on the carefully curated moments they've chosen to share in snapshots, when in reality, the relationship there is nonexistent."

In truth, the actual worst thing I can think of carries this idea one step further: that false intimacy can lead to obsession—and when the public at large shares that same obsession, it sparks a lucrative pursuit by the paparazzi.

It didn't end well for my father. I've been reluctant to embrace the same level of visibility.

Marissa moves on to Millie. "Millie, I know this takeover is all about the show, *but* we can't resist the opportunity to talk to you about your pivot toward pop these last few years. You dropped your latest single overnight and it's already at the top of the charts. Can you speak a bit about 'Midnight'?"

It's no wonder Millie's been buzzing all morning—her first albums received mixed reviews, many people unable to get past the fact that they'd known her primarily as Natalie St. Croix since she was five years old. None of her songs ever came close to topping the charts.

"Thanks, Marissa," she says.

I might be imagining things, but I think she's picked up on the voice-lowering thing Sasha-Kate does to make people take her more seriously.

"It's been a surreal day, to say the least! I'm so happy the single is resonating with people—we worked harder on this one than ever before, so it's nice to see it taking off."

They talk for a minute more about her inspiration, about her decision to pivot toward music from acting, about if she can give any more hints about her upcoming album.

"Actually, I'm glad you asked!" she says with a mischievous smile to the camera. "'Meet Me in the Garden,' my next single, will drop sometime in the next few days—there are some hints already in my feed, and there will be more. If you think you've figured out the hidden message, which is a lyric from the chorus, tag me in a story. First to figure it out will win some signed merch!"

"You heard it here first, friends!" Marissa announces excitedly. It's a win for both of them: more traffic to Snapaday, more exposure for Millie—whoever advised Millie to drop her single right before this takeover needs a raise, because it was undoubtedly part of their strategy, to keep Millie front and center of the reboot and this press moment.

Marissa checks her watch, an analog timepiece with a strap made of sunny-yellow silicone. "I had a few more questions, but I think that's a great place to leave it. We've got twenty minutes until we go live for the Q and A—why don't you all take a break, get some snacks, and we'll meet back here at five to noon."

Sasha-Kate abandons her director's chair before the words are even out of Marissa's mouth, stalking across the room like she can't get away from us fast enough.

"What's with her?" I say to Millie before I think better of it—the last thing I want to do is pour fuel on our old feud.

Millie rolls her eyes. "It's my fault," she says. "First thing she said to me when I got here was, 'Congrats on hitting number one, Hālo's *pissed.*'"

"Well, congrats on pissing off Hālo," I say cheekily, and she laughs. Hālo's reign at the top of the charts lasted a solid ten years—Millie's dethroning her is no small feat. I absolutely get why Hālo would feel threatened by it.

Millie pulls out her phone, reminding me I have a missed message of my own, probably Bre or Attica with some last-minute reminder for the interview. But no—it's Ransom—I'm still not used to seeing his name on my screen again after all this time.

I swipe it open, and my screen fills with an extreme close-up of Ford and Ransom together, making a pair of faces so over-the-top serious they're hilarious.

you've got wardrobe after your snapaday thing, yeah? if you've got time for lunch while you're near the studio, ford and i are headed to the diner—we'll do our best to snag the haunted booth just for you ;)

I laugh, despite myself, and Millie briefly glances up from her phone. I'd forgotten all about the haunted booth.

Tell Ford he's going to break his eyebrow if he arches it any higher, I write. *And yes—count me in.*

SNAPADAY LIVE: Q&A #GIRLSTALKGIRLS TAKEOVER

@Bianca_OnTheVerge
they look so cute, ahhhhh

@readloveslay22
ugh why does it keep freezing

@readloveslay22
or is that just me

@Dan_and_Xan_stans
not just you, @readloveslay22

@hamstertroll
FIX IT, come on, it's not like this is your own
platform or anything

@abbeyyyyy17
be patient, guys, it's just cause there's like
50,000 people crashing it all at once

@Bianca_OnTheVerge
75,000 now

@GOTV_fanboiiii
ok its working now EVERYONE STOP
WHAT YOURE DOING OUR QUEENS HAVE
ARRIVED

@purrmaid2007
Liv where did you get those shorts

@arianaventi
I just wanna know if Ransom's single yet
orrrrr 👀

@abbeyyyyy17
ransom's not doing the q&a tho
@arianaventi

@authoremilyquinn
Loved hearing all their answers in your
stories this morning, @Snapaday @haileyg
@marissasanchez—thanks for doing this!
Excited for this Q&A!

@arianaventi
@abbeyyyyy17 yeah but maybe they know

@MillsMillsMills
MILLIE I LOVE MIDNIGHT

@hamstertroll
anyone else notice their hashtag could be
read girl stalk girls

@spinderella
@arianaventi no i think they got engaged

@arianaventi
@spinderella I know there are ~rumors~
about that but has anyone actually seen
them together all week???

@spinderella
@arianaventi yeah good question, now i wanna know too

@abbeyyyyy17
@spinderella @arianaventi ohmygahhhhh can we just forget about Ransom for TWO SECONDS and listen to the girls? #GirlsTalkGirls not #GirlsTalkRansom

@arianaventi
@abbeyyyyy17 @spinderella fwiw i would absolutely tune in to #GirlsTalkRansom, can we do that instead

@spinderella
@arianaventi HARD SAME @abbeyyyyy17

@abbeyyyyy17
agree to disagree, y'all are a good example of why we even NEED a chat like this but ok @arianaventi @spinderella

@Bianca_OnTheVerge
anyone else think sk's interview made it sound like honor totally picked the dream job in new york over staying in cali with duke? sorry not sorry for the spoilers if anyone here hasnt gotten to the series finale

@GOTV_fanboiiii
ughhhhhh @Bianca_OnTheVerge I hate it but you have a point

@Abbeyyyyy17
@Bianca_OnTheVerge @GOTV_fanboiiii
maybe she found a way to take the job *and*
stay with duke

@GOTV_fanboiiii
@fanline @Bianca_OnTheVerge
@Abbeyyyyy17 WE NEED ANSWERS

The diner and I go way back.

It's as close to the studio as you can get without being inside the gate, perched on a side street at the back edge of the lot—a hidden gem that managed to stay off the radar for most of the time we were on the air, frequented almost exclusively by studio employees. My mother and I originally heard about it from one of the producers at my audition.

We took the corner booth at the back that day; I was such a jumble of emotion I couldn't eat. Even my mother, who adores a good hidden gem, hardly took two sips of her coffee. Our food went cold, but she left a generous tip.

Two months later, I found myself at the diner again, ravenous after a marathon day of shooting. This time, Ransom and Ford and Sasha-Kate joined me in the corner booth, just the right size for the four of us. It was the perfect oasis amid so many days that blurred into each other—until late in our fifth season, anyway, when some PA brought his daughter to work and she blasted it all over the internet when she saw us.

Now, upon arrival, I'm immediately greeted by a familiar face, leathery and crossed with a lifetime of wrinkles—Marjorie was already on the older side back in the day, but she's still got a spark in her eyes, even if their blue has faded with time.

"Liv!" she says, reaching up to embrace me. "The boys told me you were on your way. Nearly gave me a heart attack, seeing them here after all these years."

Marjorie leads me back to the booth where Ransom and Ford are seated. Ransom's hair is disheveled after trying on who knows how many outfits at his wardrobe fitting.

I slide into my usual spot, my bare leg brushing up against the soft fabric of Ransom's joggers. It's familiar and new all at once.

"Oh man, I'd forgotten about that sandwich," I say to Ransom by way of greeting, nodding at his open menu. A glossy photo of a chicken sandwich piled high with provolone, avocado, and pineapple takes up more than half a page, titled—in gigantic all-caps text—THE RANSOM SPECIAL. "Didn't you eat it, like, twenty days in a row?"

"Twenty-two," he says, "but who's counting?"

"I bet I know exactly what you'll be having, Liv," Ford says, and Ransom joins him in unison: "Two scrambled eggs with only one yolk, no butter, black beans, extra salsa, two slices of avocado, and berries on the side."

"It *is* the perfect meal," I say, laughing. "You're one to talk, Mr. Please-Put-the-Pineapple-*Between*-the-Avocado-and-Cheese!"

"It's *practical*," Ransom insists. "Keeps the bun from getting soggy. Can't help it if I know exactly what I love," he says, grinning.

His eyes linger on mine with a look that makes me feel like he's talking about much more than just a non-soggy sandwich. A beat passes between us, and another, and I think maybe I'm reading this exactly right because he's gone as quiet as I have.

I need a distraction, fast. "Hey," I say, nudging Ford under the table with my toe. "What's with you? You're awfully quiet." Now that Ransom and I are equally silent, it's clear he's in one of his rare taciturn moods.

"Starving," he says, not looking up from the menu.

Ford's always starving, but he's not usually like this. "And?"

"Haven't heard from Juliette since Tuesday," he says. "Cast has her on a pretty strict shooting schedule."

"Doesn't help that they're shooting all the love scenes this week," Ransom adds with a grimace.

"Ahhh," I say, glancing at Ford, who continues to stare into the menu like it holds all the secrets to the universe. "Who's playing opposite her again?"

"Ethan . . . bloody . . . Miller," Ford says, exaggerating each syllable, still not looking up.

Ransom and I exchange a look. "I'm sure you have nothing to worry about with Juliette," I say. "She seems incredibly professional and not at all like the sort who would . . . well, you know. Not even with Ethan Miller."

"It's not Juliette I'm worried about," Ford says simply.

Ransom pulls the menu from him. "You don't need this thing. You know you're going to get exactly what you always get—shrimp tacos, a pile of fries, and a cookies 'n' cream shake."

"Gotta admit, nothing else sounds as good," Ford says, with the hint of a smile. Finally.

"And you guys give *me* a hard time about never ordering anything different," I laugh.

"What I want to know is, why is Ransom the only one who gets a menu item named after him?" Ford arches an eyebrow. "I think 'Ford's Favorites' has an intriguing ring to it, personally."

"Marjorie always did love Ransom best," I say. No one argues because it's true.

It hits me, suddenly, how strange it all is, that we're all here in this booth again like old times—how strange it is that at this time next week, we'll be on set and shooting a brand-new episode.

Marjorie returns to take our orders; Ford gets his usual, and Ransom takes the unexpected route with a grilled chicken–and-kale salad with ginger-peanut dressing. It feels like *someone* should order the Ransom Special, so I go out on a limb, too.

"How'd your Snapaday thing go this morning?" Ransom asks, once Marjorie moves on and it's just us again. I'm surprised he remembered what I was up to today, especially since we never explicitly talked about it—I definitely don't know what's on his schedule for the week unless it's something that involves both of us.

"It went well, except Sasha-Kate was in a big mood over the whole Millie situation."

"Her new song?" Ransom guesses, while Ford sings what can only be a line from the chorus.

"Yeah, apparently she knocked Hālo out of the number one spot," I say. "Sounds like Hālo's *thrilled*."

A little while later, when our food arrives, Ford immediately takes an enormous pull on his milkshake. "And this is on the house," Marjorie says, sliding a strawberry shake across the table to me.

"Wait—it's not September, so it's not her birthday," Ransom says. "And it's not April, either. What's the occasion?"

"Missed a lot of birthdays since the last time you lot were in," Marjorie says with a wink as she shuffles back to the kitchen. "You're next, hon. Hope you still like cookies 'n' cream as much as that one."

I assume she means Ford, but I can't stop staring at Ransom. I'm not at all surprised he remembered my birthday—he always made a point to make a big deal out of it. But he remembers April, too: how, each year on the twelfth, we'd split a strawberry shake in honor of my father, who should have been celebrating another year around the sun.

"For the record, I remember your birthday, too," Ford says, stealing a sweet potato fry from my plate. "September ninth. And Ransom's is—"

"December eleventh," I fill in. I never could forget, even the years when I wanted to.

"And mine?" Ford says, stealing two more fries.

"Ju . . . ly?" It's a wild stab in the dark. A wrong one.

"November twenty-eighth." Ford gives me a look of faux disappointment. "Not even close, Livvie."

Suddenly, an all-too-familiar sound starts up from the wall just behind our booth, a subtle and rhythmic creaking not audible from anywhere but our beloved corner. Ransom and I turn to each other on instinct, wide-eyed with delight.

"Guess it's still haunted," Ford says, reaching for yet another of my fries.

"Would you like the rest of these?" I say, pushing my plate across the table.

For the longest time, none of us knew what to make of the creaking—until one day, Ransom accidentally walked into the single-room bathroom on the other side of the wall while it was very much occupied—by two people. A postage stamp–sized bathroom in a hole-in-the-wall diner hardly seemed like the ideal place to fulfill unresolved romantic tension, but I guess desperate times called for desperate measures. Long days on the lot and limited privacy meant those hookups happened way more often than you might expect.

Marjorie returns with another cookies 'n' cream shake, sliding it over to Ransom. "Better get started on that before it melts," she says to me, spoken like someone who's never had to endure the joy of a wardrobe fitting where everyone has an opinion about your body.

My milkshake is beautiful and decadent, served in a tall, frosty glass with whipped cream and a fresh strawberry on top—completely Snapaday-worthy. I've been trying to take more opportunities to post, per Attica's requests, so I pull out my phone and open the app.

A little notification pops up that indicates new followers, and it's a dizzying number—*six digits* of new followers since I last opened it yesterday—

"Everything okay?" Ransom asks.

"It's . . . yeah." I tilt the phone so he can see, and his eyes grow wide.

"Guess the Snapaday chat really did go well this morning," he says. His eyes—his smile—they're so close to me, so unexpectedly gorgeous that my breath catches. If he notices, he doesn't show it.

I snap a quick picture of my shake—it's definitely starting to melt—and then take a sip. It's heaven in a cup.

"Want to give them something to *really* go crazy for?" Ransom goes on, with a mischievous grin. "Let's do some stories. Post your shake, post one of Ford, and then let's do one together. They'll love it."

He's right—it's exactly the sort of thing Attica would suggest. It's also what makes me hesitant. Where's the line between posting what's happening in my life versus posting my life for the sake of making people talk? Like everything else that's begun to blur lately, the boundary between what's private and what's not feels less clear than it always has.

I snap a photo of Ford, who's purposefully exaggerating his look-off-into-the-distance-while-sipping-a-milkshake pose. It's hilarious, and honestly, it's this that decides it for me: this isn't a date—so it's not crossing any romantic lines. And it's not some manufactured publicity stunt. It's slightly outside of my comfort zone, but it's going to be fine. I make the rules for what I'm comfortable with, and I decide when to break them.

It's just that I've never broken them before.

"Here, lean in," Ransom says, putting his arm around me, pulling me so there's no space between us. The warmth of him, the weight of his arm, all of it sends chills coursing down my arms. He's so familiar, even though it's been a million years since we've sat like this. Never as more than friends.

We were so close for so long, but now there are parts of him I don't know yet. Parts of him, despite our history—despite the small voice in my head telling me it could be a mistake to let down my guard—I want to know. I lean closer, breathe him in. He smells like ginger-peanut sauce and, underneath that, fresh laundry.

I center our faces on my screen as we give our best smiles to the camera, then snap. It's a great shot, a keeper on the first try.

"Tag me," Ransom says. "I'll share it, too."

"Same," Ford says, right before stuffing half a taco in his mouth.

My fingers fumble over the screen—why are my hands shaking? I silently count to five, calm myself. When I'm steady again, I post three quick stories, no captions, tagging them in each. It's done.

"I should probably get going so I'm not late to my fitting," I say, noticing both the time and a missed notification from Jimmy saying he's waiting outside.

"Beware of Tabitha and her straight pins," Ford says, in a considerably better mood than when he sat down. "Ask for Melody if you get your pick."

"Noted," I say. I take a few final sips of my shake, stopping just short of brain freeze. "Thanks for inviting me, guys, this was a blast." I pull out my wallet, looking for some cash to leave for the bill.

"Don't worry about it," Ransom says as I slip out of the booth. "You can get mine next time."

I'm quite certain Ransom isn't hurting for cash, so I take him up on it. "See you tomorrow at Dan and Xan's," I say. "Thanks again."

I feel faintly buzzed as I leave, even though I haven't had a sip of alcohol all day—only half a strawberry shake and a strong dose of proximity to Ransom. My mind is caught on his last two words to me: *next time*.

Pull it together, Liv, I tell myself as I slide into the car. We've got an entire show to shoot over the next week, and it's never going to work if I start looking at him as anything but my costar. We're still relearning how to be friends.

My phone buzzes inside my handbag—it's a text from Attica that simply says, *Brilliant move* ☻

Brilliant or reckless, I think. Possibly both.

Spotted:
Handsome Ransom + Lovely Liv

By Zenia DiLitto // Editor in Chief, Pop Culture, DizzyZine.com

Hello hello, my lovely Spinners—and thank you all for playing along with my game of ~speculation~ this week re: the Gemma Gardner Situation, as I've taken to calling it! It's heartening to see it's not just yours truly who suspects things might have taken a turn for the rocky—or at the very least, the murky—between Ransom and Gemma . . . though I do appreciate those of you who chimed in to assure us that Gemma is looking well as ever in her recent Snapaday posts.

I can't resist the opportunity to note, though, that there's still been no *evidence* that she and Ransom have actually been in the same place lately. Regarding that one post that wasn't a selfie, there's no proof that the second coffee cup pictured actually belonged to Ransom—THOUGH before you @ me, I will reluctantly admit (a): if Gemma has been through a recent breakup, I want whatever she's using to still look like the glowing queen she is, and (b): I am aware that Ransom's drink of choice is a mocha with cinnamon on top, which is exactly what was pictured. BUT STILL. NO *ACTUAL* EVIDENCE OF HIS PRESENCE. Ahem.

Now that we've got that straightened out, can we talk about that story drop in Liv's feed? In case you didn't see it, check out the photos below. Look how cozy she is with Ransom—and that strawberry shake, could she have *picked* a more romantic-looking beverage?! It screams "we're having a BLAST and I want you ALL to KNOW IT!" Well, we know it now, don't we? Don't lie to me, Spinners, I know this is what we've all not so secretly been hoping for since the episode where we saw Honor and Duke kiss for the first time (and, honestly, we all knew that kiss was inevitable for YEARS before it finally happened) . . . seeing everyone's OTP looking legit cozy with each other in real, actual life? I don't know why it's so comforting, but it is. It's like all is right in the world—tell me it's not just me. Be still, my fangirl heart!

Let the speculation begin below! If you spot anything out in the wild that might be of my interest, you know where to reach me. (Or, if you don't, it's spinnerspotted@dizzyzine .com!)

10

It's Friday night, more than twenty-four hours since I finished at the costume fitting, and I'm still sore in the spot where Tabitha jabbed me. Fortunately, getting dressed for the cast-and-crew party Dan and Xan are throwing at their house tonight requires zero straight pins.

I've picked out the perfect outfit, something that strikes the right balance of cool and casual: black skinny jeans, stylishly ripped at the knees, with a soft gray sweater and a vintage black leather jacket on top. For the finishing touches, I'm wearing a layered silver coin necklace, black ballet flats, and a white handbag from my closet; my hair is down in waves that look natural, as if I haven't spent an hour getting them just right.

Bre drills me on lines as I get ready for the party, going over scene after scene. Even though the table read isn't until Monday, I want to make sure to nail the emotional beats, so we've been drilling off and on since I got the script. This episode is classic Dan and Xan—solid and streamlined, but with heart, subtle in the way that makes the writing look *easy*.

"Ready for the last one?" she says, flipping to the bedroom scene I've intentionally been avoiding.

It's not like Ransom and I have never filmed anything intimate before—we have. But that was then, before things changed between us for worse and for better. At the moment, my mind is entirely stuck on *for better*: the way Ransom's grown into himself, every inch the blazing-hot action star who's single-handedly responsible for a myriad of sold-out midnight premieres. His five-o'clock shadow, permanently there no matter the time of day. That new scent on his skin, citrus and cedar and spice. How warm his fingertips felt as they grazed my bare back the other night on the red carpet—

The world might see images of him—of us—but how it *feels* to be near him? It's like a secret, something up close and personal that only I can know.

"Liv."

I look up, startled, and Bre laughs—she's giving me a *look*, eyebrows raised, the script facedown on the bed beside her.

"Is there something you'd like to tell me?" There's a lilt to her voice just like the other night, on the way home from the Fanline dinner—she knows exactly where my mind is.

"No idea what you're talking about," I say, attempting and failing at nonchalance. "Why?"

"I happened to notice the internet going crazy yesterday about a certain photo you posted?" she says casually.

"Oh yeah?"

"Mm-hmm," she says. I'm not looking at her, but I don't have to be looking to know she has one eyebrow raised and a number of questions—just as I'm certain she knows I'm trying my best to hide the blush creeping into my cheeks, the smile on my face.

"I've been in a cave ever since I posted," I admit. A blissfully silent cave where the memory is mine alone and I don't have to share it with millions of fans who want a milkshake to mean more.

"People are loving it," she says, and I finally glance her way. She looks every bit as enthusiastic as she sounds. "Attica's beyond thrilled, to say the least—she started texting me when you went too long without answering."

I turn back to the mirror, put one last finishing touch of mascara on my lashes. "Well," I say, the grin practically plastered on my face now, "that *was* a particularly gorgeous strawberry milkshake."

She laughs. "Yes, it most definitely was."

Was his face really as close to mine as I remember? Was his smile the same one he uses at photo calls, the one he wields with precision like a scalpel, carving out exactly what he wants in the world—or was it the other one, the spontaneous one he gives on instinct when he laughs? I feel an overpowering urge to find out the answer *right now*.

But if I look now, Bre will ask all the questions I know she's been stifling. If I look now, I'll have to answer them—even if I'm silent, my silence will *be* an answer. I trust Bre, I absolutely do. I'll tell her everything, when and if there's something I should tell.

Which there isn't. There can't be.

Ransom and I were friends first, and then we were ghosts. I'm still learning what we are now.

"We're drilling this one first next time *or else*," she says with a grin, opening the script to the bedroom scene and leaving it faceup on my bedside table. "You're off the hook for today."

✦

Dan and Xan's house is a major upgrade from the one I remember from previous cast parties. Their old place was like a private oasis—small and secluded, the perfect place to make memories with their twin daughters—but this one is a sprawling mansion complete with palm tree–lined drive and a wishing-well fountain in the front driveway. By our final two seasons, our collective representation had negotiated lucrative deals for the entire principal cast and the writing team; between that and the success they'd had even before *Girl* broke out, it's safe to assume the Jennings estate is doing more than fine.

Millie and I arrive at the same time.

"This place is gorgeous," she breathes as a smartly dressed attendant opens the door for us.

The foyer stretches to the stratosphere and is immaculately clean, decorated sparsely in dark gray and emerald to offset the white stone tiling. I can hear music and voices off in the distance.

"You'll find everyone out in the backyard," the door attendant says, as if reading my mind. "Go straight, then take either path at the end of the foyer—you won't be able to miss it."

We walk the long hallway, then turn into a spacious open-concept living area where the back wall is basically one huge window. For good reason: the backyard looks *massive*. Even from here, I can see a pool and another wishing-well fountain and manicured hedges that could rival a Disney theme park's, all of it lit with tiki torches and glowing lamplight under the dusky evening sky.

"Okay, Dan and Xan win best house," Millie says. "This is total goals, Liv."

My own home feels like a tiny beachside cottage in comparison—but honestly, I wouldn't trade it. I'd get lost in so much space, living all alone.

We make our way out into the backyard, where silhouettes mill all across the grounds. Servers, dressed in the same black-and-white uniform as the door attendant, weave down the pathways carrying trays of rosé and cheese and crackers. When they come our way, I take a glass and a plate full of each.

Millie's chatting my ear off—running commentary on the flowers, the lights, the cheese, the wine—when my eyes lock with Ransom's. I hadn't even seen him standing across the way, but then someone shifted and he turned his head and his eyes were just . . . *there*.

I take a healthy sip of rosé, nearly flooding my lungs instead of swallowing. *Steady, Liv.* All these years, I've tried to convince myself it was for the best that we took a step back. That I could eventually get over him, that maybe in time my feelings would fade—that maybe I'd blended fiction with reality and my feelings for him were never real at all.

But of course they were real. He's everything a person would be attracted to, and it's no use pretending I'm somehow exempt. He's beautiful, he's intense, he's funny and kind and sincere.

He's headed this way.

"Ooooh, where'd you get the strawberries?" Millie says by way of greeting, plucking one straight off his plate.

Ransom laughs. "Petite redheaded server at six o'clock," he says, and Millie's halfway across the backyard before the words have even left his mouth. His eyebrows shoot up. "She's got *energy*."

"She's been talking my ear off since the moment we arrived—girl must've had a vat of coffee this afternoon."

He grins. "I wonder how different all of this feels to her," he says. "She never went through it like we did back in the day."

"I had the same thought yesterday," I say. Millie definitely had a healthy fan following, but it was nothing like the unrelenting attention Ransom and I experienced. "She was absolutely swarmed by photographers when she arrived at our fitting. I got Tabitha, by the way. Or, rather, Tabitha got me—I've got the bruises to prove it!"

He winces but laughs.

"Nice outfit," he says.

I blush, so distracted by the compliment that it takes me a moment to realize he and I look like we coordinated for tonight. He's wearing slim-cut black jeans—which look *good* on him, might I add— with a gray sweater almost the exact shade as mine, sleeves pushed up to the elbows. It looks soft, and I suppress the instinct to reach out and touch it.

"Where's a photographer when we need one?" I say, grinning. "You clean up nicely yourself."

"Care for some bacon-wrapped figs?" a server interrupts.

"Those smell incredible," Ransom says, taking one for each of us.

It's a logistical challenge, eating an entire bacon-wrapped fruit in a way that's both graceful and doesn't require me to stuff the entire thing in my mouth like Ransom does. It turns out to be more than he bargained for, and he struggles to polish it off. I take a delicate bite— there's honey involved, too, as it turns out, sealing the bacon to the fig—and now we're both laughing, and sticky, too.

I take a long sip of rosé once it's over with. "That," I say, "was entirely worth the hassle."

"We did *not* think those through," he says, laughing.

"*Nobody* thought those through!"

I hear a howl of laughter across the yard, over by the fountain, where Sasha-Kate has managed to crack one of the stoniest Fanline execs.

"Only Sasha-Kate could get Bob Renfro to drop his guard like that," Ransom says. "Did I ever tell you what happened when I first met him?"

No, I want to say, and we both realize at the same time that of course he hasn't told me—Bob Renfro and all things Fanline only came into our lives this year, and until very recently, our text thread was silent. I might be imagining things, but I think Ransom's cheeks look a little pink.

"I was all set up to do one of their original series," he goes on, "a spy thriller that eventually fell apart, and Bob was sitting next to me in one of the meetings. I was shifting through some paperwork they wanted me to look over and accidentally spilled my water in his lap. Like, *all* of it. Ice included."

I can't help it, I laugh. "What did he do?"

Bob Renfro is the most prim, uptight man I've met in my entire life. A total silver fox—but an emotional vault.

"He was wearing these wiry little reading glasses, and he gave me this . . . this death glare over the top of them. It's a miracle he gave us the green light for the reunion, knowing I'm involved."

"I'm certain that man loves his bank account much more than he hated a pile of ice in his lap."

And now we're both laughing, and his eyes—his *eyes*, they are absolutely magnetic, all those shades of green—I can't look away.

"It's been really good being around you again," he suddenly says. "And I wanted to make sure you're okay—we haven't really had a chance to talk, just us, since the Fanline dinner—and—"

He cuts himself off. He's definitely blushing now—I've never seen him like this, nervous. Nervous around *me*.

"No, yeah—I'm good," I say quickly, and his relief is visible. "Better than good." We lock eyes. "Better than expected."

He holds my gaze a little longer—a minute, an hour, who can say? "Has it been hard?" he asks. "The interviews, I mean. You haven't done them in so long."

"Have you been looking for my nonexistent interviews all these years, Ransom Joel?"

He grins, dimples deepening. "More than I should probably

admit." His tone is light, but his eyes see right down to my soul. "It's been okay this week, though? No one else has crossed the line?" *Like that reporter on the red carpet*, he doesn't have to add. Like what happened years ago, too, in our final season.

I shrug. "You know how it goes. They've dug a little deeper than I'd like, but not so much it hurts." Yet. "How about you?"

He lets out a long exhale. "It's getting harder to keep the breakup a secret," he says. "Everyone wants to know about Gemma, what she's up to, where she's been. 'Busy season for both of us' just isn't going to cut it for much longer."

"I'm sure our diner photo didn't help," I say. He doesn't have to answer for me to know I'm right.

"I've kept quiet because that's what she wants, but it's going to get out eventually," he says. "The press has been swarming her for a while now, and she's always been so overwhelmed by it. She couldn't even get to her bookstore without paparazzi once people thought we were engaged, and it didn't help when she found out there was no substance to the rumors at all—so—yeahhhh." He drags the word out with a grimace. "She's had a rough few weeks."

"So," I say, at a loss. "Mutual, then?"

"Would have been, if she hadn't broken it off first." He looks right in my eyes. "You and Ford were the first people I told."

We've had a thousand moments just like this, scripted, but no less intense. But this: this is real.

"I'm still shocked you've actually managed to keep it quiet," I say, a small surge of pleasure at the knowledge that he trusted me with the news.

"It won't be pretty when they find out," he says. "They always make my exes the villains no matter what I say. I hate that for her."

He's right. Everyone loves to love Ransom—and by extension, they love to hate on anyone who hurts him. If Gemma couldn't bear the attention from the press when they thought she'd gotten engaged to Ransom, how much worse will it be when they find out she broke up with him? They won't care if it was mutual. They'll spin everything in favor of their golden boy, and Gemma will take the heat—I've seen more than one of his exes labeled a heartbreaker even when Ransom hasn't seemed heartbroken at all.

"It's good of you to care about that," I say, finding his eyes again. "Not everyone would be so kind."

Something shifts in him, something subtle—a spark in his already intense expression, like we're seeing each other for the very first time. Of all his many layers he's shown me over the years, this is a peek at something I haven't seen.

"Can I ask you—" he begins, but is immediately cut off by a piercing crest of feedback coming from one of the nearby speakers camouflaged as a large garden rock.

"Oops, so sorry about that! Is this thing on?" I hear Xan's voice before I see her, holding a wireless mic over on the patio near the pool. "Thank you all so much for being here this evening—on behalf of Dan and myself, I just want to take a brief moment to welcome you to our home!"

Xan is radiant as ever, ten feet of personality packed into a petite five-foot-four frame. She's wearing a black pencil skirt with black wedge ankle booties and a bright red top that perfectly complements her skin tone and dark wavy hair.

She goes on to thank the caterers, then gives us an overview of how dinner will work—there's a buffet set up at the far back edge of the yard, there are tables, it's eat at our own leisure—and continues on for more than what I would call *a brief moment*. I love Xan, but I want to know: What was Ransom about to ask me?

By the time she finishes, everyone is eager to move around and mingle again—I don't manage a single word before Ford appears and drapes his arms over both Ransom's and my shoulders.

"I heard there's someone juggling fire back by the buffet!" he says with enthusiasm that reminds me of the puppy my mother adopted a few years ago. "*Fire*, you guys!"

And that's when I know our moment is well and truly broken. Hopefully Ransom and I will get another chance to talk, alone, before the night is over.

We follow Ford down the path to the buffet—and, apparently, not one fire-juggler but three of them—picking up Millie and Sasha-Kate along the way. Sasha-Kate is wearing an especially dramatic scarlet jumpsuit, a backless halter with a plunging V-neck and wide-leg pants. Her greeting toward Millie is measured, lacking in warmth, but at least it's not the silent treatment she was giving her yesterday.

"This looks amazing," Millie breathes. A long table is set up at the back of the yard, draped in a thick black tablecloth. A gleaming row of silver chafing dishes holds everything we need for a fusion Hawaiian taco feast: tortillas in one, black beans and rice in the next, all followed by a bounty of mahi-mahi and fried coconut shrimp and some sort of vegan option; trays of papaya and strawberries and mango wait at the end, where there are also bowls full of fresh cotija cheese and lime wedges and soy sauce and pineapple pico de gallo and a sweet-and-spicy sauce that smells divine. I absolutely love a good taco bar—tacos are amazing in that you could eat them every day for a week and never have the same meal twice.

We soon get pulled in four different directions, so we don't actually get to eat together. Ransom ends up in a conversation with Shine Jacobs and Bob Renfro, Ford looks genuinely interested in whatever Pierre Alameda is talking his ear off about—probably the up-and-coming tennis star he's been coaching lately, who made it past the first round of the French Open—and Millie stands by while Sasha-Kate chats up our producing team, Nathaniel and Gabe. I'm the lucky one: I end up with Xan.

"So how was it working with Vienna Lawson, Liv?" she asks between bites of taco. We're standing at a tall table under a gorgeous weeping willow that sways gently in the evening breeze. "Your performance in *Love // Indigo* was really something special. You two were obviously a collaborative match made in heaven!"

I blush; I can't help it.

"Thank you," I say, stalling for time. Xan practically built my career, and I'm so grateful for it. Working with Vienna was an entirely different sort of experience, though—more creative input on my part, a more mature role requiring range I never knew I had—and I'm not sure how to describe it in a way that won't sound like I liked Vienna better.

"It was . . . it was a singular experience," I finally say. "Simultaneously more relaxed and more intense than anything I've ever worked on before."

More relaxed, in that Vienna and I regularly hung out in my trailer until two in the morning with a full pot of coffee, trading ideas about how to approach shooting the next day's scene. More intense for the same reason.

Xan nods thoughtfully, working on a particularly juicy bite of papaya. I assume she's read the various articles and interviews floating around about Vienna's creative process; it's no secret Vienna holds her ideas loosely and is always open to testing them, no secret that this often leads to plans being flipped on a moment's notice in a way that stretches into long days and longer nights. It's such a different world from the one Dan and Xan inhabit, where they bounce things off each other and bring a fully realized script to the table week after week.

"I heard from a mutual friend that she's been working on a secret new project," Xan says, and I can't hide my surprise—a large coconut shrimp falls out of my taco and onto my plate. "News to you, then? I'd bet money she's writing something with you in mind."

"I'd be lucky to work with her again, honestly. She's brilliant."

Xan shakes her head. "You make your own luck, lovely. Dan and I have spoken often, privately, about how *Girl* wouldn't have become what it did without you."

"I don't know about that—I had some exceptional material to work with on the show. Did you know there are entire college courses devoted to you and Dan?"

She makes a face, and I laugh. "The college courses I love. But if I get *one more email* from a high school sophomore saying their English teacher is requiring them to interview a writer, I cannot be held accountable for my actions! What kind of assignment is that, anyway? Bless their hearts." She stabs a slice of mango with her fork. "The students, I mean. Not the imbeciles who assign those things."

This is why I love Xan. She's brilliant and confident and grounded, and it's always been primarily about the work itself for her, not other people giving her recognition for it. She and my father got along well when they were both up-and-coming in the industry—he was the same way.

"If Fanline gives the green light on our reboot," she says, an abrupt subject change, "we'd go into production as early as August. If Vienna reaches out to you about whatever she has in the works"—ahhh, that's how we got onto this topic—"all we ask is that you don't commit before clearing it with *Girl*'s shooting schedule, okay?" She says it with a smile, but there's an unexpectedly hard undercurrent to her tone.

"I—oh," I stammer, totally caught off guard. She's assuming I'm a yes for the reboot, if it happens at all, even though I've been careful not to get anyone's hopes up. I especially dislike the way she's implying *Girl* should take priority over all other potential projects on my radar, and the insinuation that I might jeopardize the reboot by accepting a role elsewhere. I don't know whether to be flattered or insulted.

"Don't worry," I go on, smoothing my words out until they're seamless. "My agent is on top of my schedule and will work it out if there are any potential conflicts. There won't be any issue."

Even as the words leave my mouth, though, I know they sound more solid than they feel. More committed than I am. Hypothetically—*if* I were to commit—the shooting schedule for *Girl* might be fixed and predictable, but Vienna Lawson is anything but. She could get an idea tonight, draft it next week, and have everything all set up for an on-location shoot by next month—or it could take as long as a year, maybe two, for her to feel ready to go. At the very least, if she's writing a project with me in mind, she might hope for intense collaboration in the months to come, which could become a point of contention if it started to interfere with *Girl*.

I need to take a breath and a big step back before I get too far ahead of myself.

"If you'll excuse me, I need to make a quick phone call. Good to chat, Xan—thanks for tonight!"

We both know my "quick phone call" is an excuse—I should definitely touch base with Mars about what just happened, but it can wait. I follow a winding path lined with tall tropical trees, their leaves wide and green, and find a quiet corner. Dan and Xan really do have a phenomenal backyard, I think, taking a moment to just *be* here in this peaceful little alcove. It's like its own private room under the stars, a ceramic birdbath its focal point, walled off by coral honeysuckle and moonflower vines and a thriving lot of wisteria, all of it lit by a lamp-post straight out of Narnia. It's lovely, romantic. Relatively quiet.

Quiet, that is, until I hear the soft crunch of footsteps on the gravel path behind me. I startle at the sound like I've been caught doing something I shouldn't, like I'm somewhere off-limits—but it's only Ransom.

"Hey," he says, with a little half grin that tells me I am 100 percent, absolutely, no question about it in trouble, especially if he moves any closer.

He takes a step closer.

"Everything okay? You left Xan sort of abruptly back there."

"You saw that?"

"I saw enough. Wanna talk?"

I grin. *Wanna talk?*, with that specific cadence and inflection—it's a line straight out of so many episodes of *Girl*. Ransom stole it a long time ago for our real-life heart-to-hearts, just like the ones Duke and Honor had on the show except without as much stage makeup (most of the time). Hearing it, here and now, brings me back to so many moments, so many feelings, so many days where Ransom and I were inseparable on-screen and off-.

We lock eyes, and *oh*—this is new.

In all the times I've looked at him as more than just a friend, I've never seen those feelings reflected back at me with such sparkling clarity. I thought I had, years ago, on that flight to Shanghai during our world tour, when I was sure he was going to kiss me. Whatever I saw then, though, was only a shadow of what is unmistakably happening now. This is so startlingly more substantial than any look he's given me, ever, and it nearly knocks the wind out of me.

Ransom and I have so much history: hundreds of mornings of laughter and *Wanna talk?* midnights, thousands of moments full of his smile, his moods, even his silence. *Years* of silence, gaping in the wake of all that happened in our final season. We've been embers and ashes for so long, but never entirely dead—from a distance, he kept up enough to know I've hardly given an interview in more than a decade. From a distance, I've watched his edges sharpen over the years, cheekbones and jawbone and the cut of muscle under his smooth bronze skin. There's no distance between us now.

As it turns out, all it takes is a single spark to flare embers and ashes into something wild and blazing.

"I . . . don't think I feel like talking right now." My voice comes out quieter than I mean it to, not much more than a whisper.

He takes another step, and I close the gap between us, and before I know it his hands are resting on the dark denim at my hips, pulling me in close. I rest one hand on the strong stretch of muscle between his neck and his shoulder—his sweater is every bit as soft as it looks—and curl the other around the back of his neck. We've done this countless times as Duke and Honor. It's as natural as breathing, being this close to him, but at the same time: it's entirely new as Ransom and Liv.

He grins, biting his bottom lip in a way that says we are absolutely on the same page here, so close now I can smell the sweet scent of papaya lingering on his breath—

But then his phone starts vibrating in his pocket, startling us apart.

He stifles a curse. "I'm so sorry," he says. "My agent keeps calling, and I've already sent her to voice mail three times. I should probably . . ."

"Oh, yeah, totally," I say too quickly, my heart still racing, my mind still catching up to what almost happened just now. "I get it." It's part of the job, urgent phone calls at odd hours, a trade-off for all the perks we enjoy.

He gives a slow grin, trademark Ransom, and I melt a little. "See you at the table read?"

"Can't wait," I say. "See you Monday."

He heads back to the din of the party.

I almost kissed Ransom Joel.

Ransom Joel almost kissed *me*.

I need to get out of here before it happens again—I need to be *sure*, sure we're not making a huge mistake.

Gemma Gardner, Heartbreaker!

By Lila Lavender // Staff Writer, *You Heard It Here First!*

Psssssst . . . you're gonna want to lean in close for this one, y'all! Are you ready for it? Are you sure? Get ready to see this bit of news blasted to even the darkest, dustiest corners of the interwebs: we hear from a trusted source, Gemma Gardner's purported good friend Clare Holbrook, that press-shy Gemma has dumped everyone's favorite first crush, Ransom Joel— and we have the receipts to prove it! Guess she's not the soft-spoken sweetheart we all thought she was, yeah? Allow me to present Exhibit A: screenshots submitted by this so-called friend half an hour ago. (!!!) It just keeps getting better and better, amirite? We suspect "friend" is not the term Gemma will use for Clare Holbrook after this, if they were ever close at all—and after reading this exchange, I have my doubts.

June 15

Gemma

6:58 p.m. Look, Clare, I'm sorry I can't come . . .
I'm dealing with some big stuff right now

Wait, big stuff? DID HE
PROPOSE   6:59 p.m.

7:12 p.m. Uh, no.
x2sy3ww.jpeg

[Editorial note, for those of you whose screen reader won't describe that JPEG as well as I will: It's a photo of Gemma holding her engagement-ring-less left hand in front of her face, which is undeniably hers and undeniably busted in a way that says I HAVEN'T STOPPED CRYING IN DAYSSSS. Former friend Clare, what were you thinking selling Gemma out like this? 😭]

                              GIRL   7:12 p.m.

                              GEMMA MARIE GARDNER   7:12 p.m.

                              WHAT HAPPENED AND
                              WHY AM I ONLY JUST
                              NOW FINDING OUT
                              ABOUT IT   7:12 p.m.

7:27 p.m.   We're over

                              WHAT
                              W H A T
                              W   H   A   T   7:27 p.m.

                              I need DETAILS what
                              happened   7:27 p.m.

                              Do I need to go hurt
                              somebody orrrrrrrrr . . . ?   7:31 p.m.

7:51 p.m.   No, I broke up with him

7:51 p.m.   Four weeks ago

                              FOUR WEEKS AGO, and
                              I'm JUST NOW hearing about
                              this???   7:51 p.m.

7:58 p.m.   I'm holding up as well as I can,
              thanks for asking xo

[Editorial note: THE SHAAAAAAADE of that last line, you guys. Gemma might look sweet as cherry pie on the outside, but wow. That's some A+ passive aggressiveness right there—not that I blame her, since Clare apparently couldn't take a hint from the time stamps and über-short answers that Gemma had ZERO interest in confiding in her, and probably wouldn't have said anything at all had Clare not pressed so hard for the info. I also, for the record, would not be surprised if this was what pushed Clare to one-up said passive aggressiveness with some retaliation of her own.]

                          What HAPPENED tho   7:59 p.m.

                          Gemma?   8:15 p.m.

                          Okay then, I'm here to listen
                          but if you don't wanna talk I
                          guess I can't make you   8:21 p.m.

Sooooo yeah, you guys. Looks like Gemma's got some fires to put out in her personal life this week, so if you see her around town, remember to be kind! And if you see Ransom Joel, buy him some chocolate hazelnut gelato if you can—I can almost guarantee he won't be single for long. Maybe you'll be the lucky girl? (If I don't get there first, that is.) ☺

As always, send your juiciest tips to lila@youhearditherefirst.com and you could win a $500 gift card to the store of your choice in our monthly drawing. Or, you know, sometimes we straight up buy it for a lot more . . . just ask Clare!

11

At five minutes to nine on Monday morning, we're all crowded into one of the studio's meeting rooms for our table read. Things have changed quite a bit since we last did this—it's been nearly fourteen years, after all, and the studio has clearly put their significant fortune to good use. Compared to the old gray room with too many fold-out chairs crammed around a not-quite-big-enough table, this one feels like a palace.

Slate-gray walls stretch at least twenty feet high, adorned with the occasional wooden shelf and lavish green plants that spill from terra-cotta pots. The focal point table is a solid slab of reclaimed wood, sanded and stained, surrounded by leather chairs the color of warm caramel. Overhead, six fishbowl pendants hang in a dramatic row, illuminated by Edison bulbs. It's calm and energizing in here despite the distinct lack of natural light.

I'm five minutes early—my version of *right on time*—and most everyone is here already. Millie and Ford and Ransom are chatting with Laurence and Annagrey, while Sasha-Kate talks animatedly to Bryan and Nathaniel. Pierre Alameda is over with our other producer, Gabe, and a trio of new-to-me actors who'll be playing minor characters. They look a bit intimidated, if I'm honest—the girl who'll be playing Sasha-Kate's roommate is dabbing surreptitiously at a coffee stain on her peach-colored blouse. At the far end of the table, Dan and Xan are already in their seats, flipping through script pages and jotting last-minute notes in the margins as usual. But this time, Dan's hair is silvery gray, and his wire-rimmed reading glasses sit low on his nose; it hits me all over again how surreal it is that we're celebrating *twenty years* since our premiere, how familiar this all is and also how much has changed.

I head straight for my seat. Bryan likes to start precisely on time, and sure enough, as I make my way to the table, he makes the call: "Everyone, we've got sixty seconds to settle in—please find your way to your seats!"

Ransom turns his attention from whatever Annagrey was saying, and his eyes light up as they lock on mine. I feel heat creeping into my cheeks, the memory of Friday night so fresh I can almost feel his hands on me all over again.

Stop it, Liv, I tell myself. *Focus.*

I found a text on my phone late Friday night after I'd already settled in bed with the Emily Quinn novel. *sorry about tonight*, he'd written. *dealing w a bit of a mess right now—catch up session soon?*

Yes please, I wrote back, though it didn't stop me from analyzing every word. His *sorry about tonight* message: Sorry that what went down between us happened at all—or that it ended so abruptly? Everything felt so clear in the garden, what we both wanted.

But I've misread him before.

I stayed mostly offline all weekend, going over my lines and finishing the Emily Quinn novel—I got so into it I couldn't put it down. Mars and I talked last night about all the decisions I'll need to make soon, and about my uncomfortable conversation with Xan.

"The *nerve* that woman has," Mars said when I told her, and I could practically hear her rolling her eyes. She doesn't know Xan like I do, isn't quite as generous in giving the benefit of the doubt. "Don't waste one second worrying about this Liv, I'm telling you—*if* there's a conflict, which is a big if at the moment, it will work out in our favor. I'll make it work." She promised to put out feelers with Vienna's assistant, too, see if she can find anything out about the new project Xan mentioned.

Mars has always taken a *they don't have to like it* approach, and it's worked out well for this long. The network always bent to her demands because we had leverage—*I* was leverage, the star of their show.

Now, though, it's a different situation. With a reboot, they could find a way to restructure it without me. I may not have decided if I want to commit yet, but I definitely don't want to burn bridges—not with Fanline, and not with Vienna. Not with the fans, either. I'm not ready to think about what it would mean for *Girl* if it came down to me having to choose between projects.

"Just focus on the reunion show," Mars told me. "I'll do my job, and you just keep being brilliant at yours."

All of this brings us to today.

Ransom settles into the seat across from mine. I try to focus on the first page of the script, the scene that opens on the two of us down at Aurora Cove—the fictional beach where our infamous finale cut to black in the middle of my last line—but my eyes keep drifting up to his face.

He seems to be having the same problem.

This . . . could be a challenge.

"All right, everyone!" Bryan stands at the head of the table, the far opposite end from Dan and Xan. "Thank you all for being prompt this afternoon—we'll need to be efficient with our time this week, starting now. I'd like to request that any comments that aren't absolutely crucial be saved for our discussion after the break. Are we ready?"

The rustle of paper fills the room as everyone flips to the first page, giving collective consent that yes, we are ready.

Bryan's eyes land on me. "Liv and Ransom, take it away."

EXT. AURORA COVE BEACH - SUNRISE

PRESENT DAY

> It's dawn at Aurora Cove. The sun peeks out over the horizon, cutting through the fog that lingers over the sand and surf. The secluded beach is empty except for a lone figure: DUKE BEAUFORT.

A camera sits on a tripod, facing the
ocean. Duke adjusts the settings, peers
through the finder.

We see HONOR ST. CROIX join him on the
sand. Duke is too preoccupied with his
camera to notice he isn't alone.

                    HONOR
          Hey, stranger.

Duke goes still.

                    HONOR
          Seen anything good yet this
          morning?

Duke turns. For a moment, he's
speechless.

                    DUKE
          A few sea lions. Dolphins.
            (long beat)
          You . . . you're back home?

                    HONOR
          Needed a break. Can't get this
          in New York.

Honor grins, but it doesn't take long
to fade.

                    HONOR
          Looks like you're doing
          well, then? I saw your last

film. The Hawaiian monk seal
documentary -- it was good,
Duke. It should have won.

Duke looks away, back to his camera.
Adjusts a few more settings.

                    DUKE
          How's the magazine?

                    HONOR
            (with a half-hearted laugh)
          Better than I ever imagined it
          would be.

Duke finally looks at her again.

                    DUKE
          I saw you went to Santorini?
          And Positano?

                    HONOR
          They always send me to the
          coasts.

                    DUKE
          They send you here now?

Now it's Honor's turn to look away. The
sun is fully above the horizon now, the
waves glittering under its rays.

                    HONOR
          I'm here because I've missed
          this place.

```
                    (beat)
          I've missed you.


     Duke is quiet, but can't take his eyes
     off her.


                         HONOR
               None of the places they sent
               me felt like this.


                         DUKE
               Freezing with a side of fog,
               you mean?


     Honor gives a small smile, tucking her
     hands deeper into the front pocket of
     her thick hoodie.


                         HONOR
               None of the places they sent
               me had you there.
```

"Brilliant, brilliant, on to the next," Bryan says, pulling me out of what has suddenly become a rather intense moment.

The next scene centers on Sasha-Kate, and I'm thankful for the breather—holy *wow* was that some next-level eye contact with Ransom during those last lines. He's feeling the tension, too, I can tell—just the thought of being so close, having this intense conversation on the beach while the waves roll in, has me wanting to crawl across the polished wood of this table and finish what we didn't quite get the chance to start in the garden the other night.

I catch Ransom's eyes on me when I glance at him over the top of my script. The corner of his mouth quirks up, subtly enough so as not to distract Sasha-Kate and Millie as they work through their scene. I force my eyes back down to the page, and it's a good thing, because this scene is ending and I've got the first line in the next one.

We work all the way through the rest of the episode like this, flipping from Liv and Ransom to Honor and Duke and back again, each glance, every quirk of his lips unraveling me a little more—and that's not to mention the mid-episode scene that's brimming with close-to-kissing tension between Honor and Duke, which has a few people fanning themselves just from the way we've read it on our opposite sides of the table. By the time we finish the final scene and our break rolls around, no one but us seems to have caught on that it's more than just lines on a page. No one but us knows what almost happened in the garden.

The secrecy of it lights me up from the inside: it's almost unbearable, standing here with Ford and Millie and Ransom during the break, eating a cranberry orange muffin like it's any other day. I have the sudden urge to lick the crumbs off Ransom's lips, taste the sugar on his tongue. From the way he looks at me when our eyes meet, it's safe to say the feeling is mutual.

I've got to get out of here. Five more minutes until Bryan will expect us at the table again—it's more than enough time. I make a beeline for the ladies' room. As soon as I enter, though, I hear a voice echoing from behind one of the locked stalls: Sasha-Kate. Her tone sounds secretive, even a little sultry. She must have heard me, too, because a second later she says, "Gotta run—I'll call you back after."

I duck into the second stall before she comes out and things get awkward. I'm not in the mood for small talk, not with her, not while feeling all the things I'm feeling for Ransom, and especially not after overhearing enough of her phone call to know it sounded much more suited to a private hotel room than this very public bathroom stall.

Just before I head back out, my phone buzzes. Ransom: *this is torture* *Agreed*, I type back. *Still on for catching up later?*

The typing bubble pops up, then disappears. A moment later, he writes, *think we can get away with gelato on the beach without anyone noticing?*

Another message immediately follows: *also come back now, bryan's giving your empty seat the death glare*

I laugh out loud, and it echoes from the tile. *On my way*, I tap out as I walk. *And I've got beach at my house, let's use that*

I hit send before I fully think through the implications of what I've just done. The idea of Ransom in my living room, on my back porch, on the stretch of sand between my house and the Pacific Ocean, all of it—suddenly I'm a tangle of anticipation, of nerves and excitement and the *on purpose* of it all.

But it's not a date, I remind myself. He wants to catch up, which is fine, totally fine. It's been fourteen years and we've only just reconnected. There's a lot to catch up on.

Everyone's seated when I return. Bryan trains his death glare on me, not my seat—his eyes are so lovely and kind until they're staring intensely down his narrow, picture-perfect nose at you, and then they're lasers. Worse, he doesn't acknowledge me verbally—there's no *Nice of you to join us, Liv* to distract from the glare, nothing to soften the hard silence. Once I'm seated, he simply says, "Now that we're all here, let's begin."

Despite that uncomfortable moment, the rest of the afternoon soon turns into one of the best I've had in a while. It takes forever to go through the feedback—so many pages of notes from Dan and Xan all the way up to the Fanline executives—but overall, everyone is thrilled with the table read, especially the performances given by Ransom, Sasha-Kate, and me.

When all is said and done, Ford stretches his arms out over my shoulders and Millie's, who's sitting on the other side of him, and pulls us into something resembling a seated side hug. "You *killed* it today, my dudes," he says, seemingly unbothered that the production team was decidedly neutral on his own performance.

"Liv killed it, anyway," Millie says. If that's bitterness I detect in her voice, I'm pretty sure it's not directed at me. "I sound 'like a heartless extraterrestrial who was picked up off the street and handed a script five minutes ago,' apparently."

Yeah, ouch. Production was decidedly less neutral about Millie.

"I'd like to see Bob Renfro try singing 'Midnight' while wearing four-inch heels," Ford says under his breath, and Millie laughs—but Bob Renfro's comments, though scathing, were spot-on. Millie wasn't exactly cast for her acting skills back at age five, and they haven't improved much since then.

Ford unsuccessfully tries to get a group together for dinner—Sasha-Kate rushed out as soon as we finished, and Ransom says he has plans. My heartbeat picks up in my throat, knowing *I* am the plans.

"Livvie? You in?"

"Can't tonight, Ford, sorry. Rain check?"

"Holding you to it," he says. "Guess it's just me and Millie, then."

Millie's cheeks are on fire. "I wish I could, but . . . um . . . public places have become a logistical nightmare this week."

Ford wisely doesn't push it. With the amount of publicity Millie's getting these days, his personal life would be a wreck if they were caught out together just the two of them, even as friends—no one cares about truth, only headlines. And those headlines would absolutely make their way to Juliette in a heartbeat, even on a remote film set in Iceland.

Which is precisely why, even though my phone lights up with a text before we've even left the studio—*your place it is, how about 7:30?*—Ransom and I leave every bit as separately as we arrived. I don't want us in headlines.

Not when the fandom is still reeling over Gemma, those leaked texts blasted to every corner of the internet this weekend.

Not when there's not even an *us* to be written about.

My place at 7:30 sounds perfect, I reply as I slip into the back of Jimmy's Mercedes. *Should I pick anything up for us?* Too late, I realize my phrasing sounds a little too close to date territory, like I'm suggesting dinner.

It's not a date.

To snack on, I'm about ready to add, but his text comes back so quickly it's like he was waiting for mine: *got it covered, see you tonight*

For this not being a date, I'm feeling surprisingly fizzy inside.

The first time I felt feelings for him start to flare up, so many years ago and especially on that flight to Shanghai, I had to train them out of me when it was clear he didn't think of me like that—as anything more than a best friend, a particularly close costar. He never would have gone after Kylie, the tour director's daughter, if he had; never would have confided in me all the details of his feelings for her from first hookup to messy breakup.

I spent so many months back then trying to convince myself we were better off as friends, *best* friends who also happened to have incredible on-screen chemistry. As best friends, we could enjoy each other without risking a messy breakup. As costars, we could enjoy countless inside jokes and endless days on set together, all while making bank off of said chemistry. Why risk ruining it all?

Except then, in our final season, our scenes were more intimate than ever, blurring the line between fiction and reality all the more. So many times on set, it never felt like acting. We were closer than ever off-screen, too, both of us confiding things in the other we'd never told anyone else. He was my best friend, and I was his, and it sometimes felt like we were teetering on the edge of more.

But I was wrong then, too: one thing led to another, and one step back turned into a total break.

Then came the end of the show. With it, the end of us.

Now that Ransom and I are together on set again, the years between us feel like a long, looping detour: it's like we've picked up at the exact same spot. We're older now, our skin thicker—but underneath it all, we're still Liv and Ransom, whose foundation was each other for so, so long.

I feel the exact same spark between us, the exact same chemistry.

More of both, if I'm honest.

And though I try not to think about them, I feel the exact same fears, and new ones, too: that I'll let him in—even closer than before, at the rate we're trending—only for us to be torn apart in spectacular fashion all over again.

Rumors of Fanline Merger with CMC/Snapaday

By Anna Lindell // Associate Editor, Arts & Entertainment, *Sunset Central*

Rumors began to circulate this weekend after Fanline founder and CEO Shine Jacobs was spotted at bougie brunch spot Travelō with Marco Ferracora, CEO of television giant CMC (known most recently for their multimillion-dollar acquisition of social media site Snapaday).

Jacobs, who became a household name three years ago after taking Fanline from simple online media hub to the premier streaming service in the industry, has notoriously refused a handful of acquisition offers in the past, to her obvious benefit. But could this brunch signal a change in the wind? And if so, who would be acquiring whom?

It's tough to say. Some speculate there may be trouble beneath the surface of Fanline's flashy neon logo: that their acquisition of the rights to *Girl on the Verge*'s upcoming twentieth-reunion special—and a rumored, still unconfirmed reboot to follow—was a last-ditch effort to draw viewers to the platform. Others insist they wouldn't have been able to acquire said rights in the first place without significant resources; we need only reflect on <u>the cast's infamous salary negotiations</u> to surmise that's definitely a point in favor of Fanline doing much better than its detractors might argue—that not only are they surviving in this present market, they're thriving.

Enter CMC.

The California Media Corporation, or CMC, has been
gathering up speed this past decade and expanding its
acquisitions far beyond the coast for which it is named—
prior to the Snapaday acquisition, CMC snapped up a
trio of print, broadcast, and film conglomerates based in
Milan, Bangladesh, and São Paulo. With Snapaday, they
expanded their social media footprint; now, the only horizon
left unturned is a streaming service. Most of Fanline's rights
catalog is a bit dated, though—and while said catalog will
be a perennial vein of rich income for decades into the
future, some say they need a current hit to do more than
break even, especially after dropping such massive bank on
the Snapaday deal.

We've reached out to both Fanline and CMC about this
potential match, but for the time being, spokespersons for
both have declined to comment. More updates to come as
the situation develops.

12

What does one wear to a nondate on a beach that happens to be in your own backyard, with a guy you once knew as well as yourself until you suddenly didn't, who—not for nothing—also has lips you inexplicably want to lick the sugar off of at the most inappropriate of times?

This is the question I've been mulling over in my closet this evening. Ransom's seen me in literally everything, from red-carpet glam to slouchy tour joggers and sweatshirts to silky camisole sets while shooting bedroom scenes together, yet here I am, overthinking this as if it's the very first time he'll see me in person at all.

In the end, I go with beach casual—light-wash denim cutoffs, a faded oversized V-neck tee and a chunky-knit cardigan at the ready in case it gets breezy, leather sandals and a fresh coat of polish on my toes, an armful of friendship bracelets sent to me by fans over the years, my hair loose and wavy—and dig out an indigo beach blanket my mother gave me as a housewarming present back when I first moved in.

There's a knock on my door at precisely seven thirty. Like me, Ransom has also changed clothes since the table read and is now wearing a pair of slim-cut dark chinos with a chambray button-down shirt that's cuffed at the elbows. I can't help but notice how handsome he looks in the evening light. His forearms have always been glorious, the sort of effortless lean muscle gym rats would kill for, and his chunky analog watch—dials upon dials, three knobs, matte black fixtures against an olive-green band—only enhances the appeal.

He smiles when he sees me, a full-wattage thing that's entirely contagious. "Hi," he says simply.

"Hi," I echo, heat blooming in a variety of places. "Come in?"

Only as he edges past me do I notice the backpack he's carrying, a
dark olive green that matches his watch. It appears to be stuffed to the
brim. He catches me eyeing it and says, with a grin, "Told you I had
everything covered."

Not. A. Date, I remind myself.

It feels like a date.

Down on the beach, we slip off our shoes and settle onto my indigo blanket, which is soft and comfortable under my bare legs. The
beach is otherwise deserted thanks to the stretch of private residences
on both sides of my property—my immediate neighbors are even more
reclusive than I am when they're home, and off enjoying the beaches of
Bali and Saint-Tropez when they're not. Still, Ransom pulls on a dark
ball cap, just in case. It isn't the best disguise, but speaking from past
experience, every little bit can help. At the very least, it puts us both
more at ease.

"This should be perfect timing," he says, nodding to the sky. The
sun has dipped lower in the time since we've come out here; soon, the
sky and water will be a riot of pink and orange and gold.

From his backpack, he produces a paper-wrapped loaf of artisan
sourdough, then an insulated bag. Inside the bag are a variety of cheeses
and meats wrapped in the same paper, along with a variety of fruits—
blackberries, strawberries, mango, and honeydew—and even a small
jar of kalamata olives. He pulls out a plank of smooth cedar from the
pocket that would normally hold a laptop, then begins arranging it all.

"This looks incredible." I've always loved a good charcuterie board
but have never had one on the beach. "I've got some wine inside," I say,
against my better not-a-date judgment. "Should I go grab it?"

He grins, then pulls out a bottle of sauvignon blanc from the backpack, too. "Only if you'd rather have a different kind."

"No, this is perfect." I mean it. "Let me at least get us some wine-
glasses?"

He probably has a pair of those stuffed in his Mary Poppins backpack, too, but I'm halfway back up the stairs to the patio before he can reply. When I return, he pours us both a glass.

"So," he says. "Tell me all the things, Livvie."

"You want the long version or just the sound bites?"

He laughs, eyes sparkling in the sunlight. "I'm not in a rush. I want to hear whatever you want to tell me. What was it like for you after the show?"

The years I disappeared, he doesn't have to elaborate.

"I found a place in Montana," I reply, the answer fast on my tongue. "A little cabin with a lake and a valley full of wildflowers, no neighbors for miles, all the books I could fit on the shelf, and almost entirely unreliable access to the internet. It was glorious."

"What made you decide to come back? Too lonely out there?"

I shake my head. In truth, I thrived on solitude after so many years in the spotlight. "I missed the work, loved it too much to let it go forever. And—I don't know. I kept thinking about my father. He loved acting so much, you know? He would have hated that I cut myself off from it when I loved it so much, too." I've never spoken these thoughts out loud to anyone, but if there's anyone who will get it, it's Ransom. "He would have hated the press for making me want to quit."

"He already hated the press," Ransom says. "And he would have loved you no matter what."

His words are cool water to the parched parts of me that will never stop missing my father. It was the perfect thing to say.

We sit together in silence, so close the space between our shoulders is electric, watching the waves as they lick the shore. A nest of shorebirds— snowy plovers, I think—has taken up residence just down this deserted stretch of beach, all tucked into a sand dune. Otherwise, it's just Ransom and me and the light, gentle breeze coming off the ocean.

"I can't remember the last time I watched a sunset from the beach," he says, breaking our silence. He spears a slice of mango with his fork, takes a bite. "I can't remember the last time I sat on a beach, period."

"I bet you get absolutely *swarmed* at the beach," I say as I fill my plate with berries and cheese and olives, and he laughs. I love an ocean view, clearly, but I've learned the hard way to avoid the more populous

beaches like the plague. Too many starry-eyed tourists—it's impossible to get a run in without getting stopped, even when I've gone full
camouflage in my ball cap, sunglasses, and low side braid. Somehow
they always know. Yet another reason I love where I live: most of my
neighbors have been famous longer than I've been alive, so I'm mostly
left alone.

"Well, the view here is amazing." His gaze flickers from the sparkling sea and lands on mine; a flush of heat warms me to my core. "If I
lived here, I'd never want to leave."

I take a sip of sauvignon blanc. It's crisp but smooth, cooling me
off from the inside. "I should really come out here more often," I say.
"It's been way too long since the last time." All this sand at my disposal,
and I hardly ever venture past the chaises on my patio. My beach blanket still looks brand-new, even though it's more than a decade old.

Ransom takes a long look at me, his eyes bright even under the
shadow of his ball cap. My words hang in the air between us.

"I'm glad we get to do this," he finally says. "The show, the press
tour. *This*." He holds up his plate of fruit and cheese in one hand, his
wine in the other, gesturing to the sun as it dips lower on the horizon.
Another beat, another breath. "I'm glad we get to do this *together*."

Together.

I savor this moment, take a mental picture: this stillness, the peaceful crash of waves on the shore, the sand and the sea and the shorebirds,
the singular focus in his eyes that says there's nowhere on earth he'd
rather be right now.

"Me too." My voice catches, raw and quiet in my throat. "It's good
to be together again. I've missed you."

His hand shifts on the blanket, so close to mine I feel the heat
radiating between our pinkies. "I've missed you, too, Liv."

I hold my breath, not sure what I'm hoping to hear, but very much
aware of how invested I am in what he's about to say.

"I know I had no right to be hurting as much as I did when I was
the one who suggested we take a step back, but holy shit, Liv, it felt like
the world ended when we stopped talking. I've wanted to call you so
many times since then."

I don't have to ask why he didn't—I can see the memory all over his face, can hear my own words like the slap they were. *You probably shouldn't call me anymore, then*, I told him, swallowing harsher words, truer words. *We can take a step back if that's what you really want.*

"Everything just felt . . . so . . . *empty* without you," he goes on.

"You seemed to manage okay," I can't help but say. "Lots of girls willing to step in and hang out with you." I keep my tone light and airy in a way that says I absolutely did not keep up with all the headlines from my little cabin in Montana whenever the internet actually decided to work.

"Those girls were fun and all, but no one knew me like you. No one even tried to, honestly, not until Gemma—and even with her, there was still something missing." He looks back out to the sea, where the sky has just begun to explode into a thousand shades of rose-tinted fire. "I lost part of myself when you and I stopped hanging out, Liv, and I kept looking for it in every place but the right one. When I saw you at the Fanline dinner, and we started talking like we never stopped, it was the first time in years that things felt right again," he says, turning back to me. "I've never felt more like *me* than when I'm with you. You make my world make sense."

I take in his words. It's the perfect way to say it—I've always felt that way, too.

It's why I can't resist the pull between us, why I can't stay hurt: at the end of it all, I've missed him too much. I've missed *us*. I've missed myself—the feeling of knowing there's someone out there who radically accepts me for who I am on days when I'm grieving and seething and haunted by shadows, not just everyone's favorite girl-next-door who can do no wrong.

"I kept hoping it would feel worth it," I say. "The step back."

He shakes his head. "I never should have listened to my dad. It was his advice."

His words sink like stones, shifting the landscape of my memory: it was his dad's idea, not his. I should have known.

When my father died, my mother was my fiercest advocate, working with Mars to keep me grounded, protected. She knew Hollywood would eat me alive if my own grief didn't, and she was determined to be a safe space for me.

Ransom's dad was just as involved in his career, but my mother was always wary of him. *Textbook stage dad*, I overheard her saying one night on the phone when she thought I wasn't listening. *It's like he thinks Ransom is his own personal show pony.*

If life were fair, I would have gotten more time with my father, and Ransom would have gotten a better one.

"I have a question," I say, because I've always wondered. "Why did you go the blockbuster route?" He's talented enough to have scored multiple award nominations by now, maybe even wins.

Ransom lets out a long exhale, his expression clouded by something I can't quite read. "After the show, everyone had all these plans for my career—my publicist Andrea, and my dad—he's still my manager. Everything they put in front of me seemed great on paper, and worth the time, at least in theory—"

"And lucrative?" I interject.

He grins. "Very lucrative," he agrees. "So I took the roles they found for me, did what they thought would put me in the best position to . . . you know."

"Make every human with a heartbeat fall in love with you?"

His dimples deepen. "Stay relevant, as they say." He says it light-heartedly, but underneath, I sense an undercurrent of tension. "At some point, the line started to blur, and it was hard to tell where Ransom Joel the action star ended and the real me began. What *I* wanted, not what everyone else wanted for me."

"And what *do* you want?" I ask quietly as a cool breeze picks up between us.

His gaze lingers on mine, the golden flecks in his eyes lit up by the sunset. "I think I'm finally starting to figure it out."

I've looked into these eyes ten thousand times but never like this, where time stands still and I'm afraid to move for fear of breaking the magic of this moment. His gaze flickers down to my lips briefly; to the bare skin of my legs stretched out on the blanket.

"Tell me about these?" he says quietly, tracing a finger over one of the four friendship bracelets loosely knotted at my wrist. His skin brushing against mine sends shivers up my arm.

"I've received hundreds over the years, but these are the only ones I kept," I say, finding my voice. "That summer-camp episode we did started it—you know, the one with the shy girl and the canoe?" And the clique of mean girls that left her stranded out in the middle of a lake, I don't have to add: my character made her a friendship bracelet at the end of that episode, and I've been receiving them in my fan mail ever since.

His finger moves on to one of the thicker ones, diagonal rows of cornflower blue and seafoam green. My pulse picks up beneath his touch.

"So why these in particular?"

I think back on the letters I received, so many notes sent by so many people over the years, and not just girls: *This show literally saved my life*, more than a few of them read. *It sounds stupid, but* GotV *was the only thing that got me through the year after my mother's death*, another said. Letters like those stood out in the sea of autograph requests and endless handwritten notes boasting *I'm like THE biggest fan, no seriously, for REAL, I love you, Livvvvv!*

"These . . . they're the ones that remind me to be grateful, even for the harder days." They're why I feel such love for the fandom despite my hatred of the paparazzi. No one's ever asked me about my bracelets—most of the time, they live on my nightstand, not on my wrist. "These are the ones that remind me that what we do is bigger than a show for some people."

I watch my words sink in, take root in his mind. The corner of his mouth quirks up, and he says, "I think you and I receive two *very* different types of fan mail."

"I can only imagine." I shudder to think what he's been blindsided by, if the images people tweet at him are any indication—I've gotten my fair share of those, too. Fortunately, for me, those have been few and far between.

We settle into a mutual silence, watching as the sun slips behind the glittering sea on the horizon. Shades of deep purple blend to pink and orange and gold, chasing the rays as they shift in the sky. My skin feels electric under the heat of his touch, where he's still lightly tracing the bracelets at my wrist. It's a moment of perfect clarity: I want this. I want *him*.

I'm not sure I ever truly stopped.

The breeze picks up, cooler now that the darkness is creeping in. I hug my knees to my chest and wrap my bulky cardigan over my bare skin. Without a word, Ransom closes the gap between us and puts his arm around me, pulling me in tight. The hand that had been tracing lines on my wrist finds its way to my hip, thumb hooked into a belt loop, and I rest my head on his shoulder.

"Better?" His voice is quiet, his breath hot in my hair.

"Much," I reply.

And then the sun is gone, and the stars come out, and the next thing I know, we're not looking at the sky at all but at each other. I turn my face up to his, ready to close the gap—but a sudden gust of wind has other plans, tearing his ball cap away and carrying it down the beach. I stand on instinct, rushing to retrieve it.

Ransom follows me, both of us barefoot; I just manage to snag his hat before a retreating wave pulls it out to sea. My toes sink into the sand, soft and silky under the cold water. He catches up with me, wraps his arms around me from behind, both of us laughing—he's solid and warm and strong, a nice contrast to the sea. I turn to face him, and we're close, so close I smell the sweet scent of mango on his lips.

"It's a little wet," I say, an understatement, as I hold up his dripping hat.

He smiles, bright in the darkness—and in one swift motion, he takes his hat and places it backward on my head. I shriek, laughing, which makes him laugh, too. I don't even care that it's cold and wet, don't care about the wind whipping through my hair even though it's freezing.

"I'd say I'm sorry, but it just looks so *right* on you." He laughs, absolutely and obviously not one bit sorry. He's got a playful gleam in his eye, and it can only mean one thing.

"Ransom Joel, don't you *dare*—" I start, but it's futile. He dips his hand in the water and splashes me before I even have a chance to turn away. "Oh, it is *on* now!"

I dip his hat in the water, scooping up as much of the sea as possible before attempting to dump it on him—but the wind has other ideas, and blows all the water right back onto me.

"Wouldn't try that again, Latimer!" He laughs, darting away as I scoop up another hatful. "Even nature's on my side!"

I try to slip around him, but a wave catches me off-balance, and next thing I know I'm up to my neck in ocean. I don't even care, though, because I've managed to pull him down with me.

We're both shaking with laughter, especially when Ransom pulls *seaweed* from my hair—I'm mortified, and he's laughing so hard now he's practically crying. I splash him good this time, right before another wave completely obliterates me.

I'm soaked to the bone and starting to shiver. "Let's get you inside," he says, pulling me close as we make our way out of the water. It won't be long before the temperature drops a degree or twenty. A change of clothes and a fluffy blanket sound very appealing right now.

He grabs the wine, the plates, and what's left of our charcuterie board; I shake out the beach blanket and carry it, along with the wine-glasses, back up to my patio door. Luckily, he's got a change of clothes in the car—I'm not at all surprised he's prepared for the gym on a moment's notice. I take a lightning-fast shower and slip into my favorite yellow Lululemons and a soft gray racerback tank.

When we're back inside with fresh refills and dry clothes, we settle into a corner of the couch and get comfortable. For this not being a date, I'm sitting a bit closer to him than is strictly necessary—and his arm is stretched out along the back of the couch, not quite touching me, but almost.

"Have you ever seen *The Goatherd*?" Ransom suddenly asks.

"That's the one with Ford in it, isn't it? The mockumentary?" An image flickers in my mind: dozens of goats chasing Ford—clad in head-to-toe Gucci and a pair of oversized sunglasses—down the side of a mountain. "I've only seen the trailer."

We've got an early call time tomorrow for our first day on set, but we queue it up on my big screen anyway. It's only half past eight right now, more than enough time to watch the entire movie and then some. Ransom will head home by eleven at the latest, we agree. I set an alarm on my phone just in case we get . . . distracted.

Halfway through the movie, we're curled up under a thick blanket, my back pressed up against the hard muscle of his abdomen. His arm migrated from the back of the couch at some point and is now wrapped around me; I lean my head back on his shoulder, and he rests his head on mine. It feels perfect; it feels right. I'm so at home beside him, so comfortable and warm, that I drift off before the end of the movie—which I will absolutely not tell Ford—and wake up to total darkness.

"Ransom," I whisper, nudging him awake, trying to find my traitorous phone, which I now see is buried under a pile of blankets on the floor, battery completely dead. "It's one in the morning—Bryan will kill us if we're late tomorrow."

He mumbles a curse, still half asleep. "Why must this industry insist on six a.m. call times?"

"Any chance you packed your script in that backpack? You can just stay here, if so." An unexpected thrill courses through me at the idea of him spending the night—and at the semiconscious realization that I just spent half a night curled up beside him on my couch.

"No script," he says. I don't even have to look to know his eyes are still shut tight, resisting the inevitable.

Even though it wouldn't be hard to obtain an extra copy, I know him well enough to know he's got notes penciled in every margin—and on top of that, word would get back to Bryan, and that would be a disastrous start to the shoot. We're at the top of the call sheet and want to stay there. Tardiness, unpreparedness? Neither is an option.

His arms tighten around me. "I should go," he mumbles, still half asleep.

"You should," I agree. "Otherwise, you are definitely going to get stuck here, which would be terrible."

"Awful," he says into my hair, breath hot on my skin. He lingers there, long enough that I'm well and truly tempted to blow straight through our call time—we both are, clearly—but then the clock hits 1:15, and reality sinks in.

"Tomorrow is going to be brutal," he says, finally extricating himself from our little nest on the couch.

"Brutal, yeah."

And yet, right now, it feels anything but.

A "Garden" Party to Remember: Ransom Joel Superfan Ejected from Gemma Gardner Bookstore Event

By Lila Lavender // Staff Writer, *You Heard It Here First!*

Well, hello, my sweets: we meet again! And can I just take a minute to say THANK YOU for the outpouring of messages that hit my inbox after That One Article I Posted, in which I spilled the beans about the split heard 'round the world? (Except you, Dave. You can stop it with the daily emails shaming me for my true and timely reporting on actual facts that everyone but you is clearly interested in. Readers, I'm not *saying* you should do a scavenger hunt through the thousands of comments on that last post just for the sake of finding Dave's inaugural problematic comment and telling him how very much you appreciate what we do here at *YHIHF!*, but . . . I'm not *not* saying that, either. Dave, you reap what you sow!)

Ahem. ANYWAY.

You may recall, from said previous post, my speculation that sweet-as-cherry-pie Gemma Gardner has a certain amount of tartness to her, too—after <u>her supposed "friend" sold her out</u> and the incident I'm about to share with you, it's not hard to see why a stronger, more forthright side of her is starting to come out.

Case in point: the restraining order she just took out against one of Ransom's more . . . enthusiastic . . . fans. Did it ever occur to you, dear readers, that the best way to express your displeasure at someone for breaking the

heart of the stranger you love *might* just be to show
up to <u>the independent bookstore she runs</u> (Snapaday:
@thegardenbygems), dressed in custom-designed fabric
printed with said heartbreaker's face all over it AND HER
EYES X-ED OUT, and proceed to make a gigantic idiot of
yourself while trying to make a point? No? Well, good for
you, because that means you won't be sharing a restraining
order with this, er, special someone (pictured below in
numerous Snapaday posts from eyewitnesses).

Around here, we're allllllllll for a friendly roast—as you
know—but please think twice before actually entering
someone's space in a way that threatens both their business
and their existence. (Keep that in mind while roasting Dave,
please.) Let me just say, in case it isn't clear: I have nothing
but respect for this no-nonsense Gemma and fully support
the actions she's taken to protect herself.

If you're losing sleep at night over how anyone could toss
Ransom Joel's heart aside, hey! Look at the silver lining—he
has yet to be seen around town with anyone else, right? You
could be next!

A word of caution, though, if you do turn out to be his next
special someone—just keep those superfans in mind! You
could be next in that sense, too, if you follow in Gemma
Gardner's heartbreaker footsteps. A good rule of thumb:
if you see someone who's gone to great lengths to craft
an outfit covered in your face, eyes x-ed out or not, that's
always a bad sign.

Until next time (hit me up at lila@youhearditherefirst.com with
all your juiciest tidbits so there can *be* a next time)!

xo, Lila

Despite my best efforts, I sleep through yet another alarm in the morning—I could have sworn I turned the volume up while plugging in my phone last night, but apparently not.

I have eight missed calls from Bre before I finally pick up. "How bad is it?"

I stuff my script in my bag, along with a slim cylinder of ibuprofen and a banana that's already developing brown spots. The digital clock on my microwave reads 6:32—I was supposed to be on set half an hour ago.

Bryan's going to kill me.

"Bad enough that I had to stop in the middle of my Peloton ride," she says, a touch breathless. Translation: quite bad. "Bryan called me four times in a row. Everything okay?"

I think back to the beach, the cold water lapping at my ankles. Ransom's eyes sparking gold under the setting sun, laughing until we cried out in the ocean. Waking up together on the couch, him finally heading home just over five hours ago.

"Ransom was over pretty late," I admit, unable to keep it to myself. It's Bre, for one—and it also feels more than a little relevant. "Not that I'm going to tell Bryan that."

"Liv Latimer! I need to know *everything*!" she squeals, and I know I'm forgiven for the interruption to her workout. "I mean, uh. You know. *After* your first big day on set. Which, I'm sure, is on hold until you get there. I'll call Bryan back for you in a minute and report that you're on your way—right?"

I peek out my front window, see Jimmy's Mercedes idling in my driveway. He's got a thing for thrillers, and I can see his latest read open and resting on his steering wheel. Still, I feel bad for making him wait, and that I didn't hear either of his two attempts to call me.

"Yes, please and thank you." I tighten the lid on my water bottle, sling it into my tote with all the rest of my things. "Could you also do me a favor after that?"

I tell her about a book I recently saw advertised on Snapaday, a new release by Eric Zhang that comes out at the end of next month—I've spent so much time in Jimmy's presence, the algorithms in my social media have started giving me ads for his favorite authors. I ask Bre to work whatever magic she possesses that will make an advance copy of the book appear on my doorstep.

"So sorry I'm late," I say to Jimmy, which I'm sure is only the first time I'll say that this morning. By the time I'm on set and settled in at hair and makeup forty minutes later, I've definitely said it at least six more times.

"You're not the only one who was late," my hairstylist, Emilio, says conspiratorially. "Your boyfriend rolled in at six twenty this morning. I thought Bryan was about to lose his mind when neither of you showed up on time."

My heart leaps into my throat until I realize he's only talking about Ransom in the context of being my *on-screen* boyfriend and that he has no clue anything more could be going on behind the scenes.

"Well, I'm glad I'm not alone," I say smoothly, hoping it isn't written all over my face that Ransom was at my place last night.

By some miracle, we're not too far behind schedule—Emilio made quick work of my hair, and my makeup artist, Gretchen, is some sort of wizard whose gifts allow her to simultaneously bend time *and* make me look effortlessly luminous. I get a death glare from Bryan when I walk on set, but that's it—Sasha-Kate and Millie are mid scene on whatever he shifted around to shoot instead of the scene Ransom and I had been slated to do first thing.

Ransom's hanging out on the far side of the soundstage near craft services, sliding a pile of doughnuts onto his plate; an assistant around Bre's age looks on hungrily with heart eyes—at Ransom, not the doughnuts. I doubt she even realizes she's staring.

I slip across the room as silently as possible so as not to interrupt the scene. "Morning," I whisper once I'm close, loud enough that only he can hear. He gives me a lopsided grin, the same montage flashback from last night clearly playing across both our memories.

I join him in front of a tray of tropical fruit. At the sight of this particular fruit mountain, my stomach unleashes a startlingly loud growl—I whip around to make sure the noise hasn't interrupted the shoot, but in doing so, I accidentally knock a pair of tongs from the table. They hit the floor with a clang, which earns me yet another death glare from both Bryan and Sasha-Kate. She and Millie were in the middle of a quiet, serious moment, and I've just ruined it.

Sorry, I mouth in their direction.

Ransom passes me a clean pair of tongs, and I pile a sunny selection of mango and pineapple on my plate. This day needs a turnaround, and *fast*. It isn't like me to show up anything less than perfectly on time— had I actually delayed the schedule instead of just causing it to shift around a bit, I would be getting more than just a series of not-so-subtle death glares from Bryan. I've seen extras fired for less. Even though no one would ever fire me from *this* particular production, there are other ways to remind a girl who's running the show. If anyone—from Bryan all the way up the chain to Bob Renfro and Shine Jacobs—decides I'm not taking this seriously, word could spread around town and affect the reputation I've worked so hard to earn.

We should have been more careful last night.

Sasha-Kate and Millie knock out their scene after only three more takes, and then it's our turn. To my credit—especially after the morning I've had—I'm rock-solid in our first scene. I don't miss a line, don't miss a beat.

Unfortunately, the same can't be said for Ransom. The man needs a solid six hours of sleep to be fully functional, minimum, and he must have gotten, what—three or four?

The scene is nothing short of a disaster. We're not shooting in order—Bryan set the schedule up according to our big set pieces and which ones would be the most efficiently grouped together each day. Today's scene falls toward the end of the episode. It's supposed to be a pivotal, emotional moment between Duke and Honor, but every single one of Ransom's lines has fallen flat so far—and that's when he hasn't missed his cue or forgotten his lines altogether.

"Let's take it from the top," Bryan says, not so subtly checking his watch. "Again."

I can feel the tension radiating from him, the frustration he's not even trying to mask. His frown deepens, so much so that it can be hard to remember that off set, he's actually an incredibly chill guy. It's a good thing, too, because otherwise his blood pressure would pose a serious health risk.

Ransom and I lock eyes.

You've got this, I think, wondering if we've been through enough hours on set in our lives for him to read my mind.

He gives a subtle nod and takes a long, slow breath.

Even the clapper loader seems irritated as he aggressively snaps the clapboard shut, our signal to begin. Again.

> **INT. DUKE'S BEACH BUNGALOW - LATE AFTERNOON**
>
> Duke ties his running shoes and slips a pair of wireless earbuds in his ears. He's on his way out, a little distracted by the music app on his phone, but when he opens his front door, there's Honor.
>
> HONOR
> Sorry, is this a bad time?
>
> Duke pulls his earbuds back out again, tucks them in his pocket.

                    DUKE
          (beat)
I thought you were flying back
to New York.

                    HONOR
I couldn't do it -- not after
last night.

                    DUKE
But your assignment on the
Adriatic . . . ?

                    HONOR
Croatia can wait.

                    DUKE
So can I.

                    HONOR
You've been waiting for me for
too long already. One summer
in New York was never supposed
to turn into this many years.

                    DUKE
Do you want to come in?

Duke steps back from the open door;
Honor follows him inside. She pauses
to take in a display on the wall --
an old typesetter's drawer full of
seashells -- and beside it, a vintage
map of the California coast. On a
nearby bookshelf is the first Emmy

Duke won, for one of his marine
documentaries.

Duke wraps his arms around her from
behind and slowly pulls her into a bear
hug. She fits perfectly with him and
tips her head back to rest it against
his chest.

                    HONOR
          I should have been with you
          when   you   collected   these
          shells. You picked them all up
          while filming?

Duke points to a calico scallop.

                    DUKE
          Found that one the day I saw
          a   pod   of   dolphins   up   near
          Monterey. And that one, there,
          was when I filmed the harbor
          seals up in Half Moon Bay.

Honor sighs, still resting against him.

                    HONOR
          I think I'm going to quit my job.

                    DUKE
          You love it, though, don't you?

Honor's still looking at his seashell
collection. Duke can't catch her eye.

                    HONOR
          I do.
             (beat)
          But I love you, too.

      Finally, still wrapped in his arms,
      Honor twists around to face him.

                    HONOR
          I've seen the whole world, it
          feels like -- but on my last
          trip to the Amalfi Coast, I
          couldn't stop wishing you were
          there with me. I don't want
          to watch my life go by from
          behind a camera lens, alone.
          And I don't want the whole
          world at my fingertips unless
          you're in it with me.

Ransom closes the space between us, and I'm holding my breath—this is the first time we've made it all the way through the scene, finally, and there's just one little bit left.

"I don't want you to give up your dream job for me," Ransom-as-Duke says, looking deep in my eyes.

Heat spreads through me, and it's all I can do to stay in character right now, to be Honor-rewriting-her-life-story and not Liv-who-wants-last-night-and-more-*pronto*.

"But I'm with you whatever you choose, okay? You'd make an incredible cinematographer—we could go on location together for the next project." He buries his face in my hair, takes a deep inhale. "No pressure, though. I mean it."

He pulls away, just far enough to look at me. His eyes spark, hot as fire, and the position we're in isn't helping, no space between us from the waist down. We're in danger of slipping into territory that's much more appropriate for a scene we're slated to shoot later in the week.

"Thank you," I say, the first words of my final line barely making it out before I lose it. I close my eyes and we press our foreheads together like the script calls for. "I think I'd like that."

We stay like this for several beats, so close it's torture: I want to be *closer*.

"Aaaaand *cut*!" Bryan calls out, after what feels like an eternity. "Good, good. That'll work. Coffee has finally kicked in, I see."

It's about as close to a compliment as we're going to get from him today, and it's actually *quite* a nice one considering we threw a wrench in the schedule and took a ridiculously circuitous path to get here, what with Ransom tripping over so many of his lines this morning.

Bryan tells us to take twenty—well, technically, he tells *Ransom* to take twenty, since I'm not in the next scene—a shorter break in the name of trying to get the shoot back on schedule.

"I'm sorry I was such a wreck," Ransom says under his breath as we make our way off set.

I wave him off, even though it is kind of a big deal, and I do appreciate him acknowledging it. It's also partially my fault. "We're good," I say. I glance at him, find his eyes already locked on me, and he grins.

"Do you want to—" I start, at the same time as he says, "Your trailer or mine?"

"Yours," I manage, just before we're intercepted by the same assistant who was eyeing him over doughnuts this morning. *Evy Langford*, her badge reads.

"Hi, Ransom," she says, falling into step beside him. No greeting for me. "Just wanted to let you know your lunch will be delivered to you ASAP, since you don't have much of a break. Would you prefer the barbecued chicken or the coconut curry?"

"Let's go with the curry today," he says. "Thanks."

She passes the message on via walkie-talkie, keeping pace with us even after he's answered her question. "Great work today," she says, and like the nice guy he is, he takes the compliment.

It's a good thing she only has eyes for Ransom—I have to bite my lip to keep from laughing. I adore Ransom, but I'm not blind. That was one of the worst mornings on set he's ever had, if not *the* worst. This girl has it bad.

"I'll wait here to make sure there aren't any issues with your food," Evy says when we get to Ransom's trailer.

So much for my plan to follow him inside.

"That won't be necessary," he says. "I'm sure it'll be fine."

Evy doesn't get the hint. Like me, she can't resist Ransom's magnetic pull.

"Oh, I don't mind at all!" she says brightly. "It's totally my job."

I feel the seconds slipping away with every word she says. Ransom gives a polite nod, even though I know he must be dying for a moment of privacy. If we can't be private together, the least I can do is help him get a private moment alone.

"Hey, Evy, want to join me for some coffee? My treat. That sludge from this morning isn't cutting it." I strongly suspect Bryan withheld my usual flat white as punishment for being late.

Her eyebrows practically go through the roof—this isn't a thing we do, usually, mixing cast and crew on breaks, and even though she's new around here, I can tell she knows enough to appreciate the offer.

"Let me just— I need to ask—"

I wave her off. "I've got you." We won't be gone more than fifteen minutes—there's a good coffee shop right here on the lot.

Ransom gives a small wave and mouths a relieved *Thank you* when he's sure Evy isn't looking.

Thank me later, I mouth back.

He grins, eyes sparkling as he shuts the door between us.

Later can't come soon enough.

#5Facts: Rising Star Millie Matson!

By Octavia Benetton // Staff Writer, *Love & Lightning Rounds*

Hey heyyyy, Lightning Bugs—welcome back to this week's edition of #5Facts, featuring everything you never knew you needed to know about rising star (and former scene-stealing child actress from *GotV*) Millie Matson! Unless you've been living on the moon for the past week, you've no doubt heard Millie's latest single, "Midnight," which skyrocketed to the top of the charts. And it's only gaining traction—understandably, as it is one SERIOUSLY catchy melody that somehow makes you love it more every time you hear it. SO! With that in mind, even though Sasha-Kate has been our *Girl* obsession for years, we thought we'd do something a little different and give some love to Millie, who's gone a bit under the radar for too long. We have a feeling her star might just outshine the others in her orbit soon—and that's truly saying something, coming from us.

1. Millie wrote all her own songs for the upcoming *Midnight* album! Unlike her first two ventures—*Bubblegum!* and *Peaches*—Millie took a three-year break between albums, handpicked a new producer to collaborate with (and might we add, his musical sense is as hot as he happens to be), and wrote every single song herself. You've already heard "Midnight," but we were given an exclusive preview of three more songs on the upcoming album, and let us just say: you are NOT ready for them, they WILL be on repeat for the rest of this year, and you're going to love every single second. Be on the lookout for sparse, sexy, infectious late-in-the-album track "Spark," as well as the wild ride that is "Tiger Queen," and—of course—the next single set to drop, "Meet Me in the Garden."

2. Millie masterminded her own launch strategy for this album, which is debatably even more impressive than the fact that she wrote every track. It's clear she's intent on taking the reins of her career in her own hands, and even clearer that she's incredibly competent at it. From her Snapaday presence (anyone else following along with the hints she's been dropping?) to the makeup look themed specifically for this album (please tell me I'm not the only one who spent an hour picking silver star-and-moon confetti from my carpet after a particularly vindictive cat knocked the tube off the table) to the timing of when/how she drops each single for maximum effectiveness (hi, yes, how many of you are only just now hearing about *Girl on the Verge* *because* of Millie's music/Snapaday account? THOUGHT SO. On the flip side, I suspect there's an equal number of *GotV* viewers hearing about Millie's *music* because they're fans of the show. Girl's got good instincts.), Millie's had a hand in every step of the way. Her approach is clearly working.

3. Millie is single! In all the photos we've seen since "Midnight" blew up—and there have been A LOT of photos—there hasn't been even a hint that she's seeing someone. Unless, of course, you count her ever-present new security guy, who I've affectionately named Paolo. Doesn't he look like a Paolo, y'all? (I hear his actual name is Thomas, but you know. Details.)

4. Millie loves the Alps! Although she lives full-time in Los Angeles for ~obvious reasons~, Millie's favorite place on earth is France's exclusive luxury ski resort Courchevel 1850—she and her family vacation there for Christmas every year, thanks to a mix of family connections and, we assume, her *GotV* earnings. Check out Millie's gorgeous Snapaday posts from her last trip—don't you just want to climb through the phone and live in those photos forever???

5. Millie's got a green thumb! Rumor has it that Millie's favorite way to unwind is . . . wait for it . . . to drink mint iced tea grown from seeds in her very own garden, while walking around barefoot in said garden watering her various plants. Knowing what you now know, you might assume her next single "Meet Me in the Garden" would be pretty tame, buuuuuut . . . let me be the first to say: no. No, no—tame it is not. Millie clearly enjoys *other* ways to unwind in her garden, if you catch my drift. ;)

OKAY! Aaaaaaand that's it for today's #5Facts—hope you enjoyed this special Millie Matson–focused edition! Question of the day for you: If you're new around this blog, which did you hear of first, Millie's music *or* *Girl on the Verge*? And for everyone, which of Millie's singles are you most excited to hear? Sound off below!

14

We're back in ten minutes—the coffee shop was quick today. I'm headed for my trailer, finally ready for a moment to myself after parting ways with Evy near the soundstage, when Bryan intercepts me.

"Liv, hi," he says, falling into step beside me. "I need you to do something for me." He doesn't wait for me to ask questions. "We're about to start shooting, but I need to make sure Ransom's good for it—can't handle any more delays today. He's not in the first half of this scene, so I want you to go run lines with him until I need him."

I take a long sip of my flat white, an excellent disguise for the smile creeping onto my face.

"Sure, yes, of course," I say. "I'll head straight there."

"Great, Liv, thanks." His pace is quick, his slick leather soles staccato against the pavement. "Oh, and Liv—don't miss another call time."

Without another word, or even a backward glance, he turns and heads toward the soundstage. Warnings like that used to sting, back when I was expected to be as perfect as Honor. Now, though, I tuck it deep in my mind. It won't happen again.

I knock lightly on Ransom's trailer door. The smell of coconut curry is strong, even from here. When he opens it, I know we're in trouble—he's shirtless, not quite fully changed into his costume for the next scene. There is absolutely no way we're going to manage to simply *run lines* the whole time. If we spend half the time rehearsing, it will be a blazing success.

"Bryan sent me to run lines with you," I say by way of greeting, my voice cracking. I'm working really, really hard to keep my eyes from wandering down to the abs that earned his most recent millions—to the waistband of his pants, low on his hips, the very tip of the tiny triangle tattoo peeking out from underneath. This is decidedly *not* the same body I knew in our last season on set, proof in the flesh that some things get *much* better with age.

He smirks, his lopsided grin telling me we're on exactly the same page. "Oh, is *that* what we're calling it now?"

I slip inside, quickly, before someone sees—even though we've literally been directed to spend time together, it's good to be careful. Bryan isn't a fan of on-set romance, and I don't want to invite speculation.

I set my coffee on a table just inside the door and rummage around my bag for the script. I should at least *try* to focus—

Or that's my plan, anyway, until I look up and see the way he's looking at me.

"What?" I say, a blush creeping into my cheeks.

I'm not sure I've ever seen Ransom Joel speechless.

"I don't know how we went six seasons doing scenes like the one we just did without us ever ending up like *this*." He swallows. "Together."

Something Bre said the night of the Fanline dinner floats up to the surface of my memory: *What if he just never realized he was in love with you? He might not have realized how into you he was back then, but he is definitely into you now.*

I lean back against the trailer door, hear it click shut behind me. "We have had some pretty epic scenes," I say, grinning as he takes a step closer. His trailer's one of the bigger ones, but right now, it feels perfectly intimate.

"I was so distracted on set, Liv—I could *not* stop thinking about you." He presses me gently against the door, buries his hands in my hair. His lips are dangerously close to mine. "I've wanted to do this all morning."

I've wanted to do this for forever.

"Logically, I think you *have* to kiss me now so you're not as distracted during your next scene, right?" I say.

"I like the way you think, Livvie. It's a good thing I actually know my lines for this one."

"It's a good thing I'm not going to be on set to distract you for this one," I counter, and he grins.

I settle my hands at his waist, his bare skin hot beneath my palms. "Better that way," I say, the husk of my last word barely making it out as he closes the distance between us.

His lips are soft and warm, sweet with a trace of coconut still on them. It's a deep, slow kiss, with infinitely more dimension than its countless scripted counterparts we shared over the years. It's incredible how different it feels, just us, alone together; how every kiss on camera was just a shadow of the real thing. There's a hungry tension between us now—a clear and mutual desire to explore every new angle, but at a pace that lingers—though the lingering is quickly giving way to something ravenous. I want *more*, and I want to savor every minute of it.

Ransom clearly wants the same. He's got one hand in my hair, one hand on my hip, and from the sounds he's making, he doesn't mind one bit that my hands are equally interested in exploring; I trace the lines of his stomach with my fingertips, feel him press harder against me when I do.

He presses a kiss into the curve of my neck, sending a spark of chills coursing through me. I run my hands up the length of his muscular abdomen, his skin hot beneath mine as I pull him even closer. He plants another kiss just under my jaw, then finds his way to my mouth again, and time is a glittering, intoxicating blur. It's dizzying and perfect and everything I never knew we could be together—

Until a knock sounds from the other side of the door, a mere inch and a half of metal and vinyl separating whoever it is from my shoulder blades, pressed up against it. We break away on instinct, Ransom running a hand through his disheveled hair, my kisses still swollen on his lips. It is a *look*.

"Ransom?" Evy's voice is the aural equivalent of a Valentine's heart, sweet and hopeful and—in this moment—entirely irritating. "Bryan's ready for you on set. Should I wait to walk you there?"

"Oh, thank you," he calls out. "No need to wait—just tell Bryan

I'm on my way." And then, more quietly, his striking eyes holding steady on mine, he says, "You are gorgeous, Liv, did you know that?"

It's all I can do to not pick up exactly where we left off before Evy interrupted us. "You're not so bad yourself," I reply, understatement of the millennium.

We stand absolutely still, waiting to move until we're sure Evy's not right outside his door anymore. One glance at the clock tells me time has *flown*.

"I hope you really do know your lines," I say, as Ransom slips a thin, mint-green V-neck on. I will never cease to be envious of how easy guys have it when it comes to getting ready for a shoot.

"Eh, I'm about fifty-fifty," he says, with the dimple I know means he's only saying it to make me laugh. "I'll be fine. Text you later?"

"Yes," I reply. "Yes, *please*. Now, get to set before Bryan comes down here and kills us both."

✧

At precisely five o'clock, Jimmy drops me off outside the London West Hollywood, a posh Beverly Hills hotel whose delightfully se-cluded rooftop pool has become a regular meeting spot whenever Mars, Attica, Bre, and I get together for dinner and drinks to talk business. It's the sort of place where we can talk freely—mostly—as no one has ever blinked twice at my presence, especially not the wait-staff, who've seen far more famous people than me. From what I've observed, anyone else around is either just as well-known or wishes they were; those in the first camp don't bother to eavesdrop, while those in the second speak so loudly it's obvious they're hoping some-one will.

When I step out of the elevator, the hostess directs me to a table in the far back corner. I've been here so many times, but I will never get over this view: skyscrapers off in the distance on one side, Hollywood Hills on the other. The rooftop itself is its own little oasis, with the sparkling blue water of the pool its focal point, surrounded by rows of pristine white pool chairs and umbrellas, all of it set off by accents of greenery in the form of hedges, neatly manicured strips of grass, several palm trees, and a wall of ivy at one end of the pool.

Attica waves me over when she sees me, mid-sentence as usual, ever the multitasker. Mars sips chilled water from a glass, studying the menu even though she knows it by heart; she takes off her oversized sunglasses when I settle in at my seat and gives me a closed-lip smile.

"Liv!" Bre exclaims. "We ordered you that same chardonnay you raved about last time—hope that's okay! I'll drink it if you want something different." She gestures to the wineglass in front of me, fresh and full, the glass frosty with condensation. It must have arrived just before I did.

"No, that's perfect, thanks." Even if it hadn't been the longest day on set in history, it would still sound great—crisp and refreshing and cool for this touch-too-warm summer evening. I take a sip, and it hits exactly right.

"How'd it go this afternoon?" Mars asks. Presumably, Bre's filled the others in on my disastrous start to the day. I texted a quick update on my break earlier about how we'd had our fair share of first-day set-backs but left out the fact that it was Ransom who'd slowed the shoot down this morning—and I definitely didn't mention that I'd played a significant part in how hard he struggled today.

I also might have left out certain other details about Ransom.

"Better than this morning, but honestly, that isn't saying much." I take another sip of chardonnay. "My scene went well, though."

As well as it could, given that the scene we shot this afternoon was one of the so-called "jarringly flat" family scenes—the good news was that everyone seemed pleased with my performance. The not-so-good news was that we had to take an extended break after Millie botched the same line sixteen times in a row.

I'm in the middle of telling them about it when our server stops by to take our order—Attica is the only one who doesn't know what she wants, no surprise there. I order a spicy tuna roll and truffle fries, my usual.

"So, let's get to it," Mars says, once Attica has finally settled on a baby spinach salad topped with avocado, mango, shrimp, and a drizzle of sesame oil. "Lots of ground to cover today. First things first, Liv: I spoke to Vienna Lawson's agent this morning, and you'll be pleased to know she is indeed breaking a new project and wants to set up a meeting with you as soon as possible."

"Oh!" I say, surprised mostly at the formality of it all, pleased that she's going through my agent for a new project instead of just texting me at two in the morning. "That's wonderful news. I'd love to meet up with her, just say when."

Bre jots a quick note in her planner—it'll be her job to work that out.

"The fact that she wants to meet with you, and so early in the process, bodes well," Mars goes on. "The sooner we can get a meeting on the books the better, especially since it looks like there's a good chance Fanline will give the reboot a green light."

"On that note," Attica cuts in, even though she knows full well Mars likes to finish giving the rundown before going off on tangents, "I heard some things from Caroline Crenshaw that we should really discuss."

Bre looks up from her planner. "Sasha-Kate's publicist," she fills in before I can even ask.

Attica scrolls through her phone, then holds up a screenshot of a text exchange for all of us to see. "So Caro says they're talking about shifting focus for the reboot, equal screen time for Mills and SK and Liv instead of it just being mostly Liv's story. Any of you heard about this yet?"

"I—I'm sorry, what?" I can't help it, I laugh. Giving Sasha-Kate more screen time is one thing, but after Millie's work at the table read, I cannot imagine a world where they'd want to give her *more* scenes. "When did you hear that?"

Attica checks the time stamp, takes a sip of her grapefruit cosmo. "Two hours ago."

"No way," I say. "That's not happening." It comes out a touch more defensively than I mean it to. Not that I don't want good things for Millie—or Sasha-Kate, even—but this has never been an official idea floated my way before. Apparently I have *feelings* about it.

"I haven't heard a word about that," Mars says evenly as she tries to gauge my reaction. "But if it's true, it implies certain complications."

She doesn't elaborate, and my mind is reeling. I never thought I was the type to crave the spotlight—to crave it *at the exclusion of others*—but she's right, the idea does imply some significant things to consider. The money, for example: I don't know exact figures, but it doesn't take a rocket scientist to figure out that the studio would most likely split their original budget for a lead—what they would have paid only to me—into three easily digestible pieces, rather than give Sasha-Kate and Millie massive payouts to match mine.

It's about more than just money, though. Between my inheritance, original salary, and the residuals from all the years we've been syndicated, I'm set for life—a privilege I don't take for granted. But money is symbolic in the film world: it's an expression of how much you're valued on any given project.

Or how much you're not.

"Before you start stressing over this, Liv," Mars says, and it's only now that I realize they're all staring at me, "let me reach out to Shine and find out the facts. Even if they're not what we want to hear, rest assured, at the end of the day I will make sure you're in a place where your talent is *appreciated*."

Her emphasis on *appreciated* tells me everything I need to know—we're on the same page on all fronts, financial and otherwise. She has a stake in this, too; we all do. I'm the bank that pays their bills. Another reason why, if we're given the green light, I would struggle to say no.

I think I've been hoping, just a little, that maybe our green light won't happen at all. I haven't missed the intense attention I experienced at the height of the show's popularity, the constant scrutiny. More than that, I crave the challenge of learning how to bring new characters to life, how to give them subtlety and depth.

I love *Girl*—I do. But I could also love something new.

Still, I'm torn: I don't want to think about *Girl* happening without me.

"Thanks, Mars," I say, slipping on a smile that says, *Easy, breezy, nothing to worry about*. "Let me know what you find out, okay?"

She knows me well enough to know I've got an iceberg of concerns beneath that smile, but in typical Mars fashion, she simply gives a deep nod. "In better news, there's been some progress on the Emily Quinn project—they've got Elina Atravaya attached to adapt the screenplay, and I think she's a smart choice. She worked on the first two seasons of *Lunar Eclipse*, as well as that spy thriller set in Alaska—"

"The one with the sled dogs?" Attica cuts in. She's obsessed with dogs.

"Yes, the one with the sled dogs," Mars says. "But yes, Elina is a solid choice for that script, so things will probably start moving quickly from here—which means we'll have some decisions to make. You're still their first choice for the lead, so they're willing to give us time as we nail down next steps with Vienna and Fanline, but the more people they attach, the harder it will be to make sure we have a say in the shooting schedule. So. If you're on board, I can give them a tentative yes—but I understand if you need a little time to weigh your options."

"A little time would be great, thanks," I say, an understatement. The commitments I make in the coming weeks will affect the next few *years*. A thousand actresses would kill for the chance to star in any one of these projects, let alone have their pick; even for me, this is an unusual deluge of high-quality opportunity. All the more reason I need to stay focused on set—a deluge can turn to drought in a heartbeat. Hollywood's brutal like that.

Bre's engrossed in her planner, making quick notes. Sensing that Mars is finally done with the bulk of what she wanted to cover, Attica pounces on the silence.

"So, Liv, I've already been thinking about this for a little while, but if what Caroline says is true, I think it's even more important we make the most of all our opportunities here—do you think you could post some more content of you and Ransom together on your feed?"

I cough a little as my chardonnay goes down the wrong way. Bre glances up from her notes, a look on her face I can't quite read.

"People are still talking about your last photo together," Attica goes on. "If we're concerned about Fanline minimizing your role on the show, what better way to remind them the fandom wants Honor and Duke front and center than to have the entire internet losing their minds at the sight of the two of you together?"

Bre shakes her head. "I don't know if a publicity stunt like that is the way to go right now, Attica," she says, glancing my way. "Especially so soon after Ransom's breakup with Gemma."

Attica knows I draw the line at sharing my romantic life in public— but she has no idea there's any romantic life to speak of with Ransom.

Ransom's hands tangled in my hair, his lips on mine, his skin hot beneath—

"That actually makes the timing *perfect*," Attica replies, and my thoughts turn to dust. "It would only complicate things if he was still with Gemma—now that he's not with her, that's one less obstacle in the way."

"Maybe what I meant to say is, do you really think a publicity stunt like that is the way to go . . . at all?" Bre's set her pencil down entirely now. She doesn't usually get so involved in discussions like this. "People see through those things."

Attica waves her off. "People see what they want to see—and we can *use* that."

My stomach twists at the idea, never mind the fact that what they'd be seeing between Ransom and me is actually real. I cling to my father's words like scripture in moments like these: *People will take as much as you give them, Livvie. Be careful to keep some things for yourself.*

Our server arrives, a welcome distraction that leads to an even more welcome subject change. Attica and the server get to talking about the small dog someone brought with them to dinner, seated all the way on the opposite side of the rooftop, and Bre jumps on the opportunity to steer things back around to business.

"If Vienna's free tonight, Liv, would that work for you? You've got a somewhat early morning on set"—to her credit, she doesn't give me the Look to remind me that I absolutely cannot be late again tomorrow—"but if she's available on short notice, maybe you can head her way right after we're done here?"

I'll have to push my plans back with Ransom: his place tonight, plans I'd very much love to keep. I haven't caught Bre up on the latest with Ransom, though, so I can't just come out and say that—telling them about my plans would only add fuel to Attica's publicity stunt idea.

"Yes, that would work." Disappointment flutters in my stomach. I know Ransom will understand, and I'm beyond thrilled to get the chance to sit down with Vienna about a new project—but still.

"Perfect," Bre says, pushing away from the table even though she's barely made a dent in her food. "I'll put in a call right now, back in a few!"

Forty minutes later, I'm in the back of Jimmy's Mercedes, full of spicy tuna roll, truffle fries, and chardonnay, thankful the outfit I chose today will work for an impromptu meeting with Vienna at her secluded bungalow up in the hills.

So, so sorry to do this, but I have to cancel for tonight, I type out to Ransom. *Last minute meeting scheduled (WITH VIENNA LAWSON) (!!!!!) . . . rain check for tomorrow night instead?*

He writes back immediately, just a GIF of Vienna Lawson from the Oscars several years back—the look on her face is pure joy, a moment caught just after she found out her friend Jude St. Stephens won Best Costume Design. Not everyone realizes this GIF was from the same year Vienna was snubbed by the Academy. That she could show up amid the controversy and be that happy for her friend, not a trace of envy on her face, makes me respect her all the more.

It's the perfect reply from Ransom, especially paired with his follow-up text—just an unbroken string of exclamation points, more of them than I care to count.

absolutely, yes, we can take a rain check, he writes back in a new bubble. *liv, this is amazing! today was torture, though, wasn't it?*

I grin, even though he can't see me. *100%,* I type. Hit send. *The best sort, though.*

Just thinking about how close we were today, how much longer I could have stayed there, makes me want to cancel my plans and head straight over to his place.

Are we sure I shouldn't rain check Vienna instead? I write, very much wishing I could be in two places at once.

go do the thing, liv, he writes back. *i'll still be here tomorrow xo*

Spotted: Flirty, Fiery Ford

By Zenia DiLitto // Editor in Chief, Pop Culture, DizzyZine.com

Ohhhhhhh, Spinners—do I have a tasty scoop of gelato just for YOU: Ford Brooks (best known as *Girl on the Verge*'s Tyler Thatcher) was spotted this afternoon down at Manhattan Beach looking hot and cozy (emphasis on the hot, because heart eyes for dayyyyyyys) with a blonde who's very much NOT his longtime girlfriend-from-across-the-Atlantic Juliette Wells. I don't know about you, but I was totally under the impression that Ford and Juliette were in it for the long haul.

Now? We here at *Dizzy* aren't so sure.

Find, here, THE EVIDENCE.

We submit for your perusal Photograph #1: Gorgeous Not-Juliette, laughing as she takes a bite from Flirty Ford's soon-to-be-melted double-scoop cone of mint chocolate chip gelato. Also worth noting, Ford's eyes are crinkled in that totally genuine way that says, "YES, Gorgeous Not-Juliette, I'll give you absolutely anything you want!" Just try to convince me that isn't the look of someone falling hard—and *fast*! Really, go ahead and try. I'll wait.

Next, Photograph #2: Flirty Ford with his arm around Not-Juliette. Now, we fully admit this is a pretty G-rated exhibit of arm draping—no thumb hooked into the back pocket of her quite-short shorts, and I've definitely experienced this very casual sort of bro hug on numerous occasions from my actual brothers. BUT STILL, do you see the way she's looking at him? Whether he meant to get her hopes up or not, Not-Juliette 1000% wishes he'd pull her in even closer. Tell me I'm wrong.

Finally, Photograph #3: Flirty Ford morphs into Fiery Ford in an instant—specifically, the exact instant where he realizes he's being watched and photographed. Would a guy who's *not* cheating on his girlfriend look *that* upset at being caught out with another girl? Uhhhh . . . we think not.

It appears Juliette's time on set with Jonathan Cast up in Iceland is causing trouble in the lovebird nest she and Ford have built together. . . . You'd better believe we'll be following this as it unfolds! Until then, we wish you all the mint chocolate gelato your heart desires (and someone who'll look at you the way Not-Juliette's looking at Ford)!

15

As far as trekking across Los Angeles is concerned, the drive from the London West Hollywood to Vienna's hilltop bungalow in Silver Lake isn't the worst. The house is a tiny, secluded little thing, and from the road, you'd never guess a renowned filmmaker like Vienna calls it home. Probably the exact reason she was drawn to it, now that I think about it.

"Liv!" she welcomes me, flinging the door open wide. "It's been *ages*—you look stunning! Come in, come in."

Vienna and I are close to the same age—she's actually a year younger—but it sometimes feels like she has five or ten years on me. She knows *exactly* who she is and makes no apologies. Nowhere are those qualities more evident than in her work—that she trusts my creative input still feels like a mystery—but the decor here in her new place also feels carefully curated. Every wall is bright white, clearly designed to make the room look airy, and the floors are an immaculate blond wood. The overall feel is crisp, clean, and minimal, neutral grays with the occasional pop of jewel-toned accent colors, potted plants scattered in all the right places to add a touch of warmth and life.

All of this is the perfect backdrop to Vienna herself, who is anything but neutral. She radiates light and creative energy, from her messy topknot to the light denim cutoffs unraveling at a length that accentuates her toned, tan legs to the oversized cardigan knitted from thick wool she probably commissioned from someone on Etsy (someone, no doubt, who dyes their own yarn with indigo and henna).

"Have you eaten?" she asks, leading me into her postage stamp–sized kitchen. "I made a big batch of soba noodles with peanut sauce and lime—you're not allergic to peanuts, are you? Or, hmm, let's see . . . just made a trip to the farmers market yesterday, so I've got lots of produce on hand if you want something like that. Or I can make us tea? My sister sent me the most amazing shortbread cookies if you'd like to try those; I've got some plain ones and also some with orange zest that've been dipped in chocolate. Really, you're welcome to anything, everything!"

I take her up on the tea, and ten minutes later we're settled in on her back patio. Like the rest of the house, it's minimalistic, a simple gray deck with walls made of stained wooden slats and some modern bohemian outdoor furniture. What it lacks in size, it makes up for in view—the LA skyline looks incredible from this vantage point, high up in the hills.

"So, Liv, thanks so much for meeting with me on such short notice," she says, as if *she* were the one who initiated this and not the other way around. "Mars mentioned you've got a number of projects on your radar right now, so I'm happy to fill you in on the ideas I've been tossing around."

Over the next twenty minutes, she cracks open the door to her brain, and it's like being exposed to a sliver of white-hot sunlight, intense and sparkling and luminous. I drain my tea down to the dregs, listening to her vision for the project—a love story set in a cabin in some rainy woods, with an element of mystery and the sort of nonlinear, innovative structure where the viewer gets bits and pieces of the story in a strategic order that will require a good deal of nuance and subtlety on my part, and whoever is cast opposite as my love interest.

"I want to call it *emit // time*," she says, jotting it down haphazardly on a page in her blank Moleskine sketchbook. "It's a play on the structure and the theme, see? *Time* backward—it's *emit*, which I kind of love, even though people will probably think it's a really strange title. Honestly, that's part of why I love it. And it's a nice parallel with *Love // Indigo*, with the slash marks there. . . . I'm thinking you and I can title all our films together with this pattern from here on out, like a signature for our collaborations!"

My stomach flutters at the mention of *all our films together* and *like a signature for our collaborations*—she's clearly several steps ahead of herself, seeing as how I have not yet been officially approached to sign on for even *this* project, but it's flattering and exciting nonetheless. Even though she's been talking nonstop for half an hour now, I know from past experience that it would be a true collaboration, as it always is with us.

"So?" she asks, finally taking a sip of her tea that's surely gone cold by now. "What do you think?"

I think it's brilliant.

I think it would show my range as an actress, and Vienna has a particular talent for drawing out the best in me.

I think I want to do it.

And . . . I think I should probably ask some questions. Not to mention, have business affairs at the agency look over the fine print.

"It sounds incredible," I say, careful not to say anything along the lines of *Yes, sign me up yesterday*—she'll take it as a commitment.

"So you'll do it?" she says, practically leaping out of her seat. "Ahhhhh, this is going to be *perfect*, Liv, it's just so rare that you find a collaborative relationship like we have that I almost forgot we hadn't actually *talked* about it yet until your agent reached out."

"Yes, and speaking of," I cut in before she can get another word in, "Mars asked to see the paperwork before I sign or commit to anything. You know how that goes."

She freezes, only for a split second, just long enough that I can tell she forgot there are a number of dull hoops to jump through before I'm officially attached; Mars is a saint for always sorting all that out. But then Vienna breaks into a wide smile and says, "Of course, yes, I'll have the producers get that to her before the end of the week for *sure*. Here, you have *got* to try this shortbread—it's utterly seraphic!"

I take one of the chocolate-dipped orange-zest cookies from the plate, and she raises hers together with mine as if we're toasting champagne.

"To us!" she says, startling a lizard that's just fallen asleep in the dirt of a nearby potted succulent. "And to my star, who might just win all the awards for this one!" Her energy is contagious—it's one of the things I've always loved most about her. She has this uncanny ability to make even the loftiest dreams feel like they're just close enough to take hold of, to make them feel like a sure thing.

And the thing is, she's almost always right.

The first bite of cookie isn't even halfway down my throat when I realize: the contract could be a prison sentence, for all perpetuity, as extends to the far reaches of the universe, and I'd probably still sign it.

Again, I say: Mars is a saint.

✧

By the time I get home, it's just after ten and I'm exhausted. This day feels like it's lasted a thousand years—it seems impossible that Ransom was here, on my couch, less than twenty-four hours ago, impossible that we were on set just this morning and late into the afternoon. My head is spinning from everything I talked about with Vienna. It also doesn't help that sound bites from my dinner conversation with Mars, Attica, and Bre are chasing themselves in a loop: all the bright, sparkling possibilities, followed by deep shadows of doubt, followed by hope and worry, and—finally—back around to the reassuring reminder that having so many potential options can only be a good thing.

Rinse and repeat.

My phone vibrates on my bathroom counter, loud against the white marble, as I wash the day off my face. It's Ransom: *missing you tonight, can't wait for our rain check tomorrow . . . wanna hear all about vienna!*

It was amazing, I reply once I've dried my hands. *Will tell you all about it tomorrow xo*

speaking of tomorrow, he writes back, *your call time is at 6am, too, yes?*

Yes . . . why? I glance at the clock on instinct, mentally calculating how much later I can afford to stay up before crashing tonight. Forty-five minutes—an hour, max, if I want to be fresh tomorrow. And I need to be fresh.

i've got an idea, he writes back. *meet me at the studio at 5:30? will text details in the morning*

If that won't get me out of bed on time, I don't know what will. Suddenly the crack of dawn can't come soon enough. *I'll be there*, I reply.

As I hit send, another text comes in, this one from Bre. *Sooooooo when do I get to hear about Ransom at your place last night?* 👀 *Please tell me this was a date??! I wanted SO BADLY to ask you about it earlier*

"Hey, Siri," I say, as I dot my face with moisturizer. "Call Bre."

Two seconds later, she picks up, laughing. "Aren't you so proud of my restraint, Liv? It was so hard to sit there with all the secret things burning a hole in me. Also hi, how are you?"

I laugh, too, feeling lighter already. "Such a long day, but I'm good. Thank you for suffering in silence on my behalf!"

"So?" she says. "Is there anything you'd like to tell me, Liv Latimer?"

The question alone fills me with butterflies, like I might somehow ruin everything with Ransom just by talking about it—like if I say it out loud, it will become a *real* thing that's happening. Real things have the tendency to fall apart.

Even so, I don't think I can hold it in.

"It wasn't a date," I say, the words falling out of my mouth before I can stop them. "But it kind of felt like a date. And it's possible he kissed me today in his trailer?"

She's silent on the other end, for just long enough I start to wonder if I've made a huge mistake. "I'm sorry," she finally says excitedly, if a little tentatively, "I thought I just heard you say *Ransom Joel kissed you today*."

Now it's my turn for silence—where to even begin?

"Liv. *Liv*. You're serious right now? You and Ransom—really?! As in, real-life kissed you, not TV-kissed you?" Her smile is so infectious I can practically hear it through the phone.

"*Really*, really," I say, and I can't help it, I'm smiling now, too. I had no idea how different a kiss with Ransom could feel, just us, no scripts and no cameras. It was like we'd never done it before at all.

"We had the best time last night, Bre. Clearly, since we were both late this morning." Heat floods my cheeks as soon as I say it because it sounds like we were doing *much* more than falling asleep on the couch while watching a movie.

"Okay, okay, I'm gonna need you to back up to the beginning. I'm getting some popcorn, okay? This is amazing. Tell me *everything*."

I turn out my bathroom light and climb into bed, phone still on speakerphone.

So much for going straight to sleep tonight.

Snapaday story by @GOTV_fanboiiii / 11:06 p.m.

> legit dying over here waiting for the GotV reunion, looks like im starting the series over

Snapaday poll by @GOTV_fanboiiii / 11:07 p.m.

> anyone else lowkey worried we wont get any actual answers in the reunion ep
>
> 73% theyll give answers but not the ones we want
>
> 27% the writers are trash we will never get answers

Snapaday poll by @GOTV_fanboiiii / 11:14 p.m.

> ok ok i hear you, too doom and gloom, is this one better
>
> *IF* we get answers do you think
>
> 55% honor chose duke
>
> 45% honor chose new york
>
> fwiw she better not have chosen new york

Snapaday story by @GOTV_fanboiiii / 11:15 p.m.

who am i kidding this show can do no wrong
and ill stan no matter what

16

I arrive at the studio ten minutes early. It's just before dawn, still dark out—but that doesn't stop two dozen photographers outside the gates from snapping a hundred shots of me on my way in. I toss my hair and give them a subdued smile; I'm feeling generous this morning.

"Liv! Over here!" one shouts. "Liv, can I ask you a question?"

"Just did!" I say with a cheeky smile. They never like that answer very much, but this one seems amused to have gotten a response at all. With a small wave, I duck inside the studio door and leave them behind.

Everything is quiet and still, even the normally bustling espresso bar. The other café on the lot opens at five, but the one here in our building won't open until quarter to six. It's only just now 5:28—how early did Ransom *get* here, anyway? I glance down at the directions he sent ten minutes ago. In the corner is an unassuming door marked with the universal signage for a stairway; I slip inside and head all the way up to the top.

As it turns out, there's an entire rooftop terrace up here I never knew existed—another upgrade in the latest studio remodel, no doubt, with posh orange patio seating and Edison bulb lighting that's currently as sleepy as the rest of the building. Ransom's leaning on the railing, his dark silhouette framed by deep lavender sky and the last bits of starlight.

"Well, *this* is lovely," I say, and he turns. Even in near darkness, his smile is brilliant.

I meet him at the far end of the terrace. On the frosted glass table beside him are a pair of insulated coffee mugs and a plate of double chocolate biscotti.

"It's about to get even better, and not just because I brought your favorite flat white." He grins, and so do I. Everyone knows my drink, so it's not that surprising he'd remember, but that he went out of his way to get one—especially at such an early hour—makes me feel a rush of affection for him.

The sky is turning lighter by the minute, pale lavender now, bright enough that I can see all the distinct shades in Ransom's eyes. "We don't have a lot of time, but I figured we could start this day off right, and start it together." He twists open the lid to my flat white and hands it to me, along with the biscotti, remembering from years ago how much I love to dip them in before taking a bite.

"It's perfect," I say, and I mean it—I couldn't have asked for a more thoughtful start to this day, a more romantic place to watch the sunrise together. He slips his arm around me, a warm shield from the early-morning chill. We sip our coffees in silence, taking in the view as golden light overtakes the sky.

I could live in this moment forever.

It won't be long before it ends, but neither of us breaks the magic by saying so. We linger as long as we can, soaking up the silence and stillness before things turns intense with the day's shoot. Eventually, his phone alarm vibrates in his pocket—I feel it, too, pressed up this close against him.

He turns to face me, dips his forehead to rest against mine. "We should probably go," he says quietly.

I bite my lip, not ready for this to end. He's right, of course. "Yeah. We probably should."

He leans in, presses a soft, slow kiss to my lips. When he pulls away, I could swear he's taken a part of me with him. "Come to my place tonight, since last night didn't work out? I'll make you dinner, and I want to hear all about Vienna."

"Yes," I say immediately, with one more quick kiss for emphasis. "But only because dinner's involved, obviously."

"Obviously," he says, with a lopsided grin I'll be thinking about all day.

He gathers our empty coffee tumblers, shoves them along with the plate into the depths of his backpack, the same one he brought to our hangout on the beach. A few minutes later, he disappears into the stairwell, promising to text me an all clear so we aren't seen leaving the terrace together.

When I slip back in to reception, Ransom's long gone. No one seems to notice me, as the few people in the room are over at the window, eyeing the crowd that's doubled outside the studio gate.

"Millie must be on her way, then?" I comment to anyone within listening distance. At the moment, that includes a couple of interns and Gretchen, my makeup artist. If they're surprised to see me, they don't show it.

"She dropped another new single overnight," one of the interns says. "It's already stuck in my head."

Our barista, who'll get his own line in the credits for keeping us caffeinated, appears from the opposite hallway, a fresh flat white in hand. "Made it a triple this morning," he whispers conspiratorially, "to make up for Bryan punishing you yesterday." His eye roll is over-the-top dramatic, and I can't help but laugh.

"You're the best," I say, not about to tell him I've already had an entire flat white courtesy of Ransom.

"Ready when you are," Gretchen says. "Didn't see you slip in this morning—how'd you manage that?"

"Got here extra early today," I say, hoping she doesn't notice the heat blooming in my cheeks. "Couldn't risk being late again."

She laughs. "Yeah, good call."

A little over an hour later, when she and Emilio have turned me into a very fashion-forward version of Honor for the brunch scene we'll be shooting, I head out to the golf cart that will deliver me to our outdoor set on the far side of the lot. It's been done up to look like a cute little café; Sasha-Kate and Millie are already there when I arrive, waiting on its patio.

It doesn't take long to tell a storm is brewing. Sasha-Kate is seated

at an iron table on the patio, scowling, absently toying with prop packets of sugar. Upon closer glance I see her iPhone jammed up between
her ear and her shoulder. Meanwhile, Millie's chatting with the actress
who'll be playing our server—just close enough that Sasha-Kate can
most definitely hear every word—eating up the actress's effusive praise
about her latest single.

This should be fun.

"Liv, so nice of you to join us on time today," Bryan says pointedly, breaking away from the director of photography and a handful of
lighting guys. I suppress an eye roll. "Sasha-Kate, end it now, please!"

She glances over at him and holds up a single *Just a sec* finger.
Clearly, she's forgotten about the time Bryan threw Ford's phone in a
koi pond when he took too long to put it away.

Bryan stares at her, arms crossed. When she still makes no move
to end the call, he walks over to the table and pulls up a seat. He leans
back, watching her as she continues to listen to whoever's on the other
end.

"Yeah, I've gotta go," she finally says, not breaking eye contact with
Bryan. "Talk soon."

A gust of wind blows a packet of sugar off the table—Bryan catches
it in midair. He crumples it and tucks it into his pocket.

"Now," he says, clapping his hands together, "are we ready?"

The shoot gets off to a smooth-enough start: it's a sister brunch
put together by Sasha-Kate's character, Bianca, to celebrate Honor's unexpected visit to Aurora Cove after traveling the world for so long—but
in typical Bianca fashion, she talks more than she listens, so she has no
idea Honor's thinking of quitting her job.

It's a testament to Sasha-Kate's acting skills to see her flip so thoroughly into sincere-and-supportive sister mode, especially considering
she flips back to agitated envy every time the cameras stop rolling. For
Millie's part, she must have spent a good long while going over her lines
last night, trying to make them sound natural—her performance is a
marked improvement from yesterday's.

So far today, our delays are entirely weather related. The wind is a
problem for everything, from the sugar packets to our hair, and on top

of that, it's incredibly hot with the sun directly on us—all three of us are starting to sweat through our makeup. It's such a problem we have to stop and wait for Gretchen, Emilio, and two more hair and makeup people to hop a golf cart to come freshen us up.

"Congrats on the new single," Sasha-Kate says while we wait, too saccharine to sound sincere.

Millie takes it at face value, as if it were one of the myriad genuine compliments she's received from her rapidly growing fanbase. "Thanks!" she says brightly. "It's one of my favorites on the album!"

A flash of irritation sparks in Sasha-Kate's eyes. "Oh, hey!" she says sweetly—sugar laced with poison, no doubt. "Hālo told me a few days ago that Shine called her people, interested in possibly securing the rights to 'Hallowed' for our closing credits! Maybe one day you'll get to do something like that, too, Millie!"

Millie's smile hardens by just a fraction. She's more aware than she let on before—she's figured out that Sasha-Kate gets this way whenever she starts to feel outshined by anyone, and that it's not really about Hālo at all. Millie's doing an impressive job at keeping her cool.

"Hālo will be disappointed to hear about the meeting I had with Bob and Shine just this morning over breakfast, then," she says, picking up Sasha-Kate's overly sweet tone, "where I signed the contract for 'Meet Me in the Garden' to be our official closing credits song, and in all the promo spots. You're sure it was *our* show Hālo was thinking of?"

Sasha-Kate's mouth falls open, speechless for once. Mercifully, our hair and makeup teams pull up in their golf carts before she can give a reply. Emilio blasts some synthy disco-pop from his cart's Bluetooth speaker—a welcome distraction.

The stylists have their work cut out for them in this heat and wind, but they chatter away with one another as they touch up our hair and makeup. Meanwhile, where we're concerned, it's a tale of three phones: Millie, beaming as she scrolls through what can only be more praise for her new single; me, surreptitiously checking Ransom's feed and wishing very badly that I could crawl into the frame and curl up beside his gorgeous, shirtless body; and Sasha-Kate, scowling at her screen.

"Okay, everyone," Bryan says with a loud clap a few minutes later. "Let's get rolling while you're all fresh."

I tuck my phone inside the prop handbag, take a second to try to forget the past fifteen minutes, and slip back into Honor's headspace. Honor, who loves her sisters even when they're frustrating.

It's not easy, and we're all a bit edgy, but we manage to knock out a flawless scene in only two more takes—a miracle, and not a second too soon.

"Love it, love it!" Bryan says as soon as we stop rolling. "Where was this yesterday? Great work, everyone!" He gives Millie a pointed nod, and she blushes. She worked hard to up her game overnight, and it shows.

Ford and Ransom arrive in a golf cart as we wrap up—they're shooting a scene together on another outdoor set in this section of the lot. Ransom's eyes lock with mine, the cool drink of water I hadn't even realized I needed.

"What is *up*, ladies?" Ford greets us, leaping from the back of the cart before it's even fully parked. He claps Bryan on one shoulder in a move so bro only Ford could get away with it, then proceeds to shake his hand. "Now I get why wardrobe apologized when they put me in *this* today." He gestures to his skinny man jeans and the sleeves of his button-down shirt that are rolled halfway up his forearms. "Bryan, can I improv a fall into the fountain to cool off, by any chance?"

Bryan laughs, then snaps to a straight face with perfect timing. "Don't even think about it."

Ford is the best person to work with on set—he never takes himself too seriously, and it tends to rub off. I've got scenes with him tomorrow and Friday, which will be a welcome change on so many fronts.

Ransom comes to stand beside me, nudging my arm with his in greeting—to everyone else, it looks like any other day, hopefully. To me, it feels like agony, his skin on mine in broad daylight. Everything in me wants to wrap my arms around him, pull him close.

"How's it going so far?" he says quietly.

"A bit tense, but we made it work."

"You look great."

I laugh, holding out my arm to show the sheen of sweat clinging to my skin. "I look hot."

"You *do* look hot," he agrees with a playful smile, brushing his fingers lightly over my outstretched wrist.

"Liv?" Sasha-Kate says, with a tone that says she's most definitely repeating herself. "Are you riding back with us?" Her eyes flicker from me to Ransom and back again.

"Oh. Yes, I just need to—yes." I pull my hand away and rummage around in my bag, making sure everything I brought with me found its way back in. "Ready when you are."

"I'll text you later," Ransom murmurs, his back to the girls, with a mischievous grin that doesn't help anything, not one bit. I can't hide the blush in my cheeks, can't stop myself from grinning back in response.

"What was *that*?" Sasha-Kate asks when I'm settled in beside her on the golf cart, one eyebrow artfully raised. Millie's in the row behind us, attention firmly on her phone.

"What was what?" The breeze picks up as we pull away; I tuck a wayward bit of hair behind my ear.

I feel her eyes on me, studying me. She doesn't press it.

She knows, though, I can tell—and from just that single, tiny exchange with Ransom. In hindsight, how did I ever think we could hide it? I forget that she knows us every bit as well as Ransom and I know each other. Every mood, every subtle shift of our expressions.

I only hope she keeps it to herself.

I can think of a million reasons why she won't.

New Vienna Lawson Project on the Horizon

By Gregor Ives // Senior Editor, Books & Film, *West Coast Daily*

It's been more than two years since indie darling Vienna Lawson's stunning debut *Love // Indigo* made waves at Sundance, Tribeca, and SXSW, with not so much as a hint as to what she's dreaming up next—a longer wait than her devoted fans hoped for, but hardly a surprise to anyone familiar with her creative process.

Soon, that wait will be over. After hearing whispers around town about a potential new project on the horizon—boosted by the fact that Liv Latimer (Lawson's starring-actress-turned-close-collaborator) was spotted leaving Lawson's Silver Lake residence this week—we went straight to the source: the filmmaker herself.

"It would be a dream to work with Liv again," Lawson said. "When that sort of magic happens in a partnership, the kind we had for our first project together, you just sort of hold your breath a little and hope things will fall together for you to do it again sometime. It's taken a while to figure out the perfect follow-up to my debut, but I think I've finally found it. I love it; Liv loves it. Nothing's official yet—but I'm hopeful we'll get the chance to make magic together again."

We hope so, too. Liv Latimer is in high demand, thanks to all things *Girl on the Verge* and <u>another potential film in the works</u> (an adaptation of a survival novel set in futuristic

Antarctica), and for good reason—the daughter of three-time Academy Award winner Patrick Latimer has inherited his innate talent in spades. Whatever projects she takes on, it's safe to say they'll be worth the wait.

We'll be bringing you the latest updates as they develop; follow us @WestCoastDaily for up-to-the-minute news.

17

When I arrive at Ransom's place, I'm struck by two things.

One, how I couldn't have dreamed up a more perfect house for him if I'd tried: black painted brick, accents of pine stained the color of dark honey, raised flower beds dotted with cacti and lush greenery spilling over the edges. His property is tucked behind a gate, one that requires a code. Aside from that, his two-story home is subtle, not your typical sprawling Hollywood mansion—anyone could live here. It's perfectly modern, perfectly stylish. Perfectly Ransom.

Two, the car parked in his circle drive is anything but subtle, at odds with its surroundings.

I've been anticipating tonight ever since I last saw him on set. His touch on my wrist was so light, barely there in the moment, but it's stuck with me all day. We haven't crossed paths since—while I had two more scenes to shoot and am coming straight from the studio, he had a light schedule this afternoon.

Ransom answers almost as soon as I knock, swinging the door open wide. He grins.

"You look amazing," he says. "Come on in."

He looks pretty great himself, and I almost manage to say so, but then an intense urge to kiss him kicks in and I barely make it inside before giving in. He goes along with it, his lips hot against mine—and now that we're finally together, alone, I can't get enough. It's such a relief to finally do this after only having a handful of minutes together this morning.

He settles his hands at my hips and tugs me closer. His five-o'clock shadow is delightfully rough under my fingertips, sending a current of sparks straight through me. I taste a hint of basil on his tongue, or maybe it's mint—something earthy and sweet. I could stay right here all night.

"You feel *good*, Liv," he murmurs between kisses.

Clearly, we are on the same page.

My hands find their way down to his chest, solid muscle beneath his soft cotton shirt. "You too," I reply, barely more than a breath. I kiss him harder, deeper—

But then Ransom suddenly pulls away, at the exact same time I hear someone clear their throat from the far side of the room.

Oh. Oh *no*.

"Nice to see you again, Liv," says the throat-clearer. Time has been kind, to put it mildly: Ransom's father has hardly aged a day. If this is any indication of what Ransom will look like in twenty-five years, he'll undoubtedly be gracing magazine covers for at *least* the next few decades.

"Hi, Mr. Joel," I say, glancing from him to Ransom. I'm calm on the surface, but just underneath I'm frantic—what is his father doing here?

"Dad was just leaving," Ransom says with a pointed glance.

"Yes, sorry, things ran a bit long," his dad replies. "You know how business meetings go, I'm sure."

Ransom had mentioned a meeting, but it was supposed to have started around four—it's quarter to eight right now. Ransom's father quickly gathers his things, tucking an expensive-looking document portfolio into a Saint Laurent leather satchel.

"I'll touch base tomorrow," he says on his way out the door. "Think about it."

Ransom gives him a tight smile. I think back to what he told me on the beach two nights ago, about the little say he's had in his own career. Mr. Joel climbs into the car I noticed on my way in—a black Bugatti that looks like it time traveled straight to Ransom's driveway from some century far in the future—and like it would push the budget, even for someone like Ransom.

"Nice car," I say, the car as flashy as Ransom is not. I knew it seemed out of place.

"He bought it used," he replies. "And he'd kill me if he found out I told anyone."

"Long meeting."

"Well, he was over two hours late. I told him we should reschedule, but he ignored me and came anyway."

"Wow." I follow Ransom out of the foyer and into a gigantic kitchen. "Does he do that often?"

"It's gotten worse the past few years." He rummages around inside his fridge; his kitchen is spotless, practically glittering under the bright overhead lights. "His word has always been the final one, but it wasn't as obvious when I was younger—back then, it felt more like he was just a parent looking out for his kid. But now . . ."

"You're not a kid," I finish, when his voice trails off.

"Exactly."

He pulls two balls of—dough?—from his fridge, along with some fresh mozzarella, basil, and a jar of marinara sauce. "You okay with a little homemade pizza?" He grins, and his eyes twinkle on cue. How does he *do* that? "I have pineapple, too—I know how much you love that on pizza."

I laugh. He knows full well how much I *hate* it on pizza, but I love that he remembers to tease me about it.

"This is amazing. When did you learn how to do this?"

"Oh, you know," he says as he slices the mozzarella. "Somewhere in between fighting off velociraptors and zombies and solving a number of international crises. As one does."

"It's too bad they never thought to combine all of those into *one* of your movies—velociraptor zombies *would* make quite the international crisis." I steal a tiny bit of mozzarella and pop it into my mouth.

"Don't let my father hear that idea," he says, suddenly slicing a bit more vigorously. "He might pitch it."

We work together quietly, rolling out the dough and building two personal-sized Margherita pizzas. He doesn't have a pizza stone or a pizza peel, just a deep cast-iron Dutch oven, so we cook them one at a time, narrowly avoiding burns from the 500°F heat.

"I thought we could eat outside by the pool," he suggests, a sudden reminder that while I know thousands of things about Ransom himself, I know practically nothing about this home I'm in, where he lives. I just wish I'd thought to bring a suit.

Ransom smiles, grabbing a bottle of merlot and a pair of wine-glasses; I take our plates, on which he has placed a simple pile of greens in addition to each of our pizzas.

His backyard is small but immaculately kept—and very private. Whereas my home's privacy is implied by its proximity to nature and ultra-reclusive neighbors, his has been carefully and purposefully crafted, walled in by ivy-covered enclosures that stretch as high as his two-story house. It's green, green, and more green—the trees, the ivy, the perfect sort of grass for running barefoot—except for the travertine pool deck and the pool itself. The pool glows turquoise in the twilight, with a backlit waterfall spilling over a stony cliff. His backyard is *incredible*.

I arrange our plates on a simple stone table, fill our glasses with wine; meanwhile, Ransom works magic in a nearby firepit, and a blaze flares to life in its smooth iron bowl.

"This . . . your place is amazing." I take a bite of the pizza, close my eyes—it's possibly the best thing I've ever eaten in my life. "And so is this. Holy crap, Ransom! I think you missed your calling!"

He gives a shy smile. It's so new and refreshing and rare that I can't look away.

"I've gotten really into dough," he says, like it's a secret he's admitting to. In a way, it is: I imagine the list of people who get to see inside these high walls is very short. Me, and—I assume—Gemma, before.

"It's relaxing," he goes on, "and the possibilities are endless. There are so many different kinds of dough, and to do it well requires this weird and precise mix of science and intuition. Don't even get me started on sourdough."

I laugh. "This is really amazing, Ransom. I mean it."

"Only downside to learning how to bake is that the craft services croissants now feel barely edible in comparison."

"They're not the best," I agree, an understatement. They're actually kind of the worst.

A fly buzzes near the rim of his wineglass; he swats it away.

"So it was tense on set today?" he asks.

"Let's just say I'm very much looking forward to doing scenes with you and Ford over the next few days. The whole Sasha-Kate and Millie dynamic is exhausting."

"Yeah?" He's thoughtful for a moment. "Yeah, I can see that."

"Why is it never enough for Sasha-Kate to just, like, appreciate the love she gets from her fans? And why can't she just be happy for people when they do well? It's like she needs to be loved the *most*, and make everyone else as unhappy as she is."

Ransom's heard me vent about Sasha-Kate more times than I can count. More times than either of us probably even remembers.

"How has she been around you?" he asks.

I shrug, my mouth full of pizza. "The usual," I say a moment later. "A little better than usual, actually—she's used to competing with me for the spotlight, but Millie becoming a massive star overnight wasn't really on anyone's radar, so I think she's preoccupied with that right now."

It's like I'm watching a brand-new feud sprout up right before my eyes—I can tell our original distaste for each other still has roots, too, though, like a weed looking to take over everything good.

Ransom sips his wine, studies me. "How was Millie in the scene today?"

"Better than before," I say, but then I remember everything Attica brought up at dinner yesterday and make a face. "My publicist heard a rumor that they're thinking about making Sasha-Kate and Millie more prominent in the reboot."

Which would make me less.

"I . . . hmmm," he says, several questions crossing his face. "I'm struggling to find a nice way to say, 'They want to give Millie *more* screen time? Really?'"

I laugh. "My thoughts exactly. She did pretty well today, though, actually."

"You think you'll still sign on if they go in that direction?"

I wrinkle my nose, not sure how to tell him I'm on the fence about signing on at all, especially since that decision will affect him, too—what would happen to his character if mine wasn't in the show?

"I have a lot of potential projects in the works," I say carefully. "Another film with Vienna Lawson, maybe also an adaptation of one of the books I read recently."

He has a thoughtful look on his face, one I can't quite read. "Would those shoot here in LA?"

"The Vienna project is set in a remote cabin in the woods, and she said last night she wants to shoot on location, so I already know I'd be traveling for that one. And the Emily Quinn novel is set in Antarctica—so—yeah. Even if a lot is shot on green screen, I imagine we'll need to do some stuff in the actual ice and snow."

"How would those fit with *Girl*? It seems like they'll green-light us any day now."

I know he's right. My social media following has been growing by the hour, and word around set is that our old episodes are shattering records left and right among Fanline's streaming catalog.

"I'm honestly not sure," I admit. "Mars assures me it'll all work out, if I say yes." I sip my wine, glance at the glittering blue water of his pool. "I haven't really told anyone this, but I'm having mixed feelings about returning to the show . . . like . . . at all."

"Oh, wow, Livvie, that's huge." He goes quiet for a moment, the look on his face unreadable.

I take another sip of wine, give him some space.

"The reboot wouldn't be the same without you," he finally says.

I'm not sure there would even *be* a reboot without me, but it feels immodest to say so. "Do you—" I start, then take a moment to re-organize the question in my head. "Are you pretty sure you'll sign on if it happens?"

"It never even occurred to me to say no." He bites his lip, like there's something he wants to say but isn't sure he should.

"Are there any other projects you're looking at?" I ask when he doesn't say more. "Whether you sign on for *Girl* or not, I mean?"

He grins, but it doesn't quite reach his eyes. "More of the same. I know they've got another Hunter Drew script in the works, so I'm probably looking at Belgium or Prague for a couple of months at some point. And I'm sure my dad has a lot on his radar he hasn't mentioned yet."

"Like that apocalypse thriller with the velociraptor zombies?" I joke.

He cracks a genuine smile.

"*Exactly* like that, Livvie. If you weren't in such high demand, I'd definitely fight to get you cast as my costar," he says, laughing. "Seriously, though, it's amazing you have so many incredible roles to choose from."

Suddenly I'm all too aware of how this is a very specific and fortunate problem to have—too many movies, too many good roles, too many amazing locations that could potentially cancel each other out. Just because Ransom and I had twin career tracks to begin with on *Girl*, it doesn't mean we still do, doesn't mean he'll relate to every twist and rise in mine. He's plenty in demand—but for his looks, not for the depth of substance we both know he can bring to the table.

"I'm grateful," I say. I want to add more, but there's not a way to add *But I don't know how I'll choose* without rubbing in the fact that I have such compelling projects to choose from in the first place.

"Well, you've earned every bit of it." His smile is sweet, sincere, but with just a touch of sadness. He probably thinks he's hiding it.

An idea hits me out of nowhere, and it's the best one I've had in ages. "I wonder if Vienna has anyone in mind for the love interest yet— you would be so perfect!" I blurt, before thinking twice. It might be a little out of his comfort zone, but I honestly think he'd bring so much emotional depth to the role.

His face lights up, surprised. He's totally and obviously intrigued by the suggestion. "You think that could work? Are you close enough to her that you could bring it up?"

"I'm *positive* I could bring it up."

"That would be amazing, Liv. Wow." He stares into the pool, eyes reflecting its sparkle. A role like this could seriously transform his career.

All at once, he reaches for my hand and pulls me up to standing in one swift motion. "Have I ever told you how much I like you?" he says, wrapping his arms around me.

I put mine up around his neck, pull him closer. "I think you might have mentioned it." I say, grinning. "But I don't mind hearing it again."

The next thing I know, his lips are on mine, soft and gentle but hungry. A wave of heat floods through me as I press a little harder, tasting blackberries and spice from the merlot. I already knew his heather-gray V-neck was soft to the touch, but only once my hand is on his stomach do I notice how *thin* it is—I feel every chiseled line underneath, every solid curve.

His fingers trace the thin straps of my romper. It seemed like a good idea at the time—it's a super-flattering cut, fitted at the waist, and the paprika-red color looks fantastic with my skin tone and hair color—but now it only feels like an obstacle, one we're probably both all too eager to remove.

"Can you swim in that?" he whispers, breathless between kisses.

"Can I? Probably." Another kiss, another stolen breath. "Should I? Probably not the best idea for the ride home."

And that's how we end up in only our underwear behind the waterfall in his pool, which has a hidden alcove with a bench cut into the rock. It's romantic and beautiful and louder than I expected, every crash of the water echoing from the rocks. This is hardly the first time we've been this close while wearing this little clothing, but it turns out context is everything: this is far from being on set, acting out scripted lines for the whole world to see, and I am *into* it.

Unfortunately, it quickly becomes clear that the design of the hidden alcove isn't super optimal for much of anything other than sitting side by side. The bench is narrow, and the rocks behind us are rough—still, we try to make it work. Ransom plants kisses down the length of my neck, but we both end up laughing because the position is so awkward. He slides off the bench to give us more room—we're in the shallow end, and he's tall—but he immediately gets a face full of waterfall, which makes us laugh even harder, so loudly the neighbors can probably hear it echoing from over Ransom's high ivy walls.

Suddenly, the thought of other people hearing us, even though they'd have no way to know it's me out here with Ransom, pulls me out of the moment and straight back to reality.

It was such a *good* moment. I hate that I'm about to ruin it.

"What?" Ransom says, sensing the shift. "What happened?"

"I think Sasha-Kate knows about us," I say. "And your dad . . ."

He runs a hand through his sopping-wet hair. Neither of us is laughing now. "People will have to find out eventually, right?"

My heart swells: it's still too soon to know exactly what's going on between us, but his words feel weighty to me—whatever this is, he doesn't see it as a fling, or a secret to be kept for any reason other than the pressure it will put on us both.

"Obviously," I say with a smile, hoping he can see how very badly I want us to last, that I have no interest in flings or secrets for secrets' sake. "It's just . . . the fandom is going to go *wild* over this, right? Remember how things blew up when we posted a single selfie together? And, I don't know. You can't please them all, and I know it's not the point to please them all, but it's just nice having others out of the mix. For now, at least."

Forever, if I had my way, but even I know that can never be our reality.

I don't say this, because I don't want to make him worry for no reason, but what's happened to Gemma in the wake of her breakup with Ransom is legit terrifying—what if things don't work out between us for some reason? What if the fans turn on me like they've turned on her? And honestly, that could happen even if things do go well. I've noticed a worrying number of comments from random people who are convinced they're meant to be with Ransom, and feel threatened by anyone who stands in their way.

This is why—one reason, anyway—I prefer to keep private things private. No one else should have a say in who we love, how we love. If we ultimately decide we're *not* in love.

He pushes up to sit beside me, sighs. "You're right. I wish you weren't."

We sit in silence, watching the waterfall crash into the pool, alone together in our secret alcove for at least a little while longer. He's right, too—if this continues, we'll have to tell people. Probably sooner rather than later, especially if I'm going to go out on a limb to ask Vienna if he can play my love interest in the new film.

For now, all I want is to sit here and enjoy him, us, *this*.

I weave my fingers through his, find his lips with mine; his other hand slips over my skin, both of us slick from the pool. It isn't long before we find our way out of the alcove, find more of each other. Everything begins in crisp, vivid focus—the pool, crystal blue and glittering under the dark night sky, and the way the lamplight catches on the beads of water rolling off his skin, and his eyes his smile his lips his tongue—

And then it all becomes one sparkling, beautiful blur.

Spotted: Sasha-Kate Kilpatrick
with Mysterious Silver Fox

By Zenia DiLitto // Editor in Chief, Pop Culture, DizzyZine.com

Ohhhhhhh, Spinnersssss, do *I* have some *news* for *YOU*! Around here, you know we're on 24/7 SKK watch, because she's always serving up some new tantalizing and delicious treat—well, I hope you're extremely hungry this morning, because I am about to present you with a FEAST.

It will come as no surprise (to anyone paying attention) that things have come to an end between Sasha-Kate and her most recent boyfriend, Nikola Milošević. Their relationship started as abruptly as it ended, we hardly ever saw them together, and lo and behold, he was spotted out clubbing last night with his longtime party-bro Luka Kilpatrick (SK's brother, and her original connection to Nikola) along with a pair of stunning brunettes. It's safe to say he's either quite over Sasha-Kate, or he's trying his best to forget her.

And THAT is merely the tablecloth for our breakfast feast, friends. Grab your mimosas and take a seat!

While Nikola, Luka, and the stunning brunettes were getting ready for their night out on the town, Sasha-Kate was doing her best to slip out of it in secret. It's not unusual for SK to take a one-night escape to ēclipse, her posh island resort of choice that's just an hour up the coast—she often visits the resort as a guest of Garbiñe Itiriti (famed heiress to the ēclipse chain) for the occasional R&R spa day with her group of girlfriends. This time, however, we have on good authority that Garbiñe is off at ēclipse: Turks and Caicos chairing a fundraiser this week, which means she was very much not in California hosting a girls' day. So what brought Sasha-Kate to the resort?

All we know is that Sasha-Kate was spotted climbing into an unmarked helicopter, not too far from the studio where she's been shooting scenes for the *Girl on the Verge* reunion special. Flight records show the helicopter landed at the resort at around one in the afternoon and returned in the dark, early hours this morning; flight records (and a good bit of digging) also reveal the charter went to great lengths to keep their identity a secret.

From the photo, we can easily see the iconic celebrity incognito look—stylishly slouchy gray hoodie, short denim cutoffs, oversized sunglasses, baseball cap over messy braids. We also see her holding the hand of someone already inside, and (here's the juicy part, y'all!) leaning in close for a kiss. Although we can't make out the face of the lucky guy from the photo, that shock of silver hair tells us enough to know he's quite a bit older than the guys Sasha-Kate usually goes for. Anyone else have a hard time remembering she's *thirty-three* now? She'll perpetually be Honor St. Croix's little sister in my mind.

ANYWAY. Here's where YOU come in, Spinners! We do love a good mystery around here, but what we love even more? A good SOLVED mystery! If you have any idea who SK's mystery silver fox might be—or any connections at ēclipse who are willing to defy their rock-solid nondisclosure agreements to spill the beans (good luck, definitely already tried that, definitely did not work)—you know where to find me!

18

It's past nine in the morning when I wake in my own bed, my phone vibrating on my nightstand. Sunlight streams through the windows, a welcome sight after having predawn call times all week. It's my first morning to sleep in, and I definitely needed it—Ransom dropped me off sometime around midnight, despite best efforts to tear ourselves apart earlier. (Okay, maybe not *best* efforts. Moderate efforts. A bit of effort?) He wasn't as lucky with the call sheet and is probably dragging on set today.

"Do you want the good news first, or the not-so-good news first?" Mars asks half an hour later, after I'm up and reasonably clearheaded. I'm still in one of my favorite pajama sets, a blush-pink camisole with shorts to match, curled up with a leisurely cup of coffee on my back patio. The waves roll in, one after another, crashing on the sand before retreating back out to sea.

"They both go hand in hand, actually," she goes on before I can answer. "So I'll just tell you: the reboot is on. But, unfortunately, what Attica heard is true—they want to center it on the three of you this time."

"Wow," is all I can manage. I don't know what to say.

"I know. When I asked Shine for insight, she said the producers were hesitant to hang the entire reboot on you, given that you're all but committed to the Vienna Lawson project—Xan's been in their ear, apparently, and it looks like Vienna gave some comments about it. They've decided to preemptively green-light the reboot in hopes of locking you in to a schedule that's on *their* terms. I've gotta say, Liv, I don't like it."

A seagull swoops low over the water, then takes a sudden plunge, snatching an unsuspecting fish. "And the money?" I ask.

"As you'd expect."

I take a long pull on my coffee. None of this bodes particularly well. I especially don't like the implication that I should give up the chance to star in a potentially award-winning film for the reboot when I wouldn't even be its main focus. I hadn't realized how much I was starting to come around to the idea of doing a huge production like *Girl* again—the reunion has been a good experience so far, and under the right circumstances, the reboot could be amazing.

These are not the right circumstances.

"This might be hard for you to hear, Liv, but I honestly think we might want to consider passing on the project. Hear me out—they know you're in high demand elsewhere, and they're trying to manipulate you into a suboptimal commitment because they know you're emotionally invested in the show, what it's meant for you. Fanline *has* the resources to pay Millie and Sasha-Kate more, as much as you would have earned as the sole lead—they're about to close on an acquisition of CMC/Snapaday, but you didn't hear that from me. But *because* of the merger, they're trying to cut corners where they can and pass it all off as a decision to go in a fresh direction creatively."

"Even Shine is on board with what's going on?" I ask.

Shine Jacobs built Fanline's empire out of nothing all on her own and has given countless commencement speeches and keynotes about her commitment to empowering women.

So much for empowerment: I feel power*less*. Like Fanline is convinced I would never say no after all the show has done for me. After all I've done for the show, though, the way they're trying to pin me down—while at the same time diminishing my role—makes me feel entirely taken for granted.

The coffee suddenly feels too sour in my stomach, the taste too bitter.

Mars sighs. "Unfortunately, when a company becomes a monolith like Fanline has, not even its founder has the final say on every issue, especially once the investors get involved. It's difficult in this case because Shine is actually fully in favor of the fresh creative direction—which is a hurdle of its own for us. She insists she's not done with the financial conversation, but as it stands now, she's been backed into a corner with the shareholder votes and a handful of issues that have more to do with the merger itself than the show."

"This is a lot to take in at ten in the morning," I say, an understatement. I have to leave for the studio in an hour—I wish I had the entire day off to process.

"Take your time, sit with it for a bit."

I hear a clinking noise through the phone, imagine her stirring a glug of cream into a fresh cup of coffee; who knows how long she's already been up this morning, dealing with this.

"I know there's a lot wrapped up in the idea of walking away—but there's also a lot for you to walk *toward*, Liv. I'll support you in whatever you decide, but I would be doing you a disservice if I didn't give you my honest gut feeling, okay?"

"Yeah. Thanks, Mars."

It's one thing to think theoretically about walking away—but now that it's a real decision I have to make, I feel a little sick.

"I'll check back with you about it," she says. "Don't talk about what's going on with anyone until we settle on a decision, not even Bre or Attica."

Not even Bre or Attica: this is the moment it hits me how big the implications would be if I were to say no—I can't let on to *anyone*, not even to the rest of my team, that I'm considering walking away from *Girl*. It's too late to keep it from Ransom, thanks to our conversation last night at his place, but hopefully he knows better than to mention it. If there's a chance I want to stay, despite everything, we can't take any risks with it getting back to Fanline. This has the power to cause significant rifts.

After we end the call, I stare out at the water for longer than I really have time for, turning the decision over and over in my head. It stings a bit to know they want to shift the focus away from Honor, but at the same time, they've told her story, and—thanks to our new reunion episode—she and Duke will finally have the happily ever after the world has been begging for. It makes sense to explore the other sisters; I get it.

What bothers me more is the way they're going about trying to make it happen—betting hard that I'm too attached to the show that launched me to superstardom, too emotionally indebted, to even consider walking away. It isn't right. They're expecting me to make big decisions with my heart instead of my head.

The line where sea meets sky blurs. Walking away would affect more than just me; all my worries from last night start to resurface. Would Ransom have a part in the show if I wasn't in it? Would there still *be* a show at all? Would the fandom support my work on other films, or would they turn on me for ruining a thing they love? I think of those friendship bracelets on my nightstand, of the people who sent them. It's so much more than a show for so many people, and the show is so much more than just me.

Right now, it feels like I alone have the power to ruin it.

My phone vibrates, startling me out of thought: *James Robertson will arrive at 11:03 am*, it says, the automatic notification alert from the GPS in Jimmy's Mercedes. That's only fifteen minutes away, I realize with a panic. I'm still in pajamas—I somehow haven't even eaten breakfast.

I take a deep breath, watch as the seagull dives back toward the water for another catch.

The fish never saw it coming.

✧

In the time it took us to drive to the studio, I practically could have walked. I'm over an hour late when I finally arrive, thanks to an extraordinarily bad wreck on the 101, and the mood on set is tense. It doesn't help that my own mood is a bit volatile, between the traffic and my call with Mars and the six texts I've received from Attica asking me to post various things on social. I've been looking forward to today's shoot all week—a scene with Ford, Ransom, and an actress named Cassidy, who's playing Ford's girlfriend, all taking place at a shabby little diner set made to look like it's just off the beach of Aurora Cove—but it's immediately apparent this is not going to be the chill, relaxing day I've been hoping for.

I'm barely inside reception when I see Bryan leaning against the back of the sitting room's plush pink couch, arms crossed. It's a bad sign: that he's not mid-shoot means I've seriously disrupted the schedule.

I hold my head high as I shift my sunglasses to rest on top of my head and look him straight in the eye. "Morning," I say with an easy smile, as if I can make Bryan forget it's technically past noon.

"Your watch looks entirely too new to be broken," he replies, giving my rose gold Cartier a glare.

"Thank you," I say. "It was a gift."

The barest hint of amusement crosses his lips before he catches himself.

"Maybe you can send a gift to my kid tonight when I miss dinner? It's going to be a late one."

"Don't act like you wouldn't be staying late anyway, Bryan." I'm skirting the edge of a razor-thin line, knowing I'll only get away with it because it's true—and because I can always tell when he's irked at the world at large and not just me specifically. Right now it's mostly the world.

He runs a hand over his face, closing his eyes, making no effort to hide his exhaustion.

"You have no idea. Because you are hideously late." He gives me a scolding look, but it's toothless—I'm in the clear. "But between you and me? I needed the break."

I grimace. "That bad?"

"Ransom's head is in the clouds," he says. "You know how he gets when his father's on set."

"Mr. Joel is here? Today?" My mind spins, grasping for any memory of Ransom mentioning it last night.

"His publicist, too, and don't get me started on her," he says. "She's making even *me* lose focus."

"Sounds like a winning combination."

After a whirlwind trip to hair and makeup to make it look like I've just come off an afternoon at the beach—not hard, given the state I arrived in—I get to experience the strained vibe on set for myself. I slide onto the bench of a red vinyl diner booth, and Ransom settles in next to me. We begin as soon as I'm ready.

Our producers, Nathaniel and Gabe, are also here today, silently observing from the shadows, which always adds a layer of pressure. And then there's Ransom's dad and publicist, both breathing right down Bryan's neck. The publicist, Andrea, looks chic in her black pantsuit and stilettos, sun-kissed and luminous and extremely confident. She's so confident, in fact, that she's not afraid to hover over Bryan's shoulder during the shoot, reading the handwritten notes from his clipboard. When she's not reading, she's watching Ransom, appraising his every move.

Numerous takes later, we're all on edge.

"Cut!" Bryan calls out *again*. I've lost track of how many times we've had to start over, how many fresh milkshakes the prop department has had to prepare because they keep melting under the lights. Bryan wasn't exaggerating about Ransom's head being in the clouds. "Everybody, take five."

He bolts from his director's chair, clipboard tucked tightly under his arm. Nathaniel and Gabe follow him out.

"Sorry, guys," Ransom says under his breath, sliding out of the booth. "I need a minute."

"Please," Ford says, holding up his cookies 'n' cream shake. "I'm living the dream, ten of these in one day!"

Cassidy laughs. "If I have to pluck one more maraschino cherry off the top, though, I might throw it at someone instead of popping it into my mouth." She's a welcome addition, at ease with all of us despite the generally uncomfortable mood in the room.

I slide out of the booth, too, ready to follow Ransom, but before I get too far, Andrea intercepts him. His dad approaches his other side, putting an arm around his shoulders in that subtly patronizing way that's always gotten under Ransom's skin. Moves like that embarrassed him enough at sixteen; I can only imagine what he's feeling now.

Instead, I head over to my bag, pull out my phone. I've missed three more texts from Attica—two additional requests, along with one *I know you're shooting right now, but it would be ideal for those behind-the-scenes stories to post in the next hour or so!*

I take a deep breath. *Busy day on set*, I write back. *I'll do my best.* I have to make a conscious effort to unclench my jaw.

Switching into my message thread with Bre, I scroll back through our history to remind myself what she's up to today. *Any chance you want a behind-the-scenes look at the show?* I type out. *Ransom's dad and publicist are wrecking the shoot, and I need help keeping my chill.* I hit send, then add, *Also, I'd love you forever if you could post some stuff to my stories so Attica will stop texting every five minutes*

Three dots pop up immediately. *Going that well?* she sends, along with a stressed-face emoji.

I think at this point Bryan would welcome an earthquake to get them to back off, I reply.

Yeah, they sound SO helpful, she writes. *Okay, be there as soon as humanly possible. I'm not far but you know LA* 😵

It takes Bryan a full ten minutes to return to set, despite the fact that he was the one who called us off for five, with Gabe and Nathaniel close behind. Andrea and Mr. Joel are still over in a dark corner, talking Ransom's ear off in hushed, harsh tones. Somehow I don't think this is what he had in mind when he said he needed a minute.

Cassidy appears at my side. "This . . . is not what I expected," she says, seeming absolutely unfazed by my presence. "Is it usually like this?"

"Yeah, no. It's never like this."

Never is a stretch—I can remember a handful of tense days like this in our later seasons, coinciding with the weeks it took to negotiate our massive salary increases. Mr. Joel was on set more often than not in those days, watching every scene, giving Ransom direction from the wings. Bryan tolerated it, but only because Mr. Joel's instincts were usually spot-on. Andrea wasn't in the mix back then, though. Neither were two decades' worth of fraught history between Ransom and his dad.

"You're holding your own really well," I tell Cassidy.

Heat floods her cheeks. "It's easy to act like you're attracted to Ford Brooks when he was your childhood crush," she says, grinning. "The hard part is making it look like acting."

I laugh. "So, I have to ask—which phase of Ford's hair was your favorite?"

"Honestly? I'm loving this current look more than any so far," she says. Production was all over the short-at-the-sides, longer-and-swooping-on-top look they gave him for the *EW* cover shoot—he'll be stealing some of Ransom's fanbase for *sure*. "I've gotta admit, though, I was most definitely into his man bun back in the day."

"I will never not love that his hair was the sole reason for a massive trend," I say, "especially because as easygoing as he is, he hated that man bun so, so—"

"Would you just *drop it*?" Ransom's voice booms from the far corner of the set.

Everyone freezes. Everything's still.

Everything, that is, except for Ransom himself, who turns on his heel and walks away from Andrea and his father without a backward glance.

I've never heard Ransom raise his voice like that. Never.

Old instincts kick in, and I run to catch up with him—neither of us ever left set alone in tense moments.

"What happened?" I ask, but he keeps walking, like I haven't said anything at all. "Are you okay?"

He turns then, his eyes empty of their usual sparkle. Empty of everything, really. "It has been a *day*, Liv, and I don't want to talk right now." His words slap so hard they sting.

I stop in my tracks, stunned.

Watch as he turns a corner. Disappears.

In the twenty years I've known him, I've never known him like this.

✧

"Ransom did *what*?" Bre says, twenty minutes later when she arrives on set. We're in a bit of limbo at the moment, with Ransom stewing in his trailer and Bryan meeting behind closed doors with Nathaniel and Gabe. "Any idea what could have set him off?"

I glance over to the far corner of the soundstage, where Mr. Joel and Andrea are sitting in a pair of director's chairs, scrolling separately on their phones. "Definitely something to do with his publicist and his dad, I think."

My phone buzzes at my hip. It's Attica—again.

Post something with Ransom, too, if you can!

I close my eyes, take a deep breath.

"Here, let me take a couple of shots of you on set," Bre says, accurately interpreting the source of my increasingly irritated mood.

I touch up my lipstick to match the sparkly red vinyl of our set's vintage diner booth and settle in for a quick pose. Bre takes a few more candids, then suggests we get a few in my trailer for good measure. We're almost all the way there when Ransom's door opens; his trailer is right next to mine.

We lock eyes when he steps out, but he immediately averts his. "Bryan wants us back on set." He holds up his phone as if to show me proof of the message, but all I see is his lock screen: the photo of us with the strawberry shake, the one that went viral.

"Are you okay?" I ask, putting a hand on his arm. He doesn't pull back, but when he meets my eyes, all I feel is distance. That, and the confirmation that whatever set him off is most definitely not over.

"I can't—" Ransom starts, but cuts himself off, takes a deep breath. "Let's talk later. I'll text you, okay?"

It should be reassuring, and yet. It's not like *I* did anything to set him off—so why can't he look me in the eye for more than half a second?

"Yeah, okay," I manage. "Sounds good."

It sounds better than silence, anyway. Any explanation at all would be nice.

Wow, Bre mouths, once we're on our way back to the soundstage, Ransom trailing behind us.

"Yeah," I say under my breath. "This afternoon should be . . . interesting."

Interesting is an understatement, as it turns out. More accurate would be *disaster*. Ransom's clearly struggling to get his head in the scene. His eyes are void of their trademark sparkle, and his lines—when he remembers them—are flat. The chemistry that usually comes so easily between us is nowhere to be found, and it's starting to spiral, bleeding into my own ability to focus. We do take after take, each one worse than the last. By the sixteenth attempt, even Cassidy and Ford are starting to founder, Ransom's dark mood an anchor dragging us all to the bottom of the sea.

"*Cut!*" Bryan calls, but it isn't half a second before Mr. Joel starts speaking over him.

"Cardboard would perform better than you right now, Ransom," he says, eyes steely and dark. "Pull it together."

I feel Ransom tense beside me, see his knuckles go white. He glances across the table, at Ford, who subtly shakes his head in solidarity.

"We're going to take five," Bryan says with authority, his voice even but terse. "And in those five minutes, we are going to remember how to leave our personal lives out of our professional ones. We will try this scene *one* more time, and if we can't manage to get it right, we'll shoot it at five in the morning tomorrow. Five minutes starts *now*."

As soon as we're all out of the booth, Ford drapes a casual arm across Ransom's shoulders and pulls him off set, presumably to some quiet place where Ransom's father and publicist can't escalate things any further. I make a beeline for Bre in hopes she can calm my fraying nerves—but as soon as I get close, she looks up from her phone and I see stress all over her face.

"What?" I ask. "What's wrong?"

She flips her hair over her shoulder, closes whatever she was looking at on the phone, and puts on the most obviously fake smile I've ever seen. "Nothing! Nothing. Everything is fine."

"Bre."

She sighs. "Okay. Everything is not fine. But. It's nothing you need to worry about right now, okay?"

"I'm only going to be *more* distracted now that I know something's going on. What is it?" Maybe it will explain what's going on with Ransom and his team.

"You're sure you want to know *right now*? I really think it would be best if—"

"Just show me." The more she builds it up, the more I'll worry, so I might as well know now.

She nods, unlocks the phone. Hands it over.

The first thing I see is my name in big, bold letters, with the purple-pink-orange *YOU HEARD IT HERE FIRST!* logo just above the headline: LIV LATIMER IN LOVE—EVERYTHING YOU NEED TO KNOW ABOUT HER SECRET ROMANCE WITH COSTAR RANSOM JOEL!

This—what—

"Aaaaaaand *time*," Bryan says, slicing through the dizzying haze as I read back over the headline.

"Liv. You've got this." Bre looks me straight in the eyes, one hand on each of my shoulders. "You do *not* want to have to shoot this scene at five in the morning tomorrow. Dig deep like I know you can—I know it's hard, but I promise you can do this."

I blink, take a breath. My head is spinning.

People know.

"You can do this," Bre says again.

I nod, swallowing down everything I want to say, every question I want to ask. She's right. I can do this, I *can*. I close my eyes, slip into Honor's world. Her thoughts, her feelings. Not mine.

It doesn't come easy today. It takes *effort* to slide into the booth with Ransom, to put love in my eyes when all I have are questions. It's like an out-of-body experience to hear Honor's lines coming out of my mouth, to *laugh*, when all I am inside is numb.

It works well enough until Mr. Joel opens his mouth again.

"Son, you can do *better*, I know you can."

And that's it, it's over. Whatever thin thread was holding Ransom together snaps. "Get your cardboard cutout, then," he says. "I'm done."

Liv Latimer in Love— Everything You Need to Know About Her Secret Romance with Costar Ransom Joel!

By Lila Lavender // Staff Writer, *You Heard It Here First!*

You guys.

YOU GUYS.

Your eyes do not deceive you, and you are not misreading that headline.

LIV LATIMER AND RANSOM JOEL.

TOGETHER.

THEY ARE A THING.

Apologies in advance for any car wrecks, falls down stairs and/or from balconies, and any other general mishaps that may or may not result in hospital bills from this news—this is a reminder that you read at your own risk, and we are not liable for any pain/suffering you might experience as a result (physical or emotional or otherwise).

BUT YES. That sound you hear? It's the glorious sound of two parallel universes colliding in perfect harmony!

Everyone's favorite teen heartthrob ship, Honor St. Croix and Duke Beaufort, is finally sailing off into a Snapaday-worthy sunset on a sea of shimmering rainbows IN REAL ACTUAL LIFE. Does any more perfect relationship exist??!

How do we know this particularly tasty bit of news, you ask?

Insert all the winky faces and zipped-lips emojis here—sorry to say the source has asked to remain anonymous, and in the interest of getting alllllll the juiciest tidbits dropped in our lap in the future, we're doing our best to ~honor~ it (pun intended, because how could I not?). Take it from my BFF Raina, though, who practically had to retrieve my jaw from where it landed—all the way down on my flip-flops, for the record (and not just because of the news itself, but also because of who delivered it)—when a Certain Well-Known Someone *quite* close to the lovebirds called in to blast the news: they've been on set this week with Liv and Ransom, and they've clearly SEEN some behind-the-scenes things.

Take, for example, this picture of what appears to be our favorite couple, nestled together on an undisclosed rooftop to watch the sunrise! (Apologies for the grainy image quality—near-darkness and iPhone zoom lenses don't quite do justice to distance shots, especially when shot from street level and its subjects are several stories up!)

SO. I've got QUESTIONS, and I'm sure you do, too.

One: Did this new development have anything to do with why Gemma Gardner dropped Ransom out of nowhere recently? (In other words, is it possible our lovable Ransy was cheating on her? I know, I know, it pains me to type that all out like that, and I honestly don't think he would, BUT a girl has to be thorough in her journalism, amirite?)

Two: When did this *start*? They've known each other for *twenty years* now—did they secretly date back when the show was on the air and we just never knew about it? Or did one—or both!—have feelings for the other they never acted on in all this time? Orrrrrrr—and I hate to go there, but again, this is me Being Thorough in Serious Journalism—is this all just a carefully orchestrated publicity stunt leading up to the *Girl on the Verge* reunion special? Think about it: they're either being verrrrrry careful in how/where they see each other, or they're . . . not . . . actually . . . seeing each other. I trust my source more than I have all-caps SUSPICIONS, but *shrug* the lacking-in-quality evidence raises questions, is all.

Three: If this is indeed real, do we think it will last? I, for one, do NOT care to see Ransom Joel's beautiful, beautiful heart broken again—especially not by Liv Latimer, the most perfect butterfly of an actress to ever exist. Honestly, it would ruin the entire show if they split in real life, IMHO . . . and I hope they realize what ruining the entire show would do to the fans who've been with them since Day One. (Okay, personal confession time: Did I ever tell you guys about the friendship bracelet I made for Liv after those episodes where they were at camp? She even wrote back, and it was legit, not just one of those prewritten things they send to everyone who writes in—I was going through some stuff back then, and getting that letter was EVERYTHING. SO. Stakes are high here, at least for me, personally. Liv, if you're out there, please don't ruin this—I'll have to throw away the friendship bracelet you sent back if you do, because UGH I will not be able to handle it. Okay? Okay.)

Sorry not sorry for that large and unexpected dose of Highly Personal Information, a thing we try to steer clear of here at *YHIHF!* (except, of course, when it comes to *other*

people's highly personal information, without which this site would not exist ☺). In this case, though, it needed to be said because UGHHHH the stakes are just so, so high with this one. It's not just me who feels that way, right? Sound off in the comments if you, too, are all up in your feelings over this and are also in danger of possibly losing your collective sh*t if this ship goes up in flames!

xo, Lila

1,347 COMMENTS

@GOTV_fanboiiii
wait, WHAT—i don't know how to feel, this is too perfect, listen to lila and DONT RUIN THIS FOR US OKAY

@arianaventi
Personally, I think it's irresponsible for you to not tell us the source. How are we supposed to believe this is even a ~thing~ without knowing if the source is credible? And without *good* photos? I'm sorry, but that hardly even looks like Liv and Ransom. Headline is misleading, says "EVERYTHING" we need to know, and, like, this entire article is just full of stupid questions? Still holding out hope Ransom's single bc he could do so much better with, oh, say, this cute girl I know who's just right down the road in Manhattan Beach ;)

@abbeyyyyy17
ohmygahhhhh, lila—liv made you a friendship bracelet??! and this is the first we're hearing

of it? i would wear that thing all the time, how amazingly special! (ps: i'm with you, will be devastated if this is just a publicity stunt or if they break up. this show was the only thing that got me through the year my parents divorced)

@Bianca_OnTheVerge
They are too pure, we don't deserve them. Which is why they'll probably go up in flames, tbh.

@hamstertroll
anyone else sick of hearing about this show i kinda want to punch that guy's face, wish this site would go back to posting about actors from this decade instead of washed up hollywood trash

@GOTV_fanboiiii
@hamstertroll YOU SHUT YOUR MOUTH, WHY ARE YOU EVEN HERE

@LilaLavenderYHIHF
@hamstertroll Cleeeeeeearly you're trying to pick a fight here, but can I just say, it says a lot that you make a point to seek out and comment on each and every one of my GotV posts—your dedication is admirable, and it's okay, none of us are going to give you a hard time for being a grown man who wept like a baby at the series finale. ;) (Yes, I know how to play this game, too, and you can 100% bet I found those secret blog posts you published that

you probably didn't realize were connected to your Flitterbird handle via simple search algorithms. It's okay. PS: For anyone who wants to check out Nilbert's blog, <u>here's the link</u>! He'd probably LOVE if you left him a comment or two!)

19

"Don't read the comments," Bre says, once we're back at my place and she's given my phone back—she confiscated it on the way home. Now we're on my patio, decompressing from today's shoot with enough sushi to feed a small film crew.

Comments are the worst, and this isn't my first rodeo.

I scroll through them anyway.

Bre saves me from myself, slipping my phone gently out of my grasp. She shuts it off and puts it facedown between us. "I swear, I wasn't the one who told."

It hadn't even crossed my mind that Bre *could* have told. She would have never—and to shut the door on any doubt I might have otherwise had, her gut reaction to the post was most definitely of the *Oh no, how did this get out?* variety and not a thinly disguised *Ohhhhh CRAP, I told someone and now it's in headlines* panic. It isn't Bre I'm worried about.

Besides, there's no possible way Bre could have taken that photo. There was a crowd of paparazzi that morning, as always, but Ransom and I weren't facing the gates—whoever took it was on the studio lot.

"I don't understand the existence of this photo," I say, zooming in on our (admittedly obscured) faces. It really is a terrible shot, but it could definitely be us if someone suggested the idea and you were to squint in just the right way.

"Wait, that's *real*?" Bre squeals. "You had a sunrise date with Ransom and you didn't tell me?!"

It seems like ages ago. "Quite real, unfortunately. And yes—it was actually incredibly sweet, he brought my flat white and every—"

The coffee.

On no planet would Ransom ever order a flat white for himself. Everyone knows it's my drink, especially the cafés on the lot. The one in our building hadn't opened yet that morning, and there's only one other place Ransom would have gone.

"Liv?" Bre says tentatively, and it's only now I realize I must have the strangest look on my face.

"The coffee," I say, dazed. "It could have been one of the baristas, maybe? From the café near the studio?"

We weren't facing the gates that morning, where all the paparazzi were, but the café is most definitely on the perfect side of the building for a shot like this. If I were to stand just outside the front doors of the café, I could almost certainly replicate the camera angle. Hardly anyone else was on the lot that early—I can't think of another way someone could have figured out we were there together.

"Okay," she says, her mind clearly working on fitting the pieces together. "But it says whoever dropped the story was 'a Certain Well-Known Someone' and that they were on set with you. That doesn't sound like a barista."

She makes a good point.

"Could a barista have sent the photo to someone, you think?" she suggests. "Someone else on the lot?"

"It's possible," I say, because what other explanation could there be?

Bre shrugs. "Maybe someone paid them upfront to watch out for anything juicy? I'm sure a photo like that could be worth a small fortune."

"Good theory," I say, running through every moment Ransom and I spent on set this week. We weren't *that* obvious—could Evy have picked up on the spark between us? Doubtful, but not impossible. "Only two other people knew. Sasha-Kate figured it out on her own, I think—and Ransom's dad, uh, saw us kissing."

If Ransom's dad leaked our news, that would certainly explain the tension between them. But then again, his behavior on set would have been enough all on its own.

"Okay, let's consider Sasha-Kate first," Bre says. "If she's the one responsible, what's in it for her?"

Before Bre even gets the question out, I know the answer in my bones: I can't think of a single thing Sasha-Kate would stand to gain by spilling our news to the world, other than the petty satisfaction of doing it just because she can. Why would she want to remind the world how much they love seeing Ransom and me together—especially when it finally looks like she might get her moment to shine in the reboot? Not even Sasha-Kate would jeopardize her own chances like that.

"I'd bet money it wasn't her," I say. "She's too self-centered to care about blasting my love life to the world."

"What about Ransom's dad, then?"

"I think he's definitely a possibility."

Something Ransom told me on the beach surfaces in my memory, though: *I never should have listened to my dad.*

"Actually, I'm not sure," I say, turning the thoughts over in my head. "I found out that Ransom's dad was the one who suggested the step back we took when *Girl* ended—I'm not sure if he was just trying to keep Ransom from being tied down at all, or if he disliked the specific idea of Ransom being with me."

"Wow," she says. "Yeah, if he didn't like the specific idea of *you* for some reason, it wouldn't make sense for him to tell the whole world you're dating his son."

"Exactly."

Bre bites her lip but says nothing.

"What?" I say.

"I don't want to be *that person*, but as your best friend, I think someone needs to say it," Bre says. "Do you think there's any possibility Ransom might have set you up?"

No, is my immediate gut reaction, followed just as quickly by another less certain word: *Maybe.*

Ransom knows I'm on the fence about signing on for the reboot—a real-life love story between the two of us could make us invaluable to the show and give us significant leverage in negotiations. He also wants to move into more serious work like I have, break away from the type-casting his father's built an empire on.

Linking himself to me publicly is a good move for him any way you look at it.

I push down the memory of how deserted the lot was that morning, other than us. The perfect illusion of privacy.

"We *just* talked about keeping it quiet last night," I say. "We both agreed it was best that way for now."

Even as the words leave my mouth, I wonder—did we, though? I think back on his words, his actual words: *You're right. I wish you weren't.* And before that, *People will have to find out eventually, right?* He's always been so much more comfortable with the press than I have. The press never caused *his* father to die in a fiery crash.

I rest my face in my hands, accidentally digging the heels of my palms so firmly into my eyelids that I see stars.

I can't stop thinking about the thing I don't want to think: this situation feels all too familiar.

"Tell me what's in your head right now," Bre says gently. "You're going to get through this, I promise. Okay?"

I nod. "Remember how I told you there was some epic drama on set during our final season? And how Ransom had a girlfriend that year, and they broke up over me?"

I've never confided the details about what happened to anyone—I could never find the words.

"Her name was Zoe," I begin before I can talk myself out of sharing. "She was a regular on set, new that season. She was territorial and possessive and didn't like how much time he spent with me."

"I dislike this already," Bre says, a sour look on her face.

"She was pretty vocal about how much she disliked our friendship," I go on, "and eventually demanded that Ransom cut me out of his life entirely."

"Drastic, much?"

"Seriously. He didn't, of course. It would have been impossible, anyway, since we weren't finished shooting the season."

"I'm sure she loved that."

"She was furious." I was, too. "So she tried to drive a wedge between us instead. She spilled private details about me to the press when she didn't get her way—apparently he talked about me kind of a lot. More than he should have."

And that, right there, is what feels familiar: I know he never meant for that information to become public news, because he's always been fiercely protective over me and my privacy. But he trusted Zoe and wasn't as careful around her as he could have been. Even today, he could have been more careful—anyone could have seen the lock screen on his phone, that photo of us together.

Anyone could have asked questions. Jumped to conclusions.

"Please tell me he dumped her immediately?" Bre says, making a face, pulling me out of my thoughts.

"Oh, yeah, he definitely did."

"But he still suggested a step back anyway?"

"He did," I say evenly.

If a girlfriend asks about you and me, it's only fair that I'm honest about why we're such close friends, I can still hear Ransom saying. *Either that, or we need to not be such close friends in the first place. No one's ever going to want to date either of us if they think we're in love with each other.*

I decided then and there that no one else would ever have to ask.

But things have taken an unexpected turn. Not even fourteen years of silence could keep us from falling back into step, on our way to being closer than ever before. Closeness comes with a risk, though: he had good intentions back then, but I still ended up hurt.

Good intentions aren't always enough.

"Wow, okay, that's a lot," Bre says, when a few minutes have passed and I still haven't found words. "Let's set aside the question of *who* for now and think about the news itself. People knowing about you and Ransom doesn't have to be a bad thing."

I want to believe that, really—things would be so much easier if I didn't care about people knowing. It's too soon for this much pressure from all the fans, though, too soon for this much pressure from *myself*. We're still learning what it means to be *Liv and Ransom* in a relationship and not *Honor and Duke*—and I was hoping to learn that in private, in our own time, without the added weight of anyone else being invested in it. I want the freedom to make mistakes if we have to without everyone expecting me to be the perfect girl I played on TV, the one who always knew exactly how to deal with every ditch in the road, every detour. That girl knew the endings ahead of time. Every line of every script.

I want this to work. I want *us* to work.

The memory of how distant Ransom was today—his words like a slap, the sting of being pushed away after finally allowing ourselves to get closer than ever before—it comes sharp and quick, and twists like the knife that it is. The idea that it might have been him who sold us out, after all our history—

The writer's words burn like the space left behind when you've stared too long at the sun: *Liv, if you're out there, please don't ruin this—I'll have to throw away the friendship bracelet you sent back if you do.* I only sent four friendship bracelets of my own back out into the world, and only to those who'd written letters that absolutely broke my heart.

"Liv," Bre says, waving her chopsticks in front of my face. "Liv, hey. Whatever you're thinking, stop, okay?"

I fight the urge to follow my thoughts as they spiral down, down, down.

"Look," she says. "I'll do some digging, see if Attica has any connections that can get them to tell us who spilled, okay? I'll also get in touch with the café on the lot and see if I can find out who was working that morning. For now, maybe lock your phone in your safe and take the rest of today to try to focus on you. Not Ransom, not strangers writing posts about your personal life, not the decisions you'll have to make soon about what comes next—just try to forget it all and be a person who does whatever she wants today, okay?"

It's tempting. It's not like all those things will just go away if I ignore them, though. "What if Mars tries to get in touch?" I ask, my conversation with her from this morning about potentially walking away from the *Girl* reboot still fresh on my mind.

"Don't worry about Mars," she says. "I'll give her a heads-up." She gives me an encouraging smile. "It's only a few hours, yeah? Nothing is so pressing it can't wait that long."

She looks so earnest, so hopeful that her suggestion will help. "I really hope you're right."

✦

Half an hour later, I'm in my tub, neck deep in lavender-scented bubbles. I can't remember the last time I treated myself to time off like this, all alone in my own house with nothing on the schedule, with clearing my head my only goal. I have to admit, Bre was right. It's not the worst way to spend an afternoon.

I take a sip of rosé as the most recent Hālo album echoes from the tile. The music is chill in a way that calms my mind, yet with an undercurrent that brims with energy—a combination that leaves me feeling lighter than before. I'm soaking up the vibe in peace until the chorus on track seven brings that to a screeching halt.

You and me, me and you
There's nothing we couldn't do
In deepest dark or brightest light
In endless desert on the coldest night
You and me, me and you
Don't know much, but this one thing's true
The world is against us but how's this their fight?
In our secret oasis, everything's all right

Ugh, ugh.

Hālo sings, every word a string that pulls me right back down to reality. Finally, the song ends and transitions to the next, but it isn't much of an improvement—it's a song called "Lullaby" that sounds calm on the surface but is all about anxiety and insomnia resulting from a sudden breakup. She's halfway through the lyric "Finally let you in, after all this time / Now I'm all alone and there's someone else in line / For my place beside you, sheets still warm / But silence sings my lullaby" when

I give up on my bath and run to change the music, not even bothering to towel off first.

So that was a bust.

I navigate out of Hālo's album, but once I'm in my song library, Millie's face stares back at me—her latest singles are an acute reminder, too, of everything I'm trying to forget: the *Girl* reboot, the massive increase of attention and pressure she's only just started to face in her career. She has no idea what she's in for. She won't be able to leave her house without an escort, won't be able to make a single choice without strangers offering their unsolicited opinions. She'll get messages she doesn't want, drama when she blocks, backlash the second she makes an all-too-human mistake. Fame is an elusive diamond, sparkling and shimmering and just out of reach . . . until it's not. By the time you're close enough to hold it, it's blinding.

I make my way downstairs after throwing on some soft pink leggings and a longline bra to match. I'm too restless to sit on the couch and watch a show, so I go to the kitchen instead. I rummage around for a snack, settling on mozzarella pearls with basil and cherry tomatoes. I've just popped the first bite in my mouth when I notice my beach blanket, still draped over one of the chairs, right where I dropped it when Ransom and I came inside after our splash war down in the surf.

It's no use trying to escape. I can't.

I wish he were here with me now, despite everything—there has to be another explanation for the article, the photo—and I wish I felt no doubt. I've got so many questions, and I'm itching to see if he's texted me like he said he would. It's not quite five o'clock, though, and I promised Bre I'd stay off my phone until six.

Screw it.

If I can't escape, and I can't forget, the least I can do is try my best to dwell on something *good* instead. I grab my beach blanket, fill a bottle with chilled water, and head down to the exact spot on the sand where Ransom and I sat to watch the sunset. That night was entirely good, and no matter what happens next—no matter what's happening *now*—the thought of it sends a warm rush all throughout my body. My thoughts flicker back to last night in the pool, just the two of us under the moonlight, behind those thick ivy walls. His smile, his laugh—his hands—his lips—his—

I take a long drink of water; it goes down cool and smooth.

Last night was perfection. I need to stop thinking about it before the horror show that is today tarnishes the memory.

I tie my hair back into a ponytail, smooth out my blanket. It's cool for late June, especially at this time in the afternoon—it's one of those rare California days where it looks like a storm might be brewing off the coast. A layer of low gray clouds have started to roll in, filtering the late-afternoon sun.

It's been ages since I did yoga, but I don't have a better idea for how to distract myself for an entire hour, so I settle into a plank, then push up into downward-facing dog. It isn't long before muscle memory takes over and I slip back into the daily practice I maintained half a decade ago. The breeze coming off the ocean, the rhythmic crash of waves, the occasional seabird swooping low over the water: it's calming, all of it. For the first time all day, the tension melts from my neck and I'm finally able to just breathe.

I stay at it for so long I don't realize how dark the sky has gotten until it breaks open. Raindrops fall fast and hard, soaking me in five seconds flat. Normally, I'd run inside immediately just to protect my phone, or my hair. Today, I let the rain wash over me, unhurried as I attempt to shake the sand from my blanket, watching as it peppers the ocean. It's beautiful.

My house feels frigid after all that time outside, especially seeing as I'm drenched. I grab a kitchen towel, trying my best to dry off a little—and that's when I hear the knocking on my front door, muffled by the storm.

"Liv?" I hear between knocks, as I rush to the front door. It sounds like Bre. "*Liv!*"

I whip the door open and yes, sure enough, there's Bre, her fiery-red hair dripping. I've always told her she bears a striking resemblance to a certain little mermaid, and now it's especially true in her soaking-wet teal-and-purple workout clothes.

"What are you doing?" I say, pulling her inside. "How long have you been here? I'm so sorry!"

"Probably fifteen minutes or so?" she says, teeth chattering. It's high sixties out there right now at best, and my air conditioner isn't helping. "I tried calling first, because I wasn't sure you'd actually go through with locking your phone away, but it looks like you did it— aghhhhhh, I'm so sorry about your rug!" I follow her gaze and see she's trailed spots all over it from the front door to my living room.

I wave her off. "No worries about *that*. Are you okay? I was doing yoga on the beach."

We hadn't made plans for her to come back, and in fact, she specifically mentioned a Peloton ride she'd been looking forward to all week, a special live event featuring Hālo's music.

Her eyebrows raise at the mention of yoga—she never knew me during my extremely dedicated yoga phase, but I had quite the intense streak going for a couple of years until I went on location for a project and it threw off my entire routine.

"So, okay, I did some digging," she says. "First of all, it definitely looks like one of the baristas was involved. I talked to a girl named Mattea, and she said her coworker Dex opened the café on his own yesterday morning. She also said he's had money trouble lately, and when she tried texting and calling to ask about the photo, he ignored her entirely. So. That's a promising lead. As for the website, no one would talk." She follows me to the guest bathroom down the hall, where I toss her a towel. "Thanks. So, yeah, they're keeping their sources locked down tight—but I still got some useful info out of the call. The girl I talked to made this comment about how this was her 'best day on the job *ever*!'" Bre puts the phrase in air quotes and does her best super-green intern voice to match. "She just happened to mention she'd talked to '*Sasha-Kate Kilpatrick*, like, *right* before this!'" She gives me a look, and the pieces fall together.

"Which means," I say slowly, "that if she's committed to keeping their source anonymous but willing to spill that Sasha-Kate called only a few minutes before—"

"And that the Sasha-Kate call happened *today*," Bre adds, "not yesterday before the article ran—"

"That means it had to be someone else who spilled," I finish. "Ransom's dad feels like the most logical answer."

It's the answer that would sting less, anyway.

"Or Ransom himself," Bre says, ever thorough.

"Or Ransom himself," I echo, but am quick to add, "but I'm, like, ninety-five percent positive he wouldn't have told."

"Ninety-five percent," she says flatly, with a *look*.

"Okay, ninety-five might be a little high," I admit. "Ninety percent. Eighty-five." I shake the ideas out of my head before I go any lower. "The point is, with our history, and especially after last night in his pool—"

Her eyes go wide. "Wait, last night *in his pool*?"

"I only meant that we talked about keeping our relationship a secret for now," I say, though I can't keep the heat from flooding my cheeks, or the ghost of a smile that pulls at the corners of my mouth. "But yeah, um. Last night was good in other ways, too."

"Okay, *that* is a conversation for later!" she says, but then the sparkle falls out of her eyes. "If you still want to have it after what I'm about to show you, that is." She takes a deep breath, exhales loudly. "I'm not saying Ransom's the one who told, okay? But some more stuff popped up today that made me wonder."

All the calm I worked so hard to cultivate is gone, replaced by what feels like an avocado pit in my stomach. A roll of thunder swells outside, the rain really picking up. A few taps later, and her phone is unlocked, open to a new headline.

She hands it over, and I begin to read.

Ones to Watch: Ransom Joel Team Neck-Deep as Offers Pour In

By Gregor Ives // Senior Editor, Books & Film, *West Coast Daily*

On the heels of today's breaking news regarding former teen heartthrob Ransom Joel—he's finally taken his on-screen romance with *Girl on the Verge* costar Liv Latimer off-screen—we hear his agent's phone has been ringing off the hook all afternoon.

Joel has stayed firmly in the public eye ever since the show that put him there went off the air nearly fourteen years ago. While his acting skills are undeniably solid, ask any teen with hearts in their eyes—or their parents, for the record—what comes to mind when they hear the name Ransom Joel, and the answer is almost always: *It doesn't matter what he's in, I'll watch it.*

This current era of Ransom Joel has been one long string of blockbusters after another. We've watched him transform from lovable boy next door (<u>surrounded by literal kittens</u>/ photo credit: ASPCA) to one of the hottest tickets in Hollywood. From his first foray into action, playing alongside Lara Starling as her reluctant boy-next-door hero, to his most recent stretch of record-breaking espionage thrillers (in which he stars as titular character Hunter Drew), to a wide variety of one-off hits in which he's faced off against—and subsequently defeated—threats such as zombies, velociraptors, and a hacker who single-handedly wreaked havoc on the world economy via an intricately coded cyberplague, it's safe to say Ransom Joel has his pick of films.

Rumor has it, though, that Joel isn't entirely content: he's looking to diversify his already robust résumé and break out in a more serious way—with some potentially Oscar-worthy roles, if we had to guess. Linking himself publicly to indie sweetheart Liv Latimer is a strategic step in the right direction, if so, and it sounds like today's news has had the intended effect: we hear it's caught the attention of none other than Jonathan Cast, who's currently on set in Iceland filming his latest, which will no doubt be a serious contender for awards across the board once it eventually debuts.

In the meantime, catch both Joel and Latimer in the upcoming *Girl on the Verge* reunion special, which will be released exclusively on the Fanline platform at the end of next month. More to come on Ransom Joel's next project as the situation develops.

20

I stare at the phone.

I'm *a strategic step in the right direction*—it sounds like a line straight out of a publicist's mouth. And after watching Ransom's publicist in action on set earlier, it isn't hard to imagine this line coming from her, specifically.

The words swim in my head, not to mention the insinuation: that Ransom's motives in hooking up with me had less to do with his actual feelings for me and everything to do with changing the trajectory of his own career.

I want to believe the best in him.

I want to believe he had nothing to do with this article, or the one that blasted our news to the world—just like he swore he had nothing to do with the article that tore us apart in our final season, everything his girlfriend spilled to the press.

I want to believe it's real this time. That even though I was wrong in the past whenever I thought there might be something between us, that this time is different.

He's a good actor, though. And things aren't adding up.

There are only so many places they could have heard "rumors" of Ransom being unsatisfied with his massive commercial success, and I sure didn't spill about it. No one would look at his résumé and think, *Oh,* there's *a guy who's lacking for opportunity!* I know all too well, though, that there are secret sides to success—that we don't talk about the darker parts of being in the public eye because we're expected to be grateful for all of it, even when it's painful. I know for a fact that Ransom is unsatisfied. I heard it straight from his lips, right before he kissed me.

My own publicist suggested we use Ransom as a publicity stunt, so of course it makes sense that his would do the same. It's hard to imagine Ransom being so calculating on his own—but even if it wasn't his idea, I have to consider the possibility that he agreed to let it happen. If all he wants is to ride my success to places he hasn't been able to go on his own, it definitely seems to be working. Even Jonathan Cast has reached out from a remote set in Iceland, according to that article.

I feel a little sick at how readily I offered to go out on a limb for him with Vienna; I left her a voice mail last night on the ride home from Ransom's house.

"I have to be missing something," I say numbly. "This can't be what it looks like. It can't." I *know* Ransom. I know him, he wouldn't do this—any of it.

"I hope there's a good explanation," Bre says, and my head snaps up. I'd forgotten for a minute that I wasn't alone, thinking out loud. "For everything."

There has to be.

I'm itching to text him, and itching to see if he's texted me, but my phone is still locked away in my safe, upstairs in the back corner of my bedroom's closet. Surely by now there'll be something.

"Back in a minute," I call over my shoulder as I rush upstairs. "Feel free to make some tea, or coffee, or . . . anything."

A low rumble of thunder rattles the house. My bedroom is dark and moody thanks to the storm, not the usual sunny haven I'm used to, and my office-sized closet feels even more like a cave. I kneel in front of my safe, tap in the code.

I scroll through all the missed texts—several from my mom, a stack of them from Vienna with only a mysterious *Call me* visible on the top message, a dozen from Attica, two missed calls from Mars, more missed calls from my mom and Vienna and Attica and Bre and even Shine Jacobs.

It's a dizzying mix of names—who's in the mix, and moreover, who *isn't*. I scroll through again, making sure I haven't missed anything: nope, nothing from Ransom.

A brief memory surfaces from late last night, though, along with a flicker of hope. I have the vague recollection of turning off notifications for Ransom's texts on the ride back to my house. After our perfect night in his backyard, I fully expected some texts today that would have given us away—one glance at my phone from the wrong set of eyes and our secret would become the biggest news in Hollywood.

Ohhhhh, Liv of yesterday, how sweet and optimistic you were.

I open my phone, certain I'll find a novel's worth of messages waiting beside the crescent moon icon by his name.

But . . . no. Nothing new, nothing since our messages last night after he dropped me off, confirming he'd made it back to his place, telling me to sleep well, a couple of kiss emojis from me and a shy, blushing emoji from him.

I tap into Snapaday against my better judgment, ignoring all the other messages still waiting for me. I also ignore the notification bubble that pops up—though its stratospheric new comment and follower counts make me do a double take—and head straight to search.

When Ransom's profile pops up, it's obvious he's also seen a major boost to his following today. There's a new post in his feed, and new stories, too—he clearly hasn't had his phone locked away all afternoon like I have.

The new post is black-and-white—he's staring straight into the camera, eyes sparkling even in grayscale. The caption is simple: a single black heart. I'm about 90 percent sure it's his publicist's handiwork. His latest story, though—it's definitely something he posted, a selfie taken by the pool in his backyard, no text or tags. He's not exactly smiling, but he doesn't look like his entire private life has just been blasted all over the internet without his permission, either.

I'm still staring at it when it disappears, and another story takes its place, an overfiltered shot of the waterfall in his pool. In tiny text, an artful italic serif, the words *only missing you* are positioned just off to the side, white letters against a shadowy stone background, punctuated with a simple white heart.

Are these words for me? Why didn't he discreetly tag me, if so? There are a number of places where the text color could blend seamlessly with the photo. Maybe he simply left this story as a reminder of last night while working through all that made him so angry on set today.

Or, maybe this story is for everyone and no one all at once, another carefully carved facet of the whole Ransom-in-love narrative that's been spun up today.

I close my eyes, put my phone facedown on the carpet. I want to go back to yesterday. I need to talk to Ransom, but right now, I just can't stomach it. The fact that he hasn't reached out at all since the news broke feels like a flaming red flag, a sign that I'm absolutely right to question whether everything between us has been one big publicity stunt for him.

And all those missed messages, especially that mysterious *Call me* text from Vienna—in my voice mail to her, sometime around one in the morning, I proposed the idea of having Ransom play opposite me in her upcoming film.

I was so careful not to mention the fact that I was *seeing* Ransom, for the sake of having her consider him as a talented actor in his own right, and for my own credibility as a collaborator. As comfortable as I am with Vienna, I know she has a specific vision for every single aspect of every single project; for me to suggest Ransom as my costar felt like new territory in our working relationship. But I believed in Ransom, and—if I'm honest—the idea of going on location with him to a remote cabin in the woods thrilled me a little.

Now I don't know what I want more: for her to hate the idea or for her to love it.

Reluctantly, I tap back into my messages app. Vienna's texts are . . . very Vienna. In other words: short, cryptic, ultimately betraying no clues about her reaction to my late-night message. No voice mails from her, either. She's always been a minimalist when it comes to anything but direct interaction, but just this once, I wish I knew what to expect when calling her back.

I'm just about to put the call through when I hear a soft knock outside my closet door. It's Bre, with a steaming cup of tea in hand. "Everything okay?"

She steps inside, perches on my sapphire-blue velvet bench. "Liv?" she says gently a moment later, when I still haven't answered.

I sigh. "Next time I take an afternoon off from my phone, remind me to leave it with you so I don't come back to such a mess," I groan. "I don't have the energy to deal."

She holds out her hand, nods toward my phone. I unlock it and hand it over.

"What first?" she says.

"Mostly just Attica and Mars," I say, realizing that the bulk of my overwhelm is stemming from messages that *aren't* there. "My mom can wait, and I'll call Vienna in a bit."

"Oh, I know for a fact that Attica's over the moon," she says, tapping into the messages. "She sent me about a hundred messages, too. Honestly, she thinks this is as good for you as it seems to be for Ransom."

"She would," I say bitterly, and Bre laughs.

"Hey, that's what you pay her for, right? Spinning any situation with the press in your favor?"

"See, and this is why I hadn't told Attica about Ransom yet," I say. "She would have blasted the news to the far corners of the planet. She would have been Suspect Number One."

"So true," Bre agrees. She scrolls a bit, confirming there's nothing I need to *do* concerning Attica—no requests to act on, no questions to respond to. "Mars says she has an update on whatever you talked about this morning and says not to pick up the phone if Shine Jacobs calls you directly?" Her eyes grow wide.

"Well, guess that's one good thing to come out of my phone being in prison all afternoon," I say, nodding toward it. "I totally would have answered that call."

Maybe Shine's is the one call that has nothing to do with Ransom at all. She could be calling to explain the new creative direction—or urging me to commit right then and there.

"What's that about?"

"Not really supposed to talk about it yet," I say. As close as Bre and I are, she won't pry; she's been doing double duty as my assistant long enough to know I'll tell her when I can. During sensitive negotiations like this that are still in progress, there are some times when Actress Liv has to overrule Friend Liv's desire to talk it all out.

"Okay, so you should probably call Mars back, too," Bre says, doing a pitch-perfect job at hiding her curiosity. "Anything else you want me to check on while I'm in here?"

I bury my face in my hands. "If there's any chance you can make Ransom magically text me and explain what the eff is going on, that'd be *great*," I say.

My phone vibrates loudly in her hand, and she looks straight at me, wide-eyed. "Uhhh . . . your wish is my command?"

She turns the phone so I can see it. Ransom's name is at the top of my message list, a little blue dot beside his words: *can we talk?*

"I know I just gave you a raise this summer," I say, "but I really don't think I gave you quite enough."

#5Facts: Everyone's Got Heart Eyes for Ransom Joel

By Octavia Benetton // Staff Writer, *Love & Lightning Rounds*

Hey hey, Lightning Bugs! Is it just me, or have you also been glued to the interwebs so you don't miss a single minute of news re: the ever-scintillating love life of Ransom Joel? (He's reportedly dating Liv Latimer, if you hadn't heard—!!!) I'll probably need an updated prescription after all the damage I've done to my eyes squinting at screens today, but hey! At least I'm a girl who can rock the thickest of frames.

Since we're all Ransom-crazy this afternoon, I thought it would be the perfect time to do a #5Facts on him—can you believe we've never done one?! Me neither. Search my archives, tell me I'm lying.

1. **Ransom Joel *is* his real name.** It's almost as if his parents mapped out his fate as a Future Hollywood Heartthrob right from birth—and honestly, that might not be too far off. Sources say his father, Jonathan Joel (who also happens to be his manager), had a short-lived film career of his own back in the day, though you won't find many significant credits to his name. Sources *also* say Jonathan's ex-wife, Julie, was reluctant to put Ransom in front of a camera when his career first started, and that it drove such a wedge between them that it led to their eventual divorce.

2. **Ransom's activism has led to more than 100,000 kitten adoptions worldwide, according to the ASPCA.** Ransom

famously modeled for a kitten calendar back in the day, and you can still find the photos online—but good luck trying to snag an actual, fresh copy! If you do happen to find one, though, be prepared to hand over your firstborn and a pair of kidneys to the cruel, heartless people who put those things up for sale. Don't they know true fans might actually try to *part* with both kidneys (not to mention our firstborns, who haven't slept through the night in EIGHT MONTHS thankyouverymuch) for such coveted memorabilia?

3. **Ransom's love life wasn't always a public spectacle.** The second Gemma Gardner came into Ransom's life two years ago, the news was everywhere—and is there a person on Planet Earth who *isn't* familiar with his long line of gorgeous girlfriends in those years just after he wrapped filming on *GotV*? Before that, though—while he was still on the show—it's all but impossible to find any record of him dating anyone. Was he single all that time, or just extra talented at keeping quiet about it? INQUIRING MINDS WANT TO KNOW! (Show of hands, who here believes Ransom was actually into Liv all that time, and that's why he never dated anyone?)

4. **Sources say he's as nice behind the camera as he looks in front of it.** Word on the street is that Ransom is always kind to everyone on set, not only his famous costars—according to an intern who worked on one of the Hunter Drew movies, he was always doing thoughtful things for people on the lot. "One time, he bought a brand-new MacBook Pro for one of the other interns who'd ruined her ancient laptop with a cup of coffee," the intern told us. "I also remember this other time when he stuck around for hours helping production clean up—we'd been shooting a sequence where it looked like a bomb had gone off, and someone was stressing out about how they might miss their kid's birthday dinner that night,

so he asked permission for the whole cast to stay and help. He's a good guy."

5. He turned down an opportunity to go skiing with the Canadian prime minister because he'd already committed to working in a soup kitchen. Yes, you read that right: Ransom Joel *turned down* an opportunity to spend time with the *PRIME MINISTER OF CANADA* and, instead, spent his time serving soup to the hungry who were spending the holidays alone on the streets of LA. The prime minister was reportedly so impressed that <u>he canceled his own trip and, instead, spent a long holiday weekend working in a soup kitchen up in Ottawa.</u> (They eventually did vacation together up in Whistler, but it says a lot that it was the ski trip that got shoved aside, not the soup kitchen. Bravo, boys!)

And that's it for now, everyone! It's one of those days where I wish this bit were called #10Facts, because my well of random Ransom tidbits runs deep. This just means I'll have to do Part II someday—I know you're all dying to find out about one of Ransom's more memorable interactions with his fans! (Spoiler alert: it involves a dazzle of zebras and some cans of whipped cream . . .)

For now, I'll let you all get back to refreshing your various internet windows mining for new updates on Ransom and Liv . . . and I'll be right there with you!

21

For once, I'm in my own car—a 2022 BMW X4 M in white—navigating the highways of Los Angeles alone. I've hardly driven in a month. I *can* drive. . . . I just strongly prefer not to. My father always preferred to drive himself everywhere, and it ended up killing him, so I have Jimmy. Jimmy's off tonight for his daughter's birthday, though, so I'm on my own.

It's twilight as I make my way down the Pacific Coast Highway. Malibu to Silver Lake is not a short drive, but at least tonight's sky is glorious, remnants of storm clouds lit up by the last purple-pink rays of sunlight on the horizon. This stretch of highway calms me like no other, usually.

Tonight, I can't stop thinking about Ransom.

Even with the sunroof open and some new tracks playing in my speakers, my nerves are on edge. I've talked myself in and out of so many potential explanations.

I'll come over, I eventually replied to Ransom's text, after workshopping options with Bre.

ok, sounds good is all he wrote back.

Five songs in, I turn the volume down. "Hey, Siri," I say to my car's connected dashboard as I turn onto I-10 at Santa Monica and leave the ocean behind. "Call Vienna."

She answers on the first ring.

"Liv, hi, I was worried!" she says warmly, taking the edge off my nerves. I imagine her sitting cross-legged on her patio, surrounded by plants and sipping on a hot cup of tea, the elusive scent of rain still hanging on the air. "Is everything okay?"

"It's been a long day," I admit. "Took a break from my phone all afternoon—so sorry I missed your calls."

There's a long pause on the other end, a rustling of papers. Conversations with Vienna are never the linear, rushed sorts I'm used to. She takes time to think, and to answer. It's much less awkward in person.

"Listen, Liv," she says. "I got your message last night—now it's my turn to apologize for missing your call, I was deep in the zone, working on our script." Only Vienna would apologize for not answering an incoming call at one in the morning. "I've been thinking all day about your proposal."

I try to remember my exact words, but the only thing I can clearly recall is a *feeling*: an intense attempt at persuasion steeped in urgency and optimism.

"Some rumors have found their way to me today," she says. "Is it true that you and Ransom Joel are together?"

No use lying about it, not to Vienna. But what's the *truth*?

I sigh. "We've been seeing each other, yes," I say. "Not long enough for me to feel comfortable with the whole world knowing."

"Mmmm," she hums. "Do you know how I spent my morning?"

"Sleeping, hopefully, since it sounds like you were up all night?"

She laughs. "Sleep, sleep," she says, and I can almost see her waving the idea away. "I'll do it again sometime when this draft is finished. But no—I was watching Ransom in *Velociraptor X*."

Of all the films she could have picked. I feel the urge to defend him, because there are much better showcases of his acting skills than the one that spawned a thousand memes, but she goes on before I have the chance.

"I know what you're thinking," she continues. "But you know what? You're right. He's good. Far, far better than anyone gives him credit for—it's in the details, his choices. I can tell he's making the most of what he's been given, and I can see in his eyes that he wants more."

Only Vienna would pick up something like that from a film like

Velociraptor X. Despite how this day has gone, despite every unknown right now with Ransom, I feel the sparkle of hope. He *is* talented. He's so much more than a beautiful face and sculpted muscles and—

My face flushes with heat just thinking about him, and I remind myself why I'm driving to his place right now at all: I need to hear his side of the story, though there's a very real possibility it won't be what I want to hear.

"I can absolutely see him in the role of Evan," she says. "And I think your chemistry would work well." There's another long pause, and I sense what's next before she says it: "But."

"But?" My heartbeat picks up, driving spikes through my confidence.

She hums noncommittally. "How do I say this?" she says. "There's no doubt he's talented—but now that I know you're in a relationship, it makes me nervous to cast him opposite you. I don't want to say it, but what if you break up? It could cause problems, Liv, and as talented as you both are—even if we could technically still pull off the love story if you're not feeling it at all—I'm not eager to invite that kind of tension onto my set. And if I'm honest, the insinuation in some of what's been written is off-putting, that he's only using you to gain consideration for a role like this." She lets out a long exhale. "I really hope that's not the case. But I'm sure you can understand where I'm coming from."

I blink back tears, focus on not smashing into the taillights in front of me.

"Yeah," I manage. "Yeah, I get it."

And I do.

I want to defend him—defend *us*—but the truth is, whether what we have is real or he's just trying to make it look that way, it sounds like neither option will land us in a place where this project works out for Ransom. Vienna's given voice to all the things I've been too afraid to even think.

"I do appreciate you putting him on my radar, though," she says. "If anyone else comes to mind, don't hesitate to call, okay?"

She mentions she'd love to have another brainstorming session soon, goes off on a tangent about some locations she's torn between, and takes another looping detour that somehow touches on ceramic teapots, polka (both dots and music), and llamas all in one go. By the time I'm outside Ransom's gate, ready to buzz for entry, I at least feel lighter than before—I didn't spend the entire drive angsting over the conversation I'm about to have, and that's a good thing—until we end the call.

"It's me," I announce into the speaker, because I don't know the gate code.

Out of the corner of my eye, I spy movement in the honeysuckle bushes that line his fence—a photographer, no doubt. Not a surprise; I'm only surprised there aren't more. I prepared for this, putting on a bright persimmon dress with blinding-white Adidas. It feels happy and bold, even if I don't.

A moment later, the gates open, and with them, so does the pit in my stomach.

I pull around the circle drive and park in front of the trio of steps leading to Ransom's front door. Just last night, when Jimmy dropped me off (*technically* a business trip, as far as he was concerned), my body buzzed for a different reason. Now, I have no idea what to expect.

I hear the faint click of a shutter behind me as I climb the steps; Ransom opens the door before I even make it to the top. The porch lamps cast shadows under his angular cheekbones, on the curves of his biceps, and he smells fresh, like he's just climbed out of the shower.

Focus, Liv.

"Thanks for coming," he says quietly, eyes searching mine, his face difficult to read. I get the feeling he wants to kiss me but knows better than to try right now.

"Photographer in your honeysuckle," I murmur when he leans in for a side hug instead.

We slip inside his house. It's dark in the foyer, dark in his living room except for a pair of lamps. I spot a book facedown on the couch and an empty container of Chinese takeout on his end table.

I bite my lip, hovering awkwardly behind the couch. "Should we—"

"Here, let's sit," he says at the same time. "Sorry. Yeah." He runs a hand through his hair, and it sticks up, not completely dry from his shower; the thought sends a flush of heat coursing throughout my body, because my body is a traitor.

I curl up in a wide leather armchair by the window, turn my head so I don't have such a clear view of the backyard. He sits across from me, on the couch—I hope the sight of the pool gives him searing memories of all the details from last night, everything I'm trying not to think about right now.

"So those articles," I begin. "That photo of us on the roof—" I suck in a sharp breath.

I want him to say something. Anything.

"Ransom?" I try to catch his eye, but can't get him to look at me. "You were just as surprised as I was by that photo—right?"

A moment passes, and then another.

His silence says everything.

"I hate that this is happening," he says, finally meeting my eyes. "I wasn't the one who leaked our news, I *swear*. And that snapshot—I fought hard for them not to go to the press with it." His voice rises, more heated with every word.

"For *who* not to go to the press?" I ask, even though I have a pretty good guess. I want to hear him say it.

"My dad," he says. "And Andrea."

"And they knew about the photo how, exactly?"

"Dad admitted that he'd hired someone to keep an eye out, offered wads of cash for any pictures they might get." He shakes his head, jaw tight. Bre's theory was spot-on. "I should know by now that he can't be trusted with anything important—he knew something was up between us when I canceled dinner to come to your house that day."

My anger spikes, I can't help it. "*Why*, though? Why couldn't he just let us enjoy it?"

"He's livid about their plans for the reboot, that my role would be smaller," he says. "For some reason he still thinks he can storm in there and just . . . argue his way into a better deal. Obviously it didn't work. And, like, did he really think hovering over Bryan's shoulder and putting everyone on edge would make anything *better*? I guess it was his backup plan to get the fandom riled up about '*Liv and Ransom*'"—the way he twists his voice and puts us in air quotes turns my stomach—"so Fanline will realize they're making a huge mistake. I tried to tell them not to, Liv. I told them you'd be upset, but Andrea was so dismissive—they both were. They *always* are. They just kept coming back to how it'd be in your best interests, too, ultimately, to get the fans on our side."

I'm stuck on something he's just said: *I tried to tell them not to, Liv.*

His father's words from last night, the last ones he said on his way out after meeting with Ransom, resurface in my memory: *Think about it.*

I take a deep breath. "When, exactly, did you find out about the photo they ran today?" My voice is low, intense. Almost unrecognizable.

He bites his lip, stares at the floor.

"When did you find out about it, Ransom?" I watch him intently, but he still won't meet my eyes.

"Last night," he finally says quietly.

"Last night. Before I came over and spent all evening with you."

"Yes."

It's like our final season on set all over again, only this time he gets to experience the aftermath right along with me: someone he deeply trusted has just sold us out to the press, as if the private details of our lives exist solely to make theirs better. First his traitor of a girlfriend—and now his own father.

"He told me he wouldn't put it out there. He *promised*, Liv." His voice catches, eyes locking on mine. "I wanted to believe him—and I didn't want to hurt you. I hate that he lied, and I am so, so sorry. Tell me how to make this better. Please, Liv."

"And I want to believe *you*—but you have to admit, the timing is questionable."

He's always loved the spotlight. He's unsatisfied with his career.

He had years to make a move, and he chose now.

His brow furrows. "I'm not sure what you're implying."

"The timing," I repeat. "We were best friends forever, but you suddenly have feelings for me? It's too convenient. It feels like a *setup*, Ransom." My voice cracks. "Like maybe none of it was actually real."

I keep my gaze steady on his, barely holding it together.

"You can't seriously think all of this was a publicity stunt," he says with a flicker of indignation. "You can't seriously think last night wasn't real."

It's a sucker punch that knocks the wind out of me, thinking of last night when this is where we are now.

"I want more than anything for last night to have been real." I look him dead in the eye. "I've loved you since we were *sixteen*, Ransom. Since our first on-screen kiss—and since that flight to Shanghai. You were *everything* to me, my very best friend. I tried so hard to tell myself that's all we were—friends. That it didn't mean anything when you confided in me things you never told anyone else. That all our inside jokes, all the times we spent laughing until we cried—or crying until we laughed—I told myself all of that was just what best friends *did* together. I didn't want to lose you. You were my one safe place."

I blink, hard, try to clear the tears. It doesn't work.

"But I did love you, no matter how hard I tried to convince myself otherwise," I go on, "and I lost you anyway, because you decided we needed to not be so close anymore, after all we'd been through. Didn't you ever wonder why I left Hollywood for so long? Every single thing reminded me of you."

"No, no," he says, shaking his head. "You said you *agreed*."

"Well, what was I supposed to say? You said no one would ever want to date either of us if they thought we were in love with each other—it implied you wanted *space*, Ransom, not for us to be even closer. You said you wanted a step back, so I gave it to you."

"I never knew how you felt—"

"I never told you because I didn't want to ruin it." I'm breathless, my words half hollow. "By the time you asked for a step back, it was too late. How could I admit I was in love with you after that, when you'd all but told me you didn't think of me that way?"

He takes it all in, his face unreadable. I don't wait for him to respond.

"I've spent so many years trying to convince myself my feelings for you weren't real—that none of it was real. That I misread myself and not your mixed signals." I take a breath, steady myself. "But now, seeing you again after all this time, it's like we never spent a day apart. And it truly felt real this time, like we were finally on the same page. Like you finally saw me as more than just a friend."

I should stop, I really should. I can't.

"But here we are—I just don't know if I can *do* this, Ransom. I want to believe you'd never intentionally hurt me, that you'd never set me up. But I honestly don't know what to think."

I've finally run out of words, and the silence between us is electric. It feels like one too-sharp breath could spark an explosion.

He turns his eyes on me now, and they're emptier than I've ever seen.

"Anything else?"

It takes a minute to set in, the pain: I imagine it's like the white-hot, searing sensation that radiates down to the bone after the initial numb shock of finding your hand in fire. Never in a million years did I imagine confessing my love—confessing *everything*—to Ransom and having this be the fallout.

I blink, over and over, hoping it will clear the blur. It doesn't. "I think I should go," I say, standing. "I can't be here right now."

He's too quiet, too still. He definitely doesn't try to stop me.

I leave him alone in the glow of lamplight, let myself out the front door. I'm so focused on getting out of there, on putting one foot ahead of the other until I find myself somewhere that isn't completely falling apart, that I forget what's waiting for me outside.

An ambush of flashbulbs, bright and blinding, catch me on my way out. They're so disorienting I nearly slip on Ransom's front steps, but I manage to steady myself before breaking an ankle or worse.

"Liv, Liv!" they shout, an ambiguous chorus obscured by foliage and the thick iron bars of the property's perimeter gate.

Where's Ransom, Liv? Did you break up? Are you still together? Were you ever *together? Liv! Over here, Liv!*

It takes all the energy I have left to force my face into something resembling easy peace, especially knowing it's far too late for that—the damage has been done. No one will be posting Serene Liv on Her Way to Her Car when they've captured frame upon frame of Angry Blind-sided Liv Nearly Breaks Her Face on Front Stoop.

I climb into my car, slam the door, and start the ignition. Slowly, I ease down the drive. One particularly stubborn photographer stands firm beside his camera and tripod just outside the gate, which opens in toward me instead of brushing him aside. He doesn't move, daring me to stay locked in this prison of public humiliation. I flash my brights at him, a warning, but he still doesn't move.

Okay, then.

I press my foot on the accelerator, wincing as thousands of dollars' worth of equipment are ground to pieces under my tires with a sickening crunch. At least its owner had the good sense to move out of the way.

Spotted, Live!:
Handsome Ransom + Lovely Liv (!!!)

In this brand! new! feature!, we here at *Dizzy* magazine will bring you *real-time* updates as we get them, straight from @ZeniaDiLitto's couch to yours! Grab some popcorn and pajamas, friends . . . we suspect this will be suuuuuuuper boring until it suddenly isn't!

(Feel free to post all your burning questions/comments below—if there's downtime, Zenia will do her best to reply!)

ZDL, 7:00 p.m.—Ohhhkay, y'all, here we go! Brand-new segment here thanks to the highly exciting information we've learned today about certain developments in Liv's Love Land (sorry, couldn't resist, promise to never use that one again). Rather than writing article upon article and forcing you into an internet scavenger hunt for the latest updates, figured it would be most efficient to put them here, all in one spot! SO. In case you're not caught up: here's the news that broke today about Liv Latimer and Ransom Joel being A THING; here is a Very Interesting Post breaking down theories about whether they've loved each other all along (or whether this is just a timely publicity stunt in the lead-up to the *Girl on the Verge* reunion special); and here, here, and here are more in-depth takes on all the developments we've seen today, complete with at least two polls where you can weigh in. Obviously, you'll find a hundred other posts on this subject, but I've done my best to curate a list of the most important ones for you to start with. More updates as things unfold!

ZDL, 7:52 p.m.—Okay, so I thought for *sure* we'd see some new developments tonight, but it looks like there's not a ton to report. At least this is giving everyone *plenty* of time to catch up on all the articles/polls I mentioned earlier. Question, while we're waiting! What's your favorite popcorn[1] topping? Mine's sea salt and cayenne pepper, with chocolate chips mixed in.

ZDL, 8:44 p.m.—Hoooooooly crap, you guys, A THING HAS HAPPENED. I repeat, A THING HAS HAPPENED. Word has it that Liv's car has just pulled up to Ransom's gate. This is about to get GOOD.

ZDL, 8:45 p.m.—My source on the ground just gave me this link to a live stream, open in a fresh window so you can watch side by side with our live updates!

ZDL, 8:47 p.m.—LOOK AT THAT LOOK. I want a man who looks at me like Ransom's looking at Liv right now, because holy wow, y'all. She looks amazing in that orange dress— she knows it, and he most definitely knows it. I kind of can't believe all we're getting is this tame side hug right now.

ZDL, 8:49 p.m.—I know, I know, we're pretty evenly split here on the possibility that this is all just one big publicity stunt, but I don't know, y'all. Wouldn't they have gone full-on front-porch make-out session if they really wanted to get us talking? That said, I can only imagine what's going on just behind that closed door . . . ;)

ZDL, 9:04 p.m.—I STAND CORRECTED. WHAT HAPPENED BEHIND THAT CLOSED DOOR COULD NOT HAVE BEEN

GOOD. NOT AT ALL. I AM STUCK ON CAPS LOCK RE:
HOW ENTIRELY NOT GOOD THIS LOOKS WTF

ZDL, 9:05 p.m.—Yiiiiikes she almost busted her gorgeous
face, did y'all see that?! Honestly hate this for her right
now :(

ZDL, 9:06 p.m.—More convinced than ever that this is NOT
just a publicity stunt . . . Liv's good at acting, but that look
on her face on her way out the door 100% screamed "we
were a thing, but now we're not" and ughhhhhh this is SO
DISAPPOINTING, I ship them SO HARD

ZDL, 9:07 p.m.—Dude, our live-feed camera guy better get
out of her way—I have a feeling Liv's not in the mood to
play right now, and honestly, I don't blame her one bit. Like,
yeah, we want to see what's going on, but now I kinda feel
like we've walked in on someone's bedroom in the middle of
the night, where she just needs to be alone for a minute with
her FEEEEEELINGS (along with the various pieces of heart
that have just chipped off thanks to whatever happened
inside that house). Liv clearly doesn't want company right
now . . . I wouldn't either . . . but gahhhh, why is it so hard to
look away??? I hate that I can't look away right now, what is
wrong with me?

ZDL, 9:08 p.m.—And—oh. Well. There goes the live feed. I
know a lot of you will probably be Team Broken Camera, but
for the record, I've decided I'm firmly Team Liv.

[1]Full disclosure: Spotted, Live! is sponsored by Pop It Like
It's Hot popcorn, but let it be known that we here at *Dizzy*
were fans first—our love for their organic heirloom blue corn
(not to mention their punny inspirational messages on the
packaging) is as pure as it gets!

22

The drive home is a blur. Streetlights, taillights, and—eventually—a bit of starlight once I turn onto PCH. If anyone was attempting to follow me out of Ransom's neighborhood, I've lost them by now.

On my front porch, I find a pint of coconut almond chocolate chip gelato tucked into a petite cooler. The note on top is in Bre's handwriting: *I hope this is melted by the time you get home. If not, please enjoy while bingeing Flower Wars, okay? Call me if you need me to come over. xB*

I strip off the day as soon as I'm inside, trading my T-shirt dress for silk pajamas, my makeup for moisturizer. My mascara is a mess; my eyes are as empty as Ransom's looked in that final glance he gave me. That look haunts me, the blankness of it. I don't feel powerful, leaving like I did. I just miss him—I miss us. I miss the us of yesterday.

Thanks for the gelato, I text Bre on my way back downstairs.

Sorry you found it so soon, she writes back immediately, punctuated by the droopiest sad emoji there is. *Want to talk about it?*

Gonna take your advice and drown my thoughts in gelato and Flower Wars, I write. *But I could totally use some company if you want to come over.*

On my way!

Bre arrives in record time, an extra pint of gelato in hand, pistachio this time. "Just in case," she says, grinning. "And for some extra good news, Bryan called off the crack-of-dawn shoot he threatened earlier, so you're off the hook until eight tomorrow morning."

"That *is* very good news," I say. "And wow, that looks amazing."

I rummage around in my kitchen, find a pair of old-fashioned sundae dishes Vienna let me take from the set of *Love // Indigo*, and give us each a healthy sampling of both flavors.

She perches on one of my kitchen island's barstools, takes a bite of pistachio. Her messy topknot tilts precariously as she leans her head back in delight.

"You're going to *die*, Liv, this gelato is so good!" She pulls out her phone and snaps a photo of it, presumably to post on Snapaday.

I tuck the half-empty pints into my freezer, then join her at the island. I try a bite of the coconut almond chocolate chip, let it melt on my tongue: it's velvety and creamy, not overly sweet. Slightly nutty, with flecks of chocolate so dark they could possibly rebrand it as health food.

It's perfect.

"This is exactly the night I needed," I say, and like the best friend she is, she lets me revel in the moment.

I don't want to dwell on today. For just a little while, I want to be Happy Liv with her happy gelato, in some sort of alternate universe where everyone's trustworthy and no one gets hurt.

"*Liv*," Bre says a moment later, eyes wide, pulling me straight back down to reality. "Did you see this? This is the girl Ford's dating, right?"

She turns her phone so I can see—it's open to a Snapaday post on *@YouHeardItHereFirst* featuring Juliette Wells, on set in Iceland, looking extremely cozy with Jonathan Cast. His arm slung low around her, hand on her hip, her head resting on his shoulder. The time stamp is from an hour ago.

My stomach flips, secondhand heartbreak kicking in on Ford's behalf—I feel it like it's my own. The aftertaste of gelato is bittersweet on my tongue.

"That's definitely her," I say. "Not sure if she and Ford will still be dating after this, though."

There's no good reason for a photo like that to exist. It would be one thing if Juliette were shooting a scene, making eyes at a costar—but Jonathan Cast is her director. They're clearly between takes, and from the angle of the shot, they don't seem to realize anyone's caught them in the moment.

Still, I know all too well how snapshots don't always tell the full story.

I slip my own phone out, shoot a text Ford's way. *Just saw the Juliette photos—here if you need to vent.*

A few minutes later, when Bre and I are finally settled into opposite corners of the couch for our *Flower Wars* marathon, Ford's face fills my phone screen: I'd forgotten how he's one of those rare people who actually prefers phone calls—he's never had the patience for texting.

"Are you okay?" I say as soon as I answer.

"Hey, Livvie. No, not really." He sounds exhausted, defeated. "Juliette's got something going with Cast now."

"You know this for sure, not just from some random photos?"

And here I thought my own love life was the only thing breaking—and being broken by—the internet.

He sighs. "I just talked to her," he confirms. "Funny how she finally found the time to call. We had a hard time connecting from the minute her flight landed, so I guess that should have been a red flag. You'd think she could have squeezed a call in here or there, even a text—she didn't even comment when I was 'caught' having a fake date on the beach as a last-ditch effort to get her attention." He laughs, but it's sad and hollow. "I kind of suspected we might be drifting apart, but I didn't know she was hooking up with *Jonathan Cast* instead. I mean, who'd pick me when an award-winning writer/director is the other option?"

Not to mention Jonathan Cast has topped the list of "40 Under 40: Hollywood Hotties Behind the Camera" for the past six years straight, but I'm not about to say so.

"I'm so sorry, Ford. It's her loss, okay?"

"Thanks, Livvie. That means a lot from you."

His words are a salve. Ford and I were close, too, back in the day. Never Ransom close—but we spent day in and day out together throughout those years, and he was my next-favorite person on set. I hate to hear him hurting like this.

"Tomorrow will be better, okay?" I say for myself as much as him.

It has to be.

As soon as we end the call, Bre sets her empty sundae dish on the side table and announces, "I'm telling *literally* everyone I know to boycott that film when it comes out, Liv, I'm not kidding. Ford is a cinnamon roll, and he deserves better."

Everyone needs a Bre in their corner.

We finally queue up *Flower Wars*—Fanline just dropped a fresh season in its entirety, so at least there's *something* good about this day. Bre plans to stay in my guest room again so we can make it a true girls' night event. Secretly, I think she also wants to make sure I arrive on set on time in the morning.

Four episodes later, I'm deeply invested in the new cast, more than happy to focus on their problems instead of my own. Grecia is going to have to pull an all-nighter if she wants to finish her ambitious project by the deadline; Cosette's flowers have all but died in the summer heat (which seems like Floral Architecture 101, but who am I to judge?); Rigsby the "villain" is unexpectedly endearing despite the fact that he's already made three people cry with his blunt, unsolicited feedback; and Hank's skill set is very much *not* up to par for the task at hand. Still, there's a moment between every episode where it's back to real life: Shine Jacobs's name pops up in the credits every time, reminding me of her missed call from earlier. I haven't spent much time dwelling on it, but it now strikes me as very odd that she'd call me directly. She's always gone through Mars before.

Sometime around three thirty in the morning, I wake up on the couch to the show's title screen, alone—I slept straight through the last three episodes of the eight-episode season—and drag myself up to bed. Bre's already up in the guest room, I assume, ever the responsible adult. I'll have to get up again in just over three hours for another long day on set.

With a start, I remember what's slated for tomorrow's shoot: a pair of bedroom scenes with Ransom that appear in the middle of the episode, one of them pretty racy. At least I have a fun run-in with Ford to shoot first thing in the morning, which should help.

But *oh*, the bedroom scenes with Ransom—I don't know how I'm going to manage them.

My eyes flutter shut, and a pair of tears slip out. All of this would be a lot easier if I didn't care so much. If I could just get past my own scar tissue, decide it doesn't matter if our private life makes a thousand headlines. If I knew for sure that I could take Ransom at his word—

And trust him to love me back.

Gemma Gardner Finally Snaps

By Zenia DiLitto // Editor in Chief, Pop Culture, DizzyZine.com

Hello, hello, my dazzling Spinners—well, this week has been an absolute doozy, has it not?!

After weeks of silence in the face of both engagement and breakup rumors, Gemma Gardner (Ransom Joel's most recent ex) has finally spoken up—and she has A LOT to say. In case you're not already following her on Snapaday, you might want to hop over to her feed *right freaking now* before she pulls a "felt cute / might delete later" on her most recent stories—is there anyone out there who hasn't woken up with regret after blasting big feelings to the internet in the middle of the night?

But never fear: if she does decide to delete everything, we've got the entire transcript below for you to enjoy. Read on for a fresh peek into the love life of Ransom Joel, with more than a few details that have never before been shared!

@gemsgemsgems via Snapaday / 3:04 a.m.

> Hi, y'all.

> It's been a rough few weeks. Sorry to go so quiet on here, I just—(sigh)

Sorry, I'm not even sure where to start. You already know Ransom and I are over. I've seen all your shade, and I guess I want to just, like, clear a few things up.

First. Everyone keeps calling me a heartbreaker. I'm not. Show me a single photo where Ransom has looked heartbroken these past few weeks, please! Go on—I'll wait. And I'll wait and wait and wait, because you know what? It doesn't exist.

It. Does. Not. Exist.

Let me let you all in on a little secret here: Ransom isn't heartbroken, because he was never in love with me to begin with.

Do I need to say it again?

Ransom wasn't in love with me. Maybe he thought he was, for a while, but I could tell there was something missing—and I knew it a long time before he did.

Okay, so I didn't know for sure. But now I definitely do.

You've seen the news by now: Ransom's with Liv.

He's loved her forever. I think I knew that a long time before he did, too.

As soon as I found out they were going to do the reunion special, I knew we were done. It was only a matter of time.

He never meant to make me feel less than special, because he's a good guy, really. He just didn't realize it, how his face lit up whenever he saw something about Liv online, or when someone asked if he was looking forward to seeing his old costars again. The way he looked at her in old photos and on the show; even though they're supposedly acting, I could always tell it was real.

I'm not Liv. No one will ever be like Liv for Ransom.

So. All this to say, I've had it with your hate mail and your harassment at my bookstore, so I am begging you to please, please stop. I never broke Ransom's heart because I never had it in the first place. I loved him—I loved him so, so much—but I ended things because I knew I could never make him happy, not truly. Please move on and let me live my life.

23

Miraculously, I show up five minutes early to my call time.

Bre banged on my door first thing this morning to make sure I wasn't late again. "Go in there like the knockout you are, okay?" she ordered. "You've got this, and if anyone makes you feel differently, screw them."

It set things off on the right foot.

I blew my hair out into billowy waves, dressed in a creamy silk top and drawstring linen shorts the color of toasted ochre, added simple-but-sparkling touches of gold jewelry—hoops as gigantic as they are thin, a stack of delicate bangles on my right wrist—and did my makeup to perfection even though Gretchen will redo it all for the shoot. I picked out my most gigantic pair of sunglasses, with sandy frames and lenses to match; they're mostly for the sake of making an entrance to remember.

Jimmy was in particularly good spirits this morning, too—Bre followed through on tracking down an advance copy of the latest Eric Zhang novel, and he's halfway through it already. I've never seen him so giddy.

It's going to be a good day, I tell myself now, as I climb out of his car and face the swarm of photographers waiting just outside the studio lot gates; I've got Millie's latest song playing in my AirPods so I won't hear their cameras or their questions.

It is going. To be. A good. Day.

I beam at the cameras, pretend I'm glowing under their attention. This way, I have as much control as possible over the headlines: no LIV LATIMER, HEARTBROKEN MESS! or LONELY, LOVELESS LIV LOOKS LIKE A TOTAL WRECK! this morning, not if I can help it.

The mood when I walk into reception is a complete one-eighty from yesterday. Sasha-Kate and Millie are chatting over in the corner, actually looking quite chummy—*they're* definitely not stressing over my love life blowing up, or the fact that Fanline wants to put them front and center of the reboot. Ford chats amiably with Gretchen and Emilio; Bryan's off by himself in one of the low chairs, his laptop open on the coffee table in front of him. He's on a call right now but gives me a nod when I come in. Starting off strong with Bryan bodes well. I need every ounce of good luck today.

Ford breaks off from Gretchen and Emilio when he sees me, and pulls me off to the side. I've already tucked my sunglasses in my bag, but now I wish I hadn't. His eyes search mine, his usual lightness displaced by something heavy.

"Get any sleep last night?" I ask.

"Define sleep. You?"

"Is it that obvious I'm running on next to nothing?" I ask, trying to play it off.

It doesn't work.

"No," he says. "It isn't. Which makes me think maybe you're working extra hard to make it look like you got a full night."

I laugh, despite myself. Count on Ford to always be more perceptive than anyone ever gives him credit for. "I hardly slept at all," I admit.

"I feel you," he says, glancing over his shoulder. "Ransom called me. He's a mess." He shakes his head. "Maybe I shouldn't have told you that, but I hate to see things go down like this. For the record, I think Gemma's take on it all is spot-on."

"Gemma's . . . take?"

He mutters a curse under his breath. "You haven't seen it yet?" He holds out his hand, gestures for my phone. "Might want your earbuds for this."

When he hands my phone back over, Gemma's face fills the screen, freshly washed, no makeup. I watch her stories three times in a row, let her words burn into me. And they do burn, everything from *he's loved her forever* to *no one will ever be like Liv for Ransom*.

I have no words. None.

After a long, silent minute, I tuck my phone away. One by one, I tuck my AirPods neatly in their case, feeling Ford's eyes on me the whole time.

"Sorry, Livvie, I thought you knew already." I hear what he hasn't said: *The entire internet knows already.* "For the record, if it helps, I've been rooting for you and Ransom to get together ever since that one flight to Shanghai on our world tour."

My heart stops. "Wait, what? What makes you say that, about Shanghai specifically?" How much did Ransom tell him?

"Please!" Ford laughs. "I agreed to the window seat on that flight, remember? I couldn't get out for three hours because you fell asleep on his shoulder!"

I had completely forgotten Ford was on my other side.

"I told Ransom to go for it with you after that—it was the perfect chance, I'm sure you know by now how long he'd had a crush on you before that. But obviously, we never knew if you felt the same way."

The world goes silent.

Surely I've misheard.

"But . . . he got together with the tour director's daughter on that trip."

"Yeah, because *you* told him he should," he says, but soon the light in his eyes dims. "Wait—you thought he actually liked her?"

"Are you trying to tell me he *didn't*? We had a whole conversation about how he was nervous to ask her out."

"That's because he wanted to ask *you* out. He was trying to get a read on if you felt the same way he did—if the idea of him dating another girl got a rise out of you, he'd know you had feelings, too." He bites his lip. "Admittedly not the best strategy, in hindsight. Sorry to say I'm the one who thought of it."

I feel dizzy. "I can't believe he couldn't tell I liked him like that," I say, but even as I say it, I remember how hard I tried to not let it show, fearful of ruining our friendship.

Yeah, of course, I told Ransom all those years ago. *You should go for her if you like her.* It was one of my finest acting moments to date.

"That's exactly what I always said. But he always went back to your interviews—you shut those questions down every time, like, 'We're just friends,' full stop, end of discussion."

My heart sinks to my stomach.

All this time, I thought Ransom was the one giving mixed signals. Never, not once, did I consider that maybe I had done the same.

"Liv?" Gretchen says tentatively, like she's hesitant to interrupt. "Hate to butt in—but we've got to get moving if we're going to stay on schedule."

"Sorry again about Juliette," I say quietly so only Ford will hear.

"Sorry about my bad advice in Shanghai," he replies, "and about everything else going on. At least we get to do a scene together today—I've been looking forward to it."

"Same," I say, forcing a smile. "And hey, forget about the bad advice. He didn't have to take it."

⟡

My scene with Ford is a fast one: we're both rock-solid on every line, every beat. We're so committed, so *on* today, you'd never guess we were both falling apart behind our makeup. The only part I don't like about doing this scene is how quickly we get a good take, and—just like that—it's over.

I haven't seen Ransom yet. Usually he'll slip in and grab a snack from the craft services table first thing, sip on his coffee while looking on from a dark corner, but not today. My stomach's been a mess of nerves all morning, especially after everything Ford told me. Two days ago, I would have been absolutely over the moon to hear Ransom's feelings for me all those years ago were mutual.

Today, I have no idea what to do with this information.

On break in my trailer, I can't stop thinking about Gemma's stories. About the irony in the step back Ransom and I took all those years ago: how, in theory, pulling apart from each other was supposed to help us get closer to our happily ever afters—but despite fourteen years of silence, my history with Ransom still came between him and Gemma in the end.

What Ford told me casts everything in a new light. If what he and Gemma both said is true—that Ransom has loved me all along, forever, just like I've loved him—maybe Ransom only suggested a step back because he thought it's what *I* wanted. Maybe he didn't want to stand in the way of *my* supposed happiness with some guy who wasn't him and did the selfless thing by giving me up.

And then I cut him out of my life. I told him not to call me. Not to reach out. He respected that for *fourteen years*. He tested the waters by texting me the day of the Fanline dinner, and has been nothing but incredible ever since. And what did I do? I went and accused him of turning us into a publicity stunt. Accused *him* of sending mixed signals.

My head hurts.

There's a soft knock on my trailer door. My stomach flips—but it's only Bryan on the other side.

"Hi, Liv," he says, unusual vulnerability in his expression. "Mind if we talk for a moment?"

"Sure, come in."

"I just wanted to make sure you're comfortable with the plan for today," he says, with a pointed—but not insensitive—glance. "Especially with . . . well. I've been informed about the Ransom situation."

My face turns such a pronounced shade of red I can see it in my reflection, even under all the makeup Gretchen caked on, even with the strategically flattering lighting built in around the mirror.

"We've already had to make some significant adjustments to the schedule, thanks to the, uh . . . various obstacles . . . we've faced this week," he goes on. *Various obstacles* is a generous way to put it, given our myriad late arrivals, Millie's acting skills, Ransom's inability to focus, and the complete halt on production yesterday after Ransom stormed off set. "We *can* rework the episode if you don't feel comfortable with the more intimate scenes we've got coming up today. But that would mean . . ."

His voice trails off, but I've been around long enough I can fill in the blanks. To cut today's scenes entirely would mean a good bit of rewriting and more scheduling headaches, to say the least. The fact that he's asking my input at all, that he's willing to go to great lengths for the sake of my comfort, that he's willing to face the ire of Bob Renfro and all the other execs for the subsequent budgetary issues and time crunch a change of this magnitude would put on everyone involved— it's significant.

"I . . . wow," I say, genuinely speechless. "Thank you, this is . . ." *Thoughtful. Ludicrous.* "It means a lot that you'd even ask. I know how much would be affected, though, and I don't want to cause any more headaches. Ransom and I are both professionals—I feel confident we can set our personal issues aside and do the scenes as planned."

I feel confident is more wishful speaking than actual truth, but even saying the words aloud makes me feel like they could be true.

Bryan's shoulders melt in relief. "Okay, yes," he says, tension no longer pulling at the corners of his eyes. "Of course you're both professionals, Liv—my sincerest apologies if I implied otherwise. Take an extra fifteen and then we'll proceed as planned."

He gives a quick little nod and closes the door on his way out.

It's just another day on set, I tell myself. *We've done versions of this scene so many times before.*

So why do I feel like I'm sixteen all over again, about to do this for the very first time?

Exclusive: Ransom Joel Parts Ways with Team Due to Unresolved Differences

By Gregor Ives // Senior Editor, Books & Film, *West Coast Daily*

Just as offers started pouring in for Ransom Joel (in the wake of <u>yesterday's surprise news</u> about his secret romance with costar Liv Latimer)—potentially a major turning point in his career—it appears this is a turning point of a different sort for the former teen heartthrob: we've learned, this morning, that Joel has severed all professional ties with longtime manager/father Jonathan Joel and publicist Andrea Moore, effective immediately; the lone member of his team to survive the cut is agent Whitney Heitz at CAA.

In a statement provided by the actor himself, Joel remarks: "I'm grateful for the opportunities and connections that have come my way, but unfortunately, I've reached an impasse with my team regarding the future of my career."

It's unclear if Joel has replacements lined up for the newly vacated roles, but what is clear is that he will be the deciding voice in finalizing a new team.

"I've spent far too long allowing my career—and my life—to shift off course from the vision I have for it," Joel adds. "I'm eager to surround myself with the sort of smart, supportive minds that are capable of seeing the whole picture of my career, what will be good for it in the long term, and not just the shine of a flashy bottom line."

If that isn't bold, I don't know what is. Bravo, Mr. Joel, on what sounds like an overdue move in the right direction—we here at *West Coast Daily* look forward to following this new era of your career.

24

I was so wrong.

This is *not* just another day on set. Not by a long shot.

It started the second I cracked open my trailer door—Ransom opened his at the exact same time. We haven't even made it five steps yet, and I already know this will go down as one of my most awkward days on set *ever*.

He gives me a courteous nod, along with a polite but tight-lipped smile that doesn't reach his eyes. "Hello," he says.

Hello. *Hello*.

It's like he's acknowledging a door-to-door salesman without wanting to encourage them to actually *stay* on his doorstep. Really, really great way to start off when you're about to climb in bed with someone to convince millions of viewers you're in love.

"Hi," I reply, every bit as awkwardly.

We walk toward the soundstage, too much space between us. I'm aware of every single inch, and all too aware of how *little* space there will be as soon as we start shooting. Did Bryan give Ransom the chance to opt out of this? Surely he must have.

I hold my head high as we walk on set, together but not quite *together*. It's as silent as I've ever heard it before a shoot, all eyes on us. I smile, do my best to project confidence and ease. Evy the intern busies herself with the pillows on the bed, fluffing them with more effort than necessary. We'll be shooting a cozy morning scene before moving on to the more intimate one; that one will have a closed set, with only the most essential crew present.

In the shadows just off to the side of the brightly lit set, we wait for Bryan to finish up a conversation with the director of photography.

"Have you seen any of the headlines this morning?" Ransom asks, his voice quiet.

I can only imagine what they're saying about us today, especially after Gemma's viral video—I can't afford to think about it or else I'll never get through our scenes. "I've done my best to avoid them."

"Excuse me, sorry," someone says, as they squeeze past us to adjust one of the lights. Ransom shifts to make way, his hand brushing mine in the process—a spark in the darkness. *Stop it*, I tell my traitorous body.

"Did Bryan talk to you?" Ransom asks, after another moment of silence.

"Yep." My *p* pops more than I mean it to, like a slammed door. "I told him we were professionals," I add, to take a little of the sting out. "We've done this before, we can get through it again."

He's quiet beside me, hands shoved in his pockets now, probably to avoid any more accidental brushes. Bryan calls us out onto the set a few minutes later, finally done working through plans with the camera and lighting crews.

The set is beautiful: both scenes take place in Duke's beachside bungalow, in his bed. The plush white linen duvet is minimalistic but luxe, and the bedroom windows are lit with a perpetually breaking dawn, sunbeams so convincing I forget they've been manufactured just out of frame.

My heartbeat picks up as I untie the thin robe Wardrobe provided with my costume for today—a matching set of silk pajamas in a soothing shade of lavender. The camisole's gorgeous, with barely there straps and a perfectly draping neckline. I strip out of the robe, the heat of the lights warm on my skin.

My eyes dart automatically to Ransom, who I catch looking at the hemline on my shorts, an unguarded expression on his face that says he is undeniably, without a doubt attracted to what he sees. His cheeks turn pink as he looks away.

This is Honor's reality, not yours, I remind myself, when I'm tempted to stare back—more than tempted, if I'm honest. Actively staring, actively attempting not to. He's down to his boxer briefs now, every glorious inch of his muscular stomach on full display.

I slide under the covers as gracefully as possible, narrowly avoiding hitting my temple on the headboard's sharp, angular edge. Ransom follows my lead. *I'm sure you know by now how long he'd had a crush on you*, Ford's words race through my mind, and Gemma's: *The way he looked at her . . . I could always tell it was real*. I flash back to every other time we've climbed into a bed like this, lights bright and cameras ready. The first time, late in our fourth season—I assured my mom I felt comfortable before we arrived on set for the scene, even though *comfortable* wasn't quite as accurate as *so excited I can't even eat* mixed with *nervous, because obviously*. There's a reason our intimate scenes always "sparked electric with teen love," as some writer once put it: those scenes never required any acting, at least not for me. It blows my mind to think Ransom might have felt the same way all that time—how maybe the only acting those scenes ever required from either of us was off-screen, pretending we only saw each other as friends.

Now, his bare leg brushes against mine under the covers, and that spark is most definitely still there. I'm going to have to do a flawless job of hiding all the contradictory things I feel: the sting of hurt and regret mixed with the persistent undercurrent of affection, despite all our complicated history.

I love him, I always have. It would make things so much easier if I didn't. Being *thisclose* to him now is like cotton fused to a raw wound, comforting so long as it isn't ripped away. No matter what, I can't let myself forget: when the lights go dark, when the cameras are off, when all is said and done—at the end of the day, what happens in this bed is all, and only, fiction.

"Ransom, Liv—get closer, please!" Bryan yells, back to his usual self. "People will wonder if one of you ate a pile of garlic in the middle of the night if you stay that far away from each other!"

I should have known Bryan's sensitive persona from earlier would have no place in the director's chair. My chance to protest was back in my trailer, and now it's up to me to be the professional I promised I'd be. I rest my cheek on the pillow, turning my entire body to face Ransom. He does the same, mirroring me.

We're not touching, but it's about as intimate as we can be—his eyes are so, so close, gorgeous as ever. The heat of his breath carries fresh mint, about as far from garlic as a girl could hope for.

Focus, Liv.

"Hi," he breathes, so quietly the microphones probably don't even catch it.

Tears well in my eyes—I can't look at him for too long or else I'm going to lose it, apparently. I don't know how I'm going to do this.

His hand finds mine under the covers, and he gives it a single firm squeeze. It's familiar and comforting the same way it used to be, back in our first season when we were both brand-new at being on camera and I used to freak out. We were so young—the full force of my crush was still a couple of years off, but even then, he was the very best friend I could ever have wanted.

"Better, better," Bryan says. "Now, Liv, if you could turn so you're flat on your back, staring at the ceiling—yes, perfect!"

A fake sunbeam streams through the window, lighting up my face just like the script calls for. I take a deep breath, try to summon the purity of Honor's feelings amid the multiple cameras that are poised and ready to capture the scene from a variety of angles.

"We're rolling in five, four, three . . . ," Bryan calls.

I could do this scene in my sleep, and—thankfully—muscle memory takes over. My voice says all the right words, in all the right ways, and Ransom doesn't miss a beat. We slip into our characters so easily after all this time: there's safety there, in Honor's skin, where nothing can truly hurt because nothing we say or do is truly *real*.

That's what I tell myself, anyway, as Ransom slips his arm around my waist. As his fingertips graze the line where the bare skin of my stomach meets the hem of my silk camisole, hidden beneath the thick white duvet. His eyes search mine, and I can't look away—not just because it's right for the scene, but because I *can't*.

"I think you should do whatever makes you happy," Ransom says, the line hitting me in a thousand fresh ways that feel all too real.

Whatever makes you happy.

What if I can't have what makes me happy? What if, after all we've been through, Ransom feels we're better off as just friends?

Or, what if I can have what I want—but despite our thousand best intentions, it doesn't last—and we both end up miserable and broken?

I swallow, knowing before the line leaves my mouth that this will be the very best one I've ever delivered, and the most honest. "I just wish I knew exactly what that was," I say.

We hold eye contact, twenty years' worth of intensity suspended in the space between us, until—snap—Bryan's voice cuts straight through the moment.

"Well, that was exceptional," he says, with a slow clap, not a hint of sarcasm. "A true one-take wonder, right there. Okay, stay exactly where you are and I'll clear the set as quickly as I can—let's capture this next bedroom scene while you've got the same level of intensity, it's absolutely perfect."

My eyes find their way back to Ransom immediately. His are still on me, lingering on the line where my seriously thin camisole strap hugs my skin, probably thinking about how one of the first things he'll do in the next scene is take the entire thing off of me. It's like we have the exact same thought at the exact same moment—his eyes flicker back to mine with a hunger and fire that was so, so absent yesterday.

"Liv, I—"

"Don't," I murmur, an attempt at cutting him off, but the word gets caught and mangled in my throat.

"I'm so sorry," he finishes, clearly not getting the message.

I can't have this conversation right now—I can't. I'll never get through the next scene.

"Talk later?" I say, my voice breaking.

He swallows, nods. "Yeah," he says quietly. "Talk later."

All at once, the sunbeam disappears from our window, and it's like we've teleported to some moonlit midnight. I realize, with a start, how quiet it is on set, how empty: only Bryan is still around, and a single cameraperson—a woman named Jules.

"Liv, Ransom, are we ready?" Bryan calls. At least he's been too busy clearing the set to listen to our every word; if he'd been listening, he wouldn't be asking.

I close my eyes, push down the surge of emotion that rushed in during the short break. *Five, four, three,* I count in my head, trying to find the line where I end and Honor begins.

By the time I reach *one,* I've found it. Only barely, but I can do this.

"Ready," I say, because Ransom still hasn't answered yet.

"Ready," he finally echoes, only the barest trace of an edge left in his voice.

There are no words in this scene; it will be a hard cut directly on the heels of another scene we've already shot. While we once had free rein to let the scene evolve naturally—within certain bounds, given that our audience isn't X-rated, or even R-rated—this time around, our every move has been pre-choreographed by an intimacy coordinator; it's Jules's job to film all the right angles without us even realizing she's there. The final version of the episode will have music, but for now, it's silent—borderline *too* silent.

"Rolling in five," Bryan says, counting us in to the scene.

Ransom's eyes go from spark to fire in two seconds flat. The hunger there feels so, so real—my body can't tell the difference, and suddenly it feels like I'm slipping on ashes, hurtling headlong toward the flames. He slides one hand into my hair and pulls me close, closer—

His lips find mine, tentative at first, and then they're ravenous. I match his hunger and then some, letting the moment take over, fury fusing with passion until they're indistinguishable. His legs tangle with mine under the covers; no one will see just how close we are in this moment, no one will know there's not an inch of space between us. The heat of his skin, his strong body pressed up against mine: he feels *good.*

I feel good.

His fingers graze my stomach as he slips them under the hem of my camisole. He pulls the soft silk up and over my head, expertly keeping all the necessary parts of me covered under the thick duvet, where the cameras can't see. Only my silk shorts and his boxers are between us now, a barrier that's simultaneously so little and so much—I kiss him deeper, my hands curling into his hair so hard it might hurt.

He pulls me in tighter. My hands find their way down to his shoulders, to the strong, solid muscles of his lats, to the cut, carved lines of his stomach that earned him every role he's taken since the last time we did a scene like this.

I'm not hating this.

Not even a little.

I force my mind into silence, trying my best to soak up the kisses he's now trailing down my neck, the hand at the small of my back. He's straying a bit from the choreographed plan, but not in a bad way; it's all very, very good. The duvet is low enough now that the audience will have a good glimpse of skin—all those hours over the years with my personal trainer will finally pay off—and a chill rips through me, possibly related to the lack of duvet, probably not.

On instinct, we both pull back at the same time, searching each other's eyes—his spark like I've never seen before, not even by the pool in his backyard. My heart cracks sharply at the memory, but I push it down. I can't deal, not now. Not yet. He tilts his head close to mine, one hand buried in my hair in a way that will flatter us both on camera, his hair soft against my forehead.

I want to do so much more.

I *want* so much more.

"Aaaaaaand *cut*!" Bryan shouts excitedly. "That was perfect, golden, I love it. Yes."

The moment comes crashing down around us, but we stay still, locked together until my heart cracks a little more, too much to ignore this time. It's all too much.

I fumble around for my discarded camisole, feeling flustered when I don't find it immediately. After what feels like an eternity, Jules hands it to me with a kind smile—it's not her job description at all, but with a closed set, no one else but Bryan is around to help.

"Thanks," I manage, my voice muffled as I slip the silky material over my head. And then, half to Ransom and half to Bryan, "I have to go."

Where, I'm not sure yet—my trailer? Home? Back in time, before everything got so royally fractured? I have to go, and it doesn't matter where. I just can't bear to stay.

✧

I can't get the shoot out of my head.

It's been five hours now, our longest day of shooting yet—more filming, some family scenes and a couple of takes to capture Pierre's one and only cameo in the episode—but I feel like I've floated through the entire thing. On the outside, I've been Honor St. Croix to perfection.

On the inside, I'm a conflicted mess.

I can't stop thinking about Ransom. His eyes on mine, the heat of his hands on my bare skin, how very little we were wearing under the thick white bedding—

How much easier all of this would be if I weren't 100 percent, absolutely, undeniably attracted to him—how I still feel a desire to be near him, despite how tangled things have gotten this week. If I didn't feel so strongly, I could just brush it off and move on.

I've never been able to move on from Ransom, though.

I thought I had, but now I see those deep-rooted feelings never truly died—they were just parched, neglected. Just because you bury something, it doesn't make it any less real.

Jimmy keeps glancing at me in his rearview mirror, probably because I've been quieter than usual ever since I slipped into the back seat. My sunglasses are on, and I've stared out the window for most of the drive. It's been an exercise of discipline to keep my phone tucked in my bag all this time—I almost always use the commute to catch up on email, texts, and calls—but I'm still working my way up to feeling ready for the talk I know Ransom and I need to have. If he's texted, I'm not sure I want to know.

If he hasn't, I'm not sure I want to know that, either.

I can't stand it anymore, though. I pull my phone out of my bag and give the stack of missed notifications the once-over. I've missed stuff from all of my usuals—Bre, Mars, Attica, and my mom—and yes, tucked in between, is one from Ransom that immediately sends my pulse into overdrive.

so you don't have to go digging, is all it says, along with a preview to an article on WestCoastDaily.com, the same one Bre sent in one of her messages with a note saying *Did you see this??!?!!????*

I click into the article immediately, scan the headline: EXCLUSIVE: RANSOM JOEL PARTS WAYS WITH TEAM DUE TO UNRESOLVED DIFFERENCES.

Wait. What?

I take it in as fast as I can, reading and rereading the quotes Ransom gave, lingering over lines like *reached an impasse with my team* and *I've spent far too long allowing my career—and my life—to shift off course from the vision I have for it* and *I'm eager to surround myself with the sort of smart, supportive minds that are capable of seeing the whole picture of my career* and *not just the shine of a flashy bottom line.* My heart swells at the sight of the writer's praise for Ransom, the bravery it took to finally do this—and now, of all times, when the offers are pouring in.

Something nags at my memory, something from one of the articles yesterday. Because I am apparently a glutton for pain, I scroll through my phone's open internet windows and find the one I'm looking for: another *West Coast Daily* article, the one about all the offers flooding Ransom's team in the wake of the news about us. When I first read it, I was too caught up in the possibility that Ransom himself had leaked the news—that he was using me as a publicity stunt for his own gain—but now the entire thing hits me from a different angle.

Rumor has it, though, that Joel isn't entirely content: he's looking to diversify his already robust résumé and break out in a more serious way.

I know, now, that it was his father and publicist who blasted our private lives to the far corners of the world—the photo of us, and, presumably, everything else—which means they haven't been oblivious to how unsatisfied Ransom's been. They knew, and they just didn't care.

His father promised him he wouldn't share that photo of us.

And Ransom believed him.

My eyes flutter shut.

Ransom might have known the photo existed before it leaked, but he was every bit as blindsided by it as I was. He fought for our privacy even before I asked him to, I realize, imploring his team to keep quiet—and I lashed out at him.

We've both made mistakes.

Mistake is not the word for what his father's done, though. What Jonathan Joel did was for his own best interests, something selfish and calculated without an ounce of regret.

And this is when I know: I feel this pain like it's my own because, like it or not, Ransom's heart has been tied up with mine for the better part of two decades now. I couldn't stop caring if I tried. That's what makes everything about us feel so right—and at the same time, so risky.

Somewhere along the line I forgot we were both human. Everyone expected perfection from me for so long I think I started expecting it from myself, too—and from him. In hindsight, it's clear he's only ever had the best of intentions.

I did, too.

I feel a sharp ache at how thoroughly I pulled back from him for all those years, a deep longing for everything we lost and might never get back again. At how reluctant I've been to get close to *anyone* after how things ended with Ransom.

I loved Ransom so much I was willing to sacrifice the most important friendship in my life if it meant he'd be happy, even if it wasn't with me. He sacrificed the same, not realizing all I wanted was *him*.

How different would things have been if, instead of taking a step back, we'd taken a leap of faith?

Maybe, then and now—just like me—Ransom's only ever been afraid of losing the incredibly rare, special thing we have.

I already lost him once. I'm not ready to lose him again.

But Ransom's world has just tipped upside down now that he's cut professional ties with his father—I can only imagine how difficult it was for him to do that. Cutting someone out of your life who's been intertwined with every single career move for twenty years, no matter how toxic, can't be anything but excruciating to go through.

Maybe what Ransom needs right now is safe.

Maybe it's all he wants.

Maybe I need to be the one to take a step back here, let him figure things out on his own for a while without me in the mix.

I can be his safe place if that's what he needs—but I can't be the one to make that choice for him.

Girl on the Verge Reboot Officially Gets Green Light at Fanline!

By Ithaca Alexander // Staff Writer, Arts & Entertainment, *Sunset Central*

Hot on the heels of today's breaking news about <u>Fanline's acquisition of media giant CMC</u>, a spokesperson at Fanline has officially confirmed recent rumors that beloved teen drama *Girl on the Verge* will be returning with ten brand-new episodes as soon as this fall. Fans all over the world, rejoice: the stars have finally aligned for the reboot we've all been asking for!

But what will that look like, exactly?

Details are still being kept under wraps, but for now, the show's creators—husband-and-wife writing team Dan and Xan Jennings—have dropped a few hints. "We've always loved collaborating with our cast," Xan told us. "You can definitely expect some familiar faces when the new episodes air this fall!"

Expanding on Xan's comments, Dan added, "We're looking forward to taking a fresh approach to the themes that have always been the heart of the show."

The official cast has yet to be confirmed, but it sounds like it's safe to assume a number of our favorite faces will be gracing our screens once more—but as series regulars or guest stars? We'll have to wait and see!

Sound off in the comments with your best fan theories; more updates to come, so follow us for the latest!

25

The next few days pass in a blur.

Lights, cameras, and long days on set keep me busy enough that I can slip into Honor whenever being Liv feels like too much. We pull a couple of twelve-hour days to make up for lost time, and at the end of the third, we're all a bit sleep-deprived. Which isn't to say we *look* it— no, Emilio and Gretchen and the other hair and makeup artists keep us looking our best, fiction at its finest.

I still haven't replied to Ransom's text. He hasn't sent any follow-ups, either. Every time I open up our text thread, I second-guess myself: it's possible he's waiting for me to reach out—but what if he just needs space? I've become a sudden expert at avoiding him except where necessary; we've knocked out a couple of scenes together, but nothing as intimate as the one I can't get out of my head.

And ohhhhh, is it ever in my head.

I can't meet his eyes without remembering that final moment in bed together, before Bryan called cut. I can't look at Ransom's hands without feeling the memory of his palms seared into my skin. When he speaks, it isn't his voice I hear but the silence in between: every unspoken thing I want to say but can't, every breath that reminds me I could be content forever just being near him—

If that's something he still wants.

I can't bring myself to ask. Not knowing isn't easy, but it's easier than it would be to find out that he doesn't want to try—that he's considered the risks and decided they aren't worth it.

That *we're* not worth it.

I'm so exhausted, and so in my head, that I don't notice Sasha-Kate coming around the corner until I slam into her, drenching us both in the frigid iced water I've sent sloshing from her glass.

"Hey, watch it!" she says, and just like that I'm pulled right back to the present.

The very cold, very wet present.

"I'm so, so sorry—wait, are you okay?"

Her face is ashen, her impeccable makeup smudged around the eyes. "I don't want to talk about it," she snaps, but as soon as the words are out of her mouth, she sighs. In all the years I've known her, I've never seen her look this tired—or this vulnerable.

She glances over her shoulder. No one's there to overhear. "I think I've made a big mess," she admits quietly, but doesn't elaborate. "You should maybe go call your agent."

My mouth falls open, but before I can figure out how to respond—to all of it—she edges past me and slips into her trailer. She shuts the door behind her, and not gently.

Okay, then.

Sure enough, when I check my phone in the privacy of my trailer, I've missed two calls from Mars. I call her back immediately.

"Liv," she says, breathless in the way that tells me she maybe sprinted across a room and/or spilled a cup of coffee to get to my call in time. "It has been a *day*. Do you have a minute? And by a minute, I really mean ten."

"I'm here." I have a break—short, but I should be safe.

"So . . . we have a situation." Mars has never been anything but direct, and now is no exception. "Shine Jacobs caught Sasha-Kate with Bob Renfro in his office today. I'll spare you the explicit details—I trust you can do your best to imagine the worst."

Wow. Whatever I was expecting, it was *not* this.

"Isn't he, like, twice her age?" I manage. Sasha-Kate's usual type is midtwenties, Gucci-wearing, questionable-hygiene-but-call-it-*fashion*, usually with some sort of accent—like Nikola, the guy she brought to the Fanline dinner. The furthest thing from Bob Renfro, in other words.

"Almost, but that's not the problem here," she says. "Bob's the one who's been leading the charge for the restructured reboot, with a more prominent role for Sasha-Kate."

"Well, *that* makes more sense now," I say.

I'm not sure what leaves a more bitter taste: that she tried to pull this at all—sleeping with an exec to advance her career—or that it almost worked.

"It does. But now Shine's in a tough spot, because the reboot's already been announced, and due to Fanline's zero-tolerance policy on relationships involving execs and the cast, Sasha-Kate's no longer eligible to have a prominent role on the show—that zero-tolerance clause was in her contract just like it was in yours."

Wow. "So . . . now what?" I'm not even sure what I'm hoping to hear.

She sucks in a sharp breath.

"Well," she says, "there are three options. One is to go back with you front and center, and I've been pushing for that, but they're on a budget thanks to the merger, and it feels like creative territory they've already covered. Two is to put the entire focus on Millie, which—I don't think I need to explain why they're not immediately leaping in that direction. Three is to find a new lead, a brand-new *Girl* to follow who we haven't met yet, and give the three of you substantially less-prominent roles, since they've already promised fans they'll see familiar faces in the reboot. So." She takes a breath, finally giving my mind a chance to stop spinning. "I've been trying to give you time to work through all the options we have on the table, but we're going to have to make some hard and fast decisions. Today, if possible. If you want to be part of the *Girl* reboot going forward, in any capacity, I need to know so I can fight for the best deal and control over the schedule. I already know you're set on working with Vienna, so all that's left to consider after that is the Emily Quinn project."

"I . . . wow. Okay." I catch a glimpse of my reflection in the mirror, the face that's become synonymous with *Girl on the Verge* for two decades now. Who will I be if I walk away?

"I know," she says. "Think it over. My best advice is to go with your gut. If you want me to keep pushing for the lead role, say the word and I'll do it. We might have to make some compromises, but you know I would never let you take a *bad* deal."

I feel a deep sense of gratitude for Mars, fiercely in my corner since day one. And then I remember Ransom, who's never had a team like mine, and I feel heavy all over again.

If we walk, it affects him, too.

Before I give my final answer, I should probably go talk to him. See where he stands.

"Thanks, Mars," I say. "I'll get back to you by tonight."

"The sooner you can let me know, the better." I've known her long enough to translate it into *I really need to know by six*, which is less than two hours away. "Talk soon, babe."

"Yeah," I say. "Talk soon."

I've got one last scene to shoot before we wrap, and there's no way I can put it off—today's our very last day on set, and it's already a day longer than we were meant to be here. On top of that, I have a press appearance on *The Late Show with Ben Bristol* immediately after we finish, which is all the way on the far side of the lot.

But I have to talk to Ransom.

Bryan's going to kill me. *I need twenty minutes*, I text, before I can talk myself out of it.

Three dots pop up, and I wait.

Twenty minutes, and not a minute more, he finally sends back.

✧

I knock on Ransom's trailer door, hoping hard he hasn't already headed home.

I only have to wonder for a moment.

He opens the door, looking at me like he's not sure I'm actually there—like I'm every bit the ghost I've become since our kissing scene three endless days ago.

I can't stop staring at the towel wrapped around his lower half, and the droplets making their way down his chest.

"Let me just—" He steps back, gestures for me to come in. "Wait here for a second, okay?"

I want to tell him I don't have a second to spare, that I might lose my nerve if I don't get the words out *rightthissecond*. "Okay," I say instead as he disappears into his bathroom, a burst of steam escaping when he opens the door.

A moment later, he returns to the small sitting area—identical to mine except for the pillows, deep emerald green instead of marigold—wearing navy joggers and a light gray V-neck. He settles onto the couch, in the corner closest to where I'm perched on his loveseat.

"Is everything okay?" he asks. "What's wrong?"

I don't even know where to start—and I didn't factor in how good he would smell, freshly showered with a hint of cologne, when preparing my speech in my head. Everything I want to say feels nebulous in the haze of him.

"Mars called," I say, the easiest way in. "I have to make a decision tonight—now—about the reboot." I take a deep breath. "I'm seriously thinking about walking away."

His face is unreadable. He studies me with those light green eyes that take center stage in all my favorite memories.

"If it's because of me, Livvie, if what happened with us is making it too hard for you to be here—if I'm ruining the show for you—"

My head snaps up. "What? No, it's not you. Not at all." For all the reasons I'm reluctant to sign on, Ransom isn't one of them. If anything, he's the reason I'm tempted to *stay*. "It's been amazing being around you again." Tears spring up in my eyes, and I will them to stay put. "Really amazing, honestly."

He gives a half laugh. "You've been avoiding me for *days*. I thought maybe I went too far in that scene, that maybe you could tell—"

He cuts himself off, looks away.

"That I could tell what?"

I want to hear him say it. I need to hear it.

"That I've been in love with you my entire life, Livvie. That I never knew how to tell you, *if* I could tell you. All I ever wanted was for you to be happy."

I let his words sink in, take a moment to truly hear them. To feel them, hot as fire as they slip under my skin. "I wanted to be happy *with you*," I finally say.

"I know that now. But I screwed everything up—"

"*I* screwed up, too, Ransom. I thought the way I felt about you was always obvious. It never occurred to me that I might be sending mixed signals of my own. And everything I said at your house the other night—"

My voice catches. I need to say it, but it's stuck in my throat.

"I'm sorry," I say. "I believe you had nothing to do with the photo, the press. Any of it. I believe all of this was real for you, every minute, and I'm sorry I didn't take you at your word."

"I'm sorry I ever gave you reason to doubt it," he says. His eyes linger on mine before falling away. After a long stretch of silence, he looks up again. "You're really thinking about saying no to the show?"

I let out a long exhale. "It's more that I'm thinking of saying yes to other things. And maybe I'm feeling like it's just . . . time."

He nods, presses his lips together in a tight line. Like there are words in there, if only he'll let them out.

"What?" I say, when he doesn't say anything.

"You've always been the heart of the show, Livvie. You steal every scene you're in, and that didn't stop when *Girl* did—you're special. Your talent is *rare*." His eyes flicker down to his hands, then back up to mine. "You're just like your dad in that way."

I blink, but the room is a hopeless blur. I'm an actress, I should be able to control this—I should.

I can't.

He takes my hand in his. It's large and warm and perfect. "Anything you work on will turn to gold. I think you should do whatever makes you excited."

"What will you do if I say no?" I say after a long, cleansing breath. "If there's no Honor . . ."

"Don't worry about me—and I mean it. Don't choose *Girl* unless it's what you really want," he says. "Not for me, not for Dan and Xan. Not for the fans. Choose it for you. Or . . . don't."

"You're sure you want to leave your fate on the show up to me?" I need to know he won't regret this if I walk away—that he's not sacrificing his own happiness for mine, as I now know we both have a history of doing.

"Honestly, I wouldn't want to do it without you. And besides," he says with a grin, "I probably need to clear my schedule if I want to star in any velociraptor zombie–hunting apocalypse films in the near future."

I can't help it, I laugh. "Not signing on for any Jonathan Cast projects, then?"

"In solidarity with Ford," he says, "that'd be a no."

In my pocket, my phone gives a short, sharp buzz. I glance at the time—I've got five minutes to get over to hair and makeup before Bryan comes to hunt me down.

We stand, lingering as long as I can afford to, fingers still entwined. He tucks my hair behind my ear, the same piece that's always falling. "I wish I could stay," I say, pressing my forehead to his.

"I wish you could, too." He presses a soft, slow kiss to my lips. "I'll find you later, okay?" he says when we break apart. "Now go kill it, Livvie."

✧

Sasha-Kate and I have our work cut out for us in this final scene. I don't envy the affair-with-executive-to-win-a-leading-role fallout she's dealing with; at least major career decisions are the only thing weighing me down while I slip into Honor's skin, possibly for the very last time.

Possibly for the very last time.

The thought hits me so hard it feels physical. This show has given me everything, for better and for worse—and the ratio of better to worse has been undoubtedly skewed toward the better.

Which isn't to say the worst parts haven't been hard. The scrutiny, the stress, the pressure: for all the good that comes with fame, the hardest parts have left indelible marks on me that far outlasted my time playing Honor on the show. People have always held me up to Honor's impossible standards and have been disappointed to find I'm only human, only unscripted Liv trying to work her way through life without knowing which lines come next. And on the flip side, when I come anywhere close to resembling Honor in my real life, I'm either a threat or a stepping stone: too successful to stay with, or someone to use. There has never been a happy medium, and I'm still discovering new, jagged facets to how my time on the show shaped me.

For better or worse, though, there's so much of me tied up in her character—and my life would not be what it is without Honor. For all the pain that's come with it over the years, I wouldn't trade it.

Who will I be if I walk away?

Who will I be if I *stay*?

All at once, with perfect clarity, I know what I have to do.

"Liv, Sasha-Kate—ready?" Bryan calls out, looking up from his clipboard to make sure we're in our places.

There's no trace of anything but fire in Sasha-Kate's eyes. Between Gretchen's touch-ups and a few minutes to pull herself together, a casual observer would never know anything was wrong.

There's something wild and untamed in her at the moment, a flicker of fear mixed in with her usual radiant confidence. It will work for this scene, at least—that sort of energy always sparks something raw and real in our most emotional scenes, like the one we're about to shoot.

We get right into it, the stage set to look like Bianca's apartment. As soon as we're rolling, I bang on her door; I don't have to dig too deep to summon the distress I'm supposed to show.

"Bianca?" I call. "Bee? It's me."

Sasha-Kate whips the door open, true concern in her eyes like the sister I never had. "What? What's wrong?"

I pace around the apartment, finally telling her what's been weighing me down: traveling the world as a photographer isn't the same without Duke, and now I'm thinking of quitting to make marine documentaries with him, the way it always should have been.

"Honor. *Honor.*" She intercepts my pacing, putting her hands on both of my shoulders and looking me square in the eyes. "Are you listening to yourself? Look, do you want me to be real with you or do you want to just keep angsting like the world's about to end?"

"Somehow I don't think you're going to let me choose 'angsting like the world's about to end.' "

"Correct. Okay, are you listening? Because I'm only going to say this once." Her features shift perfectly into a mix of compassion and fiery determination. "You *have* to go for it. Do not feel guilty, not for a single second, for taking this long to figure out what you want. He'll forgive you—he *loves* you. Have you even met Duke?"

I laugh, a genuine one, because the line is so well-timed.

"He cares more about you than about all the monk seals in the entire ocean, okay?" she continues. "He's not going to resent you for traveling the world for as long as you did—he's the one who *told* you to go for it. Do the thing. Be brave. Quit your job!" She pauses, right on cue. "Unless there's something else holding you back?"

I've had this scene memorized for weeks now, every line and all the spaces in between. This is the first time the full weight of them has hit me.

I sit in silence, curling my knees to my chest as my eyes go just the right amount of shiny. I wonder if anyone will be able to tell the difference between these tears and the fake ones I usually summon on command.

"If you don't want to go for it, don't go for it," she says plainly, when I'm silent, plopping down next to me on the oversized purple sofa. "Just don't let fear win, okay?"

I'm supposed to have a line here—a witty, non sequitur one-liner for comic relief—but I can't get it out. Instead, I improvise, looking her straight in the eye, projecting the impression that she's said all the right things, and now it's up to me to follow through. In yet another improvised move, she suddenly wraps me in a tight hug, and we sit there on the sofa, side by side, like we're in it together and always have been. She leans her head on mine; I close my eyes and hold, waiting for Bryan to call cut, imagining the camera pulling away slowly to leave us in a private moment.

I can't believe we just filmed our very last scene together—it was the perfect way to go out. We've had our moments over the years, on screen and off, and not all of them pleasant.

This is the one I want to remember.

"Aaaaaaand *cut*!" Bryan says after an eternity. "Better than scripted, ladies—perfect. We're sticking with it." He hops out of his director's chair, tucking his clipboard under his arm. "That's a wrap, everyone! Be on the lookout for details about the cast party—we'll do a private screening before the episode goes live on Fanline. In the meantime, get some rest. You've earned it."

The lights go dark, but Sasha-Kate and I are still on the sofa, frozen. Her arms are no longer around me, but the two of us are like statues, living monuments to the end of an era that has all too abruptly fallen down on us.

"I can't believe it's over," she finally says, as the crew gets straight to work breaking down the set. It feels like she's talking about so much more than just this scene, or even these past two weeks of all of us being together again.

I take in the sight of our set, everyone in a rush to take it apart. Soon, it will be like we were never here.

"In a way, though, things are just beginning, right?" I say, thinking of the call I'm about to make to Mars on my way across the lot.

"For *you*," she says simply. Tartly.

Just like that, she's Sasha-Kate again: jealous, guarded, unpleasant.

Maybe I should have thought twice before making that comment—for her, this is the beginning of gossip fodder for an entire generation of bloggers.

For the first time, I catch a glimpse of what it might have been like for Sasha-Kate all these years, living in the shadow of her character, who often got overlooked—living in the shadow of *my* character. People have a hard time separating us from our characters, I know that.

Sometimes we have a hard time separating ourselves from them, too.

The soundstage is quiet now except for the hushed handful of people bustling around. Across the room, one of the production assistants clears his throat.

"Liv?" He adjusts his tortoiseshell glasses like he's nervous to interrupt us. "We've got a cart here to take you across the lot for *The Late Show* whenever you're ready."

Not *Liv and Sasha-Kate*—just me. It's one more reminder that I've always been at the center of the machine that is *Girl*, even all these years later.

"See you at the wrap party," I say on my way out.

But Sasha-Kate's back is turned, and for all the talk of beginnings, this is an end.

26

I hang up with Mars, stow my phone in my handbag.

It's done.

I never envisioned myself walking away from the show, not truly, despite my reluctance to commit. A part of me hoped it wouldn't go forward at all—but deep down, I could never quite imagine what it would feel like to actually say no.

Never, in any of the twenty years since all of this began, did I imagine myself standing outside the studio for *The Late Show with Ben Bristol*, pacing circles as the pavement practically evaporated under the late June sun, sweat beading at my temples, on a phone call with my agent, telling her I think the show should officially recenter itself on a brand-new girl. That I would make the occasional cameo because I know the fandom will want it, but I believe Honor's story has gone as far as it needs to go.

I gave Mars the go-ahead on Vienna's new project, and told her I'd like to move forward with the Emily Quinn film, too. It'll be a much larger set than the ones I've worked on since *Girl*, and a different sort of role starring in a high-concept film with substantial action sequences—but the intensity and range I've always craved in a character is there in spades. It sounds like the perfect next step. The perfect challenge.

I take a deep breath, centering myself before making my way over to the studio door. A production assistant named Alyssa—chestnut hair in two long braids, thick clear frames rimming the lenses of her glasses, badge on a lanyard that gives her access to everywhere I'll need to be—has been waiting patiently for me, earbuds in so it's clear she's not trying to eavesdrop on my call. I've kept my distance and my voice down anyway, though, just in case.

"All ready?" she says as I make my way over, slipping her earbuds out and letting the cord dangle around one of her overall straps.

"Thanks for waiting—are we okay on time?" I give her a warm smile as she lets me in, relishing the cold blast of air-conditioning as it hits my skin.

"Not *great* on time, but we'll make it."

She leads me through a labyrinthine series of hallways.

"I know you were shooting all day, but—we've got a few minutes blocked off for a touch-up if you'd like one?" Her cheeks turn pink, probably because she's basically just told me I very much *need* a touch-up.

"Yes, please," I say, thinking of my makeup melting in the heat. I'd rather not do this interview looking like I just ran a marathon in an inferno.

She grins. A few minutes later, I'm settled into hair and makeup, sipping lime-infused water that might as well have been tapped straight from a glacier. It's glorious. I close my eyes, let the stylists do their work on me, silently grateful for a moment to process everything before going on national television. Now that I've gotten all my business decisions out of the way, it's time to focus on the second part of my plan: Ransom.

I know Ben Bristol will ask.

Even if it's not his first question, it most certainly won't be his last—it will be the question around which all other questions revolve.

It's my chance to tell my own story, to tell the world—to tell *Ransom*—what I've known, deep down, since the first time he took my hand in his and calmed me down during a shoot: I don't know how to live my life without him in it.

Volunteering this sort of information in an interview goes against every instinct I've ever had, for as long as I can remember, yet here we are. Given our unique circumstances—and my particular panorama of fears—I can think of no better way to show Ransom I'm not afraid of the world knowing how I feel about him than to declare it on national television; that I'm not afraid of the substantial risks that come with being more than friends, more than just each other's safe place. That I'm trying to face my fear head-on after a lifetime of letting it control me.

Just don't let fear win.

That final line from my scene with Sasha-Kate hit me hard. Fear has won for far too long, and it's time to stop playing it safe.

"All done," says my makeup artist, whose name is (inexplicably) Feather. "You look *amazing*."

"Okay, right this way," Alyssa says. "We've got a quick detour that isn't listed in your schedule—I promise it will be totally worth it! Just follow me."

Alyssa practically bounces down the hall in her pristine white sneakers. We make a left turn, then a right, and then—I nearly trip over a tiny gray kitten that's escaped out into the hallway.

My heart picks up. The kitten gives the tiniest *meow* that echoes off the tile, its eyes round as marbles. Around its neck is a ribbon tied into a bow, a gift tag attached with the word *GIRL* written on it in thick black marker.

Alyssa lunges for the kitten, but it makes a break for it and darts away. "I'll be back!" she calls, chasing it down the hall and around the corner.

I'm still staring after her when I hear more kittens, mewing in chorus from a little farther down the hall. I turn but don't see anything—until Ransom slips out of one of the rooms just ahead, gently closing the door behind him. He's dressed in a sharply cut black blazer with slim, tailored pants to match, a look that would be perfectly at home on a Prada runway. His face is a wonder—sparkling eyes, distinctive cheekbones, five-o'clock shadow, full lower lip—

I can't stop staring.

"What . . . what are you doing here?" I finally manage.

No one mentioned he was scheduled for Ben Bristol with me—and Ransom himself didn't breathe a word about it in his trailer earlier.

His cheeks flush pink, and he gives a bashful smile. He's nervous, too, I can tell by the way he's fidgeting with his hands.

"I did say I'd find you later," he says, grinning. "Here, come in and we can talk."

I follow him inside and see five other kittens running around the room, chasing each other with huge floppy bows fastened at their collars just like the first. One is carrying a peacock toy, and she drops it right at my feet. The tag on her collar just has a single question mark on it. Another, an orange one, darts between Ransom's legs, the word *WILL* blurring as it passes.

"Ransom?" I'm fidgeting with my hands now, too—what is going *on*? It's like Kittenpalooza 2.0 in here. "What . . . ?"

It's a little jarring seeing this posh, polished version of him next to all the kittens—he's definitely not the young, adorable, heartthrob-next-door type he once was. Jarring as it is, it somehow still works.

"Right after we talked, I got in touch and asked if I could surprise you here tonight, but there was some sort of miscommunication—they thought I wanted to surprise you *during* the show, not before it. I didn't realize what had happened until I showed up, and by then it had blown up into a whole thing, and the ASPCA was dropping off this entire fleet of kittens, and—"

He cuts himself off, glances around at the tiny creatures bounding across the room.

"Long story short," he goes on, "it's turned into something else than I meant it to be, and I told them I'd only go on during the show if I got a chance to talk to you privately first. Before we go out there, I want to make it abundantly clear that you are not a publicity stunt to me. That you're so much more."

He closes the distance between us, takes both of my hands in his. I can't stop staring into his eyes—the feeling seems to be mutual.

"Liv," he says, with more emotion packed into a single syllable than I've ever heard. "We said a lot of things earlier, but when you left, I realized I never said the most important part." His hands close tighter around mine as he takes a deep breath. "I'm so sorry for all the years I never acted on how I felt. Sorry for being so afraid to lose you that I wasn't up-front when it mattered—I've always only wanted to protect you, but ended up being the one to *hurt* you. I hate that things happened like they did."

He takes a breath, keeps going. "I'm sorry I wasn't brave enough to cut my father out of my life years ago and that his actions made you doubt what you and I have."

My heart tightens at the memory of that night in his living room: how cold I was to him, how I left without giving him a chance to explain. A sand-colored kitten curls around my ankle, its fur soft on my skin: *YOU*, reads its tag.

"When my dad leaked the news about us, I completely lost it—I wasn't thinking straight after what he did, and *how* he did it, and—" He cuts himself off, takes a calming breath. "Point is, after finally getting my chance with you, I thought I'd blown it." His eyes are practically on fire, and I can't look away. "I should never have snapped at you that day on set when all you wanted was to help."

I have no words. Not one.

"I love your eyelashes," he goes on, words tumbling out one on top of another, "and how you freak out if one lands on your cheek. I love your smiles, all of them, the hundred different ones you have in your arsenal—but especially that first one you gave me twenty years ago, when we met for the first time. I was so, so nervous, even though I was trying to act chill, and your smile—it was shy and small and I can still remember it like it was yesterday—it was the first thing that actually made me *feel* chill. Like everything would be okay. And I love the smile you gave me at the Fanline dinner, like we'd never missed a day, when the truth is I should've been in your life for every single one of them. I'm so sorry, Liv. I'm sorry for all of it, and I hope you'll forgive me, because I—I don't think I could run out of ways to tell you how much I love you if we had a hundred years together. So. Hi," he says. "Will you be my very best friend, and also my very public girlfriend? I think it's a little late to keep the news from getting out, unfortunately."

I break into the widest smile, laughing, overwhelmed in the best way by all of it. "Yes," I say, nodding avidly. "Yes, please. Yes to all of it."

"I love you, Livvie," he says quietly. "I don't care who knows it, I don't care how hard it might be to live our lives with so many eyes on us—I just want to live it *with you*."

He puts one hand to my face and wipes a stray tear away with his thumb. Each second passes in slow motion, until suddenly it can't go fast enough: I close the distance between us, kiss him like I should have all along, making up for the past week and so many years before. I've never kissed someone while smiling before—never tasted salt on a smile, either, or kissed someone with half a dozen kittens mewing in the background.

"Ransom?" I say, between kisses. "I just have one question. Why did they bring in all the kittens?"

He laughs, pulling away until it's just our fingertips touching, and then not even that. He pulls a laser pointer out of his pocket and points it at the floor—its beam is *Girl on the Verge* pink, just like our logo. All the kittens gather around it in a line, their heads bobbing in unison as he captivates them with the light.

I read their tags: *WILL MY BE YOU ?*

"Oh," he says, grinning, leaning down to the ground. "The last one's still missing." In one smooth motion, he swaps one kitten for another, and it now reads *WILL YOU BE MY ?* "The last one says *GIRL*—we can play it off as a teaser for the reunion special, if you want. I think they're hoping I'll officially ask you out on live TV, but we can keep it just between us if you're not ready for that. When you pull them out of their gift boxes during the segment on the show, though, be sure and act surprised, okay?"

"This is amazing. *You* are amazing." The laser blinks off, and the kittens scatter, except for the sand-colored one with the question mark who seems seriously in love with my ankles.

Ransom pulls me in for another kiss, and I know it will be the first of many, many more. Being this close to him is the most familiar thing in the world, but at the same time, it feels brand-new: he's my very best friend, my favorite place on the planet even if it isn't always safe, my risk worth taking—because whatever happens from here, we have to try. We've wasted too much time. Now we can start making up for it all.

There's a soft knock at the door. I break away, reluctant to end the moment, but it's okay—this is only the beginning for us. I open the door. Alyssa's on the other side, the wayward gray kitten curled up and purring in her arms.

Alyssa's eyes dart between us, bright and hopeful, but she doesn't pry for details. "You're on in five, Liv," she says. "Ready to do this?"

In only a few minutes, I'll be on camera in front of a live studio audience, under a white-hot spotlight, answering a thousand questions about my career, my personal life, and my plans. In only a few minutes, Ransom will "surprise" me with kittens upon kittens, and I'll do the best acting job of my life pretending he's caught me off guard.

After a lifetime of pretending, we're finally on the same page about what's real.

"Yes," I reply, my eyes flickering to Ransom. "I'm ready."

Epilogue

It's the most gorgeous Saturday evening in late July, the deep blue summer sky only just beginning to shift into shades of lavender, flamingo pink, and nectarine. The fountain in front of Dan and Xan's gigantic mansion bubbles with crystal clear water, and there's a gorgeous pair of flower walls flanking the front steps. I recognize the latest winner of *Flower Wars*, Grecia, standing just to the side of them, chatting casually with Shine Jacobs and our producers.

"Are you sure I look okay?" Bre whispers, eyeing the others who have just begun to arrive.

"You look perfect," I tell her, and it's true. She's wearing an emerald chiffon jumpsuit with wide legs and floaty sleeves, its deep V-neck plunging all the way to the matching belt knotted at her navel.

She grins, relieved. "Back at you."

My outfit is the polar opposite of hers—a chic pair of shorts with a fitted short-sleeved top to match, both made out of a stiff, floral-print fabric. I paired it all with a simple vintage choker, three thin tiers of gold circling loosely at my neck.

And, of course, I've got a handsome guy on my arm.

"Bre's right," Ransom says with a flirty nudge, just loud enough for only me to hear. "You really do look incredible."

I grin, nudge him right back. "You clean up well yourself," I say, a total understatement. He looks like he stepped right out of *GQ*, like maybe the entire magazine was inspired by the fact that he exists.

Ford joins us, also looking rather stylish, pulling Ransom in for a bro hug as soon as he's close. I focus on not tripping up the front steps as we all head inside, my platform wedges making things slightly precarious. Bre actually does slip, catching a bit of chiffon under her spiky heel, and Ford offers his arm to steady her. They're so at ease with each other it almost looks like they showed up together.

It's hard to believe it was only five weeks ago that Millie and I climbed these steps for the first time, for the cast party that kicked off our week of shooting our final episode. We'll be watching that episode in just under an hour, getting a first look at it before it drops on Fanline next week, all of us together again for the first time since we wrapped—and the last time before *Girl on the Verge* moves into its new era with a brand-new cast.

The backyard is already bustling when we arrive, full of so many faces I may not ever see again. On instinct, my gaze flickers straight to the back corner, to the little foliage-covered alcove where Ransom and I nearly had our first kiss.

That was a very, very good night.

"Might have to slip away from the party again," he says under his breath, reading my mind.

"Those two might beat us to it," I say, laughing, nodding toward Bre and Ford. He looks over just in time to see their faces light up—there's most *definitely* a spark there.

"Ransom! Liv!" Xan Jennings is suddenly right in front of us, a pair of clean champagne flutes in her hand. "We're so glad you could make it. Welcome. And congratulations on your upcoming projects—Dan and I heard you'll be working on a film together?"

She seems genuine as ever, but I can't forget our conversation last time we were here, the uncomfortable way she insinuated the reboot should be my top priority.

"It's true," I say, unable to help the feeling of satisfaction that rushes over me. "Ransom will be playing opposite me in one of the films I signed on for, an adaptation of a sci-fi survival novel."

"Oh, that's *right!*" she exclaims, her voice tinged with the barest hint of envy and regret. "We read about it in *Deadline*, I believe."

Deadline, Forbes, The Hollywood Reporter, Entertainment Weekly—basically anywhere with any interest in film news—there were countless articles, and the internet went into an absolute frenzy. As soon as the news broke that we'd both signed on to the project, the book shattered all sorts of preorder records.

"Liv's doing the new Vienna Lawson project, too," Ransom says, not even trying to hide the obvious pride in his voice. Whenever the subject of the Emily Quinn film comes up, this is his follow-up, every single time. He has yet to sound anything but thrilled for me.

"Oh, yes, of course," Xan says, flustered, looking like she'd really rather move on to some other conversation. "Well, Dan and I are very proud to have worked with you both all these years, and we look forward to seeing how things turn out. If you'll excuse me, I've got to go find a server—" She holds the champagne flutes up as if to finish the sentence, then disappears inside the house.

"Think she'll actually watch the Vienna film when it's done?" I say, once she's well out of earshot.

Very seriously, Ransom nods. "When the Academy sends her a screener, you know she'll totally hate-watch it," he says, in impressive deadpan before finally cracking a smile. "And then she'll vote for you to win all the things because she knows you deserve them."

I laugh, taking his hand in mine.

We mingle for the next half hour, plucking mini quiches and melon wrapped in prosciutto from the trays as they pass by, along with the most refreshing sauvignon blanc that's ever graced my palate.

Everyone from the reunion show is here, minus one notable absence—Bob Renfro was terminated immediately after his affair came to light, and apparently he said some horrible things to Shine on his way out. Sasha-Kate came out tonight after lying low for a while, now that the gossip cycle has finally started to move on. She's off chatting with one of the extras, not a silver fox in sight—the execs are clustered clear on the far side of the backyard. If I had to guess, they're avoiding her every bit as much as she's avoiding them.

Millie is surrounded by a group of interns and assistants just down the path. She looks radiant, and for good reason: her full album just dropped, and it's already solidly at the top of the charts, which is truly saying something—Hālo conveniently dropped her latest on the exact same night.

Ransom and I are in the middle of congratulating Millie when the squeal of microphone feedback cuts us off. "Sorry about that; sorry, everyone!" Bryan says, overcompensating by holding the mic way too far from his face. "If you'll all find your seats, we'll begin the show in ten minutes."

Unlike the first garden party at Dan and Xan's, a huge screen has been hung on the back side of the house, as if the house were designed with an outdoor theater in mind. Our pink *Girl on the Verge* logo is bright against a teal-blue background, projected from a machine that's been expertly hidden somewhere in the landscaping; the bright blue water of the pool suddenly dims to dark navy, and the reflection it had cast on the screen disappears.

The backyard is filled with rows of long, straight tables covered in sleek black tablecloths. Servers are delivering charcuterie boards, bowls of popcorn, and baskets of baked pretzels at regular intervals, along with plates and silverware and chilled jugs of water. I take my seat, front and center, with Ransom on one side of me and Bre on the other. I'm just about to lean over to chat with her when someone taps my shoulder. I practically leap out of my seat, barely managing to avoid a wine-related disaster.

"Oh! I'm so sorry to startle you, I'm so sorry!" says a girl with a heart-shaped face and bright amber eyes. I recognize her immediately. Her picture has been everywhere these past few weeks, right beside mine, our names together in all the articles. "I'm Clarke, Clarke Hartley—and I was wondering if I could get a picture with you?"

She gives a grin that will win over a new generation of fans as soon as they see her on-screen.

"I'd be honored," I say, accidentally breaking my own rule of never making a pun out of my character's name.

Clarke doesn't notice. "That would be— Ahhh! Sorry. I'm sorry I'm not more chill about all this. It's just that I grew up watching you, and it's just . . . all of this is really, really surreal."

I want to tell her to stop apologizing: to enjoy it all, every minute, to relish this time where people don't know all there is to know about her—where she still feels like a fan instead of being the very center of a fandom, where she'll no doubt end up as soon as the reboot hits Fanline this fall. I want to tell her it'll be the adventure of a lifetime and also the hardest thing she'll ever do.

"You're going to be amazing," I say instead. I hear they cut off the casting call as soon as they saw her audition; I can see why.

She gives me a tight-lipped smile, and I know right away that she'll be okay in this business: she's confident, but not so much it will ruin her, and she accepts my compliment without seeming at all desperate for it.

Ransom offers to take the photo for us, but I wave him off—this is selfie material. Attica has taught me well.

"Here, lean in," I tell her, centering our faces just below the *Girl* logo in the background. "Mind if I post it, too?"

Her cheeks turn pink. "That would be great," she says. "Yes, please. And thanks."

She AirDrops it to my phone, and I spend a few quick seconds uploading it to my feed. *Original Girl meets new Girl*, I caption it. I tag her, adding a quick #gotvreboot to the end. Two taps later, the post is live. My official stamp of approval will go a long way with the fandom.

Clarke thanks me again, then rushes to find her seat as the garden lights dim to nearly complete darkness. Ransom squeezes my hand under the table, bringing a sudden wave of emotion.

"Doing okay?" he asks.

This is the end of an era, bittersweet and surreal, to use Clarke's word. But then I remember, whenever an era ends, it's time for a new one to begin.

"More than okay," I say, and I mean it.

Our theme song fills the speakers for the very last time, our logo fading as the episode begins. I know our logo by heart, the image indelibly carved into my entire existence in neon pink. But I don't watch the screen: Honor and Duke, as much as I love them, are fiction—their story is over.

Now it's time for real life.

Acknowledgments

I started writing this book in March 2020, in the earliest days of the pandemic: the world was scary and stressful, and I needed somewhere fun to go in my head every day (especially when we couldn't really leave the house).

Fortunately, my incredible literary agents didn't bat a single eyelash when I told them I'd like to pivot from survival stories to the glitz and shine of a Hollywood romance—an all-caps THANK YOU to Holly Root and Taylor Haggerty at Root Literary for believing in me and my work for nearly a decade now, and for the razor-sharp instincts that landed this book at its most perfect home. Thank you, too, to my wonderful film agent, Mary Pender-Coplan at United Talent Agency, and to foreign rights agent extraordinaire Heather Baror-Shapiro at Baror International for all you've both done on my behalf over the years.

Kaitlin Olson, you have been a dream to work with—thank you for championing this story right from the start! I see your fingerprints all over it, and am so grateful to have had the chance to collaborate with you; your editorial instincts pushed me to make this project the very best version it could be. It's been a joy to be Team K. Olson² with you!

It takes a village to make a book, and I can't imagine a better one than the team at Atria, which—at the time of writing this—includes: Megan Rudloff (Publicist—US), Katelyn Phillips (Marketing), Dayna Johnson (Marketing), Paige Lytle (Managing Editor), Iris Chen

(Managing Ed Assistant), Erica Ferguson (Copy Editor), Elizabeth Hitti (Editorial Assistant), Morgan Hart (Production Editor), Nicole Bond (Subrights), Bee Johnson (Cover Illustrator), Kelli McAdams (Cover Art Team), and Lexy East (Designer). All my gratitude to every single one of you for your heart, enthusiasm, and beautiful work.

Rebekah Faubion and Tracey Neithercott, thank you both for the countless writing sprints, encouraging texts, and George Costanza GIFs that fueled the writing of this book! No one *likes* a pandemic lockdown, but you made mine infinitely better, and I'm forever grateful.

Emily Bain Murphy, thank you for being Liv's very first champion, and for reading my 100,000-word first draft in a single day—!! We've been on this publishing journey together for so many years now, and I'm so thankful to have had you by my side through every twist and turn in the road.

Emily Wibberley, Austin Siegemund-Broka, and Jenna Evans Welch: thank you for writing such incredibly smart, perfect romances over the years—I've loved/devoured your books for ages, long before I ever thought about writing a romance of my own, and your friendship and encouragement along the way has meant so much to me.

To my tennis family—especially Emily, Brandon, Constance, Whitney, Luis, my league teammates, and all the cardio regulars—all the fun we've had on the court has had a direct impact on my energy, enthusiasm, discipline, and general happiness these past several years, not to mention my eagerness to step out of my comfort zone and try new things. Thank you for always believing in me and challenging me to pursue excellence in all that I do.

To my *family* family—Hahns, Holubecs, Olsons, and Malones—thank you for being so wonderful! Specific shout-outs to my parents (Mark and Dawn) and my sister's family (Lori, Cody, Otto, and Olive) for being so incredibly supportive throughout my life: you've always made me feel I could do anything I set my mind to. Thank you!

To Andrew and James, I love you both so much! Andrew, I could not have written this book (or *any* of my books!) without your unwavering support or your steadfast belief that all the time I spend writing at my desk is time well spent. James, you are kind and thoughtful and brilliant, the very best kid I could ever have hoped for; it's a privilege and joy to watch you grow up.

Lastly—even though it might sound like the most stereotypical Oscar speech—I am sincerely grateful to Jesus Christ for such wonderful people in my life, and the fact that I'm alive at all. I believe every good and perfect gift is from above (James 1:17), and am grateful for every twist and turn, both happy and hard, that brought me here to this moment.

Okay, no, actually, *this* is the last thing: To all of you readers, I hope this book brought some sunshine to your day—in a world that can be so full of dark and heavy things, I think it's good to spend time with things that sparkle every now and then. Thank you for living in the *Girl on the Verge* universe for a little while! Now, go binge your favorite show (and don't forget to make a batch of Bre's favorite popcorn). ♥

About the Author

Kayla Olson writes stories about heart and hope, friendship and family, and the blurred lines where those things intersect. Whether writing at her desk or curled up with a good book, she can most often be found with a fresh cup of coffee and at least one cat.